DYING
WITH A
SECRET

DYING WITH A SECRET

THE DEAD DETECTIVE CASEFILES

TJ O'CONNOR

Praise for The Dead Detective Casefiles

"O'Connor's The Dead Detective Casefiles series is a must read for those who like mysteries with a dash of history, a hard-boiled twist, and a pinch of paranormal."—Heather Weidner, author of the Jules Keene Glamping Mysteries

"Tj O'Connor is a master storyteller who can have you gasping in suspense one moment and snorting coffee through your nose the next. In the Dead Detective Casefiles, he seamlessly merges mystery, humor, and paranormal so authentically that the reader never gives a second thought to the concept of the main character, Detective Oliver Tucker, actually being dead.

"I cannot put these books down. I love the characters, I love O'Connor's writing style, and while I can't wait to see what happens, I also don't want to reach the end and have to say goodbye to this engaging cast of characters."—Annette Dashofy, *USA Today* bestselling author of the Zoe Chambers Mystery Series.

Chapter One

Dying can bring out the best in people. It can also bring out the worst of secrets. Oh, not only about the dead—sure, that's when everyone starts whispering about the dearly departed. No, I'm talking about the secrets of the living who are left behind. Sometimes, those people get brazen about their dastardly deeds when someone involved in those deeds dies. They don't always keep them well hidden. Often, too, a death sheds too much light on too many people. Light others would rather not be in—like Wyle E. Coyote's oncoming train in the tunnel. It can be too revealing for some. Blinding for others. One secret often leads to another. Another death. And by another death, I mean murder.

So, if you want to know who your friends are, or what they're truly up to, kill one.

It works every time.

What makes me so sure? Murder is my thing. I'm a homicide cop in the historic Virginia city of Winchester. Winchester has a hell of a murder rate that most don't know about. I know because I've solved more than twenty murders in the last few years alone. Well, seventeen to be precise. Three deaths were accidents and suicides—not something I tell stories about. But the other seventeen—phew, what a rush. As you can see, I'm an expert on the dead.

More about that later.

At the moment, it was a beautiful August afternoon in Winchester, Virginia. As always on these beautiful August days in Winchester, it was hot as, er, … it was hot. Luckily, instead of being in the dog days of summer,

I sat in the air conditioning atop a stack of wooden crates in our local library, ogling the beautiful woman working across the room from me. Her auburn hair flowed around her shoulders like a silk veil, and her green eyes sparkled even in the dark. At thirty-eight, she had the hourglass figure a twenty-year-old would die for—and today it was wrapped in jeans and a denim shirt with her sleeves rolled up to her elbows. This lady's charm and intelligence radiated an allure that stole my heart the moment I pulled her over for an undeserved speeding ticket back in the day. Sure, sure, it was unethical. Hey, I didn't give her the ticket after securing a date.

Fortunately, the statute of limitations on cheesy pickup ploys expired years ago.

This lady was doing her best to ignore me—difficult as it was—though she wanted nothing more than to get lost in my affections. No, really, it's true.

Full disclosure. This angel was formally Dr. Angela Hill Tucker, Assistant Dean and Chairwoman of History at the Mosby Center for American Studies, University of the Shenandoah Valley. Yep, my wife. Today, she was researching a new historical find in the Lower-Level Research Room at the Handley Library, a local historical landmark. The Lower Level is actually the library's finished basement. Since it's a classy place, they call it the Lower Level.

Angel sat at a cluttered wooden desk beside crates of documents discovered in a formerly undiscovered sub-basement at the Winchester Courthouse—another historic building. Yeah, I know, we have a lot of historic buildings in town. That's because Winchester dates back to George Washington's day, and we've played a big part in American history ever since. Anyway, she had just opened one of the six large, wooden crates to begin work. The first few items she took out were more of the same as many of the other crates—folded files tied with leather straps. There were a few land maps and surveyors' drawings, and an old silver-plate photograph of a family standing around a horse carriage with grim, pasty faces.

Angel was in heaven—pardon the pun. She spent much of her life in rooms just like this one, doing what she was now doing—researching old stuff. Okay, it's historically significant old stuff. The other part of her life she spent in pursuit of her real passion—trying to be a crack detective like me. Oh, I'm her real passion, too. But don't tell her I said that. It's our secret.

All day, I'd sat with my feet propped up on a crate, bored. I had on the same clothes as usual—blue jeans, running shoes, a blue Oxford button-down shirt, and a blue blazer. Angel once called my ensemble, 'old guy sexy.' I don't know about the old guy—I'm only forty-one—but I'll take the sexy part.

"Hey, Angel," I said, stretching. "How about we go grab takeout?"

She ignored me. Not unusual. Not that she was so focused on her work, but because working at a small table across the room was her research assistant, Andy-somebody. She didn't want to fluster him, so she just made believe I wasn't around. We have this thing, you see.

"Hey, it's a beautiful summer day. Maybe steaks on the grill and wine?"

She glanced up and gave me one of those "God, I want you" looks. Okay, maybe it was a "quiet, I'm working" look.

"Angela?" The thin, shaggy-haired assistant, Andrew Pellman, walked to the stack of crates beside her. He lifted one of the crates, grunted a little from the unexpected weight, and set it on the corner of her desk. "I'm done computerizing the inventory from crates one and two. Shall I get a head start on crate four while you finish crate three?"

"No, Andrew. We'll keep to our process." She saw his face melt into a pout. Me, I would have let him cry, but she was the kind soul in the family. "Oh, all right. Go ahead and begin. Follow our guidelines closely. One document at a time. Identify, inventory, and scan what you can. Photograph any that won't stand up to the scanning process. Andrew, be careful—very careful."

His face lit up. "Sure, Angela, I'll be careful."

Pellman was a meek kid in his mid-twenties. He was working on his doctoral thesis at the university, and Angel was his dissertation advisor. I didn't like him. Not one bit. I have a sixth sense about people. When he was around, my BS meter pings like it does with politicians and faux car warranty stalkers. Andy was a new class of "some people" that I hadn't labeled yet.

"I think you should call me Professor Tucker," Angel said with an easy tone. "Let's keep this professional. Okay?"

"Yes, Professor Tucker."

"It's not personal, Andrew."

He shrugged. "Okay."

Angel flipped through a document and stopped. She retrieved another and did a comparison. Finally, she looked over at Pellman. "Have you seen any references to 'M35W?' Do you recognize it from anything you've done?"

"Why?" He walked to her worktable. "Is it important?"

She shrugged. "I don't know. It seems out of place. Like some kind of acronym or citation. Can you check your new research engine tomorrow?"

"Sure, okay. It'll give me a good test run on my changes to the algorithm." His face beamed. "Thank you."

Andrew's doctoral studies used computers to perform detailed research traditionally done by historians and doctoral students. One day, that program he wrote would likely replace those researchers with keyboards and mice—the electronic kind, not the crumb snatchers. You know, like self-checkout machines at the grocery store. You do all the work, and they charge you the same price. Then, they'll fire five clerks who the machines replaced. Great plan, Andy. I wonder how many historians you'll replace with your gadgets.

"Thank you, Andrew." Her cell rang, and she took the call. "Professor Tucker." The caller had Angel's complete attention. I knew that because she jotted some notes and checked her watch twice—all the while continuing to ignore me. So, it must have been really important, right? "Yes, of course. I'll be right up."

"Professor Tucker?" Andrew asked.

She glanced over at Andrew as she tapped off the call. "We're done for the day, Andrew."

"Is something wrong?" he asked. "I can help."

"No, it's fine. I have to meet someone up in the rotunda. We'll start again in the morning." She began straightening her papers and stuffing files into her worn, leather briefcase.

"Who?" he asked.

I said, "Never you mind, sonny-boy. You work for her, not the other way around." I winked at Angel. "Millennials, right?"

She hefted her briefcase. "Something to do with our Apple Harvest research."

"Okay." He glanced at the crates of research. "Want me to gather up your research and get it to your car? There's an awful lot here."

"Actually, yes. If you don't mind." She gave him the keypad code for her Explorer. "Leave my briefcase and the files beside it here. The rest can go in my vehicle. Please make sure it's locked when you're done. Thank you."

"Sure thing, Professor Tucker." His face lit up. "See you in the morning."

I followed Angel through the Stewart Bell Jr. Archive Room, into the Lower Lobby, and up the stairs toward the main library entrance.

"I don't like him, Angel. He's shifty."

"Shifty, Tuck?" Finally, she acknowledged me. I wore her down. "No one says 'shifty' anymore."

"It's coming back in style."

She grinned and whispered, "Is that your detective-senses talking or because he stares at me when he thinks I'm not looking?"

"He doesn't stare. He ogles."

"Yes, he ogles."

"I can get Bear to check him—"

"No, Tuck. He's fine. I don't like it when you're jealous."

Me, jealous? No. It was purely a professional irritation I felt whenever Andy was around. Truly.

We reached the first-floor hall that led into the main library rooms. There, she made her way into the rotunda at the library entrance. She stopped beside a high-back wood bench where Library Lil—the bronze statue of a young girl reading a book—sat.

A tall, thin man about thirty stepped out of one of the meeting rooms along the west hallway. He glanced around before he headed our way. He wore dark slacks and a dark sport jacket over a white, button-down dress shirt that was untucked in that new-millennial style, and penny-loafers. He strode to us and looked around his entire trip.

"That must be Special Agent Kerns with the DOD," Angel whispered. "He called just now."

A fed? Interested in her research? I asked her that.

"I don't know. He said it was about my Apple Harvest research and that it was classified. Go wait somewhere."

"I am somewhere. I'm here."

She gave me the evil eye, so I meandered to a bench nearby.

As Kerns approached, fingers began dancing up my spine—hot, pointy fingers. I didn't like those fingers. Every time they did the mambo up my vertebrae, something bad happened in the next few beats.

Kerns reached Angel, proffered a hand, and said something with a serious, tight expression on his face. Then, he hooked a thumb toward the main entrance doors.

Angel shook his hand and smiled faintly, a sure sign she was unsure of him

Those fingers reached the base of my brain and *squeezed* ...

"Angel, get down!" I lunged forward and pulled her away from Kerns, down behind Library Lil's bench.

Kerns stood there, frozen in an eerie mist. His arms shot out sideways, and he seemed to lift onto his toes. His face contorted into a stunned, painful grimace.

"Tuck?" Angel cried. "What's happening to him?"

Hell if I knew.

Kerns' entire body vibrated and shuddered. He staggered backward and collapsed onto the floor, writhing. The lights above us flickered wildly and went out. The original iron, brass, and blown-glass chandelier swayed dramatically two floors overhead. Its lights flickered and went dark.

When I glanced back at Kerns lying on the floor, I cringed.

Blood flowed from his ears, nose, and mouth. It seeped from his eye sockets, where his eyeballs looked like soft-boiled eggs stewing in their sockets. His hands and fingers were dark red and bony. His face and neck had oddly sunk, and his skin looked like it had been draped over his bones as though someone had sucked the tissue and muscle from beneath. He looked like he had melted inside.

The only thing left of him was his clothes and a spreading pool of goo.

Kerns was dead, sure enough. He'd been murdered, too, right in front of Angel and a dozen people. I knew no one had seen anything. No one heard anything. No one knew anything. Me included.

Well, that's not true. I knew something. Special Agent Kerns didn't die of a heart attack because of a poor diet. He wasn't killed by a sniper with a silenced rifle, a knife-throwing ninja assassin, or by an Amazonian's blow dart. He died of something else.

What killed him, I had no idea. But it scared the life out of me.

Chapter Two

I'm Oliver "Tuck" Tucker, detective *extraordinaire*. Homicides are my specialty—especially weird ones. I have firsthand experience in weird cases. Experience that's proven invaluable over the years. That's because murder and dead people find me like a tick finds a dog.

Yep. I said dead people.

Kerns was, without a doubt, the weirdest murder I'd ever seen. His bizarre cause of death was sure to lead to a lot of secrets—all of them bad. Remember what I said earlier about secrets.

The question was, who would the secrets lead to?

Murder and secrets are like peanut butter and jelly, Abbott and Costello, and politicians and corruption. Inseparable. That's why I look for secrets to solve murders. Some people go through life trying to hide secrets. Me, I try to uncover them. I'd say I go through life like that, too, except I don't. See, the truth is, I'm not going through life at all.

I'm dead. There it is—*dead*.

You see, late one night a few years ago, someone murdered me. I died in my home, even as my best pal tried to save me and Angel looked on. My best pal being Hercule—that's *Herk-ule* like Christie's famous detective—my one-hundred ten-pound Black Lab. He took a bullet trying to save me and protect Angel. Thankfully, he survived—unlike my killer. He's worm food. His secrets caught up to him.

Ever since then, I've been a detective for the dead—a dead detective, you might say. If I'm being honest, I'm a better detective now than in my breathing days. I work as much for the dead as the living. The only setback is, as you might imagine, the dead don't pay. At least, not in cash. Of course, I don't have expenses, and I don't pay taxes. *Shush*, don't tell the IRS, or they'll send me a bill for back taxes and penalties.

It's weird, I know.

A bull of a man in an old, worn barn coat and jeans stood staring over the shoulder of a medical examiner kneeling beside Kerns' body—what was left of it. The big man was six-four and hefty—not fat and not un-fat—just big and brawny. You know the type—strong as a bull but with a few squishy spots. He was forty-two, and despite the stress of life, gray hadn't begun to show. He rubbed his square, powerful jaw and contemplated the dead federal agent lying at his feet.

"Okay, Curtis, give," Captain Theodore "Bear" Braddock grumbled. "COD?"

COD could mean a nice, tasty fish served with French fries, or maybe the collection for a package delivered to you in the old days. But in this case, it meant "cause of death."

Reginald Curtis, one of the local medical examiners from the Winchester Medical Center, stood and typed some notes into his computer tablet. When I was alive, we used paper and a pen. You don't need to recharge a pencil. No one can hack into your account, either. Don't get me started.

"I've never seen anything like this before, Bear." Curtis didn't look up. "There are protocols for things that *look* like this."

I said, "Look like what?"

Bear nearly jumped out of his hiking boots.

Bear had been my best friend and part of my family since our early days at the police academy. We'd come up through the ranks together, and both became detectives on the Frederick County Task Force back in the day. The years formed a bond between us—all three of us, including Angel. We were more than friends. More than brothers. We were family—closer than any blood relatives could be. He had a special place in our lives, Angel and mine, and he'd stayed close after my murder. To say he loved us both might raise awkward questions about his relationship with Angel. If those thoughts come to mind, erase them. Bear was as honest and loyal as Hercule.

Okay, talking point here. Other than Angel and Bear, no one can see or hear me. Well, almost no one. Certainly not Curtis or the others milling around the library.

Bear's face flushed with anger, and he snapped a nasty look around. Oh, I should mention he can hear but not see me—much to his dismay. The scowl on his face was the hidden joy that I'd joined him on this case. No, really, it was.

"What are you talking about, Curtis?" Bear asked.

Curtis turned to him. "He sort of, um, *melted* … internally."

"Melted?" Bear blinked several times as his face screwed up. He'd been the commander of the county's Major Crimes Task Force for nearly a year now. The last commander, Captain Helen Sutter, was injured in a motorcycle accident, and voila, he got the job. Of course, the headaches of personnel and paperwork were not his forte. But they came with the job.

Kerns melting on the marble library floor promised to make him yearn for bygone days.

"He melted?" Bear repeated.

"His organs and tissue have liquified." Curtis returned to his tablet. "The autopsy will tell me more. He has severe internal hemorrhaging, evidenced by blood loss through the mouth, nose, eyes, and ears. His skin has turned from deep red from some form of fever or intrusion of something, to pale from blood loss. He melted, Bear. That's my best answer right now."

"Jeez, Curtis." Bear stepped back from Kerns' body. "Ebola?"

Ebola? I saw a movie once where Donald Sutherland tried to nuke Dustin Hoffman over an outbreak of Ebola. Some damn monkey caused the whole thing. I never went to the zoo again.

"Actually, very similar in presentation." Curtis stared at Bear as his eyes got big. "It's concerning."

"No kidding." Bear's face twisted like he'd eaten a rotten lemon. "Should we quarantine?"

Curtis looked around before leaning in close to him. "Yes, until we know for sure. We have to quarantine everyone here. Then, find anyone who's been in and out in the past twenty-four hours. Anyone who left must be sent to the hospital for testing. I'll get a medical team down here and notify the proper channels."

I asked, and Bear repeated me. "How bad could this get?"

The question froze Curtis like ice.

"If it's a contagion, no telling." Curtis pulled his plastic examination gloves off. "Worst-case, it could kill everyone in this library and spread into town, killing more. If unstopped—if we don't contain it here—it could lead to an epidemic or worse."

Worse? "Bear, you gotta get control of this place fast. There's no cure for Ebola."

"On it." Bear was on his cell phone speaking urgently and quietly to the Sheriff's dispatch.

I listened in the best I could. The words I caught, I didn't like. CDC, the Center for Disease Control, you know, the bug and death people. FEMA, or Federal Emergency Management Agency, the crash, earthquake, and hurricane people. Now, they might be the Ebola people, too. The rest was a jumble of orders and requests. Bear never panicked, but if he were to, this was the time.

While I can't die again, everyone in this town might be lined up for their first at bat. We—Bear and I—needed answers, clues, something other than a melted fed. Those answers might give us a way out of this mess. It was time to try one of my dead detective tricks. I have several, although I'm not always in control of them. They work *most* of the time.

As Curtis walked away with one of his technicians, Bear clicked off his call but kept the phone against his ear as cover to speak with me.

"Kerns was here to meet Angela, Tuck. What's that all about?"

He knew everything I did, and I said as much, adding, "He said he needed to meet with her on urgent business about her Apple Harvest research."

"Her what?"

"The Apple Harvest Project. You've read about it in the paper, Bear."

"Humor me."

Clearly, he had not read about it in the paper. Or listened to Angel and me discuss it a dozen times over the past weeks.

"Several months ago, during renovations of the town courthouse, they found six wooden crates of old archive files. They were in a sub-vault no one knew about in the courthouse basement. The crates were branded "Apple Harvest Farms." They'd been sealed and lost a hundred or more years ago. Some of the records date back to the Civil War and before."

Bear's face scrunched up. "So?"

"So—there's old land records, banking files, all kinds of stuff. Some of it came from old Winchester families, two old banks no longer in existence, and even John Mosby and Bradley M. White."

"Mosby the Confederate guerrilla fighter?" Bear glanced around to see if anyone was listening. "Our White? The rich old guy in town?"

"Yep, those two."

"White has pals all the way to Richmond and Washington. What about the files?"

I laughed. "Boy, you don't read the papers much, do you? White's already fighting in court to take control of the records and not allow Angel to keep examining them."

Bradley White was quite a local character. Rich. Powerful. Rich and powerful again. He was widely known for his pleasant, simple-man demeanor, too. No, that's a lie. He was a tight-ass, arrogant, power-monger who looked down his nose at everyone. He spoke with a slight southern drawl, and his little gray cells were constantly trying to contemplate how to restore the Confederacy.

Bear digested it all. "What about this fed, Kerns? What did Angela tell you?"

"He refused to say much to Angel on the phone, other than that his work was connected to the Apple Harvest find. That, and it was classified."

"Classified?" Bear stood staring at the body, still feigning a call. "That's odd."

"As odd as being melted?"

"No. I guess not."

"He wouldn't talk to her here, either. The minute they met, he wanted her to leave with him."

Bear scowled. "We have to find out what that meeting was all about. And find witnesses."

Yes, we did. "Keep everyone away, Bear. I'm going in."

"Going in?" He rolled his eyes and glanced around. "Ah, jeez. I hate when you do this stuff."

"I know. But unless I do the 'poof' thing, we won't learn anything from Kerns."

I learned the poof-thing early on in my dead days. All I had to do was focus on where I wanted to be—"being there"—and poof, I arrived. Sometimes, the "being there" trick was like channel surfing cable TV until I find where I want to be. Other times, like if Angel was in danger, I don't have to search; I simply arrive. There were those odd times, too, when 'poof' had an entirely different result. Like this time.

I leaned over Kerns, gripped his what was left of his hand—bone and skin—and …

Bam. Poof.

The rotunda snapped closed—dark and gone. Sparks erupted inside me like Fourth of July fireworks. Lights and images swirled around like a crazy movie—a movie starring someone else—Special Agent Kerns. His life flashed before me … through me …

* * *

Poof…

I was no longer kneeling beside Kerns' body—I was *in* Kerns' body. I was him, sharing his person and reliving his last few moments of life—before he turned to mush. My insides were unsettled, and it took a few moments to quell my thoughts and allow his thoughts and his visions to take over. When they did, it was like a rush of adrenaline that spun me in circles like a tornado in Oz. I held on the best I could and waited for the transition to end.

A few seconds more, Special Agent Kerns began showing me his story. At least, part of it.

He—with me seeing through his eyes and hearing what he heard—walked up the Handley Library's granite stairs to the entrance. His cell phone was in our ear, and someone babbled something I had to strain to understand.

"I got it already. I just spoke with her, and she's meeting me inside," Kerns said to the anxious caller. "I'll see what she knows. If necessary, I'll take her to the safehouse. She's the only one who might be able to help with Pellman. Wait …"

We hesitated on the top landing at the big, double oak doors leading into the library. We looked around. There were several people on the sidewalk. We checked each of them carefully, giving them a good, visual looksee. No one seemed to notice us. On the street, just pulling up to the curb, was an expensive, black Tesla Roadster. A young African American man dressed in a suit got out and headed toward the library steps. The car drew lots of attention and took everyone's eyes off the driver, who climbed the library steps and disappeared inside.

Paranoia was building in us, and we double-checked Piccadilly and Braddock Streets in all directions.

A mom and three young children scurried up toward us, books in hand. Mom gave them a stern warning about their conduct in the library, as all mothers do. Horns honked as somebody failed to move out of the intersection fast enough following the light change. An old woman dragged her little fluffy dog out of the corner café and down the sidewalk in the opposite direction. Fluffy wanted to sniff a car tire and nearly got choked to death for his interest.

Not seeing whatever spooked us, we returned to the caller. "I'll call you soonest I know. I've been under surveillance since I hit town thirty minutes ago. I haven't seen them, but they're here. I know it."

"Status of the meeting?" the voice asked.

"Young just arrived."

"What about El Fazi and Liu?"

"They're inside. I'll meet you later."

We tapped off the call, pocketed the cell phone, and went inside.

Inside, we stood in the rotunda and inconspicuously checked out the visitors in eyesight. There were three halls off the rotunda. The east and west halls led to the East and West Reading Rooms and meeting rooms. The center Circulation Hall led to the main, North Reading Room. We made mental notes and wandered down the west hall, found an unlocked meeting room with a glass window where we could sit inside and view the hall. We went inside.

Almost immediately, an attractive, Asian-American woman with a little girl of perhaps ten or eleven years old walked past us and headed for the east hall. The little girl carried a large picture book, and the woman hefted a heavy, oversized shoulder bag. The girl saw us looking at her through the glass, slowed, whispering something to her mom as they reached the rotunda. Mom turned back and looked directly at us as we watched them. She glanced around, spun on her heels, and continued into the east hall.

Our paranoia was simmering, and I tried to find a reason for it in his thoughts. He'd spoken of surveillance, but I couldn't conjure up any of his memories to explain that. As always happens when I do this spook-takeover—call it temporary possession if you will—I was not in control. I was a passenger. Kerns had to show me whatever he could. Most often, what I was shown was not clear. Not apparent. Most importantly, not always what I thought I was seeing. Snippets of jumbled memories and thoughts—puzzle pieces dropped on the floor to be sorted later.

Across the rotunda, Angel appeared and walked to Library Lil's high-back bench. As she looked around, we did too.

When the paranoia subsided, we left the meeting room and walked quickly to her, proffered a hand, and said, "Professor Tucker, I'm Special Agent Thomas Kerns—DOD. We need to talk. Don't be alarmed, but please come with me now."

Oh ... Oh... God ... it hurts ...

Something stabbed us inside, everywhere. No, something started burning through us—our head, our chest, our stomach—like a billion hot, searing knives slicing and stabbing. The fire moved through us as molten pain. The agony suddenly surged into burning, searing torture.

Death.

The rattle of chains overhead made us look at the antique chandelier. We glanced around the second-floor balcony overlooking us as the lights flickered and flashed out. Still staring upward, we noticed a door to one of the private offices ajar on the east side of the balcony. Someone was standing in it, watching us ... no, not a person, *something*. It protruded out the door, barely noticeable above the wrought-iron railing around the balcony hall. It was aimed at us.

The fire inside flashed. Everything went black.

I snapped out of Kerns as I felt his life succumb to the fire. My brief journey through his last moments was over.

Poof, back on the spook express.

In a flash, I was me again—just me. In the here and now. Still dead and among the living.

Chapter Three

"I'm back, Bear."

He jumped, and he spilled a cup of coffee down his chin and soaked his shirt. "Dammit, Tuck, give me some warning, will you?"

"How? Blow in your ear? You'd more than jump."

"Yeah, yeah." He looked around to make sure no one was watching or listening. "Get anything?"

"I did. You won't believe it." I told him what I'd witnessed with Kerns and what I'd overheard right up to his murder. Repeating it all sent waves of angst through me—and sadness. "He mentioned Pellman, Angel's assistant. And after what I saw and felt, it's not Ebola or any disease. It's a death ray."

"Curtis isn't sure."

Looking down at Kerns' body, I repeated seeing the object pointing out of the second-floor balcony door. "Whatever it was, it was aimed right at us—er—Kerns. He was killed with a death ray. This all has something to do with Pellman."

When I was a kid, I saw one of the quintessential sci-fi classics of all time—*The Day the Earth Stood Still*. In the opening of the movie, an alien and his robot pal landed on the Washington, DC, Mall. They were quickly surrounded by the Army. After they came out of their spaceship, some knucklehead accidentally shot the alien. In seconds, the robot retaliated with a ray gun out of his head and zapped all the weapons from the surrounding soldiers.

A robot with a ray gun didn't sound silly, given I was standing in the library over a dead guy with his insides melted. That, and I was standing there—being dead and all.

Bear's face tightened. "No, Tuck. It wasn't any death ray. There has to be a better explanation. Go keep Angela company. Leave this to me."

"Bear, this involves Angel. She was leaving with him when he was hit with some kind of death ray—"

"It's not a death ray," Bear snapped. "Go, Tuck."

He wasn't listening. "Kerns melted right in front of her. I experienced it when I was in him. You know I'm right."

"Stay with Angela, Tuck." He saw Curtis staring at him as he walked back to us. "Sorry, Curtis. I know it's weird that I still talk to Tuck. It's habit."

"Of course." Curtis grinned. "Therapeutic."

"Yeah, therapeutic," Bear grumbled. "Curtis, could Kerns' injuries and death be because of some kind of gun … like a, a …"

"Death ray," I said.

He cringed. "Death ray?"

Curtis shook his head in amusement, then stopped and glanced back at Kerns' body. His face suddenly lost all mirth. "To tell you the truth, it's possible."

I would save my "I told you so" for later. They're like savings bonds; they gain value with age.

"Possible?" Bear's face twisted. "Explain."

"I've read research on military testing of such weapons." Curtis stepped closer to Bear. "Years ago, the military perfected an anti-riot weapon that beams enhanced microwaves at people. It gives the sensation they're burning, but they are not. No residual physical damage. Lasers and other energy tools are not new science, either. Anything is possible."

"Kerns was DOD," I said. "I bet it's their ray gun."

Bear's frown deepened. "Great, anything's possible. I hate saying this … but a ray gun killed Kerns?"

"It's remotely possible, yes." Curtis cleared his throat. "The autopsy will tell me more. Something caused him to liquefy internally. While I see no scorching or burn patterns that might indicate concentrated high-energy, it doesn't mean it's not there."

"Jeez, Curtis. I was hoping for a 'no.'"

"Why do you ask about a death ray, Bear?" Curtis asked.

I wanted to hear this one.

Bear said, "A possible witness. I wasn't putting much credence to it."

"Better it's a death ray than Ebola," Curtis said. "Lab tests will rule out contagions. But that won't be for hours." His cell rang, and he waved Bear off so he could take the call.

We obliged and walked away.

Past the Circulation Hall, a team of plainclothes detectives stood with two uniformed Winchester Police Officers. All of them were casually talking until we headed their way. Then, they snapped to and turned all business. Everyone but one—a beady-eyed, snake-like detective that slid backward and sat atop an oak reading table, sipping coffee.

"What's the plan, Bear?" Spence, the beady-eyed detective, asked. "Pretty weird, right? Some kind of death ray?"

See, everyone thought it was a death ray.

"Don't start, Spence," Bear snapped.

It was always great to see Detective Mike Spence, my nemesis on the Frederick County Major Crimes Task Force. Great to see him, like Dustin Hoffman loved seeing Donald Sutherland in that Ebola movie. Spence was a short, wiry guy in his late thirties. He only reached that age because I was murdered before I could kill him. His hair was thinning noticeably—a polite way of saying "balding,"—with a few straggly blondish hairs over his ears that hampered his flirting with much younger ladies. He had a narrow face and eyes like a viper that were always looking to make trouble. So, other than his serpent looks, dimwitted personality, and sneaky, backstabbing character, Spence wasn't a bad guy.

"Got anything, Spence?" Bear asked.

"Nobody saw, heard, or knows anything," Spence said. "What's Curtis got?"

Bear wagged a finger at the four cops. "Listen up, guys—especially you, Spence. We're quarantining the building. Winchester PD and more of our deputies are coming to secure the perimeter. Everyone stays in the rooms they're in right now. Make a roster of who's where. Anyone who has left today has to be identified and transported to the hospital."

"Lockdown?" Spence looked like he had to go to the bathroom. "Really?"

"Yes. Kerns' COD is unclear. Curtis thinks it could be a contagion. We're thinking real bad possibilities."

"Not a death ray?" Spence asked.

Bear shot him a look that was a death ray of its own.

"A contagion?" One of the other cops asked. "Like the flu?"

"Worse." Bear lowered his voice. "We're planning on the worst-case scenario and hoping it's something else."

I forced a nervous laugh. "Right. Like something that melted a guy out of his clothes."

"Worst-case. Got it." Spence's normally dull, obnoxious face darkened with worry. He licked his lips, and he seemed not to know what to do with his body, shifting around like a child. "Does this mean we're staying inside, too?"

Oddly enough, I felt for him. I'm dead, and it's not like Ebola can sicken me, and I can't get zapped with a death ray and die. At least, I hope not. He and the rest of Winchester could. Fear of the unknown was the worst kind of fear. Right then, there was plenty of unknown to go around.

"Yes. We're staying inside." Bear threw a thumb over his shoulder. "Get on those rosters of patrons in and out of here. Have Clemens work the CCTV and Kerns' cell phone."

I asked, "Bear, you and I can go check that second-floor room where the ray gun poked out of."

"No," he said and quickly added, "I'll take the second floor. I want to check those rooms personally."

Spence eyed him. "What's so special up there?"

"A possible witness. I'll handle it."

"Right." Spence made notes on a small notepad. "Maybe I should go out and organize the perimeter security. Just to make sure it's tight."

"You're in here with us." I slapped Spence behind his head and made him wince. Sometimes, when I really, really want to make a point, I can communicate with others in fun ways. "I'll be watching if you try to sneak out."

As Spence flinched, Bear said, "It's a precaution. Finish those rosters ASAP. Check carefully—*real* carefully."

"Got it." Spence started to go but stopped and turned back around, and came up close to us. "Hey, Bear, I'm scared. I'm really scared."

Spence was dumb, but he wasn't that dumb.

I wasn't sure which was worse—an Ebola outbreak or a super-secret death ray that silently killed everyone in sight.

Thank God, no one could see me.

Chapter Four

Bear headed to the second-floor offices, and I went to check on Angel. While I wanted to investigate the room where I'd seen the device kill Kerns, Angel needed me more.

The Handley Library was built in the early 1900s and is named after its benefactor, John Handley, a Pennsylvania judge who loved Winchester. I'm told the structure is a Beaux-Arts architecture designed to look like an open book. I guess it does if you stare at it long enough. The building has three floors above ground and a Lower Level. Each of the levels branches off a central rotunda. The building is meticulously designed and magnificent in its own way, with original architecture left after years of renovations that give it a historical and unique style.

I assumed Angel retreated to the Lower Level, where she'd been working earlier in the Archive and Research rooms. That's where I found her.

"What are you doing down here, Angel? The ME quarantined this place. He thinks it's Ebola or something. I think it's a death ray."

When she looked up, tears had pooled in her eyes and began streaming down her cheeks. Her eyes were glossy and red. She'd been crying for a while. She was not a crying-kinda-gal under normal circumstances. These were not that.

"Angel?"

I walked over and touched her shoulder—a comforting hand. Her face lightened, and her shoulders quivered as she closed her eyes. She always responded that way—feelings consumed her like recalling a fond memory. Whether the ethereal plane or something deeper, Angel and I have a unique bond—a deep, emotional connection that binds us closer than any marital vow or physical connection ever had. After my murder, it took me time to reach her. Eventually, I found a way. I was there—'being there,' as a crusty old friend of mine would say. For me, it was pure emotion. A deep, binding tie that no bullet could end. Later, we happened upon a path where she could not only see and hear me, but she could feel my touch and I hers—I was almost alive to her. You see, a year after my murder, someone killed her, or tried to. She was dead for several minutes. After she returned to the living, we were bound deeper than when we were both among the living.

That bond was the only thing that kept me, well, *alive*. I dare say the same for her.

She wiped the tears from her cheeks and touched my hand on her shoulder.

"Tuck, I'm scared."

"I know, Angel. Me, too."

"Really?" She glanced around at nothing. "I came down here to try and focus and get myself together—"

Something banged loudly somewhere in the Lower Level.

"Tuck?" She walked to the research room door that led out to the main Archive Room. Something banged again and startled her. "Someone else is down here. I locked the stairwell door behind me, and Bear turned the elevator off earlier."

"Stay here, Angel. I'll go see."

I *poofed* out into the Lower Lobby—the central hub of the Lower Level.

I checked the elevator, and it was off. The stairwell door was closed and locked from my side, too. Although there was a crash bar on the door for emergency exit, no one could come down from the main floor.

On the lobby floor, I noticed drag marks. The drag marks looked like black rubber skids someone might make by dragging a cart with a stuck wheel. They were intermittent and each only an inch or two long. They blazed a trail between the maintenance room doorway to the elevator.

There was also a strange scent in the air—a scent I didn't like and had smelled too many times over the years. As I searched for the source of that smell, the Robinson auditorium doors banged open, and Spence emerged walking backward. He had his pistol out and was pasty-faced and nervous.

I said, "What are you doing down here, Mikey? This wasn't your Bear's to-do list."

He turned around in a slow circle with a dim, shocked look on his face. As he did, he muttered something I couldn't make out.

Something spooked him. No pun intended.

Just then, Angel walked out of the Archive Room. "Hello?"

"It's just Spence," I said. "It's okay."

He spun around and jutted his pistol at her. "Freeze."

"Whoa, Detective, it's me—Angela."

"Oh, Angela, sorry." Spence flushed, and he lowered his gun. "What are you doing down here?"

"Working. How did you get down here?" She walked to him. "I locked the stairwell, and the elevator is off."

"Well, the stairwell door was unlocked." He rubbed his head. "I came down to see if anyone was around. I was backstage in the auditorium. Someone conked me on the head."

"Are you all right?" She checked his head gingerly with her fingers. "There's no blood. No bump that I can see, either. Did you see who it was?"

A head shake. "Must have knocked me out for a second. I'll check upstairs to see if anyone saw someone coming out of the stairwell."

"Yeah, you do that, Mikey." I didn't buy it. "Angel, he probably fell over trying to sneak out that rear door. He's scared to death."

"Me, too," she said, and when Spence looked quizzically at her, she added, "I'm scared, too, Detective. Don't feel bad."

"I'm not afraid. This place is just weird." He holstered his pistol and started for the stairs. Then, he stopped and turned around. "There's a door back there that opens into a concrete wall. Two ancient spiral staircases that stop at the ceiling and go nowhere. What the hell were these people thinking?"

She laughed despite her nervousness. "They've tried to retain some of the original architecture. It's historical ambiance."

"Yeah, right, ambiance."

I said, "Angel, get your stuff. I don't like you being down here alone. I'm not sure Spence is telling the truth, but I'm not sure he isn't, either. Either way, someone else was down here recently."

She asked Spence, "Detective, would you mind waiting on me? I'll get my things and go upstairs with you."

"Sure, Angela. I'll wait."

"Thank you."

We left him and returned to the Research Room. She gathered her briefcase and files and returned to the Lower Lobby. As we neared him, that distinct odor reached me again.

"Angel, tell Spence to check the storeroom and mechanical room."

Instead, she walked over, pushed the storeroom door easily open. "Detective, shouldn't this door be locked?"

"I don't know. Maybe." Spence peeked inside, keeping his right hand resting on his pistol. "I didn't search this far."

My dead detective senses pinged off the charts. I checked inside the storeroom door that Angel had opened. The drag marks I'd seen by the elevator were also inside the doorway. They led deeper down the inner hall toward a mechanical area. I followed them in and around the corner to another cluttered workspace. There, I found a dark, dingy cavern where the furnace, water controls, and other building infrastructure resided. It was a creepy space that seemed foreign and forgotten compared to the library's friendly grandeur.

Being forgotten wasn't the real problem, though.

It was the body lying against the electrical panel just ahead.

Chapter Five

"His neck's broken." Bear knelt beside the body doing a cursory examination. "No signs of a struggle or trauma that I can see. We'll wait on Curtis to be certain."

"Well, at least he hadn't melted out of his clothes," I said. "That's good, right?"

Bear grunted.

The body lay face down on the floor, facing away from the mechanical room entrance. His hands were out to his side. He looked like he had simply dropped where he stood at the electrical switches and breakers on the back wall. He was slightly askew, sideways as though he'd tried turning as he died. He was dressed in the traditional maintenance uniform—green pants and a long-sleeved green shirt, heavy leather toolbelt still strapped around his waist, and a tool kit near his feet. He was a big man, but not fat or frumpy. His hair was trimmed short, and his face, turned to one side, showed no more than fifty years.

There was one thing out of place. In his right ear was a single, expensive earbud. Its wire disappeared inside his shirt collar and protruded beneath his untucked shirt at his waist. The earbud wire wasn't connected to anything.

I made a note. Great detectives do that, you know. They make notes.

"Geez, Bear, I never suspected anything in here." Spence was on his cell relaying a brief report to dispatch. "I was looking for stray folks and never thought to check in here. I didn't notice the door was unlocked, either."

"He missed the drag marks, too." That got Bear's attention. "He never found Angel. I think he was trying to sneak out of the building."

Bear glanced at him with not-so-friendly eyes. "Spence, the HAZMAT guys just arrived. The building is secure. No one's going in or out. Find Curtis and bring him down ... *quietly*."

"Right." He started for the stairs.

"Wait," Bear called. "Did you finish identifying everyone in the building?"

"Ah, I've got uniforms working on that. I'll check on them."

"You do that."

Spence left mumbling as he went.

"Easy on him, Bear," Angel said in a soft voice. "He's scared like the rest of us."

"Yeah, yeah." Bear returned his attention to the body. "I get that."

I asked, "Do you recognize him, Angel?"

"That's Mr. Downey," she said, "the new maintenance man. He's only been here a couple weeks. I thought he works at night."

"Night crew?" Bear checked his watch. "It's a little after five p.m. There's no rigor, and he's still warm. My bet is he was killed within the last couple hours or less. From the way the body dropped, I'd say someone came up behind him. He turned to see who it was, and he was attacked."

"Two murders in one day." Great detectives also state the obvious. You know, to make sure everyone is keeping up. "No coincidence."

"No, no coincidence," Bear agreed. "The question is, how is Downey's murder related to Kerns?"

I knelt beside Downey. "Bear, he's wearing an earbud—just one. But it's not connected to anything. That's odd, don't you think?"

He looked Downey over again. "Maybe it was connected to his cell phone, listening to music or a book or something."

"Then where's his phone?"

Angel said, "Surely he wasn't killed for a cell phone."

I thought about that. "No. Maybe he saw what made those drag marks. Maybe he took photographs. Maybe he was talking on the phone. Maybe he was involved somehow, and whoever killed Kerns was eliminating witnesses. Then, whoever killed him grabbed the phone. Maybe—"

"That's a lot of maybes." Bear stood. "Angela, I'll walk you upstairs as soon as Spence and Curtis get here. I'll need your statement to say that *you* found the body. Can't very well say *he* did." By 'he,' Bear meant me, of course. "You didn't hear or see anyone else down here while you were working earlier?"

She thought a moment. "No, it was just Andrew and me—"

"Andrew the lab rat?" he asked. "The one Tuck heard Kerns talking about?"

"My university assistant—not lab rat. He was with me the entire day. We took a couple breaks, but I think he only left once without me. Well, he was coming and going, getting boxes of materials from other rooms."

"Bear, I doubt he could break crackers, let alone Downey's neck." I gestured to the body. "Downey's a big guy. What, maybe six feet and two-thirty, right?"

"Yeah, okay. So?"

Angel knew where I was headed. "Andrew is small. He's no more than one-thirty and short. He's a pleasant and thoughtful young man."

Thoughtful? "He's a worm. He stares at you all the time. When you're not looking, he's always playing on email and his cell phone. How is that being a 'thoughtful young man?'"

She shrugged. "He's normally very attentive and diligent. I don't know why Agent Kerns wanted him."

"Guilty conscience?" Bear asked. "Something else?"

"He's a wimpy geek." Someone had to say it. "No way little Andy broke Downey's neck. Not without a jackhammer."

Bear moved Downey's collar back to view his neckline again. "No contusions from a blow. I think someone did this with their bare hands. Could a geek do that?"

"His name is Andrew," Angel said. "But no, I don't think he is capable. He really is a nice young man."

A nice young man with a crush on her. "The library only has a few CCTV cameras. We need to check the recordings and see who came and went down here."

"Cal is on that." Bear looked at Angel. "Tell me more about Pellman."

She did. "One of the town council members highly recommended him and asked me to be his dissertation advisor. He's working on research scanning artifacts like documents using computer algorithms to categorize and analyze them. It combines his computer programming with advanced research."

"Where is he?" Bear stood. "Upstairs?"

"I'm not sure." She thought a moment. "He was going to pack up my notes and put them in my vehicle before he left for the day."

"So, he could still be here." Bear pulled out a radio from his back pocket, issued orders to locate Pellman, and pocketed the radio again. "I want to talk to him."

Angel looked worried. "He may have gotten out of the library before all this happened."

"Hold it." Bear listened to the radio replies for a moment. "No one has Pellman on any of their contact lists. That means he didn't come back in."

Angel looked tired and defeated. I said, "Angel, I'll go upstairs with you. You need to sit down for a while."

"Yes, thanks, Tuck."

I turned to Bear. "Did you check out that room along the second-floor balcony? The one with the—"

"There was no ray gun, Tuck," Bear snapped. "The room was empty. Nothing. No evidence at all. Not even a shoe print."

Damn, I was so sure, too.

Bear touched Angel's shoulder. "Find somewhere to rest, Angela. Let me worry about the—"

"Ebola, death rays, and dead bodies," I offered.

His face blanched. "Exactly."

Chapter Six

Cal Clemens stood inside the emergency exit in the North Reading Room, watching the library patrons milling around nervously. He was a tall, lean, thirty-four-year-old African American. As always, he was well dressed in a business suit, open color white dress shirt, and highly buffed shoes. In all the years he'd been on the Task Force, his appearance always stood out—sharp and refined—a stark contrast to Bear's two hundred and fifty pounds of body in a two-hundred-pound outfit. Cal had been a senior detective since Bear assumed command of the Task Force. Cal was known for being hardworking and loyal, with a reputation for being a sturdy, dependable detective. Spence, by comparison, had a reputation for being none of those things.

Cal decided to do one more sweep of the library floors to ensure they'd identified everyone in the library. Everyone would have to be interviewed, and if Kerns' death turned out to be contagious, everyone would have to be medically checked.

He walked up to the third floor. This was the library's executive level, where the Director and library staff had offices. There was also the Henkel Boardroom—part boardroom and part museum—just off the rotunda.

As he passed by the boardroom entrance, he heard voices inside. Bear had told him there was no one left up there. Obviously, there was.

"Sheriff's Department," he announced, walking in without knocking. "Who's in here?"

Sitting around the long mahogany board table were four people—a fiftyish, attractive woman with short, red hair and a pale, Asian face, an

African American with a runner's physique and a neatly trimmed beard, a dark-skinned man who might easily be Middle Eastern in a dark suit, and finally, a silver-haired man in an expensive blue blazer over tan slacks and a silk golf shirt.

As Cal entered, another door at the end of the boardroom closed.

"Who just left?" he asked the four.

"What is the meaning of this intrusion?" the silver-haired man barked, standing. "Who do you think you are? Get out."

Cal was tired and sweaty and wasn't in the mood for backtalk. He walked to the other doorway, opened it, and peered out. No one was there. Then, he returned to the conference table and the four people waiting there. He took a moment to look them over, one by one, taking mental notes of each.

"I'm Detective Clemens, Frederick County Major Crimes Task Force," he said. "I need to see IDs on all of you, please."

"I think not." The silver-haired man walked around the table and faced him. His hairline had receded to the back of his head, but the back and sides were still full and immaculately groomed. He spoke with a southern drawl with a rhythm in his speech that was slow and deliberate. The only thing missing on this distinguished-looking man was an ascot. "We are having an important meeting. Leave at once."

"No, sir." Cal took out his notepad. "Your name, please?"

The silver-haired man refused to answer.

"Now, sir."

Nothing.

The African American stood and approached Cal. "Detective, this really is an important meeting. We won't be long. Afterward, we'll find you and tell you whatever you need to know."

"No. I want names and IDs right now." Cal eyed both men standing just feet away. "This is a homicide investigation. Everyone is being identified. There will be interviews—"

"Do you know whom you're addressing, deputy?" the silver-haired man said with a bite in his voice. "Do you?"

"No, sir, that's why I need IDs. And it's 'detective.' I need your details and a few minutes of your time. That's all."

"I think not." The silver-haired man waved dismissively. "I have none to share with you, *deputy*. Leave."

"Sir, this is not a request." Cal took out his radio and called for Bear. "Do *you* understand?"

"I care not either way, deputy." The silver-haired man abruptly sat.

The Asian woman whispered something to the dark-skinned man, who stood, and with a thick foreign accent said, "Detective, I am Ahmad El Fazi. I am here discussing rare books and antiques, as are my colleagues," he gestured to the Asian woman. "This is Miss Chen Liu."

The Asian woman nodded slowly and smiled.

"I'm Peter Young." The African American proffered a hand. "Please excuse our rudeness."

Cal ignored the outstretched hand and returned his gaze to the gray-haired, angry man. "And you, sir? I need your name and business here at the library. Please."

The silver-haired man stared pure contempt and said nothing.

"We're asking all the patrons the same questions."

"Oh, really?" The silver-haired man finally said. "You never answered *my* question, *deputy*."

"It's 'detective,' and if I knew who you were, I wouldn't be asking."

"*Hmmmph*. A dolt, no doubt." The silver-haired man leaned forward, and the boom in his voice nearly knocked Cal back. "I am Bradley Millwood White. I am the presiding chairperson of the White Foundation, of which I'm sure you are well acquainted."

"Sounds familiar." Cal made notes and shook his head. "How about your—"

"Sounds familiar? Clearly uneducated."

Cal ignored him. "I'd like to see all your IDs. Just for my notes."

Bradley Millwood White lunged forward—quick even for a man half his age—and plunged a bony finger into Cal's chest. "You, deputy, need manners. I will not provide you with anything."

"Then you'll be detained. Maybe arrested." Cal leaned forward against

White's finger to force its withdrawal. "This library is an active crime scene, Mr. White. There's been two murders. We're interviewing everyone in the building. So—"

Oddly enough, the mention of two murders barely raised eyebrows.

"I think not."

"Take a step back, Mr. White," Cal ordered coolly. "Now."

"I will not."

Young stepped forward and eased White back by his arm. "Come on now, Mr. White. The detective is merely doing his job. Two murders, you said?"

Cal regretted telling them that. "Yes, I'm afraid so."

White pulled away from Young's grip on his arm, stepped up to Cal again, and shoved him toward the door. "Out. I won't be badgered by the likes of you, you damnable—"

"Careful, now." Cal held up a hand at White. "If 'boy' or the 'N' word comes from your lips, you won't like my response."

White began to sputter but retreated to the boardroom table instead.

"Let's start over." Cal turned to Young. "Show me some ID."

"Ah, sure, if you must." Young reached into his suit coat pocket just as the boardroom door opened.

Bear walked in. "I got this, Clemens."

"Bear?" Cal turned. "I found—"

"I got this." Bear looked past him at the others. Then, he gestured for Cal to follow him out into the hall. Once there, he said, "I already got their information earlier. Let them finish their meeting. It's all legit. I checked."

"You said there was no one up here." Cal couldn't believe it. "That old dude all but assaulted me. He's—"

"Bradley White, Chairman—Emeritus—of the Frederick County Board of Supervisors, a dozen other things. He's the Governor's close friend. He's one of the richest 'old dudes' in this county, *Detective*. He's got big friends everywhere, including DC. I got this. Get back to the second floor and finish your sweep. Now."

Cal couldn't believe what he was hearing. "But I—"

"Now."

Cal glanced back into the boardroom at White. The man's face blossomed with a sardonic smile.

Cal's voice was filled with steel. "Emeritus-whatever doesn't give him the right to refuse questioning or assault me, Bear. What the hell?"

"No, it doesn't. I'll deal with it." Bear hooked a thumb over his shoulder. "Now go, Detective, before things get worse."

Chapter Seven

Within an hour of discovering Downey's body, the Handley Library was in full HAZMAT lockdown. Sheriff's deputies and Winchester police were outside every exit and patrolling the perimeter along the library's esplanade and portico. The doors and windows were sealed on the outside with opaque plastic tenting. People in baggy HAZMAT suits were everywhere. They looked like spacemen from a sci-fi movie. And yes, I have seen movies like that, but I liked the vintage sci-fi better.

I swear, if some robot emerges with a laser beam coming from his head …

Angel sat in a ladder-back chair inside the West Reading Room. Her face was pale and tense while she tried to keep a calm, confident demeanor. She was failing.

"Angel, it'll be okay." I had no idea if that was true. "The HAZMAT people sealed the building, and Curtis said the hospital is already checking all the body fluid samples he sent. But don't worry, really. It's not Ebola. It was a ray gun."

"Tuck, stop with the ray gun stuff. Please."

"It's true." I reminded her what I'd witnessed on the second-floor balcony when I was possessing Kerns. "I'm betting it's a—"

"It's no ray gun." She rolled her eyes and wiped her brow. "It's getting hot in here, Tuck."

She was right. Everyone around us was sweating and fanning themselves with magazines and what have you. I meandered over to two Winchester cops in the West hallway to listen in on their conversation and radio chatter. I got my answer post haste.

I returned to Angel. "The HAZMAT people shut down the air handling system and sealed the vents on the outside. They'll stay closed until they can get the air filtered properly."

"Yes, of course." She leaned back and unbuttoned her blouse an extra button. "If Kerns died of some airborne contagion, they wouldn't want the air in here getting out."

"Right, I figured that, too." I was lying. I had no idea about HAZMAT protocols. All I knew about such things I learned from late-night sci-fi. "It'll get worse."

A young Asian-American woman in her late twenties appeared from behind a bookshelf across the West Reading Room. She was the same woman who had passed Kerns just after he entered the same meeting room earlier. She had exotic looks with long, silky black hair and large, dark eyes. She had a thin, attractive frame and was dressed stylishly in a gray pantsuit and blouse. She eyed Angel, hesitated, and then turned around and beckoned behind her. A little girl appeared. She'd been with the woman earlier, too. She was a younger version of the woman, though twenty years younger. They walked over to us.

Well, to Angel.

"Professor Angela Tucker?" The woman extended a hand with a thin, nervous smile. "I'm Emily Lee-Garcia."

Angel wiped her brow. Recognition blossomed in her face. She stood and took Emily's hand. "Yes, of course—the author."

"Yes." Emily brightened. "You know my work?"

"Of it." Angel smiled at the little girl. "You write historical thrillers, right?"

"Yes, I do." Emily beamed. "Wow, it's nice to be recognized. I'm really just starting out."

"Who is this?" Angel offered her hand to the young girl. "I'm Angela. What's your name?"

"Hello." The little girl took Angel's hand and gave it an exaggerated shake. "I'm Kerrie Garcia—not Lee-Garcia like my mommy. Just Kerrie Garcia."

"Hello, Kerrie Garcia." Angel smiled a broad, welcoming smile. "How are you?"

I watched Kerrie warm instantly to Angel. "It's okay, kiddo, don't be afraid. We'll be out of here soon. I promise. Angel, Bear, and I will take care of you all."

Strangely, Kerrie glanced toward me, smiled, and looked back at Angel. "I'm not afraid, Angel."

"Kerrie, she's Miss Angela, or Professor Tucker," Emily corrected. Then to Angel, she said, "I'm sorry. She's too mature for her age and a little precocious."

"I don't mind. My husband, Tuck, called me Angel."

Kerrie grinned. "He still does."

She knows? To Kerrie, I said, "Kerrie, do you hear me?"

"Uh, huh." She grinned again. "That, too."

Too?

Angel motioned for Emily to sit beside her. "Please, sit with me. What can I do for you?"

"Nothing, really." Emily sat with Kerrie beside her. "We're a little frightened. I recognized you and just wanted to say hello. Did the police say when we'll get out of here? I understand you know them well."

"No, I'm sorry." Angel glanced at me standing in front of them. "The quarantine is a precaution. It should end soon."

I winked at Kerrie. "It's not what they think, kiddo. Someone used a ray gun."

Kerrie giggled loudly. "I know."

Now, this was *really* weird. "Angel, I'll find Bear and see if he knows anything new. I'll be right back."

Kerrie grinned and finger-waved at me.

Holy Sixth Sense, Batman.

Chapter Eight

Leaving Angel to chat with Emily and Kerrie, I made my way to the second floor. I could have done the *poof-thing* and saved my energy, but I wanted to investigate everyone and everything along the way. My first mission was to track down the ray gun that Bear and Angel thought was my imagination. Someone had been in that second-floor office watching me when I was Kerns. That person killed him. Bear said the room was empty. I wanted to see for myself. Maybe I could get a tingle or a vision or something. You know, typical dead-detective leads.

While I would love to think the killer was from Alpha Centauri or Plant X-101, I knew better. The killer was good ole' earthborn flesh and blood. They always were.

The second-floor balcony encircled the rotunda. Off the east and west sides were library staff offices and a large meeting room. On the north side were the Tween Room for young adults and Kids Place for children, stocked full of books, magazines, games, and all manner of literature-focused amusement. Dozens of adults and teens were standing around the balcony looking down at the rotunda's Main Floor, where the crime scene teams were cleaning up. A Winchester police officer stood in the Tween Room, speaking with patrons. Everyone was upset—raised voices and animated hands—and the officer was trying his best to tamp down their nerves.

Most of the office doors around the balcony were open, trying to combat the rising heat. Two were not. One of those was on the west side. The other was on the east side, where I'd seen the ray gun.

I *"poofed"* inside. The moment I landed, I knew something was amiss.

Even being dead, I smell. No, not from the lack of a hot shower in three years. I mean, I *can* smell. The scent of perspiration was thick, and it mingled with a dense, pungent odor of charred rubber or plastic. The room had a six-foot, heavy oak table with four chairs around it. The table was empty except for a centerpiece citing the rules for the room's use. The walls were lightly decorated with a few framed photographs of Winchester over the years. Otherwise, the room was empty.

I couldn't find the source of the burnt odor. It was everywhere and nowhere. As I studied the room more carefully, I noticed the floor was covered with an inexpensive, low-pile carpet. It was a deep, burgundy color. There were four indentations on it that formed a square about three feet long and two feet wide. The indentations leading out the door as though something had been pulled or rolled out. Then I touched one of the indentations with my finger, a stab of energy bit me—the bitter, heavy scent of burnt wire.

"What the heck?"

Slowly, the pieces fell into place. During past dead-investigations, events such as these often led me to evidence. Some were obvious. Others were not. This little jolt of "hello, pay attention" was the less obvious variety.

I'd seen a device peeking out of the room and aiming right at him—us. Kerns hadn't died of monkey Ebola or the Black Plague—although it killed him in much the same way. It eviscerated his body internally. Whatever it was scared me to death. It killed a man some fifty feet away, silently, among dozens of visitors. No one saw, heard, or witnessed anything. The only signs left behind were the scent of burning wire and carpet indentations.

This was the stuff of spy thrillers where the evil genius threatens the world with a death ray. The spy had to battle never-ending platoons of bad guys, destroy the death ray, and save the world—all the while distracted by a sexy double agent and expensive champagne.

I love those movies. Though now, they didn't seem make-believe.

Geez, I hope Angel will understand if I have to handle a sexy double agent. After all, it would be to save the world. Right?

Chapter Nine

"Seal this room." Bear jutted a finger at a police officer standing in the east office doorway. "This is part of the other two crime scenes. Get the crime techs in here."

I sat atop the meeting table. "You know what I'm thinking, Bear?"

"Yeah." He turned to Mike Spence, who was taking notes in the hall. "Spence, I'm thinking whatever made these indentations is connected to those drag marks in the lower level. Something heavy or bulky on a handcart with a busted wheel."

"Ah, that's what I was gonna say, Bear." It was, really. "Get everyone from all the floors downstairs. Finish the witness statements. Find out if anyone saw anyone in this office earlier."

"Okay." Spence jotted notes and never looked up. "Cal just started on the CCTV. There's not much there, Bear. He did get some footage from the outside entrance camera. He thinks someone corrupted the rest of the interior video."

"Maybe that's why Downey was killed," I said. "Maybe he caught someone tampering with the CCTV."

"Right," Bear said. "See if the library has anything we can use to keep people out of here and restrict the lower rotunda lobby—barricades or rope or something."

Spence made another note. He was probably playing hangman. He turned to go.

Bear stopped him. "Get all the evidence we've collected locked up in one of the offices. God only knows how long we'll be in here. I don't want the chain of custody broken. When you get an office to use, give me the key."

"Got it." Spence walked off.

Bear had spent twenty minutes examining the room after I'd located him and reported what I found. My keen spirit-senses proved valuable. At first, he was skeptical about the carpet indentations. But he listened. Then, we recreated what I'd seen through Kerns' eyes. We used one of the uniformed officers' ASP extending baton as a make-shift barrel. We aimed it out the door and down toward the first-floor rotunda at another officer standing where Kerns had fallen.

It worked. It wasn't an easy target, but it was doable.

After rechecking our simulation, Bear said, "You might have something, Tuck."

Why does he ever doubt me? Oh yeah, my space alien theories. Got it.

"Hey, Bear." Something struck me. "How'd you miss the indentations earlier when you were in here?"

"I never checked in here, Tuck. I told you that to get you off my back." Bear got on his cell phone to call the Sheriff. "You're driving me nuts."

Ouch.

While he was on the phone, I went snooping, *er*, investigating. I barely made it off the second-floor balcony.

"Oh, crap. Here we go again."

Chapter Ten

Yep, I should have expected this.

Standing where Kerns died, an unusual patron of the Handley Library stood looking admiringly around the rotunda. She was a beautiful woman with curly blond hair and sparkling blue eyes. She was stunning. After a moment, she looked up directly at me and smiled a broad, beaming smile. She raised her gray, gloved hand and beckoned me to join her.

Beckoned me? *Gulp.*

It's not that I don't get beautiful women begging my attention all the time. I do. But she clearly didn't belong here. Not because she was standing in the middle of the crime scene. And not because I knew she wasn't on any visiting patrons list, either. It was her appearance. She wore a white cotton Garibaldi blouse with a short, band-collar and buttoned front with full-length, puffy sleeves, and a green, floor-length pleated skirt. I'm not talking retro or some new-fashioned outfit from the mall. I'm talking, well, *antebellum* fashion—as in the *Civil War.*

The past was invading the present. I don't mean the living past. I mean the dead past.

She waved again, and I waved back. Rudeness wasn't in my DNA—*much.*

Other than the Civil War dress, something else was amiss, too. I've met a lot of out-of-towners like her whenever I worked bizarre homicides. No one in the rotunda noticed her. One police officer posted on the crime scene walked right *through her* and leaned against the wall behind her.

That's something you don't see every day. Well, I do, but you know, not many others do.

I *poofed* down to the lobby and sauntered over to this belle like we were the only two people in the place. Truth be told, we were the only two dead people in the place.

Her smile was sultry. Her blue eyes were big and bright and pulled me in like a tractor beam. I couldn't help but notice she had a face and figure like Marilyn Monroe, not well hidden from view, either. Her blouse struggled to hold her bosom in, and unless I was mistaken, she was shapely and curved like an hourglass begging to tell me the time. All around her, the scent of jasmine floated in the air. It fit her—sweet and fragrant and alluring.

As I reached her, she leaned in, kissed my cheek, and gave me a long, familiar embrace.

"Hello, Oliver." Her southern accent had me cold. "I've waited all these many years to make your acquaintance. I've been watching you for a very, very long time. Finally, we meet. How wonderful."

Yes, wonderful. "Who are you?"

"I am Sally Elizabeth Mosby." She stepped back and did a slow twirl. "Pleased to make your acquaintance."

Holy Gone with the Wind. "Nice to meet you, Sally. Any relation to John Mosby?"

John Singleton Mosby was a legend. He was a famous Confederate Civil War officer who led the Forty-third Battalion—a cavalry unit that used guerrilla tactics against the North—Mosby's Rangers. Most of his campaigns were in the Shenandoah Valley. Many around Winchester, too. While a rebel during the war, Mosby went on to become a close friend of President Grant and even the American consul to Hong Kong in his day.

Sally grinned. "Why yes, Oliver. John is my uncle once-removed."

"Uncle? Once removed?"

She nodded and flashed that brilliant smile.

Gulp.

Sally-once-removed was unquestionably the most alluring and mysterious spirit I'd ever seen. I've seen a few real honeys, too. Angel would say I only run into real honeys, but she tends to exaggerate.

"You're staring, Oliver."

How rude of me. "Sorry. It's just that, well, er … you're …"

"Why, thank you, Oliver. You're quite fetching, too." She grinned slyly. "As I'm sure your *wife*, Angela, often tells you."

Oh, yeah, Angela. Note to self—stop ogling strange spirits.

"Sorry. What are you doing here, Sally? Although I can guess. This is not my first murder. Nor my first haunting."

"That's rather complicated, Oliver, and personal."

"Personal?"

"Of course. Death is always very personal. Don't you agree?"

She had a point. "Well, yeah."

History repeats itself. So, Sally's presence told me a few things. First, whatever happened to her would reveal itself in time. Not necessarily clearly, but it would be revealed. Also, Sally's appearance meant her death—and her past life—was directly connected to Kerns' and Downey's murders. If I've learned anything since my own murder, it's that when the dead start showing up—after they're dead that is—they're connected to the murder at my feet. There were no coincidences. None.

"Sally, you were killed—murdered—right?"

"How very direct." Her face saddened. "Yes, Oliver."

"What happened to you? Why are you here?"

She eyed me with a painful, sad face. Slowly, tears rained, and she looked away. When she faced me again, her eyes were red and fiery. Her face flashed resolve and something else … *anger*.

"If you must know, Oliver, in the fall of eighteen and sixty-four, I was murdered quite brutally. All for a secret."

Chapter Eleven

Of course, she was killed brutally. If she hadn't been, she'd be off spinning her parasol and swooning over Rhett Butler in the afterlife. Wait, did Rhett Butler actually exist? Doesn't matter. You get my point.

"Care to explain?"

"No, I do not." She put on a sly, taunting grin. "A lady likes her secrets."

"Okay, how about a hint about things here? You know, like why Kerns died, in the library, with a ray gun?"

Her eyes twinkled. They were beautiful eyes—am I gushing? Yes—and more guilt soaked me. Angel was nearby, somewhere, all warm and alive and, well, real.

"Why Oliver Tucker, who is Kerns?" She glanced around the library. "What is a ray gun?"

How do I explain a ray gun to a nineteenth-century belle? I tried but failed.

"Oh, never mind. I'll take your word; it's quite mysterious." She glanced up at the stained-glass ceiling three floors overhead. "Did I tell you that I died in eighteen and sixty-four?"

"Yes, you did. But not how or why. Obviously, you were very young."

A tear formed in her eye, and like a light switch snapping off, she disappeared.

"Sally?"

Her voice was a whisper now, singsong and melancholy, and it came from everywhere around me. "Eighteen and sixty-four, Oliver. I was barely twenty-eight years of age. I had given up my entire life for my country—for my cause. It was taken from me for doing my duty. Wrongly taken from me because of a secret."

"Right. What secret?" I doubted she'd explain things simply. The visiting dead never do. "Tell me what happened, Sally."

A sniffle or two. "They're still here, Oliver. Not the same faces, mind you, but they're here. You must find them. Stop them. If you don't, then I died for nothing, and there will be many, many more dead. Their greed and depravity are monstrous."

See, not simple at all. "Stop who, Sally? How are you connected to Kerns and Downey?"

"Doc was right." An almost imperceptible giggle. "You *are* a little slow."
Ouch.

Of course, she knew Doc. He's my spirit guide and paternal great-grandfather. He thinks guiding me is best done with sarcasm and criticism instead of outright advice. Gotta love old Doc, though.

"It's easy as pie, Oliver." Her voice faded with each syllable. "My job was to find the secret first and stop them from knowing it. They were hunting for something that would have changed the tide of the war—nothing would be as it is now. I did my job. But still, they got away. Now, they're back, and they're worse. If you don't stop them, Winchester is truly dead."

Chapter Twelve

ngel walked to the circulation desk, where Bear stood speaking with Cal. As she stopped beside them, Bear asked Cal about his progress on the CCTV and Kerns' cell phone.

"Haven't gotten to the cell phone yet. I'll do that now." Cal turned to the computer where he'd been working. He retrieved a black-cased smartphone and a yellow legal pad and handed Bear the pad. "Here's a list of everyone in the library. We're almost done with the interviews."

Angel said, "Hello, Cal, how are you?"

"Hello, Angela." Cal's face brightened. He leaned forward over the desk to give her a quick hug. "I'm okay. You holding up?"

After Tuck's death, Cal had always been friendly and supportive. Not too long ago, he'd been instrumental in hunting down a killer in a local nightclub. That case nearly took her life. Most importantly, it had been a turning point in her connection with Tuck. Since then, Cal had a closer, more personal bond with *both* of them. He knew Tuck was back—though he couldn't hear or see him—and he loved taunting Bear and Spence about it.

"Well, I wish I were elsewhere today, Cal."

"I hear you." Cal put on a cheery smile. "Angela, I ran into your young assistant earlier."

"Andrew?"

Cal nodded. "He dropped a box of your files all over the rotunda a little before Agent Kerns' murder. Nice kid, I guess. A little clumsy."

"He tries too hard," Angel said.

"That's all wonderful, Cal. But let's focus." Bear looked up from the list Cal had given him. He tore the top several pages from the legal pad, folded and pocketed them. "Give me Kerns' cell phone. I'll walk it up to the second-floor office we're using to store evidence."

"I can work on the phone now," Cal said. "It won't take long."

"No." Bear snatched the cell phone from him. "Stay on the CCTV."

"CCTV is a bust. I think someone deleted it all. But our techies have to check. It's over my head."

"Keep working." Bear pocketed the cell. "I'll deal with the phone."

"But—"

Bear's hand flashed up. "Tell Spence I want all the witness statements and everything we have compiled immediately. Give them to me. I want to review everything before they end the lockdown. No one sees anything until I do. Got it?"

"Okay. Okay." Cal glanced to Angel, who shrugged. "What about those four in the boardroom earlier?"

"Nothing there." Bear had a sharp edge in his voice. "They were meeting about books and antiques or something. Do what I told you."

"Easy, Bear. Cal's trying." Angel touched his arm. "Want me to find you some coffee?"

"I'm fine." Bear's face was tight and irritated as he pointed at Cal. "Get with Spence on those statements."

"Yes, sir. You're the boss."

"I am." Bear turned and walked away.

"What's with him, Angela?" Cal whispered, watching him go. "He's always a little gruff on a case. But he's been acting weird. Right?"

She agreed. "This is a different one. Isn't it? He's worried the contagion is something worse."

"Worse than Ebola?"

Angel forced a smile. "I highly doubt it's Ebola, Cal."

"What's *he* think?"

"Bear?"

"No, like woo-woo *him*." Cal wiggled his fingers like he was scaring a child. "Tuck."

"Oh, *him*." Angel giggled, and some of the tension escaped. "I thought we agreed not to comment on *him* between us?"

"We did." Cal turned to a library worker who walked up. "Yes, ma'am?"

The woman, a middle-aged volunteer in a tan pantsuit and big smile, pointed back to the computer workstation. "Detective, I found a backup file of some of the cameras. It's not much, but it covers the side employee entrance and the visitor parking lot. Will that help?"

"It will. Thank you." Cal turned back to Angel. "Okay, Angela. You stay safe now. And tell *him* I said 'hey.'"

As Cal returned to the computer and the volunteer, Angel used the stairwell to go up to the second floor. As she reached the balcony overlooking the rotunda, footsteps echoed above her from the third floor. Bear was just walking out of view. She hurried to follow him.

By the time she reached the third floor, he was gone.

As she navigated the balcony, the Henkel Boardroom door closed ahead. Bear's voice boomed out, angry and rumbling through the heavy oak doors. He was arguing with someone who was speaking in a soft, quiet voice. She couldn't make out the details of the dispute, but it had Bear's temper up.

"Stay here, dammit. Lock the door," Bear barked. A pause, then he added, "And you, get out of here. Get downstairs with the others."

There were three in the room.

Angel made it into one of the adjacent open offices just as the boardroom door opened. She peeked out as a familiar man walked past her toward the elevator. He was an old man, almost gaunt, with thin, graying hair and piercing, penetrating eyes. Despite the signs of old age, he still had the swagger of someone accustomed to power and respect.

Poor Nicholas Bartalotta—Poor Nic to his friends, enemies, and every law enforcement agency on the East Coast. Nicholas was not someone she'd thought would be "library material." Not unless the library was a cover for a speakeasy. Nicholas was around seventy, and the years had been rough on him. When he retired many years ago, he returned to Winchester—his boyhood summer home. Here, he eased into a life of luxury, community support, and, of all things, being her self-appointed Godfather. Winchester was known for a lot of things—Civil War history, Patsy Cline, and the Apple Blossom Festival. But its single most significant footnote was having its very own crime boss—albeit a retired one.

What was he doing here? More to the point, who was he meeting in the boardroom that made Bear so angry?

As she watched Nicholas disappear into the elevator, Bear stormed out of the boardroom and back down the stairs, grumbling to himself.

She sneaked to the balcony and peered down from behind one of the archway pillars. Her inner radar pinged, and that unnerved her. Not just because of the murders and quarantine, either. It was because Bear Braddock, the normally solid, calm, and collected man she'd known for more than fifteen years, was acting downright *peculiar*.

Below her, Bear was already out of sight. She crept down the stairs to the second floor and rounded the balcony to the Tween Room and into the Kids' Place. As she entered, a door somewhere around the balcony opened and closed. She turned in time to see Bear leaving one of the offices, carrying a large cardboard file box. He checked over the balcony twice on his path and headed back up to the third floor.

Peculiar was no longer the word describing Bear. *Suspicious* was on her lips, now.

Bear?

Chapter Thirteen

"Tuck, there's something wrong with Bear," Angel said when she found me in the Archive Room. She unloaded like a Gatling Gun about Bear, Poor Nic, and someone else in the boardroom.

Poor Nic's presence piqued my interest.

"Poor Nic in a library? I wonder what he's into this time. Any idea about the other person?"

"Cal found four people in the boardroom earlier. He never mentioned Nicholas. He did tell me they were…a Peter Young, Ahmad El Fazi, Chen Liu." Angel thought a moment. "The fourth was Bradley White, a local town father."

Those names tickled my brain. "Angel, when I was, er, possessing Kerns earlier, he'd mentioned Young, El Fazi, and Liu to someone on the phone. They were there for a meeting in the library. I heard of White by reputation only—and it's ugly."

She shrugged. "Yes, I know about White, too. I haven't heard of the others. Apparently, Bear got into an argument with Cal over them."

"If Nic was one of the four, Cal would have said."

She agreed.

"Especially with two murders on our hands. Three, if you count Sally."

"Sally?" Angel's eyebrows raised. "Who's Sally?"

"Oh, a spirit from the past. You'll love her. Promise."

"Let me guess. She's young, beautiful, and a damsel in distress."

Wow, Angel was clairvoyant.

"How'd you know?"

She folded her arms. "You don't seem to be haunted by any other type. In fact, you don't seem to investigate any other type, either."

"Kerns isn't that type. Neither is Downey." Otherwise, she had a point. "Sally's a relative of John Mosby. Isn't that interesting?"

"Fascinating."

"John Mosby the Confederate—"

"I know who John Mosby was better than you."

"He's a historical figure, right?"

She looked at me with a sneer.

Wow, tough audience. "Sally's a relative of his. Or was. Anyway, this is all history stuff. You should be thrilled."

She put on her 'what the hell are you talking about' look, which I was very familiar with. My genius often confused her.

"History stuff?" I repeated. "You know, like—"

"Tuck, just because something is 'history stuff' doesn't make it unbelievably fascinating to me. What's your point?"

Perhaps watching a federal agent get ray-gunned to death, being locked up in this sweltering library for hours, and watching Bear have some kind of weird, conspiratorial breakdown was tough on her.

"Angel, she's here for a reason. We just have to figure out why."

"Yes, of course we do." She shrugged. "Any ideas? Since I mean, you've already met this sexy, hot relative of John Mosby."

It was as if she'd met Sally already. "Angel, I think it has something to do with the ray gun that killed Kerns."

"You're still on the ray gun theory?" she scoffed. "Alien invaders shooting ray guns?"

"Not aliens. A murderer." I told her what I'd discovered in the second-floor room earlier. "What do you think now?"

She considered it all for a long time. Finally, she said, "It's possible."

"Of course it's possible." Then I told her what Sally had said right before she disappeared on me.

She pondered it. Then, "What about Bear? Something's wrong with him."

"I know. I'm worried, too. I'll follow him to see what he's up to."

"I'll stay here." She gestured to her briefcase and files. "I'll do a little research. I need to think about something else for a while."

"Good." I started dialing into Bear. "And Angel, I knew you'd like my ray gun theory."

I knew she rolled her eyes even as I disappeared.

* * *

Bear stood arguing with Cal and Spence in a small meeting room off the Main Floor's east hall. I arrived just as he slammed one hand down on the meeting table and poked a dozen holes in the air with a finger.

Spence and Cal left the room under an angry barrage of orders.

"Hey, Bear, what's going on with you?" I dropped down in a chair facing him. "You need to ease up."

Instead of jumping like he normally does when I arrive unannounced, he just closed his eyes and scowled. "I knew you'd show up."

Am I that predictable? "Angel's worried about you and—"

"I'm fine, Tuck." He rubbed his eyes. "What do you want? I'm busy."

"Are you okay?"

He went to the window and tried to peer out through the opaque plastic sheathing that FEMA had affixed. He stood staring at nothing.

"Bear?"

"I'm fine." He turned and slammed a chair into the end of the meeting table so hard it broke the chair's armrest. "Are you spying on me, Tuck?"

"Spying?"

He kicked the chair and crumpled it onto the floor. "Like popping around, hiding, and listening in? You get off on that, Tuck? You like stalking people? Now you've got her doing it."

What the hell? "Easy Bear, you're going somewhere you'll regret."

"Regret? I regret not telling you what I think before. I've been putting up with it for years, and I'm fed up. Tell Angela I'm fine and to leave me alone. If she's going to act like you, I don't want anything to do with either of you."

"Do you hear yourself, partner?" This wasn't the Bear Braddock I'd known since the police academy. "What's with you?"

"Two murders. Maybe an Ebola quarantine or some ray gun bullshit. Fifty angry library patrons and a city-wide disaster. It's all on me." He headed for the door. When he reached it, he held the knob but didn't open it. "You know something, *partner*, every time there's crazy shit going on, you and Angela are right in the middle. Why is that? Huh? Why the hell is that, Tuck?"

"Just lucky, I guess." No, my humor did not soothe him. "Come on—"

"Stay away from me. That goes for Angela, too. I'm done with both of you." With that, he yanked the door open, banged it hard enough on the wall to crack the door glass, and left.

Ouch.

Of all the bizarre things I'd witnessed since dying, the worst had just occurred. My partner and best friend had a multi-level meltdown for unknown reasons. I knew one thing, though—space aliens with ray guns were not behind Bear's behavior. That would have made more sense.

Something else had changed Bear Braddock. Something that I worried would end badly.

Chapter Fourteen

As Bear stormed off, I got a tickle in my brain. It's that tickle I feel each time Angel is up to no good. Given the situation around us, that could mean anything.

I found her rooting through the Henkel Boardroom. By rooting, I mean searching under every chair, behind the historic photographs on the wall, the paintings, even the glass display cases containing a litany of Winchester and Handley Library memorabilia.

"What are you doing, Angel?" I asked, making her spin around on my first syllable. "You shouldn't be up here. Bear's already on the warpath—"

"Bear was with Nicholas and someone else up here." She continued her foray. "I want to find out why."

I considered telling her about Bear's tirade just now. Then, I thought better of it. "Find anything?"

"Yes. Lots." She pointed into the fire extinguisher case inset into the side wall. "Look there."

I went to see what she'd discovered.

Shazam.

Positioned beside the extinguisher and concealed below the lip of the glass access door was a tiny black camera lens.

"A surveillance camera?" I knelt to get a better look. "Good find."

"There's another one in the glass display case over there." She gestured across the room. "There're two microphones under the boardroom table. Everything's wireless. This entire room is bugged, Tuck."

A thought struck me. "Angel, how long has Downey worked here?"

"A couple weeks, I think." The same thought reached her. "The earbuds he wore—do you think that's why he was killed? Someone caught him spying?"

I thought just that. "We need to check Downey's background."

"I'll check the personnel files in the office across the hall—"

"Talking to yourself again, my dear?"

Poor Nic stood in the boardroom doorway with his hands folded in front of him. He had a warm, grandfatherly smile on his face. He wore dress slacks and a bright, pink golf shirt beneath a blazer. His aging eyes were bright and focused on her.

"Nicholas? I didn't hear you come in."

"That is obvious, my dear." He entered and closed the door behind him. "What on earth are you looking for? What about Mr. Downey? Spying? Perhaps I can help."

If Poor Nic was offering to help, he'd heard too much.

"No, but you might clear something up for me," she said.

"Of course, my dear."

"Angel, hold on." I moved beside him. "I know you're pals and all, but he is a mobster deep down. Maybe he's—"

"You attended a meeting earlier," she said. "Right here. May I ask what that was about?"

"A meeting?" Poor Nic was a master at interrogation—both giving and receiving—yet her question surprised him. "Library business, my dear."

Angel said nothing, waiting for further explanation.

"Purely business." Poor Nic moved closer to her as his eyes played across the room. They rested on the fire extinguisher case that was still open. "I assure you."

"Library business? I didn't know you were a library patron."

"Of course." He had those grandfather-eyes locked on hers. "I'm on the Friends of the Handley Library board. By coincidence, I was meeting here today with a colleague on that very business."

She smiled slightly. "Oh? Who? I know several board members, but frankly, I didn't know you were one."

"Oh, just recently. Very recently." He reached out and patted her hand warmly. "My dear, are you being a detective again?"

"Just following up on something for Bear."

"For Captain Braddock?" A wry grin spread on his face. "Oh, I see."

A chill suddenly hung between them.

He went on. "I understand you were with the federal agent—Kerns, was it?—when he was murdered."

She nodded.

"You were unharmed?"

She nodded again.

"Mr. Downey?"

My radar pinged. "See what he knows about him, Angel."

"Nicholas, did you know Mr. Downey?"

"Heavens no. I've seen him here, of course. But I never said more than hello to him."

"And the meeting?" She pressed him. "Who were you—"

"Angela, Angela." He feigned surprise, but his forced grin told a different story. "I thought we were well past suspicion."

"We are." She looked down sheepishly. "I'm sorry."

For a long time, Poor Nic stood scanning the room again. Finally, he turned back to her and let his grandfatherly gaze capture her. "Angela, I understand you've been researching the Apple Harvest project. Is that correct?"

"Yes. Why?"

"Have you come across any records involving Civil War bank robberies or train robberies?"

She thought a moment. "No. Not yet. But I'm just beginning the research."

He frowned.

"What's your interest?"

His eyes brightened. "I am interested in procuring any such records of any robberies you may find."

"Procuring?" She folded her arms. "You just can't buy the records, Nicholas. They're valuable historical documents. They belong first and foremost to the town and will be protected under state historical laws."

"Oh, I see." His eyes fell. "Perhaps you'd permit me copies? I'd gladly make a sizable contribution to the Apple Harvest research coffers. I'm particularly interested in any documents that reference M35W."

Angel perked up. "M35W? I saw a reference earlier. Andrew was going to check on it."

"Andrew? I don't know him."

"Andrew Pellman. My research assistant."

"Ah, I see." Poor Nic watched her closely, maybe looking for deception, maybe not. Then, he relaxed noticeably. "M35W is an old Confederate military unit. A militia with some colorful local history."

"Colorful?" she asked. "How?"

"Well, perhaps only to a collector of local lore."

Angel wasn't having it. "You want to purchase copies and won't tell me why?"

"Yes." Poor Nic's eyes softened. "As far as I'm aware, M35W was a small militia. I cannot imagine any real value other than to a collector."

"Angel," I said, "first he's a library patron and now a history buff? If this stuff is important enough for him to buy it, then it's important to someone else, too."

She snapped up her hand to quiet me. That made Poor Nic laugh.

"Are you okay, Angela?"

"Nicholas, you haven't told me your interest."

"No, I haven't." His grin widened like it did when he was trying to be disarming. It was one of his tells that I'd learned long ago. "I am aiding a private collector trying to get first rights to newly discovered Civil War material. He's interested in funding a historical foundation. Those records would be a grand beginning."

"Who?"

Poor Nic shook his head. "You do not know him. I assure you."

"Really? I know most of the historians in the area," she pressed.

Now, the old gangster squirmed. "Would it be inappropriate to allow me this bit of confidentiality? Considering our long relationship and past adventures, I don't think it's too much to ask."

I watched him trying to disarm her with a smile. He was as kindly spirited as he was deceptive and cunning. Their relationship had begun with her suspicion that he might have murdered me five years ago. Having been innocent, their friendship had quickly grown from a casual one into a godfather-goddaughter closeness. Now, he was calling that relationship as collateral for secrecy.

"Angel, push him a little," I said. "You're the only one who can."

"Nicholas, I'd have to know who's involved before I try to get permission from the University and the town council to share any content with you. Once I have that, I'd be more than happy to allow you to view what I find. After all, my research will eventually be public record."

His eyes lit up. "My colleague wishes anonymity. However, given your willingness to consider it, I'll seek his permission to reveal his name. Now, how about a fifty-thousand-dollar donation for the Apple Harvest project? Consider it a grant. Whom do I make the check payable to?"

Fifty thousand dollars? "Whatever he's after, Angel, it's big."

"Nicholas, that's very generous." She hesitated as though truly contemplating the offer. I had to remember that the next time she and I were negotiating. "Don't get ahead of yourself."

"Of course, my dear."

Her cell phone buzzed, and she glanced at the number. "I'm sorry, Nicholas, I have to take this."

"Please do." He stepped in and kissed her cheek. "I'll leave you to it. I will be in touch. Please, however, let's keep my inquiry confidential. Agreed?"

"Of course." As Poor Nic left the boardroom, she tapped on the call and put it on speaker for me to hear. "Andrew, where are you? Did you get out in time?"

"Get out in time?" His voice was hurried. A frantic whisper. "What are you talking about?"

Angel quickly explained the murders in the library, ending with, "I don't know how long we'll be stuck—"

"Oh, my God," Andrew blurted. "It's worse than I thought. They actually did it."

Chapter Fifteen

"Professor, I'm off campus." Andrew was shaky and nervous. "I was followed, too. I didn't know why. Now, it makes sense."

"Followed? Are you sure, Andrew?" Angel was worried. "You sound scared."

"I am." Silence for a long moment—an unnerving silence. "Some guy followed me from the library earlier to campus. Then, he disappeared. I headed home and he was there, waiting. I left without going in. I think I lost him."

"Angel, keep him talking. Let's get one of the officers to send help."

"Who, Andrew?" She headed for the balcony. "Can you describe him?"

Silence.

"Andrew?"

He cursed loudly as she reached the stairwell. "I'm scared, Professor. I have to tell you something. But not on the phone. I found something on Apple Harvest you should know about."

"Something to cause people to follow you?"

"It's about M35W—that you asked me about."

"Yes? What?"

"A lot." Andrew cursed again as the sound of screeching tires smothered his reply. "Oh, no."

"Andrew, what's happening?"

"Professor Tucker, he's back. He found me."

I said, "Find a deputy and tell them what's going on, Angel."

"Hold on. I'm going for help." She ran down the stairs two at a time to the second floor. "Get somewhere safe, Andrew. A store, gas station, anywhere with people. You'll be safer. Call 911."

More tires screeched, and Andrew cursed. Finally, the background noise quieted. "I can't see him anymore."

"Who was it, Andrew? What's M35W?"

He took a long breath over the phone. "I researched M35W as you asked me to before I left. It was a Civil War… Oh, shit, I see him again."

"I'm getting the police, Andrew." She ran around the balcony toward the Tween Room area. "Where are you?"

"Driving. I have to see you soon. There's a lot more I know now, too."

"Do you know who killed Agent Kerns and Mr. Downey?"

Silence, then, "Oh my god, they killed them both?"

They? Holy crap, Andrew Pellman knows who's behind the murders.

"Angel," I said, "we gotta get him into custody. He knows about the murders."

She nodded. "Stay on the line, Andrew. No matter what. I'm looking for a police officer."

"Okay."

Officer Picanti, a female officer, emerged from the Kids' Place room and saw Angel frantically running toward her.

"Professor Tucker?"

She handed Picanti the phone. "Officer, my colleague, Andrew Pellman, was here earlier. Someone has been following him since he left. I think he knows who killed Agent Kerns and Mr. Downey. Andrew's in danger. He's on the phone now. Help him, please."

Picanti took the phone. "This is Officer Picanti. Mr. Pellman, where are you?"

Nothing.

"Mr. Pellman? Can you hear me?"

Nothing.

"Mr. Pellman?" Picanti looked at the phone's screen, shook her head, and handed the phone back to Angel. "He's gone, Professor Tucker. There's no one there."

Chapter Sixteen

"All clear. All clear," the police called out, walking through the library rooms. "Gather your belongings and make an orderly line at the front entrance. There is no danger and no contagion. Thank you for your cooperation."

The all-clear boomed in the hallways and over the balconies above the rotunda. It created a cavern-like echo that barely rose above everyone's excitement.

At the rotunda entrance, four uniformed police officers stood, ticking off names on their lists of patrons as they exited. That mission was faltering quickly. People were pressing forward, massing behind Library Lil, and crushing into the officers. Tensions were exploding, and no one wanted to spend thirty seconds checking out with the police. There were over forty people inside when the building was quarantined. Now, about ten thousand seemed to be storming the doors to escape.

Okay, so my math is off.

I found Angel lying on a long bench against the wall in the Archive Room. Her face was red from the heat, eyes closed, and her head rested on her arms. She was asleep.

I sat with her for over an hour, waiting for the chaos upstairs to subside. Her sleep was restless, and she quivered and jerked a few times, scowling and mouthing words I couldn't hear. After the day she'd had, I wasn't surprised.

After a while, I ventured to the Main Floor. The crowd was gone, and the Winchester police and Sheriff's deputies milled about. I returned to the

Archive Room to wake her.

"Angel, time to wake up and go."

She slowly opened her eyes and sat upright. "Tuck? Was I sleeping?"

"Yes. They cleared the library over an hour ago. Let's go home."

"Okay, good." She leaned forward and rubbed her eyes. "I was more tired than I thought."

"Understandable." I touched her hand, and a tingle of electricity connected us. Ever since her near-death experience last year, a simple touch sent a soothing, electric wave through us. I'd seen enough ghost hunting shows to know that was a little weird, but it was our connection, and I loved it. "We can deal with this later."

"Yes, alright." She barely moved. "I need to make sure Bear's all right first."

"I'm not so sure that's a good idea." I told her about my confrontation with him earlier when he banished us. She took it hard. "He's tired, Angel. This case is getting to him. That's all it is."

Her eyes looked at the floor for a long time. She was saddened. Her exhaustion amplified her feelings, and she started to cry. "I don't know, Tuck. Maybe."

"I'll try to talk to him tomorrow. Since I'm dead, it won't hurt if he punches me."

She looked up and faked a smile. "I'll find Nicholas tomorrow, too, and see what else he can tell me."

In the old days, when I was a living, breathing copper, Poor Nic would be top of my list for murder—any murder. But he'd proven himself a fairly decent guy—most of the time—even for a retired mobster. But between his participation in the secret meeting upstairs and his sudden interest in bank robberies and historical documents, I was beginning to wonder what cookie jar his hand was in.

Angel stood. "I'll get my things and go, Tuck."

I was about to saunter off—dead guys saunter—when Spence walked in frantically looking around.

Angel called him over. "Detective Spence—"

"Angela, where's Bear?"

She said, "I don't know. I haven't seen him for a while."

"How about Cal?" He looked around as though someone was hiding nearby. "No one has seen him for a while, either. They both disappeared right after the all-clear."

"I don't know. But there is something you should know." Angel told Spence about the strange phone call with Andrew Pellman earlier and about the surveillance equipment in the boardroom. "Officer Picanti was going to have someone check on Andrew. I'm worried something's happened to him."

"Sure, Angela," Spence said, only half-listening. "Picanti. Got it."

"Andrew hasn't called me back. He dropped the call as soon as I handed the phone to Officer Picanti. I haven't heard back."

Spence nodded absently. "Sure, I'll check it out."

I said, "Angel, let's go check on Pellman ourselves."

"Hold on, Angela." Spence pulled out his radio and requested dispatch to locate Bear. A few moments later, after three radio calls to Bear with no responses, the dispatcher reported, "Negative contact, Detective."

They repeated the exercise for Cal with the same results.

Spence checked his cell phone. "I got nothing from Bear or Cal. Bear said he was going home to change and coming right back. It's been over an hour. That's not like either of them to disappear like this."

Wait…Bear change clothes? Bear was many things, but worried about his appearance during a major case wasn't one of them. Sure, I wear the same clothes every day—I don't have a choice. Bear, on the other hand, could fit his entire wardrobe into a briefcase. In the old days, we went days with little more than sticking our head under the men's room sink during a big case. Even without one, Bear wore the same clothes to work three or four days in a row. Considering this mess on our hands, I doubted he was worrying about sweaty socks.

"Angel, let's go find them," I said.

She nodded. "Detective, I'll check on Bear and Cal at their homes before going home. I'll stop by Andrew Pellman's, too."

A long, chilling tingle ran up my spine.

Uh, oh. Things were about to get woo-woo again.

* * *

Poof... I was somewhere ... gone.

For a moment, darkness closed on me like someone zipping my tent closed after midnight. This happened when I was about to leave the here and now and go somewhere else—like a vision or a visit to another time and place.

The room disappeared, and so did Spence and Angel. In their place was a dull hum emanating from the spectral void holding me. It unnerved me. Voices rose in a whisper—not Angel or Spence's, either. They grew louder until the first words were clear ... *"Who knows? Where's the evidence? Who knew you were coming here?"* Images flashed around me like a drive-in movie montage selling popcorn and greasy cheeseburgers. Bear stood over a table laden with a shoebox stacked with cash. He slammed back a very tall drink and threw the glass against a wall ... Cal sat in a chair, head down, and mumbling incoherently ... An undisguisable woman struggled against two men dragging her from a barn toward a waiting crowd of dark, faceless people. Over and over the images reeled around me—different scenes, different images all colliding. They begged me to stop their chaotic dance. I couldn't. I didn't know how. The voices chanted. The images flashed by ...

Poof, I was gone again.

* * *

And... I was back to the here and now.

"Come back. Quick, come back." It was Angel, and she was scared. "Are you there, Tuck?"

The tent unzipped, and the light flooded in, bringing me to the hall leading to the West Reading Room facing Angel. Her face was ashen. She stood against the wall with two dark-suited men beside her. Her phone was in her hand as she continued the ruse to speak to me.

"Angel, what's wrong?"

She tapped off the call and glanced from one man to the other. She looked past them toward the rotunda and threw her chin for me to follow her gaze.

Both men were silent. They were armed—I could tell from the bulge in their suitcoats. A stream of dark-suited men surged through the rotunda and spread throughout the library like locusts. A powerfully built man in a better-quality black suit strode in, barking orders.

Those orders—these strange men—were seizing the library and everything inside. Anyone still there would be detained. No questions. No apologies.

Do not adjust your set. Resistance was futile. The Men-Wearing-Black had arrived.

Chapter Seventeen

"No wonder you think you own this place." Cal watched Bradley M. White from his vehicle across the street from the library. White was speaking with the Sheriff on the sidewalk. They stood along Piccadilly Street, where police cruisers and FEMA vehicles still blocked the area. "You're up to something, Mr. Bigot. I'm the guy going to find out what."

He took out his cell phone, turned on its camera, and set it to video. Then, he put it in its cradle on his dashboard to film in front of his vehicle. The video captured White and the sheriff clearly.

"There now. Let's just watch a while."

While he sat in his unmarked cruiser watching the two exchange laughs and pats on the back, Bear called him on the radio three times. He ignored him. On the fourth call, Cal pulled the radio from his belt and turned it off. As he did, White shook the sheriff's hand with a big smile and walked casually up Piccadilly to a dark Mercedes convertible. A moment later, the car pulled around a row of emergency vehicles—waved out of the way by the sheriff—and headed down the street.

Cal sped around the rear of the library. He negotiated several turns and blew through two stop signs to catch up to White as he turned onto Amherst heading west. There, he settled into a loose surveillance position ten or fifteen car lengths behind him.

His cell rang. Bear again.

This time, he answered. "Clemens."

"Where the hell are you?" Bear was curt and angry. "I've been trying to find you."

He thought fast. "I jumped out to get a fast shower and a sandwich. I stink, and I figure we'll be working all night."

Bear grumbled something that Cal couldn't make out.

"What's that, Bear?"

"I think I'll do the same thing. Get your ass back here as soon as you can."

"Yes, sir."

"Did you get all the interviews and files I asked for?"

Asked? These days, Bear didn't ask; he demanded. Not so nicely, either.

"Spence was gathering the last of them from the uniforms. I'll be back in an hour."

"Make it thirty minutes. I want a briefing on every detail we've got. I gotta know where all the screw ups are." Bear ended the call.

Damn.

Before returning the cell phone to its dash cradle, he tapped away for a few moments on two different email messages and affixed attachments. The attachments would take a few moments to send, but he finally completed them. Next, he set his phone back to video and continued following White west on Route 50 out of town for at least ten miles. The four-lane wound into the mountains where there were fewer homes and more hills and farmland. Just inside the Virginia border with West Virginia, White turned onto a private, gravel road where a large, bold sign read, "Private Property. Do Not Enter. Trespassers Will Be Prosecuted."

"Well, at least you didn't say lynched."

Cal slowed to give White more distance ahead before following him down the gravel road. A quarter mile ahead, he reached a metal farm gate blocking his progress. There were lights and a callbox affixed to the entrance gate. He avoided those. A tall, six-foot wood fence disappeared among the trees in both directions.

Fearing discovery, he pulled off the road among the trees where the vehicle would be out of sight. Then, he left his suitcoat and tie on the front seat and popped his trunk. Next, he'd shed his dress shoes and exchanged them for hiking boots. Lastly, he donned a sweatshirt and a dark windbreaker.

Then he headed off through the trees on foot.

He hiked a quarter mile east along the wood fence, trudging through the trees, climbing steadily in altitude. The fence seemed to run forever through the woods, and he quickly tired of searching for a way across it. Just when he was about to return to his car, he found a tall tree with a sturdy limb overhanging the fence. The tree was climbable, and it afforded him an opportunity to cross the fence without too much risk of injury.

At least, he hoped.

He hadn't climbed a tree since he was a kid. This episode cost him a ripped pant leg, two skinned knees, and several scrapes on his arms and hands before he dropped down on the other side. Once across, he jogged back to within a few yards of the gravel road and followed it deeper into the mountains. He was careful to stay secluded inside the trees.

Another half mile, still moving deeper into the forest, he encountered a second, formidable fence. This one was taller than the first, and it took him another fifteen minutes to find an outcropping of rocks and scrub trees that he could use to breach it. The rocks were barely high enough for him to get to the top of the fence. Once there, he swung up and dropped down on the other side.

He leaned back against the fence, exhausted. He was tired and sweaty, but no serious injuries. Looking ahead, what he saw made his efforts worthwhile.

Secluded in the trees ahead was a compound. A half-dozen single-story, windowless buildings surrounded a two-story log home the size of a mansion. The gravel road appeared to circle the entire compound. The log home had two-story glass windows in the front, a wrap-around veranda, and a second-story porch on one side that disappeared around the rear of the house. Stonework accented the glass and wood structure and boasted money and affluence.

"Oh, Mr. White, this must be where that chip on your shoulder comes from."

Cal checked his watch and realized he'd been out of contact with Bear and Spence for too long. Both of them would think he'd turned a shower and sandwich into a steak dinner and a nap. Irritating Bear didn't really bother him—not these days. Spence, though, would be complaining nonstop until he returned. He needed neither irritation.

Cal tried his cell phone.

A signal—weak—but usable.

As he dialed Bear's number, he thought better of it. The less questions, the better.

"Okay, Cal-my-man," he said to himself, "let's go see why ol' Mr. Bradley M. White's so secretive."

He slipped from his hiding place among the trees and slithered through the darkness to the nearest windowless building. He didn't see or hear anything but night birds. Once at the building, he moved around and approached the log mansion from the side.

The mansion had several side windows that overlooked a plush garden of shrubs and trees that enveloped a stone gazebo. That would be his next point of cover.

Without making a sound, he reached the gazebo and stopped to catch his breath.

Movement.

Lights swept through the trees as a vehicle entered the compound and drove along the gravel road. It made the long, slow drive to the front of the mansion and out of his view.

Cal stayed in the gazebo's shadows to form a plan. He'd approach the house through the garden using the tall shrubs and landscaped trees for cover. At the mansion's windows, he'd try to gather as much information as he could before reversing course for escape. He'd give himself just a few minutes before his retreat.

The less time exposed, the better. Especially since he had no search warrant or probable cause to be on White's private property. He didn't want to find out exactly how far "trespassers will be prosecuted" went. In his case, he felt a rope tighten around his neck.

Of course, he'd have to deal with Bear's wrath later. But for now, White was his only concern. That guy was up to something. Something big enough to manipulate Bear into concealing it. How he'd compromised Bear, he didn't know. But Bear's actions at the library self-indicted him. First, his strange behavior in general. Then, he'd effectively thrown Cal under the bus in the boardroom with White. Yet, he knew it wasn't just his conduct at the library. Over the past several weeks, Bear had become a stranger. His attitude had changed. He was closed off—uncommunicative, other than a nod or harsh order. Quiet. Sullen. Angry.

Cal pushed him from his thoughts. His concerns were around him now. There were two murders on the assignment board. There was no way White was getting off the suspect list. No way. No how.

After another long survey of the area, Cal moved through the darkness to the side of the mansion. There, staying out of view of the windows, he set his cell phone to video again and carefully positioned it in the lower corner of the first window. He let the video run for a few seconds before withdrawing. He repeated the maneuver for the remaining three windows on this side of the mansion.

Taking a deep, nervous breath, he retreated to the Gazebo's concealment. Every moment he was inside the compound could lead to his discovery. He'd wait to review the video until after returning to his cruiser and leaving the mountainside. Still, he had to take precautions. He tapped on his cell phone and sent five emails to an account he hadn't used in years. The first two took only a few minutes. The last three languished under the load of the huge video files he attached.

He checked his watch. The emails took nearly ten minutes and were still uploading.

Movement.

Someone was behind him.

He spun and reached for his Glock holstered on his belt. The moment he slid it from its holster, he recognized the face moving up behind him and holstered his weapon.

"Hold on, now," Cal said. "What are you doing here?"

The pistol aimed at him didn't waver.

"You shouldn't have come." The voice was low and cold. "You'll ruin everything."

Chapter Eighteen

The Men-Wearing-Black rounded up the remaining library staff. As they did, they barked orders to the police and deputies to gather in the West Reading Room. All these guys—there seemed to be a moratorium against ladies in black—were dressed identically in black suits, shirts, and ties. The only thing missing were dark sunglasses. Of course, it was dark outside, and that would have just been weird, right?

The two suits nearest Angel motioned for her to stand from her chair, where she sat against the wall. She refused. They looked at one another and waved over a short, robust man from the room entrance. He strutted over and confronted her.

"You have to join the others." His tone was flat. "Now."

"No." Angel took out her cell phone. "I haven't seen any badges or identification. By what authority—"

"I'm Colonel Smith—Department of Defense. Move, ma'am."

The first thing that struck me about Colonel Smith was that I doubted his real name was Smith. That, and I doubted he was a colonel of anything— other than maybe chicken. He was stocky, with a robust frame and fireplug arms and legs. I say fireplug with the nicest intent. Most noticeably, he was bald as a bowling ball.

When Angel tapped on her phone, I took hold of it and waited for the power to fill me.

You see, electricity is my friend. Typically, I can't do physical things as a spirit-detective. Sure, I can move around, communicate with some people, and observe others. I can't pick things up or manipulate anything. Well, sometimes, when my emotions are supercharged, I can. That's rare. Now, let me grab hold of some electricity for a few seconds and *shazam*—I'm almost a real boy.

When that tingly jazz surged through me, I leaned close to Smith and blew in his ear.

He recoiled and spun around, searching for the source. His face flushed when he found no one nearby. I did it twice more and forced him to step away from Angel as he swatted at his ear.

Oddly enough, he grinned.

"Professor Tucker, you better move. I'm not asking again."

Professor Tucker? *Hmmmm*, he'd done his homework. "Angel, do as he says."

She stood and started for the West Reading Room when Smith grabbed her phone.

"We're confiscating all electronics," he said coolly. "No exceptions."

"No, you're not." She spun around. "You can't do that without a warrant or something—probable cause or—"

"Continue to the West Room, Professor." He jutted a finger at her. "Now."

She frowned. "How do you know me?"

"Just move. You'll be interviewed later."

I didn't like what was happening. "Go, Angel."

"I was already interviewed by the police." She turned and walked away. "I'm done and leaving."

Smith tried to get into Angel's cell phone. Each time he tapped on the screen, the phone's security code stopped him.

"You know, pal," I whispered into his ear. "I don't like you talking that way to Angel. In fact, I don't like anything about you."

His eyes darted around.

"*Boo*, asshole." I slapped his hand and knocked her cell phone onto the floor. Before he could get to it, I knelt and pressed my hand against it, using every bit of willpower I had to push my energy back into the device.

It worked.

The phone crackled and smoldered. It sparked several times. I think the cell companies called that "spontaneous combustion."

"What the hell?" Smith thrust an angry finger at one of his men nearby. "Get this damn thing bagged. I want it dissected at the lab."

Whose lab?

One of the black suits pulled a clear plastic evidence bag from his jacket pocket, waited for the phone to stop sizzling, placed it into the bag, and sealed it. Except these plastic evidence bags didn't exactly say "evidence." They said "containment."

Containment of what?

Cursing, Smith strode off to the West Reading Room.

I followed.

When we got there, Angel stood with Spence and Sheriff Millbert, an averaged height man in his late-forties. He, too, was bald as a cue ball. Millbert, known for his constant, friendly smile, was without it. His hands flashed up in surrender as Angel unloaded on him about Colonel Smith.

"They have no right, Alvin," Angel snapped. "Who are they? They're not telling us anything and herding us around like sheep."

Spence patted the air. "Angela, calm down."

"No. I want my phone back. I want to know what's going on. I may be a witness to Agent Kerns' murder, but I won't be treated this way by anyone."

I stopped beside her. "Damn right, Angel. But ah, about your phone. Maybe file a claim instead."

When Smith walked up, the Sheriff turned to him. "Who are you? What's going on? I'm on scene commander—"

"I'm Colonel Smith, DOD." Smith didn't even offer any badge or paperwork. "I'm taking control of your scene, Sheriff. You and your men will stay put until interviewed. I want everything they have—notes, photos, everything. I want your dispatch records, and after I receive them, you're to delete them from any electronic media. Let's start with the crime scene evidence. Where is it?"

Sheriff Millbert's mouth dropped open. "That's a whole lot of demands from somebody I don't recognize has authority. Let me see some credentials."

Smith waved over two other dark-suited operatives. "These are security agents, Smith and Jones. They will be taking your evidence and all records."

"Smith and Jones? Really?" I snorted. "I guess it's better than Agent One and Two."

"Some ID, gentlemen?" Millbert demanded again. "Or we don't turn over shit."

Smith took out a folded piece of letterhead from his pocket and handed it to Millbert. When Millbert's eyes flared as he stared at the Department of Justice seal at the top of the paper, Smith snatched the letter back and returned it into his suitcoat.

"Understand now?"

Millbert scratched his chin. "If it's real."

"Do you need a call? Of course, it will mean your detainment for impeding a national security matter." Smith lifted his chin. "I can get one of his aids on the phone."

"No." Millbert took a deep breath and turned to Spence. "Take, ah, Smith and Jones to the second floor and sign over the evidence."

"And both bodies," Smith added.

"Bodies?" Millbert bit his lip. "Sure. Of course. Spence, they sign for every damn thing—everything. Take one of our deputies as a witness. I want a paper trail, detective."

Spence started to object, but Millbert's thumb shot out toward the hallway. Spence glanced at Angel and then Smith. "Yes, sir."

Smith-the-Second, Jones-the-First, and Spence trooped away.

To Angel, I said, "This is the weirdest thing I've ever seen, Angel. That letter was from the Attorney General. What's going on?"

She repeated the question to Smith.

"That's classified." He stared coldly at her. "Once we're through with you, you will never discuss this event with anyone ever again. Clear?"

First, the Men-Wearing-Black and now the super-secret talk and die speech? "Tell him to shove it, Angel. Let's leave. I dare them to arrest you."

She shot a sideways glance at me that said—*shut up, Tuck. I don't want to go to Guantanamo.*

Our love is so deep that we can communicate with just a look.

Millbert stabbed a finger at Smith. "Letter or not, I want answers. My men will not be interrogated. Take their notes if you must. No interrogations. Got that?"

Smith was about to respond when Smith-the-Second and Spence jogged into the room.

Smith-the-Second's face was ashen. Spence, on the other hand, looked like he'd just won the lottery.

"Sir, there's a problem," Smith-the-Second said.

"Everything's gone, Sheriff," Spence blurted. "Everything but the bodies. Reports, field notes, statements, Kerns' ID, wallet, jewelry. Same with Downey. Just the bodies are left."

Millbert's face blanched. "All of it?"

"Yeah." Spence nodded. "Even the cameras and video with all the crime scene photos and recordings. Gone."

"Dammit." Millbert pulled out his cell, but before he dialed, he asked Spence, "Where's Captain Braddock?"

"Gone."

Angel and I exchanged glances. Bear's timing couldn't be worse.

Chapter Nineteen

"Who's Braddock?" Colonel Smith demanded. "One of yours?"

"He's my Task Force captain," Millbert said. "He's overseeing this case."

"*Was* overseeing," Smith said. "He and the evidence are both missing?"

"He isn't missing," Spence blurted. "He went home to change clothes."

"Change clothes?" Millbert's face scrunched up. "Get him back here, Spence."

Smith turned to his men and issued similar orders. They faced Millbert again. "If you find him first, you'll turn him over to me immediately."

Turn him over? "Angel, we gotta find Bear. This isn't right. Smith has more in mind than interrogation. Bear's in trouble."

"Colonel Smith?" Angel squared off on him. "Aren't you investigating Agent Kerns' murder? You're acting more like this is the Manhattan Project, and we're all Russian spies."

Smith gazed at her with a dull, dead stare before looking to Millbert. "You may go for now, Sheriff. Your men stay until they are interviewed."

"I asked you a question," Angel insisted. "I'd like an answer."

He walked off.

How rude. "Angel, he didn't say you had to stay. Vamoose. We'll find Bear."

"Professor Tucker, you should leave while you can." Millbert had the same idea. "Find Bear. Get him to the office and lay low. I'll be there as soon as I can. I have to look after my deputies first."

Wise strategy. I wish I'd thought of that. Oh, wait. I did.

"Of course, Sheriff." Angel wasn't happy. "I have to get my things from Archives. Then I'll go."

I followed.

At the stairwell, one of Smith's men stopped her. I'm sure his name was Smith or Jones, too. "You can't return downstairs, ma'am."

"But some of my things are down in Archives. My research—"

The man pointed away. "No ma'am. Everything's been seized."

"For what?" She refused to budge. "When can I get it returned?"

The man held his hand up with his damnable finger pointing away.

"Angel, forget it," I said. "Get out of here before someone seizes you, too."

"This is illegal." She took out a pen from her pocket. "What's your name, please?"

"Smith."

I hate being right all the time.

"Smith? Really?"

A sarcastic grin edged the corners of this Smith's mouth. "Really."

"This is absurd." She turned on a heel, stormed into the Rotunda, and left out the front door.

I ventured down into the Lower Level to see what all the Smiths were up to.

Several men were tearing apart the mechanical room and taking everything that wasn't bolted down. What was bolted down was being examined with electronic gadgets with all manner of lights, gauges, and other wizardry. One guy, a short, thin man in, yep—a black suit—was combing the entire Lower Lobby with a Geiger Counter. The counter ticked away like a metronome for grunge rock.

A Geiger Counter?

A voice in my head began to form. It summoned me. Curiosity made me obey, and I went into the auditorium. Inside, standing at the foot of the stage was the delectable Sally Elizabeth Mosby.

I am such a chic magnet.

She'd changed clothes. She had on a cotton shirt, tan trousers, and riding boots. On her head, instead of the pretty bonnet, was a floppy-brimmed slouch hat. If not for her beautiful eyes and long, blond hair trailing from beneath her hat, I could have easily mistaken her for a young man. Well, almost.

She waved as I started down the stairs toward her.

Hey, how come I've been stuck in jeans and a sport coat for three years, but she has a wardrobe change? I asked her that, and she ignored me. Maybe she was related to Angel after all.

"Oliver, what in heavens are all those machines those dreary men are using?"

"One is a Geiger Counter. That's used for testing for radiation."

"Radi-what?"

"It tests for dangerous stuff in the air."

She thought about that. "Can it find things? Like minerals? Coins? Treasure?"

Treasure? "I don't think so. Why?"

"Those men look like they are searching for something quite valuable. I even saw one of them digging around down there." She pointed a finger toward a hatch in the stage floor a few feet away. "He had a shovel and one of those strange devices. It reminded me of a treasure hunt."

Interesting. "Sally, what did you call me for?"

"Oh, yes, of course." She lowered her voice as though the Men-Wearing-Black might hear. "To warn you."

"About what?"

"Why, those men, of course. They aren't who they say they are."

No kidding. "They're some kind of military security. What do you know of them?"

"Military, yes of course." She inched closer to me. "They are like the Pinkertons of my day, Oliver. But the Pinkertons were worse. Much, much worse."

"I thought the Pinkertons were detectives? Good guys?"

Tears filled her eyes and began taking the slow, painful path down her cheeks. "Yes, of course. Some of them were employed by the Army. Some were rogue men who did horrible, brutal things. All because they could."

I put a hand on her shoulder as she wept openly. As I did, she leaned into me, and the tears touched my cheek.

Fire.

The tears first stung, then turned to hot, slicing heat that burned like acid on my face. The room began to spin. The lights flickered and went dark. Blackness devoured me.

As it happens to me far too often, the place and the time turned upside down.

Chapter Twenty

*A*nd... *poof. I was somewhere else in time and place.*

When the lights returned and things settled, I was outdoors. The overhead lights had turned to early morning sunshine. I stood on a knoll behind a dirt street lined with clapboard and brick homes. I didn't recognize anything around me, but I knew I wasn't at the Handley Library any longer. In fact, I knew I wasn't in the twenty-first century any longer, too. My best guess was in the mid-eighteen hundreds—like around eighteen sixty-four.

It was an educated guess brought on by the six men on horseback dressed in Union cavalry uniforms, looking grumpy. Dead giveaway.

The men faced a wagon pulled by a feisty, snorting white mare. Aside from their uniforms, they had swords, sidearms, and straggly beards. Holding the mare's halter was a young man, just a teenager, wearing a similar uniform that didn't fit. He was slight and meek and struggled to keep the mare still as the other soldiers slowly circled the wagon.

A Union officer, judging by his fancy epaulettes, prodded his horse forward and examined the wagon.

The wagon bed was covered by a gray canvas shroud over something bulky. The driver's face was lowered beneath a floppy-brimmed, gray hat, and he refused to look up.

"You will dismount," ordered the officer, stopping his horse beside the mare and facing the driver. "Immediately."

The driver didn't move.

"Now, or I shall have you dismounted."

Still, the driver didn't budge.

The Union officer gestured to one of the mounted soldiers. "Assist this traitor, Corporal Johnson."

Johnson dismounted and climbed onto the wagon's front wheel. He grabbed the driver by the arm as another soldier moved up close, leaned down from his saddle, and pulled the canvas free from the wagon.

Only empty apple crates, stacked three high, filled the wagon bed.

"Not here, Captain."

Johnson struggled with the driver but finally pulled him down onto the ground. The moment he tumbled from the wagon and rolled away, the soldiers jeered.

The wagon driver was a woman. Not just any woman, either.

Sally Elizabeth Mosby.

I stood on the knoll watching. I couldn't do anything else. I wasn't really there, of course. The drama unfolding wasn't really there, either. Not now. Not in my time. It was a memory or vision to show me something from Sally's time—eighteen sixty-four. Whenever I did this spirit-travel thing, I wasn't allowed to participate or interact. Just watch. As the story unfolded around me, I was no better than if I were home with Angel and Hercule watching an old movie on television.

The captain's horse shuffled back when 1864-Sally's hat slipped off and her long, golden hair cascaded across her shoulders. She climbed to her feet and stood defiantly facing the soldiers.

"What is this, Captain Little? I demand to know why I am being accosted."

"Oh, you do?" Captain Little leaned back and laughed raucously. "Why, will you look at what we got here, boys. It's little-miss Sally."

"Captain, I assure you—"

"Don't bother, girl." Captain Little waved to Johnson, who grabbed 1864-Sally's arms, pinned them behind her, and held her. "Sally Mosby, you will tell me where the bounty is."

1864-Sally tried to pull free from Johnson but couldn't. She looked from one soldier to another surrounding her. Finally, her eyes sought Captain Little. Her eyes stayed on him, fixed and cold, staring him down. Defiance.

Anger. Resolve.

"Captain Little, do not think you can bully me as you do the others in Winchester? I will not bend to you."

"I dare say not, Sally." He laughed again. "I know the Mosby clan's reputation."

She fixed her chin higher but said nothing.

"Where's the secret, Sally? Tell me, and perhaps a cell is all you'll get."

"I don't know what you're after, Captain." She tossed her hair and tipped her chin toward the wagon. "As you can see, I was bringing apple harvest supplies home."

Captain Little's face darkened. He leaned back in his saddle and stared down at her, a cold, insolent expression spreading across his face. When he gestured to Johnson again, he looked away.

Johnson spun 1864-Sally around. He backhanded her viciously across the face, knocking her to the ground. He bent, pulled her to her feet, and struck her again. This time, he hit her so hard she spun into the side of the wagon and cracked her face on the front wheel.

"Stop this, you bastards." I tried to run to her defense—but all I could do was stand there and watch. "Stop."

It was futile. I was helpless to do anything but watch. None of the soldiers heard me. None knew I was there. After all, their attack had occurred a hundred and sixty years ago. "Sally, tell them what they want. Please."

Johnson began kicking her brutally. He gave her no reprieve—a few kicks to the stomach and chest, two in the face, back down her torso as he pounded her into the ground.

Dear God, stop.

"Enough, Corporal," Captain Little ordered. He waited for 1864-Sally to roll sideways and glare at him. "Now, Sally. I know who you are. We've known for some time."

Her face flashed with fear as she coughed to regain her breath. "I don't know what you think of me, Captain, I'm—"

"The secrets, Sally. Tell me all you know."

She lay there, bloodied and defiant. She coughed several times more and managed to climb to one knee again. "Captain Little, do you know my aunt, Mary Sutter?"

"Mary Sutter?" Captain Little's eyes narrowed. "I do not and don't care to. Where is the cargo? Who are your confederates?"

"Mary Sutter? Are you sure you don't know *Mary Sutter*?" 1864-Sally's face was bruised and bloody, and her eyes fearful as she climbed to her feet. "Before you go any further, I beg you to contact your colonel and ask him to contact my aunt. She will vouch for me."

From somewhere I didn't see, two more Union riders approached. They had a third man riding between them with one of the soldiers leading his horse. The third man was hooded with a dark cloth and his hands bound behind him. They passed the wagon and continued down the knoll to a stand of tall oaks clustered beside the dirt road. In a moment, the soldiers swung a heavy rope over a tall limb and secured one end to the tree. They looped the other end around the hooded man's neck.

"Oh my God, no," I yelled. "What are you doing? Who is that?"

No one answered. No one could.

"Sally? Last chance. Where—"

"Mary Sutter, Captain." 1864-Sally lifted her chin. "I beg of you."

Captain Little turned to another of his men. "Kilmeade, there's no time for this."

"Yessir." Kilmeade backed his horse from the others and trotted down to the other soldiers and their captive. "Last words, William?"

"I don't much like that name." The hooded man struggled against the rope. "I told ya what you wanted. Why are you doin' this to me?"

Kilmeade turned and looked to Captain Little, who nodded ever so slightly. As soon as he did, Kilmeade slapped the hooded man's horse and sent it charging away.

William, the hooded man, fell away. He kicked and struggled pointlessly as he died.

"Sally?" Captain Little asked. "Your decision?"

"You'll go to hell, Captain."

Kilmeade took another rope from his saddlebags, slung it over another branch, and tied it off before going to work on the free end.

Oh, no. What was happening gripped my insides and twisted. A dark, bottomless fear fell upon me and consumed me. "Sally, tell them whatever you can. Please. Don't do this. Dear God, don't."

She turned slightly toward me as though she'd heard me. Her face fell dark like a pale shroud. As tears formed, she turned to Little. "Captain, I truly don't know what you want. Please, contact your command and ask about my aunt Mary Sutter. I beg you."

Captain Little trotted his mount to the oak beside Kilmeade.

Corporal Johnson and the other soldiers forced 1864-Sally onto her wagon bed. One of them drove it to the trees. There, they tied her hands behind her back, stood her on the edge of the wagon, and slipped the noose around her neck.

"Sally Elizabeth Mosby, where is the bounty?" Captain Little watched her with an indifferent, smug expression. "Tell me your secret."

"Captain, I implore you—"

Corporal Johnson spat on her. "Traitorous bitch."

"No, stop this. Stop. Please." Panic swelled through me like a tidal wave of heat. My feet wouldn't move. All I could do was watch and wait for the inevitable. "Dear God, Sally, just tell them."

The morning sun flashed dark. I was gone. But not before the image of this beautiful southern lady hanging from the trooper's rope seared into my memory.

My visit to 1864 was over for now. I prayed I wouldn't visit again.

Chapter Twenty-One

Poof... Thank God ... I was back on the auditorium stage. Back home. Back to my time.

"Sally?" I looked frantically around. "Where'd you go?"

Nothing.

"Sally? Are you here? Please, it's Oliver."

"She's gone, Mr. Tucker." A voice turned me around. "Don't be sad for her. She's been gone a long time."

Kerrie Garcia stood on the top landing near the auditorium entrance. She had a curious look on her face, watching me with an understanding, intent gaze.

Ah, what? "Kerrie? You can see me?"

"Of course, Mr. Tucker."

With Angel, it took all kinds of trials and tribulations to connect with her after my murder. It was only after she was attacked and nearly killed that our bond formed. After that, she could hear and see me. She knew I was back with her. I'd always believed it was a combination of love and fear—the deepest emotions—that reunited us.

This kid—all fifty pounds and four-feet plus of her—was dialed into me without any of that.

"Kerrie, what do you mean 'she's gone?' "

She giggled. "Oh, Mr. Tucker."

"You can call me Tuck, Kerrie. After all, you're pretty special."

She beamed. "Maybe. Sally's been dead for a long, long time. A lot longer than you. You shouldn't feel sad for her. She's trying to help you."

She knew about Sally, too? "How do you know about Sally?"

"I don't know." She shrugged. "I'm still learning about the things I can do."

"Do you know what she wants from me?"

Kerrie thought for a long time and finally shook her head. "I don't know much about her. Not as much as I know about you."

Gulp. "What do you know about me, Kerrie?"

"Go see the grumpy man, Tuck." She giggled again. "He'll explain what I can't. He's funny, too. I like him."

The grumpy man? "Do you mean Bear?"

She twisted around.

The auditorium doors opened and Smith and Emily walked in.

Emily called, "Kerrie, I've been looking for you, honey. We have to go. They want to talk to us upstairs."

"Now, kid." Smith took a long, slow survey of the room. "Who were you talking to?"

Kerrie said nothing.

"Come on, kid. Out with it? Who's in here?"

Kerrie glanced back at me. "No one."

"Oh?" Smith descended a few stairs toward the stage and did another survey. "Who's here, Kerrie?"

Emily came down and knelt facing her, "Is it another of your 'special friends,' honey?"

The eleven-year-old nodded.

Smith walked to her and handed her something. "Kerrie, do you know what this is?"

"No." Kerrie looked at a round, gold coin in her hand. "Is it money?"

"Yes. Very valuable money." Smith's voice lightened. "Do you see anything from this? Think hard. What does this coin tell you?"

What the heck was going on?

Kerrie stared at the coin. She hefted it over and over as if it were heavy in her small hand. After a long time, she dropped it on the floor. "No. I don't want to do that now. I'm tired. I've been doing this all day and I don't feel well."

"Do it, Kerrie," Smith demanded. "I need you to—"

"Enough. We're going upstairs." Emily took Kerrie's hand. "She needs to rest. You've had her doing this enough. You make her sicker and sicker when you push her."

Smith started to object but relented. "Fine. But she needs to get with it. We have just a few more days to wrap this all up. "

Emily guided Kerrie from the auditorium into the Lower Lobby. Once there, Kerrie turned back, finger waved to me, and mouthed, "Bye, bye, Tuck."

I waved back. After all, I was one of her *special* friends.

Chapter Twenty-Two

As Emily and Kerrie left, Smith wandered around the auditorium, stopping and listening every few steps. I didn't know what he was up to, but I didn't like it. I didn't like anything about him. When he reached the opposite side of the auditorium from me, he slumped into a seat facing the stage. He took something from his pocket—a small, square device similar to a cell phone—turned it on and waved it around.

"Come on. Show yourself."

I'd seen that gadget before. A ghost hunting detective had one during one of my earlier cases. It's called an EMF Meter—electromagnetic field meter. The theory is that ghosts and other paranormal activity—let's say me—disrupts magnetic fields and the device locates the disruption. In short, it beeps when a spirit is nearby. Or so the theory goes.

Dead-detective instincts told me to stay quiet.

I went to where Kerrie had dropped Smith's coin and knelt. I didn't have enough energy left to pick it up. Reason kept me from trying with Smith nearby.

The coin wasn't a coin at all. It was a crudely flattened hunk of metal roughly shaped like a coin, about a quarter inch thick and two inches in diameter. I was no prospector, but it looked like a good size piece of flattened gold with crude markings I couldn't make out.

Pirate treasure? Thankfully, Angel wasn't nearby to tell me how stupid that sounded. How cool would that be? The treasure, not her chastisement.

Smith moved about and climbed onto the stage to wave his EMF meter around,. He cursed at its silence.

I touched the chunk of gold. When I did, the lights went out again.

And... *poof*... off I went onto the spook express. The question was, where was my ticket taking me this time?

* * *

And... *poof*... the lights were back on.

I landed at the end of a long, cherry table surrounded by three men and a woman. They sat on ladderback chairs and held crystal brandy snifters. The room had a fieldstone floor and a high ceiling beamed with large timbers polished to a fine sheen. On the walls hung a dozen oil paintings of various men, all lit with small decorative lights to highlight the images like an art gallery.

This was no art gallery.

The voices from the table were just mumbles like my hearing aid was low on batteries. Since I'd never worn a hearing aid, I knew patience and silence would cure me.

The lady was beautiful. As Angel would tell you, I like dealing with beautiful women. She was elegant with short cut black hair and a slight but curvy figure. Her Asian face was pretty and thin with dark eyes and a petite mouth. The younger of the men sat across from her. He was an average height, slender African American with short cut hair and a neatly trimmed beard. He had bright eyes and a pleasant, engaging smile. Another man sat beside her. He looked Middle Eastern or Northern African. He was immaculately dressed in an expensive business suit that was probably cost more than Angel's SUV.

The only person I knew was the older man sitting at the far end of the table. Bradley M. White. He was a very—very—powerful man in these here parts. He had connections to all kinds of politicians and he had tons of money and power built on the backs of local farmers, merchants, and other businesses. When I think of White, an image pops into my head of an old southern land baron sitting in his big house lording over his land and money.

It struck me that those around the table were undoubtedly the same ones Cal found in the Kenel Boardroom earlier. Later, Kerns had acknowledged them on his call when I was possessing him. My, my, they did get around.

Now they were here. Wherever here was.

The reason for them to be gathered again had killed Kerns and Downey.

"Are we ready to begin?" White asked curtly, pointing a finger around the table at each of the three. "Who will deposit twenty million? All others will leave immediately. I'm sure you understand my security concerns before I show you the HEAP."

Miss Liu took a long pull on her drink and sat the glass on the table with a noticeable bang. "The product is here?"

White nodded.

"Twenty million?" asked the African American. "If it is what you claim, then I am all in. What say you, Mr. El Fazi?"

"Yes, yes. I concur." El Fazi leaned forward in his chair. "Let's get on with this. White, you are not the only one with security concerns."

"Of course, Ahmad." White tapped the table. "The three of you witnessed the events at the Library today. Do I need to remind you the value of this prize? It will have to be moved quickly. The DOD is already asking about it. Your deposits must be made immediately. The balance of thirty-million, within two days. Then, delivery will be made after two more days."

"Hold on, Bradley," Young said. "You expect cash up front and we wait on delivery? No."

"That is all non-negotiable." White's hand flashed up. "The matter is out of my hands."

"Out of your hands?" Miss Liu asked. "What does that mean?"

White seemed irritated at the question. "We all work for someone, Miss Liu. I, unfortunately, work for the supplier. In or out. Those are the house rules."

Liu, Young, and El Fazi exchanged glances. Finally they all nodded and agreed.

"All right, let us proceed," White said dramatically. "Follow me."

White stood and walked from the room.

Although I wasn't invited, I tagged along. Curiosity always kills the cat. Since I'm dead already, what harm could it do? Right?

White led us down a long, wide hall framed in fine-honed timbers and stone masonry. At the end of the hall, we made a sharp right turn and walked to a dead end where a heavy wood door waited. There, he grasped one of the stones beside the door and pulled it open like a hatch. Inside, was an electronic keypad that he manipulated.

The heavy wood door popped open.

"Inside, please," he said. "This is my wine cellar."

We filed in.

This room was similar to the first conference room. A high, beamed ceiling, fieldstone floor and walls. It was lined with dark, old racks filled from floor to ceiling with bottles of wine.

"Wow, Bradley," I said knowing no one would hear. "Nice digs, huh? I bet you have one of those Chateaus For My Feet vintages. Am I right?"

Clever commentary calmed me.

Continuing to the rear of the room, a good thirty-feet back, he stopped at the back wall of wine racks. There, he grasped the only empty wine slot, pulled, and opened the rack like a door. Behind the wine rack was another door. This one was steel and framed in concrete. He tapped in a combination on another electronic lock and opened the door.

One by one, we entered.

A small light illuminated a large room. Several steel and polymer shipping containers were stacked inside. In the dim light, there were perhaps five nearly identical containers.

"This is it?" Miss Liu asked, moving inside. "What is this, Bradley?"

"Optional purchases." White waved his hand around. "You are free to browse and if you see something you like, you may make an offer."

Young wondered inside as El Fazi brushed past him to a heavy crate against one wall. The crate was closed, but its metal twist-lock hasps were open.

I examined the containers. Each had a small, black plate affixed to the bottom edges. On the plate were the initials ADRI. Below that, etched into the plate as well, were numbers and letters. Serial numbers? Since I had no idea what was inside, I assumed the contents were all stolen property from somebody who was gonna want it back—like the DOD. Why else would they send Special Agent Kerns?

"The display sample is there." White gestured to the first crate where his guests gathered. "See for yourselves."

El Fazi deftly opened the top. His face lit up.

So did mine.

Inside the crate was a strange-looking weapon. It was a long-barreled tube with a pistol grip on the bottom and a fold-up mini-screen on the top that looked like computer tables. Along the side of the weapon were buttons and indicator lights. The weapon had a heavy wire tether that disappeared deeper into the crate.

A ray gun. Nailed it. After all, I know these things. I watch a lot of television.

"Bradley," I said, inspecting the device, "have you been watching science fiction shows again? Are you planning an interplanetary war?"

Liu looked around the room. "More of the same? There are others?"

"Not here." White grinning slyly. "The other containers have previous generations of the same device for sale. Not as compact or battle-ready as this one. My supplier is still calibrating the design. So, for now, these are for display only."

Young wandered to another crate. "Calibrating?"

White's grin faded. "It made a mess at the library. That was unintentional. The HEAP requires some, well, tuning. It will also be far more portable, too."

El Fazi turned to him. "We are to trust you that this device is genuine and not a child's toy assembled by grade schoolers? For fifty million?"

"Yes." White walked over, closed the open crate, locked it, and turned around. "I assure you it is operational. Just some fine tuning is needed."

For a long time, Liu, Young, and El Fazi exchanged glances in a subliminal discussion highlighted with raised eyebrows, twists of their mouths, and sighs.

"Fifty million?" Young asked. "And it's not tested?"

"We have only your word that it was responsible for the library, Bradley," Liu added. "That's a lot of money for promises."

"It was not speculation that eviscerated Agent Kerns," White sneered. "It was the HEAP. Twenty million in a goodwill deposit, mind you. The balance due in two days."

El Fazi aimed a finger at Bradley. "A prototype the authorities may already be looking for? Old testing models that require additional work? Moving them, let alone reselling them, will be precarious."

White never batted an eye. "Do you understand the value of such devices in the foreign markets?"

El Fazi grinned. "I am not from Cleveland, Bradley. Of course I do."

"Trust me when I say that this HEAP is far superior to any of the previous purchases you made. Those were simple traditional weapons of war. The HEAP is the future."

I leaned close to White. "Damn, Mr. White, er, can I call you Bradley? You're an arms dealer. Winchester has Patsy Cline, a mob boss, and now an arms dealer—of ray guns. Wow, the big time."

Bradley held up a finger. "Fifty million is firm. Twenty today. My employer demands the thirty million in two days."

The three did their subliminal debate again.

"Why two days?" El Fazi asked. "Will we be able to purchase more, later?"

"No," White said flatly. "In two days, sold or unsold, they will no longer be available. The store will, well, be closed."

"Close? How mysterious," Liu said. "I'm in. Fifty million."

El Fazi and Young tripped over each other to second her motion.

Sweet Damn Yankees. Fifty million ... *firm*. No backsies. What happens in two days to close White's store?

Poof... The lights flashed off and I was sucked from the room.

Chapter Twenty-Three

P*oof... back.*

I found Angel sitting in her Explorer a half-block from the Handley library. She was staring straight ahead through angry, narrow eyes. Her knuckles were white around the steering wheel and her face was flushed with worry and anger.

As I landed, she said, "Those ... those ... arrogant, power-hungry bastards." Considering the day I'd had that description didn't narrow the field.

"Which arrogant, power-hungry bastards are you talking about, Angel?"

She half-turned in the seat to face me. "Those ... those ... government men. They stole my notes and my research. They're pushing everyone around like ... like they're—"

"Arrogant, power-hungry bastards?"

"Exactly." She fumed a bit longer. "Tuck, they didn't even ask me any questions about Agent Kerns or Mr. Downey."

"Maybe they don't need to."

That thought stilled her. "Now they think Bear stole the evidence."

Well, I knew something was bugging Bear, but corruption? It has to be something else.

"I've just met some pretty power-hungry bastards myself." I told her about White's soiree and the HEAP. "White isn't just some old-south land baron, Angel. He's an arms dealer—including ray guns. Killing Kerns was a demonstration of a new weapon called the HEAP."

"HEAP?"

"I have no idea. But it *is* a ray gun."

"A ray gun? Come on, Tuck. An arms dealer in Winchester who's selling ray guns? It's hard to believe."

Was her memory fading? "Angel, I'm dead. I'm also sitting in your SUV talking to you. How unbelievable is that?"

She shrugged.

"Let's go home. I need to talk to Doc."

Her face flashed anger. "Let me guess. About Sally?"

Uh, oh. Maybe sometimes I just need to be quiet. "Earlier today, I was with her. You won't believe what I saw." I told her about my vignette to 1864 to witness Sally's hanging. "It was horrible, Angel."

"Oh, Tuck. I'm so sorry." She looked away, embarrassed. "How horrible. I'm sorry for what I've said."

"It's okay, I do have a habit of attracting beautiful—"

"I get it."

Yeah, no sense stating the obvious. "Angel, she showed me that for a reason. I just can't figure out what it is, yet." Next, I told her about Kerrie and her strange abilities. "What do you think?"

Angel thought for a long time. "Remarkable. I've heard about things like that. We both watch programs about it on TV. I always thought it was all theatrics."

What is it about Winchester that all this bizarre phenomenon happens here? Or is it happening everywhere and we just don't know it? Maybe I'm a paranormal-magnet.

"Angel, let's go home."

"Okay, but we have to make a stop first." She started her Explorer. "I want to check if Andrew's home. I pray he's there and safe."

Oh, yeah, Andrew. "All right. I'll go with you. I don't want you running around alone."

"Tuck, there's something he wanted to tell me—or show me. He was terrified earlier when he called."

"Any news about Bear and Cal?"

"No. Detective Spence is checking on them." She eyed me sideways as she drove. "Now, about Sally. Will she be waiting at home for you?"

"I don't know. But don't worry, Hercule loves hot, sexy blonds." *Oops, did it again.* "Ah, I mean, he'll keep her company."

I wonder if it hurt her hand when she slapped me and it went right through to the headrest.

* * *

Ten minutes later, we pulled in front of a split-level home south of Winchester in Frederick County. We were in a middle-class neighborhood with dozens of homes on nicely manicured suburban lots. Andrew Pellman's home was well-kept and freshly painted. It had a detached garage and a six-foot fence around his backyard. There were no cars in the drive, but the street was lined with them in both directions. His could be anywhere.

"Nice neighborhood, Angel." I looked around. "You guys pay doctoral students well."

"We don't pay at all, Tuck." She shut off the Explorer. "He must have his own money. He was offered student quarters when he arrived but turned them down."

Interesting. "Bear will be interested in him for sure."

"There's nothing wrong with having your own money, Tuck." Angel climbed out of the Explorer and walked up the driveway. "He's a nice young man. Give him a break."

As we walked toward the house, a vehicle pulled from the curb a half block down and approached us. It slowed as it passed and I took notice. It was a large, black Suburban with blacked out windows. As it passed beneath a streetlamp, I caught the license plate—PNNY1. Poor Nic's handle.

First, Poor Nic became an avid reader and a social butterfly for the Friends of the Handley Library. Now, he's part of Andrew Pellman's neighborhood watch. What a guy, that retired killer, robber, loan shark, and conman. A real community pillar.

Good thing he liked Angel.

"Angel," I said as she reached Pellman's garage. "Poor Nic just drove by."

"Nicholas? How odd." She glanced back but he was gone. Then, she got on her tiptoes and peeked in the garage window. "Andrew's car isn't here. Go into the house and do your thing, Tuck."

"My thing?" Oh, right. "Yes, ma'am."

The moment I slipped through the front door and up the short staircase to the living room, there was no question that Pellman was in serious trouble. Either Andy's house was the epicenter of a local earthquake—local to only his house—or someone had recently visited.

The contents of two large bookcases were strewn around the room. Furniture cushions were slashed open. Two cabinets were emptied of magazines and bric-a-brac that was broken and tossed everywhere. An expensive large screen television was the only unscathed item in the room. I checked the rest of the house and found it destroyed as well. It looked like the house had been shaken and its innards scrambled.

Whoever did this was looking for something or was mad as hell. Thankfully, despite the carnage inside, Andrew Pellman wasn't among it.

A noise behind me turned me around as Angel walked through the front door.

She said, "The door was unlocked. Is it safe?"

"Yeah, no one's here." I led her room-to-room. "Angel, we better hurry. Whoever did this might come back."

She looked at the debris around us. "Before you say it, this wasn't Nicholas."

Oh, no, he'd never stoop this low. Now, Bobby, his driver and bodyguard would. I said as much.

"Dammit, I can't call Andrew to check on him." She stepped over a pile of books in the middle of the living room. "Smith took my phone."

"Yeah, bad Smith." I didn't have the heart to tell her I fried it. "What a jerk."

"I'm really worried, Tuck. Can you get anything on him?"

Now I'm a radar detector? "I can try. Find something personal."

She went into a room down the hall and returned with a photograph of Andy in a small rowboat. He was laughing and holding up a tiny fish in the quintessential silly fisherman's story.

I touched the photograph like a blind man reading braille, closed my eyes, and tried to find Andrew Pellman like a cheap carnival swami. For several minutes, I focused the best I could, and twice Andrew's face popped into view. For a second or two, I thought I was on his trail. In the end, all I got was static.

"Nothing, Angel. Not even fake news."

Her face fell. "Can't you usually get a read on someone?"

"I'm no bloodhound, but sometimes."

"Nothing?"

I shrugged. "Look, it's good news, right? If there's a 'normally,' it's that I find someone when they're in serious trouble. Or I can at least sense something bad happening. I got nothing on your boy scout. Be happy."

She sifted through the clutter on the floor. "You're right. I'm sorry."

There was a plaque, broken now, among the pile of books. "Angel, what's that?"

She went over and picked up a broken picture frame. The photo inside was scratched badly but she could make out three men wearing Martial Arts gis. Their faces were badly marred by the broken glass shards, but Andrew Pellman was in the center receiving a trophy. He wore a black belt with two white stripes on the ends. "Wow, here's something I didn't know. Andrew is a second-degree black belt in Hapkido."

Scrawny, pale-faced Andy was a Martial Arts expert? "Are we talking about the same Pellman? Are you sure it's not someone else's plaque? You know, maybe he was polishing it for them."

"Come on, Tuck. Give him a break."

I made a mental note that if we found Andrew, I would not take him for granted any longer. *Much.*

As she put the picture back among the pile of books, her face fell. "I'm even more worried about him. Before I lost his call, he said, 'It's worse than I thought. They actually did it.' He's mixed up in the middle of this, Tuck."

"Whatever this is. Bear will find Pellman. Okay?"

"Assuming Bear will talk to us." She waved a hand around the room. "What do we do about this?"

"Yes, Professor Tucker," a cold, impassive voice said from behind us. "What do you do about this?"

Chapter Twenty-Four

Colonel Smith, commander of the Men-Wearing-Black, stood in the kitchen entrance behind us.

"What are you doing here?" Angel demanded. "Did you follow me?"

Smith stepped into the living room and lifted a pistol toward her. Why, I didn't know. He didn't need a gun. He was intimidating without one.

He said, "You mean 'following us,' right? I've been listening to you for a while Professor Tucker. Exactly who are you talking to? Your deceased husband? Oliver—or does he prefer 'Tuck?'"

How exactly did this guy get past my radar? Usually, I can sense danger around Angel. Not this time. Was I losing my mojo?

"What have you done with Andrew?" Angel jutted an accusatorial finger at him. "Why did you do all this?"

"Andrew?" The expression on Smith's face was half shock, have mirth. "I assure you, Professor, I had nothing to do with *this*. I came here as you did, to speak with Mr. Pellman."

"I don't believe you."

Neither did I. "Get out of here, Angel. Colonel or not, he's dangerous."

She said, "Who are you, really? I don't think you're a real Colonel."

"That's immaterial. I'm afraid you'll have to come with me, though." He waved his pistol at her. "This is twice you're in the wrong place at the wrong time. I think it's time we had a very long chat."

Oh, hell no. I went to the windows and looked out. None of his men were outside.

"Angel, he's alone. When I say, run."

She backed toward the front door. "Colonel, where are your men? Why are you here alone?"

"They're busy. But I assure you, Professor, you're safe."

"Then why do you have a gun?" She bent down to pick up a stained-glass shaded floor lamp lying in the debris. She yanked the cord from the lamp base to expose the bare wires and held the cord out to her side. "I want all my research back."

Smith laughed. "What are you gonna do with a lamp, Professor? I never expected such antics from you."

"Good girl." Angel wasn't just beautiful, she was brilliant. "Angel get him to lower the gun."

"My research, Colonel?"

"In time, Professor. We do have to chat, though. And time is short. I'm on a rather tight timeline to complete my mission. Very tight."

"Oh?" She calmed. "Have you found anything about Special Agent Kerns or Mr. Downey's murders?"

He shrugged. "Forget them. They're my responsibility now."

Oh good, everything was in *his* hands. I felt much better.

She said, "Why the gun, Colonel? Afraid of a history professor with a broken lamp?"

"Not at all." He laughed a good, hearty laugh and holstered his pistol. "Better now?"

Perfect. I grabbed the bare ends of the lamp cord in Angel's hand and held tight.

The surge of electricity was instant and euphoric. It flashed sparks into my fingers and sent a tidal wave of energy raging through me—building up speed and intensity as it surged in me. The power filled me with an energy that propelled me in all directions. It was intoxicating. Exhilarating.

Smith's eyes bulged as he stared at me. His mouth went agape.

I leapt forward, kicked a toppled straight back chair from the floor and sent it crashing into his shins. Then I grabbed the lamp from Angel and threw it at his head. It smashed into his face and sent stained glass shards stabbed into his cheeks, hair, and chest.

He cried, "*Ahhhhh…*"

"Go, Angel. Run."

She did. In a second, she was out the front door and running for her Explorer.

Smith screamed again and frantically brushed the glass from his face. He kicked the remaining lamp carcass and sent it flying across the living room. His eyes darted around—fear and disbelief flashing in them.

"Screw you, Smith. I'm not done with you." The electricity was still surging in me. I went to a pile of books on the floor and began hurling them at him like a baseball pitching machine gone berserk. "Batter up, asshole."

As he swatted the books away with one hand, he tugged his pistol with the other. He opened fire at me. Fear turned his face from surprise to shock and terror. His bullets harmlessly passed through me with a sizzle and embedded themselves in the house walls.

"Stop. I'll let her go. Stop, dammit." He emptied his pistol, tugged a fresh magazine from his belt, and reloaded. "Enough. I give."

I heard Angel's Explorer squealing rubber down the street. She was safe.

"Good, asshole. If you go near her again, books aren't all you'll get."

I went to the door, feeling heroic. The electricity had pumped me up and saved Angel. Tesla would have been proud.

The power began to fade. Smith could no longer see me. He pivoted around the room looking for a target. Finally, he holstered his pistol. Then, he did something very peculiar. He slipped out his cell phone and tapped on a couple keys.

The recording he played stunned me.

"*Go, Angel. Run.*" The sound of Angel opening and slamming the door and what followed. "*Screw you, Smith. I'm not done with you. Batter up, asshole … Stop! I'll let her go. Stop! Enough. I give … Good, asshole. If you go near her again, books aren't all you'll get.*"

He tapped off the recording, smiled, and looked around the room.

"So, Detective Tucker. It's true. You *are* back."

Chapter Twenty-Five

Smith's words—*you are back*—haunted me. He was not among those in my life who ever knew me. He was an outsider. Yet he knew I was here. *He knew.*

That cannot be good.

I poofed home and landed in my living room just as Angel uncorked a bottle of wine. She downed a pretty-tall glass, refilled it, and downed that one.

"Angel, you're okay. Really. Take it easy."

She looked at the wineglass with a sad, anxious face. "I'm worried, Tuck. The murders and Bear acting strange. Andrew is missing and in trouble. Who did that to Andrew's house? Where is he? Do you think it was Smith? Do you think they have Andrew locked up somewhere?"

Good questions all. "If they trashed his house and grabbed him, then why was Smith back? He seemed genuinely surprised to find what we did."

"Maybe he was acting."

"Maybe."

"Maybe he was still searching when we got there."

"Where'd he hide? The refrigerator? We searched the entire house."

"He frightens me." She slugged back another mouthful of wine. "All those dark suits and Smith and Jones stuff sounds like a cheap movie. A scary, cheap movie."

Hey, wait a minute. I love scary, cheap movies.

She had a point. "It's worse, Angel."

"How could it be worse?"

I explained about Smith recording our conversation at Pellman's house. "He expected me, Angel. That's why he recorded us. He said, 'it's true, you are back.' Somehow, he knows about me."

She stared at her wine. Her face was distraught—a combination of wine and emotions. She was scared. She was upset about everything that happened today. She had every right to be. I wondered how badly she was going to let the day's events stop her.

Then, she cleared it all up. "Dammit, Tuck. We can't let Smith get away with this. He stormed into the library and took over. He even threw the sheriff out. He might have Andrew and he threatened me. On top of it all, he's trying to find you. No. We're going figure this out ourselves."

Did I mention my Angel is not only beautiful and brilliant, but feisty, too?

"What do you want to do, Angel?"

"Fight back."

"How?"

"Find Andrew. Then, find whoever killed Mr. Downey and Agent Kerns." She slugged back the rest of her wine, refilled the glass, and dropped herself in one of the twin leather chairs facing the cold fireplace. "If we solve any of those three, we'll solve them all."

Woof.

On cue whenever mama needed comfort, Hercule, appeared. He trotted into the room, slowly climbed onto her lap, and licked her face. Soon as he was done giving her some Lab love, he settled down and watched over her from a comfy place on the floor.

Hercule was the quintessential companion. Always there to play ball and take walks. Always there to sooth frayed nerves and love away sorrow. Always there for a chilly winter night by the fire. And, of course, always there to share your steak, too.

My kind of dog.

"Oliver, a word?" A voice beckoned from the living room doorway.

Woof. Wag. Woof.

Doc Gilley, a tall, broad-shouldered old curmudgeon, was dressed in surgical scrubs and a stethoscope draped around his neck. He was in his late-fifties *still*—just as he had been when he was murdered in the nineteen-fifties. Long story there, but yeah, it comes with my territory. Doc was a gray-haired, ruggedly handsome man with deep blue eyes and a perpetual five o'clock shadow. He also had a perpetual scowl. Well, he did with me anyway.

As I've said, Doc's my paternal great grandfather and a permanent member of our household. He'd been around in my family home, apparently, since I moved back in over two decades ago. I didn't know it until my murder. Then, he made his first appearance and became my spirit-guide and death-mentor. Whatever he was, he was a constant pain in the ass who played word games with me in his own version of "mentoring." Mentoring also came with a healthy dose of sarcasm, ridicule, and harassment—of me. But, he had good qualities, too. He was Hercule's second best pal, next to me, and Angel's long-lost guardian angel. Again, next to me.

"Hey, Doc," I said. "I need to talk to you."

Angel glanced around the room. "Hello, Doc. Don't mind me. I'm drowning my sorrows."

He gave a perfunctory wave but didn't bother to reply. While I could see and interact with him, Angel could not. She knew he was there only from Herc's and my interactions with him. Otherwise, she was oblivious.

I said, "I met this hot sexy Civil War Marilyn Monroe-look-a-like today. I got a million questions for you before I see her again."

He folded his arms across his chest. "A hot sexy babe you say?"

"Yeah, but I was a complete gentleman."

"I'm so relieved." He didn't budge from the doorway. "Young, pretty, sparkling blue eyes and long, curly blond hair?"

Oh yeah, Sally said she knew him. "Yup, that's her."

"You behaved?" His voice was stern and grandfatherly like he'd caught me raiding the liquor cabinet at thirteen. "Are you certain?"

Angel stopped sipping her wine. "Oh good, you're discussing Sally. Take it in the den, please. I want to relax."

Gulp.

"I should hope you behaved, Oliver." Doc wandered across the hall to my den with me in tow. "Because that hot, sexy blue-eyed, blond-babe is your fourth great-grandmother."

Ah, crap. I felt queasy.

Chapter Twenty-Six

"Grandmother?" I sat at my desk watching Doc leaning against my bookshelves across the room. "Really?"

He stared with a very satisfied, scathing grin on his face.

"Good thing I was polite." Damn, the thoughts I had—*yuck*.

"How magnanimous of you."

I said, "You never told me I had a Civil War grandmother. You never told me I was related to Colonel Mosby, either."

"It's a very distant family connection, Oliver. There is much I have never told you. More than I have, actually. You simply fail to ask me important questions. It's not my place to enlighten you. It is yours to seek enlightenment."

See what I mean? He was quick with insults, I told you so's, and riddles. Straight-out facts and direction, family heritage or actual guidance … not so much.

"What's Sally's story? What I witnessed was terrible. Some Union goon squad grabbed her and wanted some secret. She wouldn't give in so they hanged her."

"She was a spy, Oliver."

Wait, what? "A spy?"

"Yes. A train robber. A bank robber. And a spy."

Holy Mata Hari. "I thought all our relatives were the good guys?"

"Why would you think that?" He chuckled. Doc rarely chuckled. "Are you forgetting Frannie?"

Oh, yeah. Frannie. She was a forties gangster who probably whacked a few folks here and there. I'm sure they deserved it. No, really, I'm sure they did.

"Right, Frannie."

"And of course, I was never totally innocent either, Oliver." Doc's blue eyes shimmered. I think he liked being a bad boy. "Your grandfather, Ollie was also a spy."

"Sure, but he was OSS." I held up a hand. "He was a good spy."

"Perhaps he was. Perhaps he wasn't." He shrugged. "Perhaps, our family situation is due to our less-than sterling history. Those that were less than sterling, died violently. Hence our history of, well, *returning*."

Our family "situation" as he referred to it was that many of my relatives, Doc for one, Frannie, my namesake Ollie Tucker, and now hottie-grandma Sally, were all spirits who haunt me from time to time. Oh, there have been plenty of non-family members who show up, too. See, my family had some crazy lives and dark secrets. I never considered that their deaths—all violent—were caused by those secrets. That those secrets resulted in their status among the dead and back club. Right there with me. Geez, I wonder what my secrets were. I don't recall any real dark things.

"Okay, Doc. No more word games. What's Sally's story?"

"What has she told you?"

"Not much. Though she did invite me to her hanging."

"Interesting." He walked to my bookshelves where he feigned interest in some volume of something. "What do you think that has to do with those library murders?"

He was well informed. "You know about that?"

"Didn't I just say so?"

"Not exactly, no." See, he's a curmudgeon. "I have no idea how it's related. A federal agent died by some death ray. Then, a janitor who probably wasn't a janitor had his neck snapped like a twig. Bear is acting odd and he might have stolen evidence. Top that with Angel's doctoral student missing. Oh, did I mention the Men-Wearing-Black swooped in and seized control of everything? They're threatening Angel and their boss knows about me, too."

Doc didn't turn around. He had pulled a book out of the rear of the bookshelves—most of them his old collections—and was reading.

Funny how he can move things and do what he wishes without electricity or some kind of juice. Unlike me.

"Hey, Doc, can you teach me to do that? Move things and such without—"

"No." He closed the book and turned. "You certainly have made a mess of things again."

What did I do? I asked him.

"You have, as always, Oliver, failed to see the forest for the trees. Things are much more connected than you see. Step back and look at everything as one big picture."

Forest and trees? Big picture? Was Plato Doc's poker buddy? "How about you step back and tell me instead?"

"Where would the learning come in, Oliver? In many of the cases you've had, I did the hard work for you. This one needs only a bit of analysis and perspective. Surely you can find some of each, no?"

Ouch. "Sure, here's some perspective. If you were hanging around the library watching everything, why not warn me? Maybe pop in and save Downey or stop Andy Pellman from—"

"*Andrew* Pellman."

"Whatever."

Doc gazed at me. He shook his head, sighed, and started to fade from the room. "You know better, Oliver. We do not intercede and change things. Never."

"I've done pretty well doing just that before."

"Oh, you think so?" He was just a misty blur now. "I'll clarify and say that *I* do not interfere and change things. You, well, you're another story."

I laughed. "You finally admit I can do something you can't."

"I didn't say I couldn't. I said I do not. You refuse to accept the rules of this existence. Many times, you've made things worse. Did you ever consider that's why you're still here?"

No, I hadn't. "I'd rather be here with Angel and Herc than anywhere else. So, I'll just be me."

He was gone now, but said, "How wonderful for us all."

Doc never made an exit—or entrance—without unloading worldly wisdom or taunting me.

He didn't disappoint.

"Oliver, Sally Elizabeth is back because she was found to have disgraced our family. The question is why now? Ask yourself the one true, guiding question that all good detectives must ask to solve a case."

"What would that be?" God, I hated asking.

"Of course you don't know." Even in the nothing of afterlife I could see his eyes roll and heard a deep, disappointing sigh. "What is the common denominator among the players? How are they connected?"

Shit, shit, shitty-shit-shit. I hate it when he's right.

"That's two questions, Doc."

"Of course it is, Oliver. But if you couldn't get the first one, I had no hopes you'd get the second.

Chapter Twenty-Seven

I stood in my den wondering what two answers I'd missed. Of course, it's quite possible I didn't miss anything and he was just giving me a kick like always. Ole Doc, what a jokester.

Wait...

I went to the book self and looked at the old leather book he'd been reading. Not reading but baiting me. As I reached for the book, a strange, ethereal magnetism gripped me. The book pulled me closer and bade me pay attention—*A Collection Of Historical Genealogy for Winchester Virginia, 1744-1950.*

As my fingers touched the leather cover, the magnetism dissipated, and in its place ...

Lightning.

The flash blinded me. The pulse struck my fingertips and seared through my being until it lifted me off my feet and spun me in circles. The exhilaration was instant and intense—power, control, euphoria. Just as I thought it would spin me away like a kite in a tornado, the room flashed black.

Poof... gone.

* * *

And... Poof.

My den was replaced by a dark room—a barn I think—that smelled of hay and earth and animals. It took me some time but my head stopped spinning and the dizziness subsided.

Sound. A faint light. Voices.

Ahead of me, deeper inside, four figures stood near their horses packing saddlebags and haversacks from a table against the side wall. They were lit by a single kerosene lantern. The light was dim and one of the men blocked me from seeing what they were packing. Whatever it was, it had their complete attention. As one of the men lifted his haversack over a shoulder, he moved and the light shown showed me the four faces.

Not four men. It was three men and Sally Mosby—the original, 1864-Sally. They were all dressed in dark work clothes—her included. Clothes of the working class in Civil War-era Virginia.

The visions I have during these investigations were rarely in order. Rarely telling just their own story. Here, now, 1864-Sally was still alive and playing her part in whatever chapter was trying to reveal itself. This event could be a day or a month before her hanging. It might not even be connected. It might be the key.

1864-Sally spoke. "I think I should know the plan. Don't you? I'm not following y'all into the night without knowing."

"Oh?" The shorter of the men, a husky man with a wide-brimmed hat, considered her. "Well, Sally. Not sure about—"

"That traitor hogwash again, Jenkins?" Her tone was biting. "I've proven myself. I've killed enough for you, haven't I?"

The other two men murmured to Jenkins. They seemed to agree with her.

"Okay then," Jenkins said. "We git to the bank in twos. First, we make sure it's empty—no night guards or soldiers 'round. Then, you and me go in the back. Wilks and Hall go in the north side. No shootin' or killin' unless it's our only way out. And then, whatever it takes."

1864-Sally's face tightened noticeably in the light. "Well, I ain't leavin' anyone behind who might know me or who sees my face. If there is anyone about, somebody better take care of them."

The man Jenkins called Hall hefted the lantern. He was tall and thin. He wore round, wire-rimmed eyeglasses that were perched on a bony nose lost in a bushy beard. "It's near ten, Sally. There ain't gonna be nobody about. So long as we go quiet and don't trip over some drunkard or something. We ain't gonna need to worry none."

"I hope you're right." 1864-Sally glanced around the barn. "If it's gold we're after, how we gonna carry it without a wagon?"

Jenkins laughed. "You let me worry about that. If we find gold—"

"If?" she snapped. "I'm not riskin' my neck on 'if.'"

"Gold comes in lots of ways, Sally," Hall quipped. "We're after papers—important papers that will lead us to that gold yer all worried 'bout."

I tried to hear the rest, but their voices got lost in the shuffle of horses. Watching, Hall waited for the other three to mount up before turning off the lantern and climbing on a tall bay.

Jenkins said, "Okay, y'all, we'll see you inside the bank. Remember, if you see any trouble, give us the catbird."

"Or a gunshot," Hall spat. "You'll know trouble if we find it."

The four started for the barn door behind me. Hall and Wilks passed by and trotted out of the barn into the night. Jenkins followed. 1864-Sally rode a few yards behind.

Normally by now, I'd get that crazy, faint feeling as my world began to pull me back. It was like a whirlwind sucking me in and sending me home—disconcerted and confused.

Not yet.

1864-Sally passed me. Then she stopped just inside the barn door. She reigned her mount around and faced me.

Faced me?

"What are you doing here?"

Ah, me? She saw me—in this vision? The twenty-first century-me and nineteenth-century her? Never had anyone in my visions ever spoken to me. No one had ever known I was among them, watching, listening, learning. Because, in truth, I wasn't. But speak to me?

"Sally? Can you see me?"

Her horse unsettled and reared. She patted his neck and calmed him with a gentle word.

"You shouldn't be here. I didn't call for you."

"You didn't? I was in Angel's office and this book—"

"Hey, now." Jenkins' voice reached us. "What the hell are you doing, Sally? Is someone back there?"

"Nothing. Nobody. My horse spooked. A rat or something."

She reigned her horse back a couple steps closer to me. "You can't follow us. I don't know how you got here, but you can't come. I guess you found it?"

"Found what?"

"My message." She shot a glance over her shoulder, guarding against Jenkins' return. "Go home."

The barn began a slow, woozy spin around me like a carnival ride. Images of 1864-Sally on her horse slid by, then gained speed and became a blur of shadows and color. The barn disappeared and at first, the night stars were overhead. Then, just void.

Hall, Wilks, Jenkins, and 1864-Sally were gone to rob their bank.

I was gone home.

Doc was right. Great grandma was a bank robber.

Chapter Twenty-Eight

Bear stood in the middle of his living room staring bullets at the man in his doorway. "It's barely seven am and I told you never to come here, Young."

"Okay, Braddock. Okay." Peter Young's perpetual grin didn't ease. He sauntered into the room, dropped himself down in an overstuffed chair, and plopped his feet on the coffee table.

"Get your damn feet off my table." Bear kicked the side of the table. "Make it fast and get out."

"Easy, now." Young didn't move. "I come bearing gifts."

"What?"

Young pulled two packages from his windbreaker pockets and tossed them onto the table beside his feet. One package was a new cellular telephone. The other was a thick, dense envelope.

Bear eyed the phone but picked up the envelope, opening it. A two-inch stack of twenty-dollar bills fell into his beefy hand. "What's this?"

"Payday, brother."

"You already gave me twenty grand. I haven't earned that yet."

"Oh, no?" Young folded his arms. "What about earlier?"

Bear's face reddened. "I don't like where this is taking me."

"Tough shit."

Bear hated what was happening. For over twenty years, he'd been a damn good cop. He'd made detective early and just a little more than a year ago, had taken over the Major Crimes Task Force. Now, friends were seeing him falter and fail. The phone call he'd gotten an hour ago summoned him to the Sheriff's office by eight. By nine-fifteen, he'd be unemployed. Maybe indicted. If things went badly, he could be in a cell by lunch.

"I got a call this morning—"

Young held up a hand. "I figured. That's the way this was headed anyway. Just play the game. If they try to lock you up, keep your mouth shut and we'll unlock the cell. Just keep quiet, Braddock. That's most important with the people we're dealing with. Screw that up and we're both dead."

"I got that. I figured it out way before Kerns and Downey."

"Then we understand each other."

"We do." Bear stuffed the money back into the envelope and tossed it on the table beside the cell phone. "Burner phone?"

Young nodded. "Don't use it for anyone but us. Got that?"

He nodded.

Young stood, walked to the front door, and turned before he opened it. "I'll call you after your meeting with your boss."

"What's next?"

"You know what's next."

Bear's face scrunched up. "I do?"

"Cal Clemens."

"Cal?" Bear held Young's eyes for a long time trying to find something behind them that would tell him what he wanted to know. "He was onto me yesterday. I thought he was under control."

"He is. Just not how we planned it."

Chapter Twenty-Nine

"Are the Men-Wearing-Black chasing us?" I asked.

Angel glanced—for the millionth time—into the rearview mirror and side mirrors. Finally, we slid through the entrance of the Frederick County Sheriff's office a few miles outside Winchester-proper.

After sleeping in until seven a.m. this morning, Angel woke in a panic. She wanted to get to Bear and tell him what we'd found at Pellman's house last night. That, and our incursion with Smith. I don't know if she was acting paranoid as a result of a wine hangover or because of Smith. Maybe both.

"What do you mean?" We skidded to a stop in a visitor parking spot. "Is someone behind us?"

No, there wasn't. "You're driving like we're under attack. What's going on with you? What—"

"University Security called me this morning. Someone broke into my office last night, Tuck," she growled. "Someone went through my things and messed the place up."

Uh, oh. I knew where this was going.

"The security guard arrived and saw a big man leaving. He tried to catch him but he got away."

"And you think… what? That it was Bear?"

Her mouth clamped so tight her lips went white.

"You do."

She pounded her palm on the steering wheel. "The guard described him perfectly. I don't want to believe it, but—"

"Then don't." It sounded lame even as I said it. "Let's just see what he says."

On the drive to the Sheriff's Office, I'd told her about my discussion with Doc. Her eyes flared as I then explained my 1864 adventure to the barn where Sally Mosby and her pals launched a bank robbery.

She had a hundred questions. I had a hundred, "I don't know" responses.

"Soon as we're done here, Tuck, we have to get back home and figure out what that genealogical book has to do with this. It might be key to figuring out what message your sweet li'l pal, Sally, is talking about."

"She happens to be family, Angel." Geez. "Sally was hanged for being a spy. She's a bank robber, too. Although those visions are backward. Maybe that's how she got caught—robbing the bank. Maybe Captain Little wanted whatever she stole from the bank."

"You said Captain Little wanted to know about her secrets and some bounty."

She didn't give it to him and he hanged her. Bastard.

Angel sat thinking for a long time. "All this seems connected to my Apple Harvest research. I had files and local journals about that period of the war in my office. Nicholas wanted to buy them, too. It all started at the library."

"Actually, I think it all started in 1864," I said. "I know you think Bear is up to his neck in this. But let's hear him out."

"Of course."

She started to open her door when Bear stormed out of the Sheriff's Office's main door. It banged on the wall and he almost ran to the parking lot's entrance. A moment later, a black Tesla Roadster pulled up. Bear climbed in. The car did a sharp U-turn and crossed the median break and drove back the way it came.

A Tesla Roadster? Hmmm, I remember that car.

"Angel, does Bear know someone filthy-rich guy who can afford a two hundred-thousand-dollar sportscar?"

"I doubt it."

"I doubt Winchester has two Roadsters in residence." I watched the sports car disappear down the road. "I saw one outside the Library yesterday."

"No coincidences, Tuck. Also, Bear's cruiser is in his parking spot."

"We better follow him and find out what's going on."

She climbed out of the Explorer. "You follow him. I'll talk to Spence and see if I can learn anything. I'm supposed to discuss my statement today, anyway."

"All right. I'll meet you later at campus." Before she walked off, I added, "Be careful what you tell them, Angel. What's going on with Bear might be innocent. Let's not pile on him."

Just as I began my jump onto the spirit-express to follow Bear, she responded, "And you try not to cause any more trouble."

Moi?

* * *

Not knowing where Bear was going, I gambled he would get his own vehicle from his apartment first. So instead of poofing around blindly, I arrived at his apartment across town several minutes before the Roadster pulled up to his apartment.

He had a lengthy conversation with the driver before getting out.

As I headed over to eavesdrop on him and get a good look at his new pal, he climbed out of the car and the Tesla sped away. He went inside his apartment. A moment later, he returned to the parking area and got into his beat-up old pickup that he called "rustic." I called it "junk."

The last time Bear and I were together, he'd been irate with me and warned me off. Whatever was wrong with him was bad. Bad enough that he abandoned years of friendship and partnership with me. He even abandoned Angel. Never in my life, or death, had I seen that coming. Fearing a reprisal for not staying away, I sat in the truck seat beside him silent as a lamb.

We made a beeline for the Super-Big Buys store east of town.

Super-B's, as everyone called it, was a warehouse of electronics and home goods of every dimension. It was one of my favorite places in my living years. I missed roaming the aisles playing with all the new techy gadgets and games on display. Angel never liked doing that with me. After my death, she still refused to go in with me because I begged her to play with the new games so I could watch.

Sure, I could have juiced up with the electricity and played a few rounds of the latest first-person shooter. But really, explain that one to anyone watching? Sometimes, being dead was no fun at all.

As Bear parked, his jacket pocket vibrated and he pulled out a cell phone. "What?"

The caller spoke for a long time.

"I know. I just got fired. Well, suspended, but it's only a matter of time. I might be in jail by tomorrow."

More from the caller.

"Fine. Okay. Jesus, I know what I have to do. Trust me. I'll take care of everything from last night. The Sheriff's pissed, but he can't prove anything—yet. For now, I'm okay. If the feds dig in, we've got problems."

The caller commented briefly.

"Dammit, I know." Bear's face tightened. "I'm the one who did it, remember? You better keep your end of the bargain. I'm not going to prison for the rest of my life. Certainly not alone."

A short response.

"I gotta go. Don't call me. I'll call you."

Before the caller could respond, Bear tapped off the call. He turned the phone off and tucked it into the console between the seats.

My head reeled and I found myself staring at the man I thought I'd known for over twenty years. Now, I wondered if I knew him at all. If I didn't, who was he all those years? Had he played me? Or was it something worse— something ugly that happened to him and pulled him to the other side? The dark side. The criminal side.

As Bear climbed out of the truck, I wondered who his new best friend was on the phone—and in the Tesla. My best guess was Bradley M. White, arms dealer extraordinaire. I hoped I was wrong, but the tingle in my brain said I wasn't.

He wasted no time heading into Super-B's. I followed closely, but quietly—not a word. I know, it was killing me.

Inside, Bear made two purchases. The first confused me—a new cell phone. Why did he need a new phone? He has one in his truck. I wanted to ask but when he bought the second item, I knew better and kept quiet. He purchased an EMF meter.

Bear bought the EMF meter to warn him when I was nearby. That means the days of me stealthily following him around were over. Beginning now. He warned me off and now he was making sure I didn't violate his rules.

We made it all the way to his pickup before he erupted. In the truck cab, he pulled out his phone, checked the string of messages his EMF meter was sending him. Then, in a sudden rage, he slammed his fist into the dash so hard he cracked the padding.

"I told you to leave me the hell alone, Tuck."

Yup, he did. "Sorry, partner, I'm worried about you. What's with the EMF? I'm offended you're trying to keep track of me."

"Offended?" He pounded his fist into the dash again. "You're offended because I want to know when you're sneaking around? That would be funny if it didn't piss me off."

"I'm not sneaky, I'm stealthy." I'd not seen him like this before. "Bear, relax. Let Angel and me help you. We know you're in trouble."

"Oh, yeah?" He pulled the device out of his pocket and set it on the dash. "What's Angela know?"

"Everything I do."

He fumed for a long time, staring out the truck window as his teeth ground.

"Just tell me—"

"Stay the hell away from me, Tuck. We're through. Get that? You. Me. Angel. Even your damn ugly dog. All of you stay away."

Hercule was not ugly. "Enough, Bear. What's going on? Did you break into Angel's office last night? Did you take the evidence from the library? Why?"

Bear picked up the EMF meter and tapped a couple buttons.

Dammit… My head began to explode. A high-pitched, shrill siren sent needles into my eyes and brain. It was excruciating. It penetrated me with a raw, agonizing intensity.

"You like that, *partner*?" He held up the EMF meter. "This is the latest version with a self-defense alarm. If a bad ghost scares me, I tap in the code. *Poof,* it sends an ultra-high frequency alarm out. It's supposed to ward off evil spirits."

I was not an evil spirit but it still worked. I felt like a dog in a dog-whistle factory. My head pounded from the screeching and wavering tones. I couldn't focus. When he tapped the keys again, I couldn't take it.

"Okay, okay, I'll go."

He turned off the device. The sounds and needles stopped.

"You're turning into a real bastard, Bear. I don't deserve this."

"Stay away, Tuck. Angela, too. That goes for any of your stupid spirit relatives hanging around."

"Bear, listen—"

"Fine. Have it your way." He tapped the device and the needles attacked my brain again. "Remember, Tuck, stay away. All of you. You can't haunt me anymore."

Chapter Thirty

Inside the Sheriff's Office, Angel didn't knock on Bear's office door. She opened it and charged in. The instance her eyes locked onto the man sitting behind Bear's desk with his feet propped lazily on the desktop, her cheeks reddened.

Spence had his hands folded across his belly with his eyes shut.

"Detective, what are you doing?" She slammed the door and jarred him awake.

Spence snapped forward so fast he nearly toppled from the chair. Righting himself, he straightened several items on the desk that he'd moved to make himself more comfortable.

"If Bear catches you in here, he'll skin you."

"Bear's gone, Angela." He cleared his throat. "What are you doing here?"

"I came to see him. But I saw him leave." Her arms snapped folded. "Why are you in here?"

"I'm looking over files for the Sheriff."

"While asleep?"

"No, I wasn't." Spence looked down at the desk, embarrassed. "Okay, sure. It was a long night."

"Yes, it was." Angel glanced around the office and settled her gaze on him. Her eyes softened and she felt a quiver ripple through her. "Detective, what's going on?"

"I can't say, Angela." He seemed genuinely concerned. "I know you guys are close, but I can't say anything. The sheriff would be pissed."

"Detective—"

"It's Mike." Spence eased around the desk. "After all these years, will you please call me Mike? After all, I was Tuck's pal."

"No, you weren't."

"No, okay." He shrugged. "You're right. But I helped solve his murder. Didn't I?"

"You thought Bear and I did it. Remember?"

"Yeah." He shrugged again. "But then I—"

"Fine. Mike." Angel relented and wondered if she'd regret it. Mike Spence wasn't nice very often without a selfish motive. Soon, very soon, she'd find out what his was. "I need to know what's going on with Bear. I'm really worried. He was acting very odd yesterday at the library. He's in trouble."

"You're telling me." Spence stood and gestured her into one of the office chairs in front of the desk. When she sat, he dropped into the other beside her. "Okay, if I tell you what I know, you share with me whatever you know. Deal?"

She swallowed. "All right."

Spence's face crinkled into a half-gleeful, half-conspiratorial grin. "Sheriff Millbert suspended him—*indefinitely.*"

Well, at least he wasn't fired. "On what grounds?"

"Dereliction of duty and misconduct." Spence took a breath. "Bear had the only key to the missing evidence that was stolen yesterday from the library last night. No one—and I mean no one—could find him last night. Sheriff thinks maybe he was ditching the evidence."

"That's ridiculous." As the words came out, she knew it wasn't. He was protecting someone. "Any witnesses?"

"There's more." Spence leaned back and folded his arms. "Clemens left ahead of Bear last night and disappeared, too. Nobody can find him. Oh, and Bradley White, that bigshot rich guy has something on Bear."

"Bradley White?" She knew what Tuck had told her, but she'd play dumb. "Why do you think that?"

"Because the last thing Cal told me was that he'd caught White in some meeting in the library boardroom." Spence poked a hole in the air between them with his finger. "When Cal tried to check them all out, including the other three with White, Bear stopped him. Have you ever seen Bear protect some rich dude before?"

"No." Angel had to look away. "Maybe there's another reason. Maybe—"

"No." Spence softened a bit. "Bears got a hundred fifty grand in gambling debts, Angela. That's just last month."

A hundred and fifty thousand dollars? "That can't be. He doesn't gamble."

"I found the betting tickets myself. We got into his computer and found gambling sites in his history. A lot of sites. A lot of money, too. Gambling more than he makes."

"Gambling? Bear?"

"Angela, I'm sorry." Spence leaned forward and gently touched her arm. A gesture she would never have thought him capable of—compassion. "I know it's tough. Bear is over his head in debt. I think White has him on a leash. There's missing evidence. Bear's in trouble. *Real* trouble."

She closed her eyes to think. She should tell him about Bear ransacking her office last night but wasn't sure she should. There had to be another explanation. Whatever it was, Bear was trying to hide it from her and Tuck. That fact, along with what Spence had just told her, terrified her to the bone. As she tried to think of one good, reasonable explanation, Spence's next words snapped her eyes wide open.

"The sheriff's investigating Bear's involvement in all this." He lowered his voice. "I think he's in deep with Bradley White. Maybe they're both connected to Kerns and Downey's murders."

"Bear involved in the murders? You've thought that of him before, Mike. You were wrong then. You're wrong now." When Tuck was murdered, Spence had been adamant that Bear was the killer—her too at one point. Since then, Bear and he never got along. Well, they hadn't been the best of friends prior to Tuck's murder. "What do you think Bradley White has to do with this?"

"He was sneaking around the library, Angela. Coincidentally, your pal Poor Nic was lurking there, too. If you ask me, those two together spell trouble."

"Nicholas is on the Friends of the Handley Library board if that matters."

She told him about hearing Bear speaking to someone in the Henkel Boardroom and about finding surveillance devices inside. She recapped her evening there and the odd things that happened, ending with her frustration with Smith taking her research. It felt a little wrong sharing it all with him and not Bear, but given the situation, she needed to tell someone. "I'm trusting you, Detective—*Mike*. Trusting you to do the right thing with everything I've told you."

"You found listening devices in the boardroom?"

She nodded.

"So, Bear, Poor Nic, and God knows who else were all there, and someone was listening in?" Spence looked at the ceiling for a long time. "There isn't a crime in Winchester old Nic isn't connected to. Man, the Sheriff's going to go apoplectic."

"Remember, Nicholas's been accused of many things and never been at fault—at least around here. He's actually helped us many times."

"Maybe. Not being able to prove his guilt is not the same as being innocent. A leopard has spots."

"Nicholas hasn't done anything wrong." Then, thinking about Nicholas being near Andrew Pellman's house last night, she told Spence about what she'd found and about Colonel Smith being there, too.

"Jesus, Angela," he said, rubbing his chin. "You should have reported that last night. I'll get some deputies over there."

"I know. I came here this morning to speak with Bear about it."

"Yeah, okay."

"Angela." He looked down, appearing embarrassed. "I can't believe I'm asking you this, but what about *him*?"

"Him?"

"Him, you know." He looked sheepish. "*Him*."

"Tuck?" She grinned. In the years since Tuck's death, Spence had never approached the subject with her. Oh, there had been the occasional barb about her believing Tuck was back, but never seriously. "He's dead, Mike."

"Yeah, but isn't he, you know, back?"

"What do you think?"

"You think he's back. So do Bear and Cal. Everyone just accepts it."

Yes, that was true. "What are you asking?"

Spence looked around the room like a schoolchild searching for the right algebra answer to the teacher's question. "Come on, Angela. He knows stuff and somehow pops around helping Bear and you all the time on cases. How about now? What's he think?"

There it was. Mike Spence, the man who'd accused her of Tuck's murder. The man who scoffed at every instance Tuck had been around and helped solve past cases. The man who loudly taunted Bear and Cal about their beliefs in Tuck was asking her for *his* help.

"He's as worried as I am."

"Crap, I knew it." His face shriveled up. "Does he know anything? Any theories?"

She thought long and hard before answering him. "He knows Bear's in trouble. He doesn't know how or about what. He's going to find out. *We're* going to find out."

"Angela, listen," Spence said in a soft, quiet voice. "The sheriff and the feds are going after Bear like gangbusters. Bear and I don't get along, I know, but it sucks. I don't think he murdered anyone. Maybe he's covering for someone. Maybe it's something else. But I don't believe he'd kill over some lousy gambling debts."

"I agree."

"I know darn well you're going to do your own investigating. Just like always." He winked awkwardly. "How about you and me work together?"

Was he serious? "Work together? You've always been very vocal about my, what have you called it, 'amateur antics?' "

Spence blushed. "Yeah, I can be a jerk. You're pretty good at this stuff. We both know that it has something to do with Tuck. I'm not saying I totally believe he returned from the grave. I'm just saying you do and maybe somehow, that helps you figure stuff out. We're talking about Bear, here. I know you'll be into this whether the sheriff tries to stop you or not."

She just watched him.

"So, what do you say? Partners?"

Partners? "Well, I have to think—"

The office door banged open and sent them to their feet.

Colonel Smith stood in the doorway. Behind him were two Men-Wearing-Black.

"Now, isn't this cozy?" Smith sneered. "Just who I was looking for."

Chapter Thirty-One

"Detective Spence, get out." Smith threw his thumb over his shoulder and stepped inside. "I need a few words with Professor Tucker."

Spence started to object when both of Smith's men entered the room and flanked him. "Yeah, sure. Okay."

"What's this about?" Angel demanded. "I want an explanation."

"Excuse me, Professor." Smith gestured to his men and waited for them to take Spence by the arms and escort him from the room. "I wish to speak with you alone."

"Alone? No." Angel moved toward the office door, but Smith blocked her path. "I wish to leave."

"I'm sorry, Professor. You can't."

Angel's eyes flared with anger. "You cannot hold me here. I know my rights."

"Oh, yes I can." Smith's face darkened. "Where's Captain Braddock?"

Angel stared defiantly, trying to keep her composure.

"I don't play games, Professor. I want Braddock."

"I don't have him," she snapped. "I don't know where he is. If I did, I wouldn't tell you."

"No?" Smith leaned forward nearly nose-to-nose with her. "Then you'd go to jail. A federal jail."

"No, I won't. There are laws."

Smith laughed. "They get a little murky around national security."

National Security? "What are you talking about Colonel? Last night—"

"Last night never happened."

"Oh?" She stepped back from him. "Last night most assuredly happened. I'll be filing a formal complaint with your agency."

"What agency is that, Professor?"

It struck her that despite the power and authority Smith commanded—even over Sheriff Millbert—she had never actually seen or been told what agency, other than the DOD, he represented.

"Exactly," Smith said coolly. "Pray you don't find out."

A chill ran through her. "What do you want?"

"Braddock."

"I don't know where he is. Detective Spence and I were just talking about that."

"Oh, I see." Smith shot a glance toward the office door. "What did you conclude?"

"That he was suspended and has disappeared."

"Disappointing." Smith wandered behind Bear's desk and sat. "First the library evidence disappears. Then Detective Clemens disappears. Now, Braddock is gone—again. See a pattern here, Professor?"

She shrugged. "All that happened right after you showed up in town. That's the pattern I see. Maybe you should explain that."

"Listen to me." Smith slammed his fist onto the desk and jumped up. "You don't ask questions. You don't point fingers. It's the other way around. I'm not tethered by any damn rule book, lady. I don't give a damn about your rights or lawyers or courts. I want answers. I want Braddock. If you don't start cooperating, I'll slam your pretty ass in a dark hole so deep you'll never see daylight again."

"You wouldn't dare." Deep down, she wondered if he would. "You do remember you're in a police station."

"Oh, please." Smith laughed. "For such a smart, educated woman, you aren't getting it, are you? I do what I want. Now, sit down."

The office door opened. One of Smith's men entered and handed him a note. He read it and afterward stuffed it in his pocket.

"Now, Professor," Smith said. "Where were we?"

"I was leaving." She turned toward the door. "You'll be hearing from my attorney."

"Jones," Smith said and the man in the doorway reached out and grabbed her arm. "Be reasonable, Professor. We find your research rather important. Help us find Braddock, cooperate, and perhaps we'll let you keep that research afterward."

"My research?" She glared at Jones gripping her arm. "Let go of me. Now."

"Come now, Professor. I told you, I'm on a short timeline—"

"You said that last night," Angel growled, trying to pull free. "What's that mean?"

Smith shrugged. "That is not your concern."

Angel stepped in close to Jones and drove her knee into his groin. As the man cried out and doubled over, she tugged her arm free and shoved him backward onto the floor outside the office. Without looking back, she strode down the hall and into the detective's bullpen for the safety of the three detectives working there.

Spence stood in the bullpen and watched the entire thing.

"Jesus, Angela. You okay?"

"Yes, I am, *partner.*"

Chapter Thirty-Two

I caught up to Angel in her university office. She was sitting at her worktable fiddling with a new cell phone. Her face was distant and blank—she was miles away.

"Angel, what's wrong now?" I asked and instantly realized it was a stupid question. "You okay?"

She glanced up and burst into tears. Then, she pounded the desk with her palm. "I'm so damn mad. Colonel Smith cornered me in Bear's office earlier." She told me the rest of the story. Every few sentences, she pounded the desk again. "He threatened me, Tuck."

Damn. "It's over. Go easy."

She nodded. "He can't just lock me up or steal my research. Can he?"

"Unfortunately, the feds get away with all kinds of tricks these days. Mention national security and the rules change. You need to stay clear of him."

"National security? What's next?"

"Space aliens." That made her smile. "You and Spence are partners now? That's scarier than Smith."

She shrugged. "We agreed we needed help, Tuck. Without Bear, Mike's all we have."

"Yeah, about Bear." I told her about Bear visiting the Super-B's and his interesting purchases. "I won't be able to get within a hundred feet of him now. He'll turn on that defense system and fry my brain before I get a word in."

"Poor Bear—"

"Poor Bear? He almost split all my atoms with that damn EMF meter."

Her face fell. "How could he go so bad so fast?"

"Gambling. He's in with White who's selling stolen technology and there's the missing evidence. None of this makes sense. Yet, there it is. Now, he's got a gadget to keep me away—away from learning what he's up to."

"What about Smith?" She pounded the table again, sending a sheaf of paper running for its life. "This is so unbelievable."

"It'll work out. Somehow."

She restacked her papers on her desk. "Sheriff Millbert and the feds think he might have murdered Kerns and Downey, Tuck. They took his badge, gun, car … even his cell phone."

If Millbert took his cell phone, what phone did he hide in his truck console? And why buy a second one?

"Bear's no murderer, Angel." The truth is everyone is capable of murder under the right circumstances. You have to have all the right ingredients— opportunity, motive, means, and for sane people, a loss of control. I couldn't see Bear meeting those requirements. "I don't believe that."

Her face lost its edginess and saddened. "As of this morning, I never thought him a gambler, either. Over a hundred and fifty thousand that we know of."

"He's in deep." I shifted gears. I explained about his phone call with the unknown caller earlier—the one where he was worried about going to prison and threatened not to go alone. "And he probably broke in here. What's missing?"

"More of my research."

"I thought it was all taken by Smith's men?"

She shook her head. "Some of it was here." She closed her eyes, thinking. "I found some old letters and journals in one of the Apple Harvest crates. They were all bundled together in an old leather valise. Among them were notes and letters involving someone named Robert Morriss. They're gone."

I searched my keen investigative mind but found no record of any Robert Morriss. I told her as much.

"I've heard the name, but I can't place it." She moved back to her computer and tapped away on its keyboard. A few minutes later, she laughed out loud. "Oh, no. It can't be."

"What?"

"This is unbelievable, Tuck." She pointed to the screen as I moved behind her to peek over her shoulder. "Robert Morriss is connected to some silly treasure hunt in Virginia."

"Treasure hunt? Like pirates?" Wow, maybe this case was going to be fun after all.

"No, a hoax that started in the eighteen hundreds."

"Why would Bear be interested in that?"

She shrugged. "Maybe there's something else in those documents worth a lot of money."

Bear was not the treasure hunting type. Of course, last week he wasn't the obsessive gambler type, either.

"Is this the same stuff Poor Nic's interested in?"

"Maybe." She rubbed her eyes and leaned back. "There must be something more in those documents that I hadn't discovered yet."

"Poor Nic's been good to you over the years. I'll give you that. But every time he's involved with one of my cases, he's never *completely* innocent."

Begrudgingly, she agreed. "Perhaps. Maybe Bear's working with him. 'Why' is the question. All the possible answers are bad."

She was right. I couldn't find a good reason for Bear's sudden, murky change. "It has to do with the meeting in the library boardroom. That meeting was assuredly about arms deals. Nic was in that meeting, as were Mr. White, Chen Liu, Ahmad El Fazi, and Peter Young, too. That's what got Kerns and Downey murdered."

"And it involves Bear."

Did it? "Well, he ran interference for White. Then he probably broke in here and stole documents about a treasure hunt. This is the craziest thing I've ever investigated."

"Could White, Nicholas, and Bear be partners looking for the treasure?" Her face blanched a little. "How does that lead to Kerns and Downey's murders?"

"Maybe it's two different things. White's selling secrets, right? He has a supplier. My guess is that supplier was in that library with him, Poor Nic, and the others. Maybe Kerns was there to arrest them. It might not have anything to do with the treasure hunt."

"Maybe." She tapped the computer monitor. "Kerns wanted to speak with me, presumably about Andrew Pellman. What do Andrew and I have to do with stolen secrets? Second, what's it got to do with a hoax treasure hunt? And, how did Bear get involved?"

Bear suddenly had a lot of secrets. Until yesterday, I'd swear he was the most honest cop I've ever met. Now, well, the jury was out.

I changed topics. "Angel, remember the genealogical book? The one that sent me back to Sally's bank robbery?"

She nodded and took something out of her work backpack.

"It's right here." She held it up. "I stopped at the house for it. You had my curiosity up. And Hercule needed cookies."

Of course he did. "Did you check the book at all?"

"I've skimmed it." She set the leather-bound book on her desk. "Nothing stands out about Winchester in the eighteen hundreds. Not yet, anyway."

"No secret clues? No treasure maps?"

"Nothing."

"No decoder wheels or spy messages? Maybe something in the spine of the book?"

Her eyes narrowed. "Nothing, Tuck."

"No disappearing ink—"

"Nothing. Nothing. Nothing."

Geez, okay, why didn't she say so? I let her relax a bit. She was obviously stressed. "Any more documents at the courthouse? How much of those crates did you finish reviewing?"

She didn't answer. Someone else did.

A voice, faint and distant, called out to me—*Tuck? Come to me. Please. Come here. Hurry, Tuck.*

I looked around but found no source of the voice. I also didn't find Angel's university office any longer. Everything was gone. Black. Empty.

Poof. The ethereal transporter swept me away again.

139

Chapter Thirty-Three

Like many of my adventures in dying, I had no idea where I was headed. The voice—faint but familiar—sounded desperate. Very desperate. Sometimes, when I board the ethos-express on my side of the afterlife, I know where I'm going. That is, unless some old leather book sends me as an accomplice to a Civil War bank robbery. This was new. The only living person that has ever been able to summon me on demand was Angel. That was our special connection—our love and life together bonded us.

Not this time.

I landed on the Handley Library's Robinson Auditorium stage.

Across from me was Colonel Smith. He was stabbing the chest of one of his Men-Wearing-Black. "Dammit, then do the scans again. Fast. Where is she?"

"She's with her mother, sir," the man said. "She's not well—sick again."

"Get her. Make sure she understands that it's time to produce. No more bullshit excuses. I want results."

"Yes, sir."

The man headed for the auditorium entrance.

As the man disappeared from the auditorium, two other men entered and climbed onto the stage. Both were dressed in dark jumpsuits and wore strange, electronic-laden backpacks. They began walking back and forth across the stage waving long, wand-like devices. The wands were tethered by wires to their backpacks.

If I didn't know better, I'd expect the Ghostbusters to appear next. The old ones, not the new ones. I like the classics.

"Hey, Smith," I quipped. "Wutch ya doing?"

He ignored me of course.

"Playing ghost hunter?"

Nothing.

Sometimes, it's irritating that so few hear me.

Detective Tucker, come to the Archive Room. Please hurry.

Kerrie's voice was clearer and louder in my thoughts than it had been before. I poofed over to the Archive Room.

Sitting on a chair at a worktable, alone, was Kerrie Garcia.

When I appeared she looked up, straight at me. She smiled a faint smile and waved me to the table beside her.

"Tuck, I'm so glad you came." Her eyes were tired and her voice meek and groggy. "Thank you."

"What's wrong, Kerrie? Are you okay?" That thought struck me. *"How did you call for me?"*

She tried to giggle but didn't seem to have the energy. "I can do all kinds of things, Tuck. You know."

I did? "Like seeing dead people?"

"Yup. Like the movie."

Yeah, the movie. How many times had Angel teased me about that one?

"What's Smith doing with you?"

She stood and slowly walked to the middle of the room and looked out the windows into the Lower Lobby. Then, she turned back to me, closed her eyes, and waved her hand around in a circle, turning as she did like the beginning of a game of tag. As she turned, she got slower and slower, stumbling twice.

"I see things. I can find things." She stopped turning and sat back down. Exhausted. "My mom was having me tested at this scary place. You know, to find out the things I can do. Colonel Smith found us. Mom doesn't have any money, so he pays her for us to live at the Institute. They study me—and others. I don't like it there. They're mean. Really mean. But I'm not important. It's you, Tuck. You have to be careful."

Me? "I'm fine, Kerrie. What do you mean Smith studies you? Is he the one who's mean to you?"

"His name isn't Smith."

No kidding. "What's his real name?"

She shrugged, folded her arms on the table, and laid her head down. "You'll find out."

"Hey, what's wrong? Are you sick?"

"When they make me do too much, I get sick. Very tired." She looked up. "My mom says we have to do it—the things he wants. She says it's our only way to get a new life. My mom did some bad things once. Colonel Smith found out and now he makes us do stuff. He scares me."

I didn't like the sound of that. "He's a bully, Kerrie. Has he hurt you or your mom?"

She looked at the floor.

I knew what that meant. "What does he make you do?"

"It's my gifts. He makes me use them for him. Sometimes, I have to watch him talk to people through funny glass. Then, I tell him when they're lying or what they're thinking. Other times, I have to find things or help him with his UEWs."

"UEWs?"

She eyed me like it was a silly question. "Ultra-energy weapon. You know what that is?"

No, I didn't. But the fact she did embarrassed me. "How old are you, Kerrie?"

"Eleven."

Damn, I wished I'd studied in science class. "What are you doing for him now?"

"I can't tell you." She leaned back in her seat. "If I did and he found out … I'm scared, Tuck. Scared for you."

I knelt down to face her. Her pretty, eleven-year-old face was tear-streaked now, and I could tell she'd been crying before I arrived.

"What is it, Kerrie? Let me help you."

"No, Tuck. You mustn't." Her eyes became frightened and unsure.

"They're looking for something—and for Sally."

"I don't understand. How could he be looking for Sally? What for? How does Smith even know about her?"

"He knows about both of you." She looked down as shame clouded her face. "It's my fault. I told him. I didn't mean to. I had to. He's looking for something really important and has been experimenting in how to find people from the past—you know, *dead people*. He caught me talking to others several months ago. Then, the other day, he caught me talking to Sally. I made a bad mistake."

"Smith knows Sally is a ghost, right?"

"Uh, huh."

"He wants to find her?"

She nodded.

"Using you?"

She nodded again.

"Then what?"

Tears filled her eyes and she wouldn't look at me. "He'll capture her and make her tell us what he wants to know."

Capture her? Was that even possible? What in holy hell could a hundred and eighty-something-year-old dead woman tell him that was so important? I asked Kerrie that.

"Important things, Tuck." Her eyes looked tired and she dropped her head on the table again. "Really important things."

"Like what?" When I reached for her arm, she went rigid. Her arms snapped to her sides and her head went back. She stared at the ceiling. Her eyes were big and round and vacant like she was in a trance. It went on for almost a minute until she finally lowered her head and slumped back in her chair, exhausted.

I touched her arm gently. "Kerrie, are you all right? What just happened?"

For a long time she said nothing. She sat, looking blankly at the table and breathing heavily. Then, she blinked a few times and looked up at me.

"Tuck, your friend is in big trouble."

What? "Who's in trouble?"

She closed her eyes. "You have to find him. They're going to make him talk. They'll hurt him if he doesn't. You have to find him."

"Who, Kerrie?" My mind raced and I looked around hoping for a clue. "Who's in trouble? What did you see?"

"He's in a dark place. He can't see or hear anything. He doesn't know where he is so I can't find him for you. He's scared. You have to find him before it's too late."

"Is it Bear? My partner, Captain Braddock?"

"No. The other one." Her eyes got big and scared. "He's trying to stay calm. He's trying not to be afraid. In his mind, he's playing the saxophone. He keeps playing songs in his head."

Cal Clemens. He was a sax player, and a good one, in a local 40's swing band. His nickname was Calloway Clemens—named after Cab Calloway, the famous blues and jazz musician. Someone had him.

"Detective Clemens, Kerrie?"

She nodded, this time in a slow, deliberate, and sad movement as her eyes filled with tears and she lowered her head onto her arms on the table again. "Yes, Tuck. He's so afraid. You should be, too."

"Who has him, Kerrie?"

She shrugged. "He doesn't know. I'll try to find out. Be careful, Tuck. You're in danger."

"Don't worry about me. Let me get you away from Smith. Then we can find Cal."

"No. You can't help me. Not yet." She shook her head nervously. "You have to stay away unless I call you. If you don't, they'll hurt me and my mom—and you."

Now I was angry. Someone had Cal. Maybe it was White. Maybe it was Smith. Smith already terrorized Angel. But to terrorize little Kerrie and her mom—that was too much. Smith and I were going to have a discussion. A very, very, big discussion.

"I'm going to fix this, Kerrie. I promise."

The door to the Archive Room opened. Emily Lee-Garcia walked in ahead of one of Smith's minions.

"Kerrie, come here. Colonel Smith wants you. You have to concentrate, Kerrie. He's very upset with us."

"Okay, mommy." Kerrie took her mom's hand. "I'll do the best I can. I don't feel good."

"I know, honey, but you have to try."

The man with them held the door and ushered them out.

As the door closed, Kerrie turned and peeked back through the window at me. Her voice—words forming in my thoughts—chilled me.

I left something for you, Tuck. Be careful. Your friends need you. Angela needs you. I do, too. Something bad is going to happen in a few days. Colonel Smith and his men can capture you if they want to. And Tuck ... they can kill you, too—for real.

Chapter Thirty-Four

The huge television screen on the wall lit up with a brilliance that blinded Cal. It flooded the stark, empty concrete room with intense light. On the screen, a cursor began to flash as words etched left to right—the rhythmic sound of typewriter keys stung his ears after so long a silence.

Tap-tap-tap … *Detective Clemens, are you ready to talk?*

How long had he been here? How many times had these people, whoever they were, tried to intimidate and question him? How long…

"Go to hell." Cal tried to break his bonds, but the effort was as useless as the last hundred attempts had been. "I'm a cop. Release me."

Tap-tap-tap … *Simply tell us about Oliver Tucker. About Professor Tucker's research. Tell us about the Morriss letters.*

The light from the huge screen was penetrating and painful in the darkness enveloping him. He squinted and mouthed, "Screw you."

Tap-tap-tap … *Cal, tell us about your friend, Oliver Tucker. Tell us about his return. Tell us, and you may go.*

Liars. The minute he gave them what they wanted to know, he'd be dead. Though he might be anyway. How long since he had water or food? He couldn't go on. Should he tell them? Should he end this madness?

Tap-tap-tap … *You want to tell us. We can see that. Just let go. Detective Tucker is dead. What harm could it do for you to tell us what we want to know?*

Yes, tell them. Make it end. What harm… no.

"Screw you," Cal managed, croaking with difficulty as his mouth would barely form the words. "I'm—"

Tap-tap-tap … *You leave us no choice, Detective Clemens. No choice.*
"Screw you, man. Screw you."
Tap-tap-tap … *No, Detective Clemens, it is you who is screwed.*
The screens flashed black, and the darkness devoured him again.

Chapter Thirty-Five

Kill me? For real? Wasn't I dead enough?

I followed Kerrie, Emily, and the man in black to the elevator and watched the door close behind them. My first instinct was to go with her, but her last words sent me elsewhere—*I left something for you.*

Returning to the Archive Room, I had no idea what I was looking for. It would have been great if Kerrie had been a little more specific. Like "I left the killer's confession on the table," or "Here's a list of Area 51 secrets." No, "I left something for you."

But then, she was only eleven.

I didn't see any photographs of the killer lying around, lists of alien spaceships, or signed confessions. I guess I had to do this the old-fashioned way and actually search the room.

Damn, what I wouldn't give for a team of spirit assistants.

I wandered about, looking over all the tables, chairs, and storage shelves. I spent a good half-hour investigating and came up with nada.

"Come on, Kerrie, give me a hint, will you?"

Nothing.

"Kerrie? A little help—"

Something tickled my brain and turned me around. The light in the room dimmed, and a slight, flickering stream of murky brightness glistened across the room near a table stacked with old files. Sitting on the table amidst some boxes was something small and barely noticeable among the clutter—a green, plastic hair tie.

Fastened to the hair tie was a tiny plastic figure of a little bear.

Kerrie left this for me?

As I touched the hair tie, something very unusual happened. My fingers closed on it, and I picked it up. Maybe that's not odd for you, but for me, it's a big deal. As I've said, I cannot physically move objects. At least, not without major focus and lots of electricity like I'd done for my assault on Smith last night. So, to pick up a bear hair tie—that's huge.

Kerrie's voice reached me again—*Be careful, Tuck. It's not who you think. It never is.*

How was it I could just pick this hair tie up? Was it her? Me? Some new, ethereal connection?

I've learned a long time ago not to take this spirit-world for granted. So, if Kerrie wanted me to have this, I'd oblige. As I examined it a little closer, the lights snapped black.

Poof... Off I went again.

* * *

And... poof, I'm somewhere new.

Kerns was below me, standing in the center of the main floor rotunda near Library Lil. The crosshairs from the targeting scope were centered on his chest. Twice, however, a figure moved slightly left and blocked my shot.

Blocked my shot?

I was aiming at Kerns using the strange, futuristic weapon I'd seen in White's secret lair—the HEAP. With practiced fingers—not mine—I tapped away on the controller sleeve affixed to the weapon's hilt. The device was exactly as I recalled it at White's arms deal—a three-foot-long barrel of light-weight stainless steel. It was affixed to a rectangular receiver with a few switches and buttons on it below the targeting scope. A thin power cord extended from the weapon's lower receiver to a small suitcase with a gauge and meter affixed.

Who was I?

The person—the body—I occupied stood in the second-floor meeting room where I'd found indentations yesterday, readying the weapon to kill

Kerns. Yesterday, I'd possessed Kerns. Now, I possessed his killer. Not possessing him. Not really. I had simply *become* the killer—sharing his body like a freeloading squatter.

I felt the killer perspiring heavily. Three times, he tapped on the command keyboard. Afterward, he stopped and wiped his eyes and brow. The scent of nerves hung in the air with a thick, pungent odor.

We—the killer and I—looked back through the targeting scope and adjusted the crosshairs back to the center of Kerns' chest. The figure that had blocked us—Angel—stood aside him and was momentarily out of the shot.

"Dammit, I need more time," we said to no one. "A few more seconds."

The readings on the bottom of the targeting scope began to settle one after the other. As they did, each indicator above the control buttons turned green.

A wave of nerves passed. The killer readied.

Just as the targeting scope displayed Angel lurch away from Kerns— yesterday, I'd shoved her clear—we pressed the trigger.

The weapon fired.

It was not a bang or a pop or even a rumble. Just a sudden vibration and hum that ended in a loud "slap" like someone's hand slapping a tabletop in excitement.

Kerns went down.

The vibration increased, and its hum grew intense and angry.

As the weapon vibrated on the tripod, I felt a surge of adrenaline rush through us. The vibration intensified rapidly. Confusion swelled in us as we frantically tried to turn the weapon off.

"What the hell?"

Panic.

The killer banged away on the controls, but the weapon continued running away on us. Finally, in a last-ditch effort, we grasped the power cord at the power pack and yanked.

Sparks flashed, and the powerpack began to smoke.

The weapon ceased its vibration and fell silent.

From below us in the rotunda, voices crew louder—desperate voices. Someone screamed.

Angel's voice rose above them.

We—the killer and I—moved swiftly and deftly replaced the HEAP in the wheeled, black plastic case sitting behind us on the table. In a moment, the powerpack was secured beside the weapon. The case was locked and its handle extended like an airport rolling suitcase. We brazenly walked out of the office and around the second-floor rotunda balcony toward the elevator.

The trip was marred by the rolley's sluggish movement. One of its back wheels was bent in and dragged every few turns. With effort, we compensated for the weight above the wheel and continued on.

There were no patrons in the Tween Room or Kids' Place areas. No one in sight.

In less than a minute, we slipped into the elevator and rode to the basement. When the elevator door opened, we casually strolled toward the auditorium.

We only made it to the door.

"Excuse me, sir," a voice called from behind us. "You can't go in the auditorium just now. I've turned the power off for maintenance. There're no lights."

Mr. Downey stood in the open doorway leading to the mechanical room.

"I need to check inside. I left a cord to my recording equipment there," we said, with an edgy whisper in our voice. "Can I—"

"Wait here." Mr. Downey held up a finger with a crooked smile. "If you give me a minute, I can turn it back on and help you look."

"That would be great. Thanks. The professor will be pissed if I lose any more stuff."

The professor? That voice ...

"Yep, I get that." Mr. Downey turned and disappeared back to the mechanical room hall, saying over his shoulder, "Just give me a moment, son."

We followed Mr. Downey into the mechanical room hall, around the corner amidst the clutter of boxes and equipment, until he stopped at an electrical panel with his back to us.

"Won't be a second, son. You're lucky, though. I normally work evenings, but I didn't finish this electrical inspection last night." He glanced over his shoulder and saw us behind him. "You shouldn't be back here. Go on out in the hall. I'll be right there."

Sitting on a folding table in the corner of the room was a small notebook computer. On it were images of the Henkel Boardroom in its center. Then, we noticed the earbuds dangling from Mr. Downey's left ear and one around his shoulder.

On the computer screen, there were people milling around the boardroom.

Mr. Downey closed the notebook, but not before we recognized the inside of the Henkel Boardroom. Mr. Downey was eavesdropping on the meeting.

We struck.

With swift, surprising speed, we moved up behind Mr. Downey, causing him to turn his head back toward us. As he did, our left hand flashed around his neck and grabbed his right-side jaw. Our right hand snapped around his head and grabbed his left shoulder. Before he knew he was about to die, we violently—viciously—yanked in opposite directions and deftly broke his neck.

"Sorry, sir. Really."

That voice …

With the turn of a switch, the room went blank.

Then, as fast as I'd joined him, Andrew Pellman and I parted company.

Chapter Thirty-Six

"Nobody said anything about killing." Bear's delivery was stern and cold. He stood in the center of a large, high-ceilinged den that was walled in fieldstone and hand-hewn timbers. He glared at the omnipotent man sitting casually behind a large mahogany desk once owned by Stonewall Jackson. Neither the antique nor the man sitting there impressed him. "Nobody said anything about tangling with those wannabe goons, either."

"Detective—"

"Captain."

Bradley White allowed a snicker, more condescension than amusement. "Of course, *Captain*. I'm sure in your investigations, you never quite know what you're getting into. Is that right?"

Bear folded his arms. "This isn't an investigation."

"Ah, but it is. You're investigating Professor Tucker's work. You're investigating the procurement of the necessary accoutrements needed for our endeavor. You're helping secure the large capital needed to search for this long-lost wealth."

"Accoutrements? Are you kidding?"

White grinned again. "It means—"

"Screw you. I know what it means." Bear decided not to wait any longer for an invitation and dropped into a large leather chair opposite White. "A high-energy laser weapon is hardly an accoutrement. You're selling stolen government research. Let's just call it what it is—*treason*."

"Not I. I am simply the middleman." White stared at the chair as though

Bear had the audacity to seat himself without approval. "Treason is such a harsh word. Let's not use it again."

"Whatever. Why am I here?"

"You are here because I require it. That is the arrangement I have with our mutual associate."

Bear forced a laugh. "Wordplay. Call Nic what he is—my slaver. He sold me to you for a few markers."

"Now, who wordplays? Quite a sizable sum of gambling markers as I see it."

Bear shrugged. "I made mistakes."

"Yes, you did. Still, you seem to have found your place in our organization. I've spent considerable time investing in you, Detect … Captain. Considerable time investigating you, too. I believe you are ready to know a few things about our enterprise."

"Whatever." Bear looked out the large windows that consumed the entire west wall of the den. "I just want to earn my markers back and move on. I gotta find another job. If you didn't hear, I lost mine today."

White raised a finger. "How gratuitous. You are in need of employment and to recover your freedom from severe vice. We, well, we are in need of someone with your skills and connections. Perhaps even someone of your beliefs. It is my mission in life to right past wrongs and rekindle my family heritage. It is not about money, Captain, it is about heritage."

Bear watched him for a long time. White was an odd bird even for an old, crusty, filthy-rich southern gentleman accustomed to being king of the hill. But there was something behind the curtain that he wanted Bear to see. He was playing a teasing game, taunting him with tidbits, waiting to see how long he would last without demanding a look.

The thing that bothered him the most about White was that White was, as he said, just a middleman. He wanted to work for the top man—Smith.

"Look, White, I didn't sign up to play butler or bodyguard or be part of your 'the South shall rise again' crap. I'm here because Bartalotta sold me to you—without asking, I might add. I've already done a lot to help you find out about Angela Tucker's research. I figure I got about half of my debt clear already. So, what's it going to take to clear the rest?"

"Ah, but my dear captain. You did not find the most valuable of Professor Tucker's research last night. Did you?"

"No. But not for lack of trying."

White slowly rose. He wandered to the windows and gazed out at the mountains. He stood thinking for a long time. When he spoke, he never turned around.

"What is your relationship with Detective Clemens?"

Bear turned to watch him. "He works for me."

"I asked about relationship, not employment."

Bear thought carefully. "We're friendly. Not friends. I don't have the power to fire him if that's where you're headed. What happened at the library isn't on the table. I took care of it."

"That is irrelevant. I'm talking about him—the man."

"I'm indifferent. Why?"

White sighed. "I'll take indifference."

"What are you getting at?"

White still didn't turn. "We have a potential role for you in our organization. It's a particularly special organization, too. Membership is rather unique—and costly."

Bear stood. "Look, White, if you're trying to recruit me into some gang of hood-wearing whackos who stomp their feet and bluster about politics and race, I'm not interested."

White turned as Bear headed for the door. "I can accept mercenaryism, too. It's the purest form of combat. Yes, you'll do, Theodore. With one more assignment, your marker is paid. After that, you'll be compensated at a rate of two hundred thousand per annum. Once, that is, you have been accepted as a member."

"Two hundred a year?" Bear stopped and turned around. "I'm no hitman."

"Good." White raised his chin, sighed, and returned to his desk. "First, I have a loose end I need cared for. I'm not looking for a hitman, Theodore. That is more Nicholas Bartalotta—not me. I'm looking for a doer. A man who will act on my authority and trust me to handle any potential consequences. Removing a threat to our organization is not murder. It is not being a hitman. It's risk management."

"Risk management?" Bear's face hardened. "Killing is killing. But I get it. I don't seem to have much choice, or you'd probably risk manage me."

White said nothing and sat behind his desk.

"Tell me about your organization. If I'm to join—"

"In time, Theodore. In time."

"What do I have to do?"

"There are tests to pass, Theodore. I must finish my assessment of you. You will be assigned a mission You will be graded on that mission."

"Jesus, more skullduggery? It sounds like a bad movie plot. You're selling stolen secret hardware. It's that simple. All this other nonsense is ridiculous."

White slammed his fist on the desk. "Nonsense, Theodore? What I am searching for is my family's legacy. It is my right to solve the riddle that has escaped men for over a hundred and sixty years. Yet, others are searching as well. I must beat him to it. He has built an army and entire team to find the treasure. My small percentage of sales will barely finance me. However, it will restore my family's honor and protect me from all others."

"A riddle? A race?" All others? What did that mean? "I can't wait to win your heart and mind and find out exactly what this silly shit is about."

White took a deep breath and settled. Then, from the top desk drawer of his desk, he produced a photo and handed it across the desk to Bear.

"Do you recognize this young man?"

Bear didn't have to look twice. "Yeah, that's Angela Tucker's assistant."

"He is your assignment."

Chapter Thirty-Seven

Oliver, come back. Do you hear me? Come back, Oliver—now.

Never had I been so happy to hear Doc Gilley's voice.

I was in my timeout place—despair and nothingness surrounded me. It held me. Keeping me from everything and everyone. It was a place I didn't understand. Just a void that imprisoned me whenever I overextended my energy or somehow got myself into ethereal trouble. My fault or not, my actions had consequences. I never quite knew when I'd end up in the void, but apparently possessing young Andrew Pellman as he killed Kerns and Downey had bought me a first-class ticket there.

Doc's voice broke through the desolation and retrieved me. He woke me, demanding and arrogant as he is, and pulled me home. When I returned, I lay on my back on my den floor.

"Oliver? Are you all right?" He stood over me with a scolding finger, stabbing at me. "Can you understand me?"

The fog dissipated, and slowly my thoughts settled.

"Oliver? Say something."

"What's up, Doc?" *I'd waited years to say that.*

"How ridiculous." His hands snapped to his hips, and he glared fire and brimstone down on me. "Get up. You're embarrassing yourself—*again.*"

Slowly, with considerable effort, I managed to stand—wobbly and uncertain—and make my way to my desk, where I leaned against it for support.

"You did it again, didn't you, dumbass?"

Dumbass? "Look, Doc, I just solved Kerns and Downey's murder. I wouldn't call that being a dumbass."

"Oh, you have?" Doc stepped back and folded his arms. "Your conclusions?"

This was going to be good. "Andrew Pellman killed Kerns with the ray gun in the rotunda. He killed Downey with some Kung Fu stuff in the mechanical room."

Doc eyed me for a long time. He turned and paced back and forth to the bookshelves and back. Twice. When he stopped, he lifted his chin. "You're certain?"

"Yes, I am sure."

"And you came by this deduction how?"

I told him about Kerrie's hairpin and my journey back to the scene of the crime at the Handley Library. After explaining about the ray gun and Pellman's attack on Downey, I slipped into my desk chair to bask in the glory.

Doc couldn't bring himself to congratulate me. Instead, he said, "It's been nearly two days since you disappeared. Angela is waiting in the kitchen. I suggest you attend to her. She is not pleased with you."

Two days? Uh, oh. Taking his cue, I popped into the kitchen to the aroma of breakfast cooking.

"Good morning, Angel," I said in my very best 'don't be mad at me' voice. "Sorry, I've been gone. I've been solving the Kerns and Downey murders."

She stood over the coffee maker waiting for a fresh cup to finish.

"Angel?"

Nothing. Ouch.

"Boy, that coffee smells good," I said to her as she sat down across the kitchen table and began to eat. "I miss coffee—and eggs. I miss eggs, too. Oh, and steak. Mostly steak. Yeah, I miss steak and eggs and coffee."

She never looked up, set her fork onto her plate alongside her scrambled eggs, and took a long mouthful of coffee. Then, she smiled a very satisfying smile and took a large mouthful of eggs, rolling her eyes in delight.

"You're doing that on purpose, Angel."

"Oh, you're home. How wonderful for us."

Ah, crap.

She sipped her coffee again. "Sorry, I love breakfast. You, on the other hand, do not get or need breakfast. Nor do you need sexy, young, blue-eyed blonds to haunt you every time we have a new case. Is that where you've been, canoodling with your grandma?"

That was just wrong.

"Angel, first of all, Sally Mosby is not a sexy, young, blue-eyed blond haunting me. Sure, she's sexy. And young. She maybe has blue eyes, but she's my great-many times over grandmother. Geez, have some couth."

"Why aren't you ever haunted by ugly spirits?"

"Lucky, I guess."

"Wrong answer." She took a big bite of her bagel smothered in cream cheese, did the "ohhh, ahhh, oohhh—sooooo, gooood" lip-sync with her mouth between bites, and raised her coffee cup to toast me. "You didn't know she was your great-grandmother when you ogled her."

"I didn't ogle her."

"You did. I hope it made you ill when you found out who she was."

It truly did.

"You think you solved the murders?"

"Yep, I was there," I told her about my possession of Andrew Pellman on his murder spree. "Now, I just have to find a way to prove it."

Her face showed a mixture of sadness and shock. "Andrew killed them? No, he's such as—"

"Kung Fu master and murderer."

"Hapkido, Tuck. Not Kung Fu."

"Same thing."

She began shaking her head. "No, Tuck. You have to be wrong. Not Andrew."

I wasn't wrong, and I told her that. Adding, "You can't argue with the facts, Angel. You never thought Bear would go bad, either. Face it, Andrew is a stone-cold killer. We just have to prove it."

She played with her coffee cup and tried to digest what I had told her. "If Andrew's the killer, he may kill again. We have to find that ray gun—the

HEAP you called it?"

"One of them is in Bradley White's wine cellar." I thought for a moment. "The crates of stolen ray guns were marked with a logo—ADRI. Find what that is, and we might find more answers. We also might find the connection between White and Pellman and that HEAP."

She left the kitchen and returned with her notebook computer. In a second, she was banging away on its keyboard. It took her only a moment longer to find what she was looking for.

"ADRI—The Advanced Defense Research Institute. It's located in Crystal City." Angel scrolled through the "About US" section of the website. "It says here they do scientific research and development for the Department of Defense, including weapons systems, communications, artificial intelligence, national security initiatives—"

"Yadda, yadda, yadda." I rolled my eyes. "Sounds all X-Files."

"You're not far off. I think we should go see them." Angel continued reading the screen. "Maybe we can get an interview with someone in charge. I bet Colonel Smith is there."

I thought about that. "That's the connection. White sells ADRI secrets stolen by Smith. Ray gun stolen from ADRI. Ray gun kills Kerns and Downey. Smith takes over the crime scene to cover it all up. It all maps out."

She agreed and tapped away on the ADRI website. "That means Bear is involved in a national security conspiracy?"

Yikes. Never thought of that. "Angel, we should go back to Pellman's house and see if we can find any link to those guys. He killed Kerns and Downey. But I don't see the link to Smith or ADRI."

There was a knock on our front door that startled both of us.

Hercule bayed a long, throaty howl and sprang to the foyer, front paws up on the door, snarling through the glass at whoever was on our porch.

"Easy, Hercule." Angel eased him off the door. "It's Mike Spence."

As the door opened, Spence stood there with a taut, sullen face. He looked totally defeated. "Angela, sorry to just stop by without calling."

"It's all right, Mike. Come on in for coffee."

He had a plastic shopping bag in his hand. "Sorry, I can't. I thought I should tell you this in person."

"Spit it out, Spence," I cawed. "We're solving a national security conspiracy."

Angel ignored me. "What's wrong, Mike?"

"First, there's this." He handed Angel the shopping bag. "I, ah, went to Bear's place looking for him. He wasn't home, so I, er, got in. I found this hidden in the drop ceiling above his bathroom."

"You just happened to be in the bathroom searching the ceiling?" I asked. It sounded like something I'd do. "Good work, Spence. You might make a detective yet."

She opened the plastic bag and found a thick, brown folder like an accountant might have stuffed with newly printed papers. "What's all this?"

"Your missing files, I think. But, Angela, there's more." Spence's face twisted into a scowl. "They found Andrew Pellman this morning—dead." Spence's lips tightened. Then, he lifted his cell phone with an image on the screen. Pellman lay face up on a medical table. His face was death-gray, and his eyes closed, bruised and swollen. A small, round bullet hole christened the top of his forehead. "This photo just came in from the local FBI Task Force. One of their informants found him early this morning down Route 81. Sheriff Millbert confirmed it. He's dead. Someone beat the shit out of him and shot him—execution style."

Angel's hand flew to her mouth. "Oh, no. Poor Andrew."

"Poor Andrew?" I said. "He murdered Kerns and Mr. Downey. Good riddance to him."

"I know he did bad things." Angel's eyes teared. "Who did this? What's next?"

"Yeah, well, a lot." Spence waited for her to wipe her eyes. "Angela, I went to Pellman's house to follow up on his place being trashed. The house was totally empty—scrubbed. All Andrew's belongings were gone. The carpets were torn up and everything on the walls removed."

"Everything?" she asked. "Most of it was broken and scattered around?"

He shrugged. "I guess they wanted to be sure no one could find any evidence they missed the first time. The entire place smelled like bleach."

"Bleach?" Angel's face scrunched up. "Why bleach?"

"To destroy evidence—fibers, body fluids, and prints. Someone cleaned up well."

She walked to the stairs and sat facing him across the foyer. All she could do was shake her head.

"Angela, the FBI is taking over the murder cases—Kerns, Downey, and Pellman. They say Pellman killed Downey and Kerns. Now they want Pellman's killer. They've grabbed the case from us. I'm out."

"But Colonel Smith took all the evidence already, right? What about him?"

"Millbert is dealing with that. There's a big pissing contest over it—Department of Justice vs. Department of Defense."

She asked, "What now, Mike?"

"Don't know that either." He shrugged and rubbed his chin. "I'm heading into the office to meet with the Sheriff. Cal's still missing. So's Bear. The FBI wants to talk to him big time. Bear's a suspect in Pellman's murder, Angela. Their *only* suspect."

"A murderer?" Angel's face contorted. "As I said before, that can't be true."

Spence shrugged. "It's what they're saying. I need to find Cal and him. I'll try to prove the FBI wrong—if I can."

I said, "Hey, while he's digging around, have him check into ADRI and find out if Smith is connected there."

She gave him a summary of what we'd learned about the shadowy think tank. When he asked her why she was interested in them, she grinned. "Do you really want me to answer that, Mike?"

"Ah, well…" He glanced around the foyer. "No. I'll just assume you got an anonymous tip. I'll add them to my list right behind finding Cal and Bear."

"Find them, Mike," she said. "Please. Find them."

Without another word, he stood and left the house.

As he drove away, Hercule barked loudly behind us. Not just one bark, but several that shook the front door windows.

"What's up, boy?" I peered back out the still-open door. "Speak of the devil, Angel. You have a visitor."

Chapter Thirty-Eight

Poor Nic walked up and stopped on our front porch with his hands clasped in front of him. He wore casual slacks and a golf shirt with a light windbreaker zipped up nearly to his chin. A Washington Nationals ballcap was perched on his head. Old people, even retired mass murderers turned local philanthropists and library patrons, get cold in the summer.

Angel stood in the doorway, smiling. She always smiled when she greeted Poor Nic. Yeah, good ole Poor Nic was her knight in shining armor too often for me to let a little thing like his fifty years of organized crime and banditry bother me. No, sir, Poor Nic was a new, improved gangster. A real lovable fella.

Oh, and he had a mad crush on her, too. Maybe that crush could shed some light on his newly discovered interest in libraries, the Apple Harvest Research, and Civil War bank robberies.

Maybe.

"Nicholas, what are you doing here?" she asked lightly. "Did I miss your call?"

He blushed. "No, my dear. I'm afraid I failed to call. Forgive me. In my defense, we were headed into Old Town, and I thought a brief visit was prudent."

Prudent? "Hi-ya, Nic. Good to see you. Kill anyone today? How about yesterday?"

"Enough," Angel snapped before she could stop herself. "I mean, enough, Nicholas, no harm done. Come in. I'll make some tea."

"Splendid." He touched Angel's arm. "The answer is no."

"No?" she asked. "No to what?"

He grinned wryly. "Those silly questions."

Silly questions? Mine?

Since my untimely murder, Poor Nic had not simply become Angel's godfather—no offense, Mr. Brando—he'd also learned to dial in on me from time to time. Maybe it was his age and nearing death himself that opened some kind of connection between us. But now and then, I got the impression he knew I was around—even heard me. Oddly enough, it didn't bother him.

Angel led him into the kitchen and fixed him a cup of tea—Earl Grey was his favorite. Then, she made another cup of coffee for herself in that damnable machine. The gadget took forever to brew a single cup and reminded me of a still.

She sat across from him at the dinette table. "What brings you by, Nicholas?"

He sipped his tea and glanced casually around like he was admiring the new wallpaper and toaster. We had neither.

"Come on, Nic," I quipped. "Out with it. We have bad guys to find. Not you, of course, we always know where you are—right in the middle of things."

Nic did a peculiar thing. He grinned as his eyes darted around the room and then chuckled to himself. "Angela, I have come to advise you."

"Your advice is always welcome. On what?"

"Bad things."

Bad things? I slipped into the chair beside him. "He's being intentionally dodgy, Angel."

"What bad things, Nicholas? I hate to push, but I must leave shortly."

His eyebrows rose. "To where?"

"To find Cal Clemens and Bear," she said, and drew another raise of his eyebrows. "They're missing."

I said, "Don't mention ADRI. You'd have to explain how you know about them."

"I see. Another private investigation, Angela?" Poor Nic sipped his tea and hovered the cup chin high. He watched her over the rim and let his grandfatherly eyes draw her in. A vampire move if ever I saw one. "ADRI is a highly classified facility. You could get into trouble. I would stay clear of those people."

ADRI? Wow.

"Nicholas," she said, "what makes you think I would go there? And how do you know about them?"

He laughed out loud and set his teacup back on the table. "Please, Angela. You are the most intelligent woman I know. No, the most intelligent *person* I know. You discovered clues concerning ADRI. No? Dangerous clues. You are planning on chasing those clues. Correct?"

Holy crystal ball, Batman.

"How do you know all that, Nicholas?" she asked.

"Ah, my sources. They tell me of the danger you are in. So, I beg you, let the authorities handle this matter."

She set her coffee down. "Since when do you want the authorities handling anything, Nicholas? What's your involvement?"

He steepled his hands in front of his teacup. He watched her through soft, old eyes. His eyebrows twitched a little, and I knew he was trying to formulate an answer that would hold up in court.

"ADRI is not a simple defense contractor, my dear. The mysterious DOD men who arrived at the library two nights ago are ADRI operatives. None of this is normal. It is by its very nature bizarre and dangerous. An unknown assailant killing a federal agent with a death ray?"

"See, Angel," I said, "even Nic knew it was a death ray."

She ignored me, of course. "I recognize how unusual this is, Nicholas. I can take care of myself. Now, is there anything else?"

"One thing." Poor Nic watched her for another long moment. "Captain Braddock. I know how fond of him you are."

She sat back.

"I wish you to stay clear of him. Stay away and leave him be. He has issues to deal with, and if you try to involve yourself, it could be catastrophic. I know men who have lost their way. It's dangerous to be near him."

Lost their way? Bear had huge gambling debts. He's a traitor if he's thrown in with White. Lost his way was a softball. "Angel, ask him about—"

"He's in serious debt, Nicholas—gambling debts. The authorities believe he's involved with Andrew Pellman's disappearance."

"Young Andrew? Oh, my." Poor Nic sat in silence for a long time. "I am sorry to hear that. I have done what I can for Captain Braddock. It is time we all stayed away."

Wait, what? "What have you done for him, Nic?"

She asked him that question.

"Angela, please." He waved in the air like a magician. "When I learned Captain Braddock had gotten into deep financial trouble, I bought his markers—his gambling debts, you see. I wished to save him from others less tolerant than me."

Being less tolerant than Poor Nic in his prime meant they would kill you *before* they put you in a meat grinder.

"What I mean to say, Angela—"

"I understand, Nicholas. What does he have to do to repay you? How much? Is that why you were at the library? Is that—"

"No." His hand flashed up. "The two are not related, my dear. My arrangements with Captain Braddock are a totally separate matter. I assure you."

"Oh, I feel so much better." I didn't, but it sounded good.

Poor Nic's hand flashed up. "Please, a little understanding here."

I'll be damned. He could hear me. I tested the waters a little deeper. "What were you doing at Pellman's the night of Kerns' murder? Did you go back with a big bucket of bleach afterward?"

For a moment, I thought I was wrong about him. Maybe his reactions to my comments were just coincidental. Then he pushed the "holy shit meter" into the red zone.

"Angela, I assure you. My presence at Andrew Pellman's residence was innocent. I was simply following you. After the events at the library, I did what I have for years. I acted to ensure your safety. Nothing more. Nothing less."

Angel leaned back. "Thank you, Nicholas. But I can take care of myself. I've been working with Detective Spence, anyway."

Kaboom—Poor Nic pushed the plunger again. "Further, I have never used bleach in my profession. In my day, we simply would have burned the house to the ground."

"Oh, Nic, I feel all warm and snuggly inside," I snickered. "Arson is so much more fashionable than bleach."

He actually smiled.

Angel wasn't done. "Tell me about Bear and Mr. White."

"White? I do not know what you mean." He stood, looking a bit flustered. "No matter, let it go."

"I can't, Nicholas." Angel stood, too. "I know you understand."

"Yes, my dear. I do." He turned and walked from the kitchen and down the hall to the foyer with Angel and I close behind. At the front door, he turned. "Angela, ADRI is what movies are made of. They are dark and dangerous. Stay clear of them—and of Captain Braddock, too. He is a very capable man. A very dangerous man. I will be watching. I take my pledge to protect you very seriously."

At least he didn't tell Angel she owed him a favor in the future.

"Nicholas, if you know anything more about Bear—"

"I do not." And with that, Poor Nicholas Bartalotta walked off.

Chapter Thirty-Nine

"How odd," Angel said, watching Poor Nic drive off. "He's never been quite that, well—"

"Secretive? Irritating?" I ran out of verbs, or adjectives, whatever. "He was on his 'I've got a secret' game, wasn't he?"

"Wait." She turned to the table beside the front door and grabbed the plastic bag Spence had delivered to her. She carried it into my den, emptied the contents onto my desk, and sat down reviewing her stash.

"Care to share?" I asked.

She lifted a thick, brown accountant's folder from the bag. "These are copies of Civil War documents. I found the originals in the Apple Harvest research the other day. I only skimmed it when I found them. Now, I think they're more valuable than I first thought."

"That's what Bear had at his house? Copies?"

"I guess." She placed the papers on the desk. "He must have taken the originals from my office and copied them."

"I wonder who has the originals?"

Her face fell. "White, maybe? One of those people in the boardroom meeting?"

"That's my guess."

She nodded, lifted a few pages, and began reading.

I sat in the leather recliner near the bookshelf and watched her. Hercule joined me. We were there for nearly two hours. If I were alive, we'd have had lunch and a snack in that time. Maybe two snacks. Anyway, it was a long time.

Just when I was getting really bored, and Hercule trotted off to find another place to take a nap, Angel sat back in the office chair. She tapped the sheaf of documents and folded her hands in triumph.

"Tuck, I found something interesting."

I sure hope so. "I'm listening."

She leaned forward. "Remember, we discussed Robert Morriss in my office? He had something to do with this urban legend treasure hunt?"

"I remember," I said. "Kerrie Garcia was trying to do something with old coins or treasure. Sally asked me about treasure, too. We talked about White, Poor Nic, and Bear maybe being on a treasure hunt. You said the treasure's silly?"

"I did. I'm not so sure now." She sorted through some papers and spread several out in front of her. "It has to do with an adventurer named Thomas Beale, originally from Virginia. Back in the early 1800s—1817, according to these papers, he and some fellow adventurers allegedly mined millions of dollars of gold, silver, and various jewels somewhere in what's now New Mexico or Colorado. Beale returned to Virginia and hid his treasure so no one could steal it until it was time to divvy it up with his partners. Then, he put the clues in an old strongbox and entrusted it to a friend, Robert Morriss, a Lynchburg, Virginia, Innkeeper. There were three coded letters leading to the location of this treasure. Then, Beale left, possibly to return for more treasure. He disappeared and never returned."

Holy Treasure Island. "So, it's real? I mean, those research papers look genuine?"

Angel read over another page to herself before looking up. "Well, these are copies, but the story seems genuine. After years sitting in that strongbox, untouched, Morriss finally opened it. Inside, he found documents that described Beale's adventure and three documents of numbers and secret codes. He tried but couldn't decipher them."

"So, no one knows it's not a hoax?" My head hurt with all this research stuff.

Angel went on paraphrasing from the documents.

Apparently, nearing his death, Morris gave the strongbox and codes to someone else. No one knows who. One of the codes was allegedly deciphered and revealed a huge, detailed accounting of the treasure. In 1885, another friend of Morriss', James Ward, published a pamphlet written by an unidentified, mysterious friend of Morriss' discussing the Beale Treasure. This publication began a huge controversy that's lasted until present day.

"People took this seriously? I mean, come on, I might believe in stuff like that, but seriously?"

"Yes, Tuck, very seriously. In recent years, even the National Security Administration's supercomputers were used to try and break the Beale codes. They couldn't. Although someone, and I can't tell from the notes here, broke one of them using the Declaration of Independence as a cypher key. That's a fact."

Did someone say National Treasure? "Angel, they made that movie out of this? Do you think it's real? Is that why Kerns and Downey were murdered? Over this hidden treasure?"

She stood and turned back to the bay window, staring out for a long time.

Finally, she said, "Tuck, no one has ever found the treasure. It's believed to be hidden in a secret vault somewhere in Bedford County, Virginia. Nicholas wanted to buy or copy anything I found about that era; in particular, bank and train robberies—"

"Bank and train robberies?" Was Sally on a treasure hunt in 1864? "Angel, do you think Sally—"

A breeze drifted through the room scented with jasmine.

"Why, Oliver, I thought you'd never ask." Sally stood in the den doorway. She was dressed in the same riding clothes I'd seen her in at the barn when she rode off to rob a bank. "I think it is time for me to take you on a little adventure."

"Another one?"

Angel stared at me. "Tuck? What's wrong?"

"Ah, Angel," I said as the room started to fade. "I'll be back soon. Sally wants me to..."

Nope. Too late. The room snapped black, and Sally Elizabeth Mosby disappeared into the nothingness.

So did I.

Poof... off again.

Chapter Forty

And... poof. I was no longer in my den.

When I landed back on terra firma, I was lost. Totally lost. Rugged terrain and dense woods flanked me on three sides. Ahead, the vast countryside played out for miles in a plush, green panoramic valley that took my breath away. I stood on a rocky outcrop that overlooked mountains and valleys beyond.

Familiar voices turned me around.

Adjacent to the overlook, a hundred yards away, were six people. Two were mounted on horseback. One sat in an uncovered wagon holding the reins of two powerful Morgan horses. Three other horses were tied to the opposite side of the wagon. The other three men—excuse me, persons— were gathered precariously close to the overlook's edge.

Other than 1864-Sally, I recognized three of the group—Jenkins, Hall, and Wilks. They were the men from the barn before the big bank robbery caper. The other two were strangers to me.

Jenkins and Hall were now working alongside Sally near the edge of the overlook. Jenkins was the husky, shorter of the crew. He took measurements with a surveyor's theodolite mounted on a tripod aimed out into the vast countryside below. Hall, the tall, thin man with the bony nose and bushy beard, aimed a telescope over the valley and scanned some wonder I couldn't guess at. While they spoke among themselves, Sally jotted notes in a leather-bound journal and read back figures to them, occasionally glancing up and out from the overlook.

They were meticulously surveying this mountain range.

Wilks sat aboard the wagon, leisurely smoking a pipe. He grumbled with the other two men, whom I didn't recognize. He was focused on Sally. Occasionally, he shot the other men looks that sent chills through me like icicles stabbing my brain.

"So glad you joined me, Oliver," Spirit-Sally said from nowhere. "You should find this very fascinating."

In an eye-blink, Spirit-Sally appeared beside me. She was distinctly different from the 1864-Sally taking notes at the cliff's edge. Different in an odd way. Spirit-Sally was just that— a spirit with me. 1864-Sally was a vision from 1864 or thereabouts. Weird, I know.

"I'm not sure I had a choice," I said. "I never do."

"Pay attention, Oliver. What we did here was very important." She led me to the overlook.

Jenkins read off a series of numbers to 1864-Sally. Hall followed along with a compass and aimed his telescope out over the mountain view.

Jenkins spoke. "Sally, before we go trompin' down these mountains any further, how 'bout you check those fancy papers you got? I don't want to get us lost if you got somethin' wrong."

1864-Sally closed her journal and tucked it into the pocket of the long farm coat she wore. "I don't have anything wrong, I assure you."

"Good fir you. Check anyways." Jenkins aimed a finger at her. "Won't cost you nuthin' but a few boot steps. Get to it, girl."

1864-Sally walked to the rear of the wagon and pulled open a large haversack. She rummaged around inside and withdrew a heavy leather satchel. Inside, she took a sheaf of papers, unfolded them, and laid them out on the rear of the wagon.

One of the two men on horseback dismounted and tied his horse to the wagon. Then, he walked over to look at what she was doing.

"These them papers from the bank, Sally?" he asked, bending down to examine them more closely. "Looks just like a bunch of numbers and letters and such. I don't read much, but I know they ain't no real words or nuthin'."

1864-Sally quickly replaced all the papers but one into the satchel. "You let me worry about that, Johnny Townsend. You worry about you."

"You a sassy one, Sally." Johnny laughed and waved at the other man. "Ain't she, Billy?"

"Sure is, Johnny. Girl's got sass." Billy, a gruff, unshaven younger man, whipped back his long, straggly hair from his eyes. "I like sassy girls, Sally."

"Sally Elizabeth *Mosby*," she corrected, slipping her left hand into her pocket. "You all don't forget my last name, either. It demands respect here in Virginia."

Johnny roared again and bowed. "Yessum. Sure, don't want to disrespect you, Sally. Mr. Wilks says you're one tough girl."

Wilks turned from the wagon seat and climbed down. "She's a tough one, fir sure, Johnny. You watch yourself."

I turned to Spirit-Sally beside me. "I don't like this, Sally. What's going on?"

"Shush, Oliver." She held a finger to her lips. "You'll learn more stayin' quiet."

That sounded like something Doc would say. Then again, Doc was usually right, too.

"Well, girl? Tell me them measurements again," Jenkins called, looking up from his theodolite. "Quick now. We might have time to reach the spot before nightfall."

1864-Sally read several numbers in sequence from the paper she'd taken from the satchel, keeping an eye on Johnny Townsend as she did. "Same numbers I gave you before. It's there. It has to be."

Jenkins and Hall huddled and rechecked their theodolite and telescope views.

Hall looked back at Johnny Townsend. "Yep, she's right. Same figures, boys. Looks like we're headed down the mountain to get rich."

Jenkins waved at Wilks. "Make the mark, Wilks. Fast and we'll git goin'."

The mark was simple, just four characters that Wilks chiseled into a large, flat rock near the overlook.

M35W.

"Sally," I said, staring at the chiseled marks. "Those marks—"

"Shush, Oliver." Spirit-Sally held a finger to her lips again. "It ain't over yet." She took my hand, and that familiar, angelic warmth instantly spread through me.

When she squeezed my hand, the lights flashed off.

And... poof... off we went.

Chapter Forty-One

Poof... landed again.

"We're here, Oliver."

We were no longer on the overlook high on the mountainside. We were lower in a small valley surrounded by forest. We stood near a wide, slow-running creek. The light had faded, and long, dark shadows covered the ground.

"Where are we?"

She gestured behind me, and I turned. A single-story, dilapidated cabin sat in a small clearing and was built into the mountainside. It was half-buried by a large field of fallen rock on one side and hidden by overgrown brush and scrub trees on the other. The five men were scattered in front of the cabin. The wagon was busted up with a broken rear wheel and sat behind the group. Wilks was looking it over as Hall examined the broken wheel.

Hall took a lantern from the rear of the wagon. "I kin fix it. Take some time. Comin' down that last slope did us bad. I told y'all this wagon wouldn't make it. Might not git us back."

"Fix it, Hall," Wilks said. "I'll take a quick look so we know if Sally is worth her wages." He went to the cabin, lit the lantern, and looked through the window beside that door that had long ago lost any glass or framing. Seemingly satisfied, he kicked in the fragile old door and disappeared inside.

"What now, Sally?" I asked. "Where are we? What are we doing here?"

"We're on the south edge of Bedford County, Oliver. Just watch."

Of course. Don't answer a straight question with a straight answer. *Just watch*. Clearly, she was my ancestor.

1864-Sally stayed mounted and moved her horse to the stream for water. Jenkins, Billy, and Johnny Townsend dismounted and tied their horses to the wagon. Johnny Townsend began pacing around the front of the cabin, occasionally peering inside and shaking his head when he looked back to the others.

"Wilks is gone, boys," Johnny Townsend said. "This here cabin done swallowed him up. Can't see him inside none."

1864-Sally reigned her horse around but kept her distance from the men. "Maybe he's found the entrance already. Give him some time, Johnny. You're too impatient."

"Impatient? Well, there's a powerful amount of money—"

"He's back," Billy called.

Wilks emerged from the cabin covered in dirt. "I found it, ya'll. I found the entrance. It's back in the cabin, hidden behind the wall there. I pulled some boards free, and there it was. Just barely there. Part of the mountain dun slipped down into it, but it's passable. I pushed through. It was there—the entrance Sally's papers dun said."

Jenkins ran to the cabin's front door and peered in. "Get the other lanterns. We best get seein' what's in there."

"Hold on now." 1864-Sally prodded her horse a few steps forward. "It's nearly dark. We need to tend to the horses. The wagon needs fixing after getting banged up coming down here. We need to rest and eat. We can start in the morning. It'll be safer after we sleep some."

Hall agreed, but Jenkins wasn't having it. "No, sirree. We need to go see. Now, girl."

"That tunnel's been there for decades, Jenkins." 1864-Sally stopped her horse a few feet away from the men. "It'll be there in the morning."

"No." Johnny Townsend handed his lantern to Wilks, strode from the front of the cabin, and grabbed 1864-Sally's reins. He yanked the horse around sideways and grabbed her by the arm. With a grunt, he yanked her off the horse and shoved her onto her back on the ground. "Girl, you don't have no more votes here. You got us to the spot. You and those damnable funny codes. We don't need you no more."

I tried to jump forward, but Sally grabbed my arm. "Sally, we should help her—help you. Don't—"

"No, Tuck," Spirit-Sally said. "It already happened. You can't change things. It'll happen again no matter what."

It did.

Johnny Townsend descended on 1864-Sally. He grasped her arm and jerked her to her feet. Billy dismounted and joined him. He grabbed her other arm. They held her tightly between them.

Hall called from the wagon, "You boys stop that. Anything we find inside belongs to The Cause. It ain't for us. You know that. Let her go."

"Yessir, stop that." Jenkins moved toward Johnny Townsend. "She's one of us, Johnny."

"Maybe, but I ain't," Johnny snapped. He released 1864-Sally, drew a long-barreled Army Colt from his belt, and shot Jenkins before he took another step. Then, he turned the revolver toward Hall and shot him. "I don't need no damn war. With what's in this here mountain, I can buy my own country out west. Right, boys?"

Billy's face blossomed with surprise. "Whoa, now."

"Yessir, Johnny," Wilks growled from the cabin door. "Git rid of her. No witnesses."

Billy tugged on 1864-Sally's arm. "Aw, not yet, Wilks. It'll be a cozy night with her. What you say now? Like she said, ain't nothing can't wait until morning. She sure is a sassy, pretty thing."

I turned to Spirit-Sally. "Don't let them do this, Sally. Not to you. Don't—"

A gunshot startled me, and I spun around. That shot startled Johnny Townsend, too. The second and third shots surprised Wilks almost as much.

Johnny Townsend lay at 1864-Sally's feet. Wilks lay in the cabin doorway. Johnny had a gunshot to his head—a large, forty-four caliber gunshot that made him unrecognizable. Wilks hadn't been killed, and he lifted his pistol to shoot her when she fired again.

1864-Sally held her 44-caliber Colt pistol and aimed it at Billy. He was stunned and staring at the bodies on the ground.

"Think hard, Billy." She calmly cocked her pistol." You don't know where you are in these woods. Do you?"

"No, Miss Sally." Billy's eyes were big and round, and couldn't break the spell that her Colt held on him. "I ain't no good at maps and such. Never was."

"You don't know much about this part of Virginia, do you?" 1864-Sally asked.

Billy shook his head.

1864-Sally waved her Colt back and forth. "This here 44-Colt will tear you apart just like it did your friends. Am I right, Billy?"

His eyes still riveted on the Colt, Billy nodded.

1864-Sally eyed him. "Then, Billy, here's the deal. You help me prove what's inside this mountain. We take that proof back to Winchester. You can't get outta here without me. You'd die here in these mountains alone. I can't carry what I think is in there by myself. There's more gold and silver than anyone has a right to. We'll only take a little to prove we found it. We're partners. Once we get back home, I'll give you some money. You leave fast and get far away. You don't have to die. Agreed?"

Billy's eyes rose from the Colt's barrel and steadied on 1864-Sally. A thin, nervous grin spread across his face. "Yes, Miss Sally. What about these fellers?"

1864-Sally shrugged. "That's your penance, Billy. You bury them. No one back home needs to know you were gonna betray John Mosby's niece and The Cause. If we bring them the location of this here treasure, they won't much care anyway."

"Truly, Miss Sally? You gonna git me outta here all safe and all?"

"Yes, Billy." 1864-Sally de-cocked her Colt. "So long as you behave and don't make me kill you, too."

Chapter Forty-Two

"I think it's time you told me what's going on, White." Bear walked into White's den. "Now."

White sat behind his grand desk, sipping a porcelain cup of tea. He regarded him with noticeable indifference.

"Did you hear me?" Bear moved deeper into the lavish den. "I asked you a question."

"No." White stood and aimed a bony, aging finger at him. "You made a demand. A rude demand. I don't respond to demands. I also don't tolerate my employees making them."

"Yeah, but we all work for someone." Bear knew that somewhere, hiding behind the curtain, was White's boss. "Isn't that right–like Colonel Smith?"

White's eyes flared. "What do you know of Smith?"

"Oh, please," Bear said with a sly grin. "I did what I do best. I investigated. Smith showed up with the same muscle dressed in black like TV characters at the library. The same guys you have around here. Kerns was murdered using a prototype ray gun—like the one in your wine cellar. I don't think you built it. Smith's a big shot at that think tank, ADRI. All in all, it wasn't a hard trail to follow to your wine cellar."

"Wine cellar?" White slammed his teacup down and broke it on his desk. Steaming liquid splashed everywhere. "How did you gain access to my wine cellar?"

Bear had him. "You learn a few tricks as a cop. Let's just say I'm better at snooping than you are with security. Now, what's the endgame?"

"Endgame? Oh, how very dramatic." A nervous look filled White's normally arrogant, self-centered expression. "You have not earned enough benefit to learn the endgame, Theodore. But perhaps you've earned something after Pellman."

Yes, Pellman. "Think again."

"Come look at a portrait in the hall." White led him out of his den and into the long hallway running through the rest of his home. He stopped halfway down the hall and pointed to an oil portrait of a Confederate general standing beside a stomping, gray mare. "What do you see, Theodore?"

Bear considered the portrait. The officer wore a bushy beard, popular in those years. He looked dapper in his gray uniform with a sidearm and saber. One hand was over his heart, and the other held the mare's reins. He studied the painting, wondering what White expected from him.

"Theodore?"

"One of those generals who lost the war and refused to concede." There, a little honesty might just motivate the old bastard to talk. "What do you see?"

For a moment, White's eyes flared, and his mouth clamped so tight his jaw trembled. Then, the anger dissolved, replaced by that confident, artificial demeanor he played so well.

"I see my ancestor, William Stanford White. He was often called W.S. to ease confusion between the three bloodline William Stanford White's all living at the time. Like Colonel Mosby, W.S. had no official military rank, though he was considered a general. He fought out of Winchester during much of the war—completely concealed from Union interference by his agricultural empire. He often provided supplies to local troops to appease them. It was necessary to conceal his identity as the leader of a special military unit. Again, not unlike Colonel Mosby."

Bear considered him. "Mosby was a raider. A guerrilla fighter. What special military unit did your granddad run? I never heard of him."

"General Lee's 35th Militia from Winchester. The M35W was its clandestine insignia. They were saboteurs. Spies. Somewhat like Colonel Mosby, who waged unconventional warfare, my grandfather ran covert operations to thwart the Union from within—provocateurs. He was masterful at his craft."

"So, he promoted himself to general?"

"Don't be insolent." White's eyes began to simmer again but cooled slowly. "Jefferson Davis promised him command of all the Confederate forces after the war—secretly, of course. A reward for his final mission that would turn the war for the south once and for all."

Bear contemplated the portrait again. "What would that be?"

"You are not very knowledgeable of Virginia lore, are you, Theodore? Come."

White led him back to his den and waved him to a chair—the first show of civility since Bear had arrived. When Bear was seated, White opened a desk drawer and withdrew a stack of documents and a leather-bound journal. He placed them on the desk between them.

"Have you ever heard of the Beale Treasure, Theodore?"

"No. Should I?" Bear searched his memory but came up empty. "Was he a pirate or something?"

"No, no." White threw his head back and laughed raucously. "Not a pirate, an early nineteenth-century adventurer."

White told the Beale Treasure story and included vignettes of modern-day treasure hunters still searching for the massive fortune. It took twenty minutes.

"So," Bear said, digesting it all. "You're telling me that somewhere in Bedford County is a hidden treasure?"

"Fifty million dollars by today's market price. Perhaps more. It is worth untold in historical value. Most importantly, priceless heritage value to me."

"No one ever found it?"

White nodded. "Yes, someone did. My grandfather." White leaned back, pleased with himself. "W.S. had many friends in Virginia. It came to his attention that Thomas Beale had documents secured in a Winchester bank just before the Civil War began. W.S. arranged for trusted members of his M35W to raid that bank and secure those documents. The Confederacy was quickly running out of money. W.S.'s plan was to find the treasure and bestow it on Jefferson Davis to help finance a new push toward victory."

"But you said the documents were all unbreakable codes."

"The original set, yes. In that bank safety deposit box, my grandfather's team retrieved two previously forgotten documents. They were far easier to decrypt, and it took him only a few weeks. They were instructions on how to locate the treasure. It was only a matter of launching an expedition to retrieve it."

Bear sat stunned. Was this old land baron really talking about a mythical treasure hunt?

"I see skepticism on your face, Theodore."

"You do, yes. If the treasure was found, then why has anyone continued to look for it? Did your granddad keep it?"

"He did not." White lifted his chin with indignation oozing from his eyes. "He sought the treasure for the good of The Cause. The Confederacy needed that treasure desperately. It was so important that General Lee commissioned my grandfather to retrieve it."

Bear leaned forward. "And?"

"W.S. sent his son and namesake, William White II—who preferred to be called Billy for unknown reasons—and a hand-picked M35W team to follow Beale's instructions into Bedford County. Most did not return. Those that did—two, including his Billy—brought back proof of the treasure. They had marked the last few miles of the route leading to it. It lay waiting for enough men and supplies to recover it and transport it to Richmond."

Bear watched White's eyes for any sign of deceit. He saw nothing but reminiscence and pride. "So, junior made it back and knew where the treasure was? What happened?"

White lowered his eyes to the papers on his desk. "It's all in there, Theodore. Everything I've told you is there in writing. My great-grandfather acquired a journal and some of the original Beale documents. It's all in those."

"You haven't answered me. What happened—"

"They were betrayed." White's face went dark. "Among the team grandfather sent to Bedford County was a woman. She returned with

Billy. She had helped rob the bank and was excellent at code breaking and cartography. Upon their return to Winchester, Union forces captured them. They were hanged before they could reveal the treasure's location to W.S."

Bear cocked his head. "All this is about treasure hunting?"

"No, my lord. It's about heritage. It's about justice. The South has a right to its heritage. My grandfather found the Beale Treasure—my ancestor. That knowledge, along with the proof, will restore pride in my family, and more importantly, in the South's heritage. The Cause might have won had Billy White lived and brought the Beale Treasure home."

Outside, the thump-thump-thump of helicopter rotors filled the air. The sound began low and distant, and soon it was right outside the house.

"What the hell, White?" Bear jumped to his feet. "Is this a setup? Was this bullshit story to keep me busy, and you called in the feds? You're a traitor—are you also a snitch?"

White stood and walked to the large bay window overlooking his rear compound. "Why, my good Captain, have faith. It is time you met the man in charge."

Bear glared. He wasn't prepared for this.

"Your detective work is quite correct. I must say, I underestimated you."

A few moments later, the rear house doors banged open. Feet shuffled loudly down the hall. Two black-clad men, dressed in body armor and military assault paraphernalia, entered the room and took posts on either side of the entrance. Behind them, a short, robust man dressed in a black, expensive suit strode in. He was stocky and bald, with an expression that froze the air in the room. He stopped inside the den and looked straight at Bear.

"Ah, Captain Theodore Braddock. I've been looking forward to meeting you."

Bear looked from the two commandos across the room to White, then finally, at the suited man. "Colonel Smith. You've made quite the stir in Winchester."

"Yes, I have." Smith didn't offer a hand or take his eyes from Bear. "And it seems you have made quite a stir as well."

Chapter Forty-Three

After leaving Bedford County and 1864, I poofed back home to good ole Winchester in the here and now. Landing in my den, I called out for Doc.

No answer.

"Doc?"

The old surgeon appeared in my den's leather chair. Hercule was curled up at his feet like he'd been there all along. Maybe he had, and he just didn't want me to see him.

"Doc, wait until I tell you—"

"Please, Oliver." He rolled his eyes. "You went back to the Civil War with Sally. You watched her and her confederates hunting for the lost treasure. There was a lot of trouble, and she was nearly killed. She got the best of them and was aided by Billy White—your new nemesis, Bradley White's ancestor. Later, if you follow your visions, they were both hanged for their efforts. Is that what you wish to tell me?"

I hated it when he did this. He knew everything all along and, for some reason, chose not to tell me until *after* I'd discovered it myself. I guess he thought it was a teaching moment or something. I just called it showing off.

"If you knew, why not tell me before?" There, I told him. "Now, tell me the rest."

Doc leaned over and patted Hercule, who instantly went twenty-toes up for a belly rub.

"What rest?"

Oh, brother. "The real rest. Why Andy Pellman killed Kerns and Downey? What Bear's up to? What's the connection to that super-secret HEAP ray gun? And finally, what's got to do with the Beale Treasure?"

"I should think it's perfectly obvious, Oliver." Doc began to fade. "As soon as Detective Spence leaves, we will chat again."

Huh?

The doorbell rang.

I also hated when Doc did that.

Angel descended the stairs, and I joined her in the foyer.

Mike Spence stood on our front porch. He looked like he'd just seen a ghost. Well, that's not all the unusual around here, but for Spence, it was kinda ironic.

Angel let him in, and he wasted no time blurting out what had him pale and shaken.

"Angela," he plopped himself down on the ladderback chair in the foyer. "I got reamed out by the Sheriff. He's threatening to fire me for checking out ADRI, White, and Smith. The good news is I got a lead on Cal."

I said, "What? Dammit, Spence, tell us."

Angel repeated me verbatim.

He took a deep breath and glanced around conspiratorially. "I had our computer guys check Cal's cellphone and email accounts. The night of the murders—after he disappeared—he sent several emails out. They pinged off a cell tower on West Route 50 along the Virginia state line."

Why was Cal in the mountains that night? I leaned close to Spence and whispered, "Jeez, Spence, what did you find?"

"Oh, lord." His eyes flashed, and he jumped up, almost toppling the chair. "Holy cow, man, don't do that."

Angel patted his arm. "It's okay, Mike. Just tell us everything. Quickly."

He stood there, staring at my desk chair as though I were in it. "Yeah, yeah, okay. My guys were able to trace the phone's activity. They couldn't grab the actual emails—Cal deleted them all. He sent five. Big ones, too. Techies said they were big attachments. Anyway, they traced the emails."

Angel asked, "Whose account, Mike?"

His face contorted a little—half smile, half frown. "His, Angela. Cal emailed *him.*"

The air around us sizzled.

"To me?" I asked. "Cal disappeared over three days ago, and his last act was to email *me*? The me who died years ago?"

Angel stepped back and narrowed her eyes at Spence. "Tuck's email account?"

In my breathing days, I'd rarely used email for anything other than work. That was before I was murdered, of course. A few months after my demise, Angel packed up my computer and stored it in the basement. She'd moved her much newer one into my den. My desktop computer hadn't seen the light of day since then. I doubted my email account even worked, and if it did, it had years of junk mail, Russian floozies looking for love, and a thousand Nigerian Tycoons trying to give me millions of dollars.

"Yeah, it's weird." Spence shrugged. "But he did it."

I said, "Angel, my old computer's in the basement. I don't remember the logins and passwords, but it was set to remember them. If it still works, maybe we'll get lucky."

"Good idea, Tuck." She gestured toward the far end of the hall and repeated my instructions to Spence. "Can you get it, please? It's in the big gray cabinet at the bottom of the basement stairs."

Looking a little piqued, he headed for the basement door.

Ten minutes later, Spence had retrieved my old computer and monitor and hooked it back up on my desk. It took Angel a few moments to boot it up. Three times we had to three-finger salute it—that's control, alt, delete for you rookies—until the system agreed to operate.

"Go to the email program, Mike."

He did. As I suspected, there were hundreds of files. Luckily, I had automatic spam filters, so the millions of Nigerians and Russian hookers were filed there instead of my inbox.

"Damn, Tuck, I can't believe your email still works," Spence quipped. "I can barely use mine."

What a shocker. Not as much as Spence talking to me, but still a doozie.

"Why would Cal send emails to him, Angela?" Spence watched her tapping away. "I mean, why not you or me?"

"Good question."

I knew. "Because he wanted to make sure no one would intercept them. Maybe he was afraid of someone's reach into the department. He worried it would put Angel in danger. Who'd ever think to check my old email account?"

Angel repeated me, and both agreed. Of course they did. You can't argue with wisdom.

"Here are Cal's emails. He sent photos." She opened the top several emails, all date-time stamped the day Kerns and Downey were murdered, but later that evening. "There are a couple video files."

"Open them." I watched over her shoulder. "Let's see what was so important he emailed a dead detective."

Angel opened the first three emails. The first one had a simple explanation in the body of the email—*Tuck, sending these to you JIC. Can't trust anyone, man.*

What he sent was more than I'd hoped.

The first few photographs were of some important people inside the Handley Library during our quarantine. I instantly recognized the likely suspects—Bradley White, Peter Young, Ahmad El Fazi, and the exotic Chen Liu. There were various shots of them together here and there, but none together. I guess they didn't want anyone to know they were co-conspirators stealing government secrets.

Another few crime scene photos were displayed—mostly of Kerns and Downey's bodies. Others were of the surrounding rooms. Cal had been ordered to surrender everything from those crime scenes. Clearly, he had cheated a little. Good for him.

The real cherry on the top were the videos. One was a clip taken from a CCTV camera somewhere atop the Handley Library. It displayed the outside building entrance, covering the main entrance and parts of both Piccadilly and Braddock Streets. Beginning an hour before Kerns' murder, there were nothing but cars and people coming and going both in and around the library. Then, we saw something that made it all worthwhile.

Andrew Pellman exited the library carrying two large document boxes. He walked out and nearly tripped down the library's stone stairs. After righting himself, he shuffled his way to Angel's Explorer parked down the street, nearly out of camera view. He dropped one box outside her SUV and took several minutes fixing it and loading it into her vehicle. Then, he closed up the vehicle and crossed Piccadilly to an old Toyota sedan, got in, and drove away.

The date and time stamp nearly blew us away.

"Do you see the time?" Spence banged his finger on the screen. "He was loading your SUV, Angela, at the exact time Kerns was murdered."

Yes, he was. But how? I was in his body and possessed him when he killed Kerns with that HEAP ray gun. Yet this video was Pellman's alibi.

"That's not right," I said. "I was there. I possessed him when he killed Kerns and Downey."

"Pellman can't be in two places at once." Angel replayed the few minutes of video where Pellman loaded her vehicle. "Tuck knows he killed Kerns and Downey."

"How?" Spence asked.

Angel explained about me possessing Pellman. I thought Spence was going to have a heart attack when she was through.

"Jeez, Angela," Spence said, staring through unbelieving eyes. "Next time I ask for an explanation, ignore me."

She frowned. "Pellman was gone from the library when I was with Agent Kerns in the rotunda. We got it wrong. This video proves he didn't kill them. Maybe the answer is in the other video."

"I don't understand, Angel," I said. "I was there. I witnessed the murders. Firsthand."

She said, "You said yourself how odd those events are, Tuck. You got it wrong somehow."

"Maybe."

She ran the next video.

This one was with Cal's cellphone. It began with him surveilling Bradley

White and Sheriff Millbert as they gladhanded each other just outside the library. Then, Cal began a slow, discrete surveillance of White as he left town and drove west into the mountains. It was often unfocused, and landmarks were hard to discern, but a few mile markers and road signs told us what we needed to know. By the time White's Mercedes turned into a private road right before the West Virginia line, the hair on my neck—if I had one—stood straight up.

Cal followed White down that road.

A few moments later, between starts and stops on the video—almost all of it too dim to see clearly—the video cleared. This time, it was a major motion picture.

Cal was outside a large log and stone building. He moved his cell phone into three windows, one at a time, and let the video run. One window showed nothing but a large, empty dining room. Another was to a great room with expensive furnishings and opulence displayed everywhere. The third was paydirt. It was an office or den framed in hardwoods and expensive trappings. However, this one was occupied.

Bradley White had house guests, and they were having a grand ole' time.

White sat behind a huge desk. In a tall-back leather chair, pouring down a snifter of something, was Andrew Pellman. Deep down, I wasn't all that surprised. But it was the third person that gut-punched me. It made Angel and Spence gasp. He was stretched out on a leather sofa across the room. A drink in one hand and a big fat cigar in the other.

I don't know what surprised me more—my friend's sudden taste for a cliché cigar and brandy, or that Captain Bear Braddock was at home among the enemy?

Chapter Forty-Four

An hour later, Spence hung up his cell and cursed loudly. He sputtered and spit fire pacing my den. Twice, he stopped to speak but couldn't. He paced again.

"What did the sheriff say, Mike?" Angel asked. "Is he sending backup?"

"No." Spence headed for the tray of booze across the room. He poured himself a couple fingers of my best bourbon—more like a fistful—and knocked it back. "Millbert suspended me. He told me, under no uncertain terms was I to go after White or Cal or Bear. If I do, I'm through."

What the hell? Not that getting Spence fired hadn't been on my bucket list for years. Still, what we'd seen on the videos should get him promoted. *Lord, that hurt to say.*

"Then we go ourselves, Mike." Angel stood from behind my desk. "He chased White into the mountains, and now he's gone. They must have captured him after he sent those videos. He's in real danger."

"If he's still alive," I added and instantly regretted it when Angel's eyes snapped closed. "Sorry, we have to consider that possibility. Kerrie warned me he was in trouble, and he's been gone almost four days."

Spence was somber—part Cal's situation and part bourbon. "Cal was my partner and friend—is, I mean. I'm going. You stay here, Angel. Maybe send Tuck with me? I can't believe I'm saying that, but you know, right?"

"No." Angel opened the lower drawer of the desk and withdrew a small-framed semi-automatic pistol. "I'm going. You can't stop me. Tuck's good for lots of things, but he can't use this."

Damn, I loved this woman.

"It's dangerous." Spence patted the air. "Think—"

"Dangerous? Really?" She laughed. "How many times have I been in danger, Mike? With Tuck? With you and Cal? I can handle myself."

Yes, she could. "Angel, one thing—"

Tuck ... Tuck ... help us. They have my mom and me ... help ...

Kerrie Garcia's voice was strong and terrified and pleading in my head. A wave of fear cascaded over me like a cold wave. Her fear.

"Angel, I'll catch up. Kerrie's in danger. I have to go to her."

The last image I saw was Doc standing in my office doorway. "No, Oliver. No. You can't ..."

Too late. Doc was gone. And so was I.

Chapter Forty-Five

"I'm Detective Spence, Major Crimes Task Force. I have a warrant to search these premises."

Angel sat beside Spence in the front seat of his unmarked cruiser. She listened to him, trying to bluff his way into Bradley White's mountain complex. She had no idea if it would work.

It was late afternoon by the time they pieced together the video clip from Cal's emails and went out to find him. They'd found the private gravel road in no time. For the past five minutes, they sat in the cruiser, blocked by a tall steel fence. They were arguing with a voice through the callbox system.

The voice said, "Hold your warrant up to the camera, Detective."

Spence hesitated, then slipped a folded sieve of documents from his jacket pocket and held them up at the window. He conveniently kept his fingers over the date and address of the search warrant. Had he not, it would have been obvious the warrant was for a warehouse in north Winchester, issued for a drug raid a month prior.

"Hold on a moment," the voice said.

Spence glanced at Angel. "Got any other ideas?"

"No. Maybe you should have—"

"Okay," the speaker crackled again. "Wait there. Stay in your vehicle. A patrol will escort you in shortly." The speaker clicked off.

"I'll be damned." Spence winked at her. "It'll get me fired and maybe a jail cell. But, if Cal is here, it'll be worth it."

"Agreed." She breathed easily for the first time since they'd started up the mountain road. "I wish Tuck was here."

"Yeah, me too."

A few minutes later, a four-by-four rolled up to the gate with two men inside. One stepped out as the gate opened automatically. He approached them. The guard was dressed in black clothing and military tactical gear. Oddly enough, there were no patches or insignia identifying any branch of service or organization.

They were identical to Colonel Smith's men who seized the Handley Library. That fact disturbed them.

"Show me your warrant, sir." The guard reached out.

"Not you." Spence shook his head. "I show it only to Mr. White. Those are my orders."

"You're serving it alone, Detective?"

A sick feeling oozed into Angel's stomach. She whispered, "Mike, we should go."

It was too late. The second guard climbed from the four-by-four and leveled an M4 carbine at them. The first guard stepped away from Spence's cruiser, drew his sidearm, and ordered them from the car.

"Mike, what do we do?" she asked.

Spence suddenly pointed skyward and grinned as he climbed from his cruiser. "Look up, gentlemen. You're on drone surveillance. My tactical team is at your back door. I suggest you lower your weapons before our sniper goes hot. No fast moves. No reason to get shot tonight."

The guard nearest him froze. Then slowly, he glanced back at his partner, lifting a chin skyward. "What do you think, Tony?"

"Are you kidding?" Tony wasn't taking any chances. He lowered his rifle. "I think only a fool would try to bluff us if he were alone, Frank. Do it."

Frank holstered his pistol. "We don't have a back gate, Detective."

"You will soon." Spence forced a nervous laugh. He glanced around to ensure there were no CCTV cameras nearby. "My team probably just made one for you."

"I still need to see that warrant," Frank demanded. "Sniper or no sniper."

With one hand, Spence handed Frank the folded sheets of paper, and with the other, he drew his Glock from beneath his jacket. He aimed at the man's face. They met eye-to-eye before the man released the fake warrant.

"Now, Frank. After you and Tony hand my partner your weapons, we're all going up to the main house to see White. By that time, the rest of my team will be here."

Angel watched Spence. Never had she seen this side of him before. For as long as she'd known him, he'd been a half-bumbling, half-passable detective. Tuck had loathed him. Bear had tolerated him. Now, Spence had shed that skin, and the man beneath was a gutsy, crafty cop.

She hoped it would last.

Chapter Forty-Six

And poof... I arrived—where I had no idea—via the spectral express into total darkness. Not the ethereal darkness I often traveled through. No, natural darkness, like a moonless night, in a windowless room, with the lights off. You know, creepy darkness.

Dim overhead lighting turned on and grew brighter—slowly, like dawn arriving. An overpowering fear gripped me. Something I hadn't felt since I was murdered.

The room—more a laboratory—around me was large and dimly lit. The walls were covered in large computer monitors that would be the envy of every gaming-obsessed fan in the country. A dozen computer stations circled a center stage-like platform where a small table and two chairs waited. The stations were occupied by several people of varying age, gender, and description. I had a hunch they were all mad scientist apprentices.

Kerrie and Emily Garcia stood across the laboratory, flanked on both sides by armed Men-Wearing-Black. Each had a gun pressed against their sides, and both were crying. Emily's face was frozen in fear, staring at me. Kerrie's was tear-streaked and sad.

Holy evil lair, Batman. What was this place?

The moment I caught Kerrie's eyes, her face blanched, and tears rained all the harder. She tried to call out, but her guard shook her and commanded silence.

I called, "Kerrie, listen to them. I'll figure this out. It's okay. It's not your fault."

Her voice cried out in my thoughts—*No, Tuck. Get out. It's a trap!*

"I can't leave you with these men. You called me."

They made me. They were going to hurt my mom. Go. Don't come back.

There was no way I was leaving this little girl and her mom behind. No way.

"Do as they say, Kerrie. I'll get you out of this."

I looked around. It struck me that the laboratory seemed focused on history. The screens surrounding me displayed photo collages of old, grainy photographs with hand-scribed documents, letters, and other artifacts surrounding them. The photographs looked like Civil War era prints—those from glass or iron plates of the day. There were scenes of people posing with their awkward, drone faces. Some were battlefield scenes. Others were townscapes. There were hundreds of them. On the far wall hung topographic maps, old street maps, and landscaping notes.

Two large displays caught my attention. They were in the center of the front wall, opposite the door behind me. The left display showed a topographic map labeled "Bedford County, Virginia." Below the map was a series of notes and smaller photographs I couldn't make out from where I stood.

The display on the right shook me.

A black and white photo filled half the display. The image was oddly clear and sharp despite having been resized so large. It was a beautiful woman with flowing blond hair and piercing eyes that held mine intently. She was dressed in riding trousers and a floppy-brimmed hat with a blouse that still revealed her womanly physique. She held a pistol in one hand and a rolled-up document in the other. She smiled widely—unlike many of the photographs around the room that showed grim, downtrodden faces.

I'd know Sally Elizabeth Mosby anywhere. After all, she was kin.

"What is this place?" I asked.

Kerrie tried to wiggle free of her guard. He grabbed her arm and dragged her backward to a doorway along the adjacent wall. He shoved her inside. The other guard pushed Emily after her. The door automatically slammed shut, and above it, a large red light flashed green.

I could hear Kerrie crying through the door.

Ah, crap. I turned toward the large steel double-door behind me. The light above it was flashing green. I had the strangest feeling that meant I was in deep trouble—like an "oh crap" sandwich.

Time to act.

I started for the door where Kerrie and Emily had disappeared.

I made it two steps.

Around me, transparent walls jutted up from seams in the floor and dropped from overhead. They enclosed me in a strange, glass cube. It encompassed the entire landing around me. The walls glistened—no, that's not right—they sparkled and sizzled. At the top was a thick black harness that descended from the ceiling two stories above me. The harness connected heavy wires the size of outdoor electric lines to each corner of the cube. As I moved toward each wall, they pulsed and lit up as though they were alive.

I reached out and touched the wall ahead. It flashed bright and powerful and knocked me on my butt. The explosion of energy was like nothing I'd ever felt. It didn't surge and flow into me like electricity. It hit me like a truck at full speed.

I was down.

It took a few moments to shake off the percussion and regain my footing. When I did, I slowly turned, looking for a way out. I saw none.

A voice spun me on my heels. "Hello again, Detective Tucker. Welcome to Building Five. May I call you Tuck?"

Colonel Smith—Man-Wearing-Black *numero uno*—appeared on one of the large wall screens facing me. He was just head and shoulders, but there he was like a talking head on cable news.

"You know I'm here?"

Smith laughed heartily. "Of course. I see and hear you, Tuck. Now everyone can. It's an ingenious invention by a colleague of mine—a cell made of a special plasma enclosed in unbreakable, transparent polymers. A colleague you're rather familiar with, too. Amazing. Isn't it?"

"Yeah, very clever. I can't wait to hear all about it."

"Sit tight, won't you?" Smith let go another diabolical laugh. "I'll be with you shortly. Then, we'll have a real chat."

I looked around the lab. All eyes were on me. Every person in the room stared at me, caught inside this strange glass prison. Some of them pointed and spoke in hushed surprise. Some of them stood pale-faced and stared. I was a hamster in a cage.

Several of the lab techs left their workstations and moved to the cube wall to gawk close up.

What, hadn't they ever seen a ghost before?

Chapter Forty-Seven

Angel was terrified. What was she thinking coming here with only Spence? While they hadn't considered finding a secure, well-guarded compound, they should have considered the possibility someone like White wouldn't be unprotected.

She and Spence made it inside White's main house by pure luck. Upon arrival at the log mansion, Spence bluffed his way past two more armed guards at the front veranda. He'd disarmed them all with the same phony warrant and threats of drone surveillance and overwatch snipers. At one point, he used his cell phone to speak to an imaginary backup team breaching the compound's rear fence.

So far, his colorful bluff was working.

Angel stood nervously watching him. He'd handcuffed the four guards using their flex-cuff restraints while she secured their weapons in Spence's trunk.

"Mike, what's the plan now?" she asked, praying he had one. "Real backup?"

"There is no backup, Angela. Not unless Tuck shows up." He looked embarrassed about bringing him up. "I'm open for suggestions."

"Where's White?" Angel asked Frank, the guard. He was sitting with the other men, where Spence positioned them with their backs against the outer mansion wall. "We want to interview him."

Frank glared at her. "I'm not saying anything. That warrant is bullshit, Spence. We all know that now. It's just you two, right? When Mr. White finds out—"

"And yet you're in handcuffs," Spence snorted, "and I'm holding the gun."

"For now," Tony added. "When we get out, you're dead. Both of you."

Spence tried to grin, but it came out a frown.

"I'll follow you, Mike." Angel pulled out her semi-automatic pistol. "We're only here for Cal."

"Right." Spence opened the front door, peeked inside, and led the way.

They made it to the first room on the right. There, inside a large archway, was a grandly decorated great room with a two-story high-beamed ceiling. She recognized the room from one of Cal's videos.

"Oh, crap," Spence whispered.

In the center of the room was a wide, glass-top coffee table trimmed in brass and decorative steel. Atop it were three large briefcases with their tops open. Each was filled with bundles of cash. Lots and lots of cash.

"Ah, Professor Tucker. Do come in." Bradley White stood near the fieldstone fireplace with a pleased, self-satisfied grin on his face. "This is a surprise."

Angel recognized three others from one of Cal's videos at the Handley Library. There was the pretty, slender Asian woman, a dark-skinned Middle Easterner, and an African American.

A familiar voice startled her. She turned around.

Standing behind her, with a gun leveled first at her and then pivoting toward Spence, stood Bear. Behind him was Nicholas Bartalotta.

Her heart sank. She felt a little dizzy.

"You shouldn't have come, Angela," Bear said coldly. "You and Spence should've listened to the Sheriff."

Chapter Forty-Eight

"Bear, I prayed we were wrong about you." Angel backed into the great room, throwing a quick glance over her shoulder at White and the others. She lifted her hands in surrender and looked unbelievingly at Bear and Nicholas Bartalotta. "You can't be doing this. And you, Nicholas? I don't understand."

Poor Nic lowered his eyes. "No, I'm sure you don't. You've made a big mistake, my dear. I warned you. Now, I am unsure what will happen."

"I'm not unsure." Spence spit the words out. "A corrupt cop and a mobster. The marriage from hell."

"Shut it, Spence." Bear prodded him with his pistol as he reached around and took Spence's away. "You were told to stay clear, and yet here you are. This is on you. Whatever happens to Angela and you is your fault."

"Well, now, we're all here." White stood near a large fireplace on the side wall. He sipped a drink in his hand. "Move them out of the way, Theodore. We'll conclude our business first and deal with them afterward."

Bear ignored him. "Stay quiet and don't give us any trouble. Either of you."

Tears started to fill Angel's eyes, but she fought them back. They wouldn't get the satisfaction of breaking her. Not now. Not after all the years that she had been loyal to them both. Their betrayal was devastating. Her naivete shameful.

"You bastards," was all she could muster. "Tuck—"

"I don't think so, Angela." Bear held up his EMF meter. "If Tuck were within a hundred feet of me, this EMF meter would warn me."

"Ah, Professor Tucker," a voice said from the hallway behind them. "Oliver will not be joining us. You see, I have him detained elsewhere. Odd as that sounds."

Angel spun as Colonel Smith walked into the room. He had a broad smile on his face that exuded satisfaction.

She stared. "What have you done with him, Smith?"

"I captured him, Professor. In fact, I just spoke with him via video chat. My equipment not only holds him, but it allows me to communicate. Isn't that grand?"

Bear looked away.

Angel thrust a finger toward Smith. "I don't believe you."

"Oh?" Smith walked toward her and turned his cell phone around. On the screen was a strange image of a large, transparent cell. Inside, pacing nervously, was Tuck. "Later, if you cooperate, you may say hello."

"No." Angel's eyes rained tears. "Please, don't hurt him. You could never imagine—"

"As long as he cooperates—and you, too—you both will be released unharmed."

She tried to respond but couldn't find the words. Fear and uncertainty took control like it had never before. The very thought that someone, somehow, had captured Tuck was unbelievable. Yet, there it was on Smith's cellphone. If Smith could accomplish that...

"Angela, it will all be well. You will see." Poor Nic walked to a decorative mahogany bar across the room and poured himself a drink. He downed it and poured another. He stood there with his back to the others, silent.

White looked from Spence to Angel. Finally, he walked over to Smith. "Are you sure about all this? I don't like where this is headed. First, that other detective. Now these two? That wasn't part of our arrangement."

"Other detective?" Spence straightened. "Cal?"

Smith grinned. "I believe I've paid you handsomely to do as I say, Bradley. Therefore, your arrangement is what I decide at any moment."

"You didn't pay me to kidnap cops and college professors."

Smith laughed now. "Oh? I believe you did that all on your own."

"Corruption is corruption, White," Spence sneered. "You're both in this. Both of you are corrupt assholes."

One of the guards strode to Spence and punched him hard in the face. "Shut it, cop."

Spence went down. A large gash blossomed on his cheek. Blood ran down his face and neck. "White, I thought you were calling the shorts. It's Smith. Is Sheriff Millbert in your pockets? Or is he in Bartalotta's pocket and Poor Nic's in yours? I get who's pulling Bear's strings—everyone."

Smith raised a hand, and the guard yanked Spence to his feet.

Smith said, "Detective, do be quiet."

"Screw you."

The guard punched Spence in the stomach and put him down again.

Smith faced White. "Bradley, you've made a mess of things. You should have dealt with the detectives and Professor Tucker on your own. Why do I need to do everything?"

"Because you're in charge—responsible for all this." Angel couldn't help it now, and her eyes raged. As she looked at Bear, the ache of betrayal swelled in her, and she thought she'd be sick. "Bear, you and Nicholas are so, so… despicable. You disgust me."

"I know." Bear waved his pistol between her and Spence. "You don't understand. Just shut it for now."

"Back to business." Smith gestured to White. "Get on with it, Bradley."

White turned to the others standing around the table of cash. "Thank you all for your contributions. We shall begin."

"Please hurry. I have other business to attend to." Liu gestured to one of the briefcases on the center table. "My government has sent me—"

"Mr. White," El Fazi said, ignoring her, "I would like some guarantees."

"Of course." Smith walked to the rear door of the den, where French doors opened to a wide hallway leading to the rear of the house. He gestured to someone inside. "Join us, won't you?"

A young man in his late twenties, thin and meek, walked in. He wore a strange, black polymer case on his back tethered to a three-foot-long tubular device in his hands. The device had a pistol grip and a series of lights and buttons along its barrel. Mounted on top of the barrel, opposite the pistol grip, were a small keypad and screen like a cell phone. As he entered the room, he tapped on the keypad and caused the lights along the barrel to flicker on.

"Andrew?" Angel stared, dumbfounded at the young man. "Is that you, Andrew? I don't understand. You're dead."

"Ha, not me." Pellman turned the weapon toward her. "I'm Aaron, Professor."

Andrew had a twin? Her stomach knotted, and she closed her eyes. "Then Andrew is—"

"Dead. Isn't he, Captain Braddock?" Aaron aimed the weapon at El Fazi. "Andrew just couldn't get his head around things. But then, he wasn't as brilliant as me."

El Fazi patted the air. "Please, what is it you do?"

"Bear? You… you… You killed Andrew?" Angel couldn't believe what she'd heard. "It can't be true."

"Ah, but it is, Professor." Aaron Pellman tapped a button on the side of the weapon. "Poor Andrew, he was such a scaredy cat. He just wouldn't join us."

"White? What is this?" El Fazi stared at the weapon still aimed at him. "I do not understand."

White began to speak, but Smith cut him off.

"Then let me explain." Smith aimed a finger toward Pellman, who instantly lowered the weapon. "This energy weapon was designed as the infantry rifle of the future. We have made it available to you through Mr. White. However, in just days, it will no longer be available."

White's face darkened. "They know all that, Colonel Smith."

"Yes, of course," Smith sneered. "Young Aaron has modified this device especially for me—er, us. The HEAP can now be used for many purposes. You all might find them useful in your purchases."

"HEAP?" Angel asked.

Aaron Pellman grinned widely. "High Energy Assault Platform. I named it myself."

"Wait, now." Young stepped forward. "Are you saying it's not just a weapon? Then what?"

"Such fools," Liu scoffed, bent down, and closed the briefcase nearest her. "What difference does that make. They say it's unavailable in a few days. That means they plan to take our money today and keep the weapon for themselves. My government—"

Aaron Pellman abruptly turned, aimed the device toward her. "I would not be so hasty."

Chapter Forty-Nine

"What is this?" Liu's eyes froze on the HEAP's barrel. "You wouldn't dare."

Angel watched, horrified, as Aaron Pellman placed his finger on the trigger. "Stop this, Smith. Please."

A sudden, electronic hum filled the room. A flash of energy struck the stone fireplace just beside Liu. The stonework—some three feet thick—vaporized in seconds. A neat tunnel a foot in diameter was instantly cut through the rock and mortar as though they were nothing.

"Oh, my God," Young cried and tugged Liu away from the fireplace. "It's amazing."

"Of course," Aaron Pellman said, grinning. "It always worked. It just needed fine-tuning."

Then, as all eyes fell to him, Pellman turned the weapon toward Young and Liu.

"Smith," Angel cried, "make them stop."

"Bradley, no," Poor Nic said from the bar. "This was not our arrangement. Hunting for treasure and murder are two different deals. There is no need—"

"The deal's changed, my friend," Smith said calmly. "White has no say in what happens. He never has. I, on the other hand, will entertain your requests."

"This is not necessary." Angel grasped Spence's arm and nearly impaled his skin with her fingers. When she looked at Bear, his eyes, too, were riveted on the smoldering fireplace. "Bear, you cannot condone this?"

"I have no say in this, Angela," Bear snapped back. "None."

Smith walked to Aaron Pellman and gently tapped his shoulder. "That is sufficient, Aaron. Take the HEAP to my chopper if you please. I'll be along shortly."

"Yes, sir, Colonel."

Pellman shouldered the HEAP. He saluted Smith and strode from the room and down the rear hall with one of Smith's men.

Smith waited for them to leave. "White, I'm returning to ADRI. I have some unfinished business with Detective Tucker. Where is the journal?"

"What? No." White held up a hand. "The journal is mine. It's been in my family—"

"The journal—now." Smith shoved him aside. Then, he walked swiftly toward the large desk in the corner of the room, where there were stacks of files and books atop it. He stopped and sported through them. "Where is it?"

White ran to the desk. "No. It's mine. It's my heritage. You can't—"

"I can, and I am." Smith lifted an old, worn leather valise several inches thick. He opened it and removed a shabby leather journal. "Ah, here it is."

Angel recognized the journal immediately. "That was in my research, Mr. White. You stole it from my office."

"It was not yours to have, Professor." White turned and tried to grab the journal from Smith. "It is mine."

"Nonsense." Smith easily shoved him back and beckoned for one of his men to intercede. They did and dragged White back to the fireplace.

"You can't take it," White screamed, struggling with the men. "After all I've done for you?"

"Done for me? You mean done for yourself, you arrogant bastard." Smith opened the journal and fanned the pages. He stopped at something and smiled broadly. "I've given you the means to fund your little Confederate resurgence club. Millions. What has it gotten you, Bradley? Nothing. No one cares about your silly family legacy. Your ancestors lost. Finding the treasure before me won't change that. No one cares about a hundred-sixty-year-old conflict."

"I care," White yelled, tugged himself free of the guard, and lunged at Smith. He made it one step before the guard seized him again and twisted his arms behind him. "My family was blamed—disgraced. All because of yours. You owed me the money. You owe me the right to retrieve Beale's Treasure and restate my family's legacy."

Smith's eyebrows rose, and he laughed heartily.

"Bastard." White's eyes closed, trying to hide his anger. "You owe me."

"I owe you nothing." Smith moved across the room to Angel. Then, he turned back to White. "Bradley, out of the goodness of my heart, you may keep some of the ADRI products in your wine cellar. However, there will be no more."

"What if I—"

"I wouldn't. Should the authorities coincidentally find their way to me, well, I'll consider you responsible and act accordingly."

Angel knew what that meant. "You'll kill him, too, Smith?"

"Professor?" Smith looked at her with a dull, unfeeling stare. "I have killed no one. I assure you of that."

"Then you ordered it." She lowered her head. If only Tuck could be here. He'd find a way to fight these men. "You're behind everything."

"Unfortunate you feel that way, Professor." Smith gestured to two men in the hallway. "Please bring Professor Tucker with us."

The armed men descended on Angel and grabbed her by the arms as the sound of the helicopter's engine rose outside. She struggled, but they were too strong.

"No… Bear… please…" Angel cried out as she struggled harder. "Don't let them take me."

"Colonel, leave her to me," Bear said. "You don't need the extra baggage."

Smith considered him for a long time. "No, I think not. She might come in handy persuading her husband to assist me. She'll come along. But I assure you, she will remain unharmed."

Bear's words were cold. "She wasn't part of our deal."

"Once again, I've changed the deal." Smith grinned. "There is an old line from a movie—pray I don't change it further."

Poor Nic crossed the room to her. "Angela, be calm. I promise no harm will come to you."

"Oh? I suppose you're giving me your word?" she snapped as the men dragged her toward the hallway. "I've really misjudged you, Nicholas. You're a disgrace. Almost as much as Bear. You both make me sick—and sad."

Poor Nic lowered his eyes and stepped back.

"You're all fools." Angel twisted in the men's grasp. "That silly Beale Treasure is a fake. You're killing and committing treason for a myth. Think about—"

"Angela, stop fighting," Spence yelled and inched toward the rear of the room. "Don't struggle. You'll make it worse."

"Stop, Spence." Bear took a step toward him. "Don't, Mike. Don't try anything heroic. It'll get you both killed."

"Screw you, traitor." Spence kept moving but stopped when Bear aimed his pistol at him. "You've wanted to shoot me for years."

Bear, oddly enough, grinned.

"Theodore?" Smith stopped behind Angel at the hallway entrance. "Clean up this mess, won't you? And I mean *thoroughly*. I will leave a few of my men here to assist you. When things are appropriately dealt with, return with them to my office. With the cash, of course."

Bear glanced at White and then at Smith. "I understand."

Smith waved to his men, and they disappeared through the doors toward the sound of the helicopter gaining power.

Outside, the rotors blew dirt and leaves everywhere. Angel tried hard to pull free of Smith's men but couldn't. As soon as she reached the open helicopter door, she turned as a gunshot from inside split the air through the rotor wash.

"Mike!"

Chapter Fifty

The bullet Bear fired smacked into the wall beside Spence's head. Spence barely flinched. The rest—Liu, El Fazi, Young, and Bradley White, all dived for cover.

"A warning shot, Spence." Bear waved his pistol at him. "Move over there by the fireplace."

Spence raised his hands shoulder-high and did what Bear ordered. "The next one in me, right, traitor?"

Bear ignored him. He pulled Spence's gun he'd taken when he and Angel had entered the house, and handed it to Poor Nic. "Nic, watch Spence very closely."

"Of course." Poor Nic moved adjacent to the fireplace. He stayed well enough back to prevent Spence from reaching him should he try. "Now, Detective, it would be wise for you to stay very still."

White ran for the French doors, but the helicopter was already airborne. "Braddock, go after them. Bring my journal and the HEAP back here. They're mine."

"I don't work for you anymore, White." Bear moved to the center table and the stacks of cash. He eyed the others. "Okay, who wants to talk first?"

The three arms buyers exchanged glances.

Young said, "Braddock? What are you talking about? Let us take our money and leave. We'll just go."

"How magnanimous of you. You're missing a key point, Mr. Young," Poor Nic scoffed. "One of you is a government informant. It would be prudent for us to find out who and what damage has been done. The rest may leave."

Liu forced a laugh. "Yes, of course. The retired mobster knows all about informants."

"What do you have in mind, Nic?" Bear asked. "I'm sure you have friends who can help."

White's face tightened with anger. "What are you talking about, Theodore? There're millions of dollars on that table. I have a basement full of advanced government research. It's worth a half-billion dollars in the right market. I neither wish to be caught with it nor lose its sale. I still have my heritage to restore—I need cash for that."

"Heritage?" Poor Nic eyed White with an evil grin. "Are you so foolish?"

"One of us is." Young looked to El Fazi, who had been silent during most of the chaos. "You've not said much. Are you wired?"

"Wired? How dare you?" El Fazi took a step toward Young, but Young struck him hard in the stomach and doubled him over. El Fazi croaked, "What is this? You dare to accuse me?"

Young shoved him to the ground and bent over him. He searched him roughly. When he stood, he produced a short, thin wire and a small plastic box affixed to it.

"He's wired." Young threw the listening device onto a stack of cash on the table. "We're all cooked, now. Braddock, we gotta act fast. Let's clean up and go."

White's eyes locked onto the listening device and then El Fazi. "You? You have entrapped us? You buy my goods and now this?"

"No, no." El Fazi got to his knees, still holding his stomach. "This is wrong. I had no device. I swear to you. This is a trick—a sleight of hand."

"Everyone, just be quiet," Bear ordered. He jutted a finger at White. "So, you just admitted that you stole classified government research and equipment. You admitted—to whoever is listening—that you sold those US secrets and weapons to foreign governments. Let's see…. We have…" he turned to Liu and El Fazi. "The People's Republic, a Middle Eastern consortium… hmmm. They won't waste a bullet on you, Bradley. You're toast."

White's face blanched. His hands flew to his face and shook as he wiped the sweat pouring from his brow. He looked from the stacks of money to Bear and back to El Fazi. He tried to speak but only shuddered unrecognizably.

Bear moved to El Fazi. "You and Liu are here illegally. You've been buying stolen US secrets and weapons for months—longer perhaps. All of you—especially you, Bradley, are guilty of conspiracy to commit murder, espionage, arms trafficking, and a dozen other federal charges."

"El Fazi and me?" Liu gestured to Young. "What of him? He betrayed his own country. Whom did he do all this for?"

"Who gives a damn?" Spence yelled. He took a step toward the group, but Poor Nic lifted his pistol and warned him back. "Screw all of you. You'll hang. Treason. Murder. Espionage. It doesn't matter. You're scum."

Bear eyed Spence and smiled. "Mike, I couldn't have said it better myself."

Young grunted something and walked to the window at the rear of the room. He waved at something outside and turned back to the group.

"Would you like the honors, Captain Braddock?" Young slipped a small semi-automatic pistol out from behind his back. "Or shall I?"

Spence's face twisted in confusion. "What the hell does that mean?"

"Theodore?" White demanded. "Why is Mr. Young holding that pistol? Why—"

"Really, Bradley?" Young aimed at White. "The wire was mine. A little sleight of hand trick, as El Fazi knows. Like it?"

White paled. "I... I... what is happening?"

Outside, the roar of vehicles grew louder until they were right outside. Doors opened and slammed. Running feet. Shouted commands. There were three gunshots as White's guards attempted to resist. It ended quickly.

"Call off your men, White," Bear said. "You can't win. It's the FBI HRT. No sense your people getting killed for nothing."

El Fazi jumped up. "This is outrageous. It is, what do you say, entrapment."

"I wish to call my embassy," Liu cried and tried to run from the room. Poor Nic stepped forward and blocked her. "You, too, Nicholas?"

"Sit down, Miss Liu," Poor Nic said casually, gesturing with his pistol. "There is nowhere to go."

Spence's eyes flared. "Bear? You? You're… you're…"

"He's with me—FBI." Young lifted a chain with a badge affixed from beneath his shirt. "I'm glad you didn't shoot him."

"So am I." Bear walked to Spence and extended his hand. "Sorry, Mike, it was national security. I wasn't allowed to bring anyone in. Not you, not Cal, not Angela…"

Spence shook his hand. "Not even *him?*"

"Especially *him*." Bear laughed and produced his EMF meter from a pocket. "I had to keep him off me. I couldn't take the chance. Smith's been hunting him. I was afraid if he was around me too much, they'd capture him. It seems they already have."

Poor Nic raised his hand. "Ah, gentlemen, we must get to ADRI and free Angela and, well, Oliver, it seems."

Bear lowered his head. "We're going, but we have to find Cal, too. Raiding ADRI is tricky. We have to ensure we can secure Angel before any raid. If we move too quickly, the rest of Smith's network will go to ground. There's more at stake than you understand."

"No, Bear," Spence growled, moving over to White. "I do understand. Screw the spies and traitors. Angela, Cal, and Tuck are somewhere. This asshole is going to tell us."

"No, I think not." White snapped his arms folded defiantly. "I wish a deal. For the right one, I will give you all you wish. The network of buyers. ADRI inside secrets. And, of course, Colonel Smith himself."

"What about Angela Tucker?" Spence demanded. "She's first on the list."

White grinned. "Of course, and there are young Kerrie Garcia and her mother, other young people, too. Smith has them all tucked neatly away at ADRI, doing research. It would be a shame if my deal was not good enough to—"

Spence reared back and punched White squarely in the jaw. His strike sent the older man tumbling onto his back. "Okay, let's negotiate."

Bear grabbed him. "No, Mike. Not this way."

"Okay." Spence drove a deep, hard kick into White's side. "How about this way?"

White grunted and gasped for air. "You don't understand. ADRI has many secrets. Where Smith will be holding Professor Tucker and her, ah, husband—and others—is secure and impenetrable. They're not at their main complex but rather a secret facility, unidentified to any outsiders. I believe it is what you would call a black site—invisible even to the DOD. Without me, you will never find them."

Spence reared back to kick him again, but hesitated. "And that takes a deal?"

"Yes, Detective. It does." White nodded. "You will not believe this, but I have only been in this for the Beale Treasure. No killing. Smith came to me with the sales of government technology three months ago. Recently, our small enterprise started on a short timeline."

"Why?" Spence asked.

Bear answered. "Because the DOD is onto him. They're going into ADRI on a major investigation. That was going to start in a week from yesterday. Smith needs to sell, collect, and run."

"Bravo, Captain Braddock. He could not afford to be caught."

"And you?" Bear asked. "You were going down with him."

"No, Captain Braddock." Now, Smith allowed a short laugh. "I was preparing for that eventuality. That is why I require a deal. I can give you everything you need. You must understand, in the beginning, Smith's offer was impossible to say no to. Imagine, saving my family name, my heritage, and the virtues of the fallen Confederacy. Finding the Beale Treasure takes money. Lots of money. I am very close, you understand. I had nothing to do with the killings or the rest. Therefore, a deal is required for my assistance. My attorney has already prepared for this day. I have the evidence you will need. I have it all."

Bear leaned down and grasped White's arm. He jerked him to his feet. "We're listening."

"Freeze," someone yelled from the hall as four armed FBI agents burst into the room. "FBI."

Young held up his badge. "Special Agent Young, WFO. I'm the on-scene commander. Secure the compound and hold in place."

"Yes, sir," one of the FBI agents barked. Then, he turned and issued orders.

Quickly, the other agents took control of Liu and El Fazi. Young waved them off when one approached White.

"Give us a few, agent." Young stepped up close to White. "What do you want?"

White looked from Young to Bear and back again. "Rights to the Beale Treasure. Not all of it, mind you, perhaps a ten percent finder's fee. And the credit for its discovery and rights to its story and public recognition. That is all it will take to change the country's understanding of my family and for me to regain my place in history. Oh, and immunity after I provide you the evidence against Smith—"

"Don't push it." Bear asked Young, "Doable?"

"Sure, why not?" He aimed a finger at White. "No cash, White. We'll talk immunity or partial immunity based on what you can give us about Smith. Now, where do we find Angela Tucker, Cal Clemens, and the others?"

White raised his chin. "My deal—in writing. Do hurry, gentlemen. Because Colonel Smith is on the verge of running once he finds the treasure. He will abandon ADRI and kill all witnesses. That includes, I'm afraid, Angela Tucker, Kerrie Garcia, and anyone else he's wronged."

Chapter Fifty-One

Things have definitely been better for me. Recently, too. Like, anytime recently.

I was trapped like a rat in Colonel Smith's wizardly contraption. The cube walls were glowing and churning with a power I didn't understand but definitely feared. I couldn't escape or poof out. I couldn't "be there" no matter how hard I tried. My prison had some kind of magnetic force field or something. I'm not talking about late-night sci-fi movies, either. I'm talking about the stuff that seared me to the bone. It made Bear's EMF meter defense seem like child's play.

Was it possible that Smith could keep me? It seemed so. Did that also mean he could kill me? For real? Forever?

What I needed was another brilliant plan. I had one, of course, and it was my super-secret plan. I just needed a chance to use it. Smith wouldn't see it coming.

The cube walls hummed and pulsated each time I neared them. As before, they twice knocked me on my butt when I probed for a weak spot. There were none. Smith was efficient if not insane.

"There is no way out, Detective," Smith cawed, walking into the laboratory from somewhere beyond my sightline. "Do feel free to try. I'll enjoy watching you drain your energy."

Just then, a hundred expletives, none repetitive, passed my lips.

He threw his head back and laughed.

"What do you want, Smith?" I ignored the other million questions I had. "This isn't just a bad episode of Ghost Chaser, is it?"

"No, I assure you it is not. Tuck—may I call you Tuck? This is not about you."

Oh? "Then who is it all about? You? Am I some kind of half-assed science project?"

"Why yes, actually."

I didn't like the sound of that. "What's the end goal here?"

He came closer to my cell. "My fourth great-grandfather left a very odd legacy behind him after the war—the Civil War, as I'm sure you understand."

"I do."

He gestured to the large screens on the walls around the room. "My father, grandfather, and all my greats before spent their lives trying to decipher the clues that would lead us to the biggest single treasure in the history of the United States."

Here we go. "That would be the Beale Treasure. Right?"

"Yes, of course." He admired his electronic screens. "It is something that Bradley White and I have in common. A thirst to find that treasure. A thirst begun by our ancestors. Therefore, I cannot allow White to beat me to it. You see, I *need* that treasure."

Well, I knew White had to be involved in this someplace. For a while, I thought he was the chief villain. Perhaps I was wrong—strange as that sounds. Ole Bradley was just Smith's flunky.

"It all began with Thomas Beale and then Robert—"

"Morriss," I interrupted. "Yeah, I know the story. Trust me."

Smith smiled an odd, all-knowing smile. "Then by now, you should have figured out your role in all this."

Nope. He had me there. "What do you want me for?"

Now, Smith was playing his cards right out in the open.

"You see, Tuck, I came across my grandfather's wartime diary. In it, he talked about a Confederate expedition that actually found the Beale Treasure. I wish to find it again."

"Good for you. I'm not a metal detector or surveyor—or a pirate."

Smith actually laughed. "Yes, I've heard of your wit. Very good. A pirate."

"How can I help?"

"Oh, come now. You're too modest." Smith's eyes went wide. "I imagine your life—or rather your death—has been extraordinary. A year ago, I would have laughed at the notion of ghosts. Now, having the science and technology to actually capture you, I dare say I'd believe anything you told me."

Terrific. I had a fan. "Let me get this straight. Your great-granddaddy, a few times removed, left you a story where the treasure is. You want me to help find it?"

"In a manner of speaking, yes."

"What makes you think I'll help you?"

"Oh, you will." The coldness in his voice was only matched by his diabolical stare. "I'm assured of that."

A deep, emotional desire to kill him began to simmer inside me.

"Okay, Smith. First, though, how'd you learn about me? I know Kerrie spilled the beans, but you were already preparing for me, weren't you?"

"I was." Smith pointed to the large photograph of me in my cop days on one of his electronic bulletin boards. Around me was a family tree with photographs and annotations on the faces. At the very bottom of the family tree was Sally Mosby. Okay, so he knew we were related. I doubt he knew anything more about her.

"Okay, that still doesn't—"

"Kerrie simply validated what I'd already suspected." He gestured to the rear door. "Her very unique paranormal talents led us to you. There were also stories of the strange, dead detective that haunts Winchester these past years. You're quite the talk of the ghost-hunting world, Detective. I simply leveraged what I knew, hoped, and voila. Here you are."

Wow, I was famous and didn't know it. A smile started to form on my lips. Then, the thought that Kerrie and Emily Garcia were held hostage by this loon kept it from fruition.

"If I help you, Smith, what do I get?"

He considered that. "Other than getting rich, my colleagues wish to continue their research on you. You have to admit, you're an amazing phenomenon. So, you get to stay around. I won't permanently kill you."

"Lucky me." I stared bullets at him. My only thoughts were how to get out and help him join me on my side of the graveyard.

"Fear not, Tuck." He sounded pleased with himself. "We'll have lots of time to chat after we find the treasure."

I didn't have a clue what to do. Instead, I watched him through my prison walls and tried to think of a way out. All I thought of was little Kerrie. She was close by. Perhaps still scared, crying, and terrified. She'd be next if I didn't stop Smith here and now.

"Detective?" Smith said. "Your decision? Will you help me?"

Silence was my best defense.

The rear doors opened, and Andrew Pellman walked in. He had a gleeful, sadistic grin on his face that unnerved me to my bones.

Wasn't this guy dead?

"Doctor Pellman," Smith called. "Detective Tucker has declined to help us, I'm afraid."

Without a word, Pellman walked to a control panel that sat on a raised workstation platform behind Smith. He sat and began dialing buttons and tapping away on a keyboard. When he looked up, he had my death in his eyes.

Till now, my cell walls had been humming and glowing with a soft, mellow energy. Now, they gushed with an angry red pulse that lit the room in an eerie hell-like mist.

The pain was instant and intense. Even when I had died, I hadn't known pain like this.

The laboratory room snapped black, light, black, light, black. Fingers of fire and needles ripped at my being and threatened to dismember me. I held out as long as I could, but when the assault intensified and tore at me from the inside, I couldn't control it any longer.

I screamed. Loud. Long. Uncontrollably.

Tears burst from my eyes as I shrieked a guttural, agonizing cry of horror. For an instant, I was back in my foyer five years ago. My killer stood on the stairs above me. I heard the shot and the excruciating pain as the bullet burst into me. My world spun and twisted as I careened toward a permanent nothing. The agony invaded me... completely.

I screamed again.

Then, as swiftly as it had begun, it was over.

The pain dissipated. The cube walls were back to their gentle quivering and humming. Strangely, they were soothing.

Smith ordered, "Clear the room."

All but Pellman scurried out.

I collapsed on the floor. I lay there, trying to get my bearings. I fought for consciousness that had nearly been shredded into oblivion. Slowly, I got to my knees.

"What now, Smith?" I groaned. "What do you and Pellman have next? Needles in my eyes?"

"I'm sorry, Tuck. I truly am." Smith walked around to the other side of my cell and peered in as though I were a zoo animal. "I never could authorize such torture if you were alive. Believe it or not, I'm not that kind of person. But then, you're not alive. It's not like I'm killing someone. Is it?"

"You should see it from my side, asshole," I grunted. "I'm not helping you do anything."

"No? Think again, *Detective*. You must reconsider. We are on a very short timeline."

Pellman joined him outside the cube wall. "We did it. I knew it would happen. It was easier than even I thought."

"I'm sorry, Oliver," a meek, distraught voice said behind me. "I couldn't let them kill you. Not for treasure."

My super-secret escape plan failed before it began.

Standing behind me, inside the cube prison walls, was Sally Elizabeth Mosby.

Chapter Fifty-Two

Okay, so my super-secret escape plan was for Sally to rescue me. Unfortunately, we were now cellmates. I had no Plan B. Might she?

"Sally, how'd you get here?" I whispered.

"You, Tuck." She looked around the lab. "I sensed your danger. Your agony. I had to come."

"Do you have a plan to get us out?"

"No. I didn't have time to prepare." She looked around again, perhaps confused by the electronics and twenty-first-century witchcraft. "What is this?"

As her eyes locked onto mine, the realization of Smith's plan gripped me.

"You see, Tuck?" Smith chided. "My plan is working. Though I must say, I would not wish to confront you and Sally outside of this containment room. Still, I've nonetheless captured you both—"

"You?" Pellman spun toward him. "This was me, Smith. You're a glorified security guard."

Wow, I didn't think Andrew was such a glory hound.

"And you're a spoiled little brat, Aaron." Smith's face reddened. "Without me, you'd have no idea what the Beale Treasure is or was or could be."

Aaron Pellman? Andrew's evil twin? I missed that one. I guess Andrew is still dead. Thank God. "Who killed Andrew, Aaron?"

"Who cares?" Aaron looked at me indifferently and walked back to his console. "He's dead. He was a goody-two-shoes and refused to help. Maybe I can bring him back like you. You know, after I experiment on you two for a while."

That didn't sound like fun. "I'll pass."

"I'm sure you're surprised at Aaron." Smith walked close to the cell again. "Everyone assumes I killed Kerns and that janitor, Downey. Perhaps even Andrew, too. I don't care either way. I'm interested only in one thing—the Beale Treasure."

"I don't believe you." Okay, Andrew was not a zombie. Aaron was a mad scientist helping Smith with his diabolical treasure hunt. Kerns was killed with a ray gun. Downey and probably Andrew Pellman were all killed by hand. Some Kung Fu master. Excuse me, Hapkido. My head was spinning. "Sally, got any ideas?"

She shook her head. Tears pooled beneath her eyes, and she was overcome by a sadness that nearly brought me to tears, too.

"Sally?"

"I failed you, Oliver. I was supposed to protect you. I failed. Smith tricked me as his ancestor did so many years ago. Some spy I am."

Huh? "Ancestor?"

"Captain Christian Little, Tuck," Smith said with a jubilant tone. "My fourth great-grandfather. My family name is Little. Not Smith. Just as Bradley White's ancestor, William White, left a stain on his heritage, Captain Little has done the same for me. Except now, he may actually save me."

Kerrie had said Smith was someone else. Now I get it. I looked to Sally, who burst into tears and dropped to the floor, weeping.

I said, "Little hanged Sally in Winchester during the war, Smith."

"He did." Smith was indifferent. "His men captured Billy White—Bradley's ancestor—her remaining ally from M35W. She and Billy made it back to Winchester with evidence of the Beale Treasure. They found it, you see. My grandfather intercepted them before they could divulge the secret to M35W's commander—William Stanford White, Billy's father. Oh, we knew White was in charge of his silly band of M35W rabble. Captain Little laid a trap, and Billy White fell into it. He tried to barter for his life by telling Captain Little about the treasure. But Billy was bad at maps and locations. All he could say was it was somewhere in Bedford County."

"Billy was a good man at heart," Sally sniffled. "Little's men tortured him unmercifully. Anyone would break under that cruelty."

"Yes, that's true," Smith admitted. "That's why Captain Little was forced to interrogate you."

"Interrogate her?" Visions of that day will haunt me forever. "They asked a couple questions and hanged her."

Smith shrugged. "I'll take your word on that, Tuck. But the war was at stake, and Sally was a rebel spy. She got what she—"

"No, Smith. Being a rebel spy was my cover." Sally wiped the tears from her face and stood, facing Smith with a new fire, a new strength in her voice. "I was a Union operative. Your great-granddaddy did not listen to my code I gave him to prove that."

"Ah, yes, Mary Sutton," he said. "He wrote that in his journal for my family. He did know."

"Mary Sutton," I said, turning to Sally. "That was a code to tell them who you were?"

"Yes, Oliver." She looked down. "Should I ever be taken by Union troops, I was to use that code. All commanders in the field knew "Mary Sutton" belonged to Union operatives in the field. It demanded my careful release."

"Captain Little was well aware of your identity, Sally." Smith sputtered a laugh. "He simply chose to ignore it in hopes he could force the treasure's details from you."

Jesus, no. Greed trumped Captain Little's duty to the Union. Treasure trumped his grasp on humanity. "Captain Little was as much of a bastard as you, Smith. Being a traitorous asshole runs deep in your family."

"Careful now," Pellman called from his perch.

The plasma in the cell walls blazed angry red.

My whole being cried out. The pain was unbearable. My limbs felt as though they'd be torn from my body. My thoughts raced and swirled, barely able to think of anything but the agony. I was back again, lying on the floor in my house five years ago. The bullet in my chest burned with fire and despair. Anguish consumed me.

Sally writhed, too. She stood on her tiptoes with her arms behind her as though bound. Her head was cocked to one side. Her eyes bulged. She gagged for her last breath. Once again, hanging from the oak tree in Winchester—clinging to life as she slowly strangled to death.

"Enough," Smith ordered and waited for Pellman to turn off the device. "You're going too far. I warned you, Aaron. Listen or—"

"Or what?" Aaron growled. "You need me; I don't need you. Piss off."

For a second, Aaron raised the intensity of his attack, glaring at Smith the entire time. Then, just as suddenly, the pain was gone.

I settled. Sally dropped to her knees, gasping.

Smith and Aaron were in a death stare contest until Smith looked away and aimed an angry finger at Sally. "Now, Sally, I want the location of the treasure."

"That's all? Then you shall have it." Sally climbed to her feet. "No treasure is worth all this, Smith. I died a traitor in the eyes of my family and country. For what? Captain Little's greed? No."

Smith seemed pleased. "You died with the treasure's secret, Sally. It's time to reveal it to me. With that one act, you can change your reputation and be the hero you should have been. And me, you shall help me immeasurably."

"Sally, don't tell him anything," I said. "There has to be another way."

Pellman tapped his keyboard. His fingers sent Sally and me back into the darkness of suffering. He let us writhe, replaying our private deaths for a long time. We edged closer to the void of no return. Finally, he released us.

"Yes, yes ... *enough*." Sally gasped for breath and crawled to the cube's wall to face Smith. "I'll tell you. But you must give me your word that you will not harm anyone else."

"My word?" Smith turned to Pellman. "Aaron?"

"I want them for study, Smith." Pellman sat back at his terminal, thinking. "I can see a Nobel in my future."

"See, Sally? We have a deal." Smith folded his arms. "I promise he'll be more compassionate in the future."

Aaron laughed. He was a sick, twisted little shit. That realization shamed me for how I believed his dead brother, Andrew, was the culprit behind this lunacy. Andrew hadn't killed anyone. He hadn't stolen anything. It had been Smith the First and Aaron Pellman, Mad Scientist extraordinaire.

"All right, Sally," Smith said quietly. "Tell me."

She did. She began with explaining the members of her M35W team—Jenkins, Hall, Wilks, Johnny Townsend, and young Billy. She explained their trail markers carved into the rocks—M35W. She told where their trail had begun in 1864, just southwest of Lynchburg. She described the cabin along the banks of a small creek that flowed into the Roanoke River. Secreted in the rear of the cabin, partially covered by fallen rocks and dirt from the mountainside, was the entrance to a cave. Within that cave was the treasure vault, buried a hundred feet deeper into the mountain.

"Show me on the map," Smith commanded in a gleeful voice. "Quickly."

Pellman tapped away on this keyboard and brought up an old photograph of a surveyor's map from the late 1800s. The map was displayed on the far wall of our cube cell. "Quickly. Show me."

Sally studied the map for several moments. Finally, she aimed a slender finger at a spot on the Bedford County line. "One of our markers will be there. I'll give you directions to find the other markers. They will lead you to the cabin."

"Excellent." Smith's face lit up. "You have done well, Sally."

"I trust you to be a gentleman, sir," she said. "You gave us your word."

"Of course," Smith sneered. "You have my word."

The laboratory doors behind Pellman's workstation opened. A young man walked in and went immediately to Aaron and stood next to him. They conversed in whispers for a moment before looking back at us.

Sweet multiplicity. The young man was another version of Aaron and Andrew Pellman. Could it be Andrew?

"Ah, Smith, I know I'm dead and all." I pointed at Aaron and his new pal. "But I'm not blind. Is that Andrew?"

"No, Detective." Smith waved at the Pellmans. "Please meet Charles. The oldest of the triplets."

Charles glanced at me sideways but otherwise seemed disinterested.

"Charles?" I couldn't resist, even given my crappy situation. "So, mommy and daddy named the triplets Andrew, Aaron, and, ah, *Charles?*"

Charles Pellman cursed loudly and gave me the death stare. "Don't speak of my parents. I am the older, and that is all that matters."

Aaron laughed awkwardly. "Of course, brother."

"Boys, focus," Smith snapped. "Charles is one of the geniuses behind the HEAP. He'll be accompanying me in the field. But we must hurry. There is so little time left."

"Thank you, Colonel," Charles said, elbowing his brother. "See, Aaron, I'm going into the field."

Aaron shoved his brother like grade school brothers scuffling for supremacy.

What the hell? Andrew Pellman is dead. Aaron Pellman is a mad scientist with a love of torturing Sally and me. Now, I wonder what Charles Pellman's secret power was?

Whatever the answer, I doubted it had anything to do with sanity.

Chapter Fifty-Three

ADRI's black site campus was tucked away in the Virginia countryside. It was camouflaged as just another beltway bandit sitting south of Route 66, a few miles from Dulles Airport. The campus had several nondescript buildings, all similar in design. Each of its buildings—four in all—was ten stories of glass and steel that reeked of power and influence. The buildings were positioned in a semi-circle around a large atrium attached by covered walkways. The atrium was protected from the elements by a four-story high glass roof and walls with trees and plants throughout that made it look like an indoor park. The entire campus was surrounded by a ten-foot security fence with concertina wire and high-pole security lights, and CCTV cameras. Mobile security patrols moved along the inside of the fence.

The main entrance looked like a military base entrance with a wide gate shack, pop-up vehicle barriers, and armed sentries.

Those sentries took notice when the convoy of SUVs approached.

Bear and Spence were in the last FBI vehicle of the convoy. They sat in the rear seat with Agent Young and another FBI man up front. They studied satellite views of the complex provided by the FBI.

Their convoy swooped off Route 66 and approached the campus down its private road. The two armed gate sentries—commandos more like—attempted to stop them, but the lead vehicle was having none of it. When the FBI Suburban screeched to a halt, three FBI agents jumped out, arrested the guards, and quickly opened the gates to allow access to the convoy.

By the time they'd reached the compound's outer parking area, swarms of black-clad ADRI commandos emerged from inside and formed a perimeter bracing against the FBI.

"Bear, they aren't really going to try and stop us," Spence said, "right?"

"They better not," Young answered. "We've got a warrant. HRT is coming in helicopters. If it's a fight they want, they can't win."

"Sure." Spence leaned forward in the seat. "But does ADRI know that?"

Young and the other agent exchanged glances.

As the four remaining FBI vehicles pulled up to the main entrance, agents jumped from the vehicles armed with shotguns and M4 carbines. They quickly approached the line of ADRI security personnel. The resistance waned and eventually broke.

Overhead, a Blackhawk helicopter appeared and hovered above the main building. Black-clad Hostage Rescue Team operators poured from the helicopter and descended on fast ropes.

"Give them time to secure." Young slipped out of the SUV to confer with one of the agents already outside.

Several agents entered the main doors and moved throughout the lobby.

"Time's up." Bear jumped from the vehicle. "Come on, Spence."

Young joined them as they entered the lobby.

There was no resistance thus far. Inside, Assistance SAC—Paula Styres of the Washington Field Office (WFO) stopped them.

"Agent Young, we've secured the first two floors. There is no sign of Professor Tucker, Kerrie Garcia, or her mother. But this place is huge. We'll need to pull it apart."

"Understood.' Young gestured toward the elevator bank ahead of them. "Boss, White said the experimental labs were in Building Five. Four floors down. We'll work that."

"Building Five?" Styres consulted her cell phone and flipped through several screens. "Agent, there are only four buildings showing on these aerials. If White is correct, Smith could have already given the order to eliminate witnesses. Find them."

"Yes, ma'am." Young turned to Bear and Spence. "We take one of my agents and one of the building security officers with us to give us access and keep the employees in line. We gotta move fast."

Styres moved off to speak to a plain-clothed security guard—not one of the tactical-black-clad commandos, but a sharp young man dressed in a blue blazer and gray slacks. When she was done briefing him, he nodded, shook her hand, and headed for them.

"Agent Young? Detectives," the security guard said. "I'm Security Supervisor Munoz. I'll be your escort. Where do you want to start?"

"Building Five," Bear said. "Where is it?"

"There is no Building Five."

"Are you sure?" Young asked.

Munoz looked sheepish. "I've only been here a couple days, sir. I'm part-time. The regular security people—those juiced-up guys in tactical gear—were reassigned for a few days. But I'm sure there isn't a Building Five."

Bear exchanged glances with Young. "Assigned to what other things?"

"That's above my pay grade." Munoz shrugged.

"This place is huge," Spence said. "Can we get White flown here in one of your choppers? He can show us exactly where we need to go."

Young shook his head. "Nope. His lawyer denied that request already. I tried to make it part of the deal. He was afraid to show his face around here. It's up to us."

"Screw it, let's go." Bear headed for the elevators. "Munoz, bring us to the lowest level of this building."

Chapter Fifty-Four

Munoz used a plastic access card that operated the elevators and most office doors to bring them down to the third basement level—B3. There, they met two FBI agents wearing raid jackets with FBI stenciled on their backs. They were talking with a short, stout Latino in the hall. He was dressed as a cleaning crew member and held a rolling trash can.

Young said, "I'm Agent Young. We need to find Building Five. Anyone see any signs or maps showing it?"

"No, sir," one of the agents said. "I'm Timoney. Hold on. This is Miguel Ruiz. He's a contact cleaning manager."

Ruiz, the cleaning crewman, waved meekly.

"You heard the agent," Timoney said to Ruiz. "Where's Building Five?"

Ruiz got a sheepish, concerned look on his face, and he looked from Young to Timoney, and then oddly to Munoz. "No. No. There is no Building Five. Sorry. Only four—"

"Hold it." Munoz stepped forward, speaking in rapid Spanish and tapping the side of his head—gesturing for Ruiz to think harder. Ruiz responded, and the two had a lengthy back-and-forth in Spanish. Several times, Ruiz looked at the others before answering.

"Maybe a different place?" Ruiz glanced around and lowered his voice as though the walls were listening. "There *is* Section Five—very, very secret. It is under Building Four, Level B5. We no go there. None of my people go there. They have their own cleaning people."

"Oh, yeah?" Spence stepped forward. "If it's so secret, how do you know about it?"

Ruiz looked around again. "All these scientists think they so smart and we so dumb. One Saturday when they cleaner off, they make big mess in their cafeteria in Building Four, Level B4. They make me come in to clean. They talk like I stupid Latino who doesn't understand English. I hear them say, 'Don't let him near Section Five. We'll lose our jobs. He shouldn't be here even.'"

Munoz smiled, patted the man on the shoulder, and turned to Young. "Section Five. Sounds close enough."

"What's the fastest route?" Young asked.

Munoz thumbed over his shoulder. "Back up the elevator, across the courtyard—"

"No, no." Ruiz touched Munoz's sleeve. "Go past elevators. Take long hall on the other side. All the way to end. There is a door that says "Cleaning Storage Uno, er, One. Go inside. That is a special hall in very back leading to Building Four. At end, go down the stairs two floors. Somewhere there is way into Level Five, I think. I have never gone down, but I see the scientists and guards go many times."

Bear extended his hand. "Thank you, Mr. Ruiz. We won't tell anyone you helped."

"Gracias. I lose my job."

Young threw a chin down the hall. "Let's go. Time might save lives."

Bear led the way with Young, Spence, and Munoz following. It took them another ten minutes to navigate Munoz's instructions and find Cleaning Storage One. When they did, it was locked with a high-security lock and electronic keypad.

Munoz's access card wouldn't open it. "Now what?"

Bear reared back and slammed his foot into the door just below the lock. It took three kicks to break it in. On the third one, the door weakened, and Bear crashed through it with his shoulder.

Bear said, "See, it's open."

Another five minutes and they emerged from the tunnel at the stairwell leading down into Building Four. At the bottom of the stairwell two floors down, they reached a metal security door. It had a CCTV camera above it and no keypad or identifiable locks on the outside. The placard in the center of the door read "Special Access Only. Deadly Force Authorized."

"Section Five." Bear turned to the others. "Any ideas how we get in?"

A voice came over a speaker in the CCTV camera.

"Gentlemen, please identify yourselves. This is a restricted area."

Young patted Munoz's shoulder. "Thanks, we got this now. You can't be part of this. Thank you, and off you go. Leave your access card with me."

Munoz handed Young the card, hesitated, and then jogged back up the stairs.

Young held up his FBI credentials toward the CCTV camera.

"FBI. We have a search warrant. Open the door."

The voice responded, "No, sir. I'm not authorized to allow you access. Please return—"

Bear tugged his pistol and aimed it at the door handle. "Open the door, or I'm shooting my way in."

A few seconds went by—a few long, silent seconds. Finally, the door clicked and popped open.

They cautiously stepped inside.

Two black-clad commandos outfitted with full tactical gear stopped them inside the door. They held M4 carbines aimed at them chest-high.

Chapter Fifty-Five

I don't know how long Sally and I had been in our glass prison after Smith and Charles Pellman left on their treasure hunt. We stood there watching Aaron Pellman at his workstation. We'd tried to discuss an escape plan. That proved pointless. Each time we considered a new one, Aaron looked up, shook his head, and laughed sarcastically.

He would gawk at us, laugh, giggle, and generally acted like he was checking out of Hotel Sanity.

"What are we going to do, Sally?" I had no expectation of a good answer. "We're trapped."

"It'll be all right, Oliver." Sally glanced at Pellman. "We'll be fine."

Sure, if I didn't mind dying a hundred times over again.

An hour later, Pellman went to the rear laboratory doors and disappeared through them. When he returned, he dragged Kerrie Garcia and Emily close behind. Each time Emily resisted and tried to free Kerrie from his grasp, he shook her. Hard. Once, he released Kerrie just long enough to strike Emily in the face. The last strike sent her tumbling down the raised platforms to the floor outside our cell.

"Leave them alone, Pellman," I yelled. "They've done nothing but help you."

He kicked Emily hard and sent her backward against the corner of a workstation desk. Kerrie grabbed him and tried to pull him away. Pellman spun her around and shoved her down beside her mother.

"You little brat," he yelled. "You've been holding out on me for weeks about these two ghosties."

"No." Kerrie's face was flush, and her eyes flared in fear. "I helped you."

"Kerrie, do as he says," I called. "He'll hurt you if you don't."

Pellman hovered over her with his fist coiled to strike. "You've been lying. I have the session recordings, and I saw the brainwave printouts. I know what you've been up to, Kerrie—you've been talking to them. You've tried to stop my research."

Emily sat up beside Kerrie. "You're mad, Aaron. Evil. All we want is to leave here and be left alone. We won't tell anyone. Let us go. Please. I beg you."

"Let you go? Ha." Pellman laughed maniacally and returned to his workstation. "You're going to help me. We're going to be very, very close. You'll see."

Sally moved to the cube wall. "Kerrie, listen to me. You know what you have to do. Don't be afraid."

Kerrie stood and turned to Sally. She slowly closed her eyes. "Okay, Miss Sally."

"Don't talk to her, kid," Pellman bellowed. "You answer only to me. You know what happens if you don't."

"Do you know what happens?" Kerrie lowered her head. Her voice was low and curt. Her face suddenly tightened with a concentration I've never seen in a child. "You won't hurt us anymore."

"What?" Pellman slammed his fist on the workstation and jumped up. "What did you say to me?"

Damn. Aaron Pellman was as batshit crazy as Smith.

I said, "Emily, don't worry about us. Protect your mom and yourself."

"Oliver, it's all right." Sally touched my arm. "Let her go."

"Aaron, I won't do anything for you again." Kerrie's face broke out in a big, mischievous grin. She lifted her chin and stared at Pellman with an ominous, laser focus. "I won't help you."

Pellman's anger boiled over. He ignited the cube's force field and sent Sally and me into hell again. Sally resumed her tiptoe dance, replaying her hanging. I was murdered again. The bullet pierced my chest and sent me to the floor. It burned in pain and made me gasp for breath as I died. Sally gurgled as her life slipped away.

"No… no… stop…" Pellman cried in a shrill, terrified voice, "Stop."

Through my own agony, I managed to turn my head to see him.

He stood behind his workstation. His hands were raised above his head as though surrendering. His entire body thrashed around uncontrollably—a marionette in convulsions. His face was contorted into a dark, red mask. His eyes rolled, uncontrollably. His mouth was open, screaming without a voice.

Standing just outside our cube, Kerrie's hands were outstretched with fingers spread wide. She stared at Pellman with pure determination. She held him in some kind of control—some kind of force—and shook him side-to-side like a ragdoll. Then, without warning, she dropped her hands and sighed.

Pellman collapsed on the laboratory floor. He tried to get up, but Kerrie pointed a finger at him and thrust her finger toward the floor. His body obeyed and smashed itself backward with a thud.

He cried out again—his voice a quiver of fright and pain.

As I watched Kerrie, the room began to fade to nothing. I was on the doorstep of my final end. The pain had driven me there, ready to push me over for the final time. For good. I didn't fight. Anything to stop the pain. Anything to let go.

Please… enough.

Angel's face flashed before my eyes. She stood with Hercule beside her. They were sad and alone. It didn't matter. I had to stop the pain. Had to …

Kerrie turned and lowered her head. She focused on our cell.

The cell shattered in a tornado of polymer and plasma.

The light rescued me just as I reached my end.

Sally dropped to her knees, gasping. She managed to crawl to me and help me to my feet.

The pain was gone as fast as it had taken me. Freedom.

"We're all right, Oliver," Sally gasped, cradling me in her arms. "Kerrie saved us."

It wasn't over. Not yet. On my knees, I saw the little girl ending Aaron

Pellman's research.

Kerrie stood in front of her mother and began a slow, steady turn. Her movements increased in intensity. She spun in a circle, one hand straight out, spinning and pointing like a child playing a game.

This was no game.

The room began to succumb. Workstations tumbled and crashed to the floor. The electronic wall screens shattered and crashed down. Desks imploded. Some crumbled into piles of plastic and metal. Others twisted into knots where they sat. All about us, electrical sparks flashed, and notebooks caught fire.

Kerrie continued to spin. "No more. No more."

The main laboratory doors flew open. Four armed men rushed in. They made it a step inside before Kerrie's torrent grasped them, lifted them, and propelled them back through the doorway.

Lights flickered. Sparks danced. The laboratory surrendered into scrap metal and debris.

Slowly, with a giggle and a broad smile, Kerrie Garcia – not Lee-Garcia, just Kerrie Garcia—stopped twirling and lowered her hand.

Somewhere, a fire alarm whooped.

"Tuck? Miss Sally?" Kerrie came to the crumbled cube walls as though she didn't notice the carnage. "Are you all right? I didn't hurt you, did I?"

"No, sweet child. No." Sally went to her and enveloped her in an ethereal embrace. "You did good. Thank you, Kerrie."

"You should go," Emily said, finally getting to her feet, "before more guards come."

"You and Kerrie come with us," I said. "It's not safe for you."

"Not yet." Kerrie pointed toward the door. "Someone needs me. We'll be all right."

"No, Kerrie." I waved my hand around the room. "You'll be in trouble if they catch you. They won't care that you're a kid."

"Don't worry, Tuck. I won't let them hurt us again." She turned to me. "You have to go. Colonel Smith took a helicopter to find the treasure. He's there now, but he's real mad. Something's wrong."

"Real mad?" I laughed—a strange reaction given the destruction around me. "Too bad for him."

Without warning, Kerrie collapsed.

"Kerrie!" I jumped over the cell debris and knelt by her. "Kerrie? Are you—"

"She'll be fine in a few moments." Emily lifted her into her arms. "She overdid it. It happens. With a little rest, she'll be all right."

I touched Kerrie's arm. "I'll stay with you, kid."

She opened her eyes and took my hand. "No, you don't understand, Tuck. I was so worried about here, I missed there. Colonel Smith has Angela. Charles is there, too. Angela's in danger. They're going to kill her."

Chapter Fifty-Six

Bear froze in his tracks. Young did the same. Spence nearly ran into them before realizing they were in trouble.

Two ADRI commandos had them at gunpoint. They stood in front of a large, chest-high security desk, weapons leveled. Their M4s were outfitted with modern site optics and, of all things, muzzle suppressors for quieting the gunfire they could rain down. They were aimed at them.

"Easy now, boys," Young said cooly. "I'm reaching into my pocket for my FBI credentials again."

"We've seen them," said a tall, beefy guy with a bushy, caveman beard. "Doesn't matter. Put your weapons on the ground and hands over your heads."

"That's not happening." Bear eyed them with an intensity that made both commandos ease back. "We've got a warrant. *You* are going to drop your weapons and step back. Put *your* hands on your heads, too."

The commandos exchanged glances. Neither complied, but they lowered their M4 muzzles noticeably.

"Stand by." The beefy guy tapped his radio affixed to his tactical vest. "Command 1, this is Five-Alpha. We have three detained—FBI. How should we proceed?"

There was a long silence. Then, someone in their command center replied. "Five-Alpha, stand by. The FBI's up here, too. We're trying to find Colonel Smith for orders."

"While we're waiting," Spence said, "how about we all put our guns at ease. I would hate to get shot by accident."

The commandos lowered their weapons a little more.

"Great." Young tapped his pocket. "I have a copy of the federal warrant. I can show it to you—"

The commandos' radios beeped, and the voice from the command center came on.

"Stand by for a message from Colonel Smith. All stations, stand by for Colonel Smith."

A few seconds ticked by before an electric click sounded three times. Then a little static before the voice came through loud and clear.

"This is Colonel Smith." It was a prerecorded message. "We are now in Security Condition 1. I repeat. Security Condition 1. No exceptions. Section Five, you will execute Broken Glass. Repeat, Broken Glass. Execute."

The two commandos stepped back and glanced at one another. Their faces drained of color as they lifted their weapons again. This time, not as surely.

"Ah, shit." Bear patted the air. "What's Security Condition 1?"

The beefy guy began sweating. "Don't worry about it, mister. Just don't make any sudden moves. If you do, we'll shoot."

"Shoot?" Young took a half-step forward and drew both rifle muzzles toward him. "I'm a federal agent. I have a federal warrant to search these premises. Colonel Smith is wanted as a federal fugitive for a variety of crimes, including treason, kidnapping, and murder. Unless you wish to be accessories, lower your weapons."

Both commandos ignored him and continued to glance uneasily toward each other.

The beefy guy shook his head. "I don't know about Broken Glass, Mitchell. I just don't know."

"Never expected it to happen, Drainer." Mitchell, smaller than Drainer but wiry and sharp-eyed, started breathing hard and sweating all the harder. "Nope. No way. I ain't killing no families."

Spence lifted a palm up. "What's Broken Glass, boys?"

"I ain't doing it." Drainer lowered his M4. "Security Condition 1 orders us to resist with all means. Total defense of this facility. But Broken Glass, well, shit—"

"Orders from the Colonel to eliminate all the research kids and their families down here," Mitchell added. "But no way. I ain't killing nobody. Especially kids."

"Okay, drop your weapons," Young ordered, eyeing them uneasily, should it be a trap. "And step back against and face the wall."

Drainer hesitated, looked at Mitchell, and waited for him to nod, and shrugged. "Yes, sir."

Both commandos slowly laid their weapons on the floor, turned, and spread-eagled against the rear wall.

Bear moved quickly to remove their sidearms as Spence and Young handcuffed them with their hands behind their backs. One by one, they turned them around and gestured for them to sit on the floor.

"Don't move, guys," Spence said, picking up one of the M4s. "You just saved your own lives."

Mitchell looked at each of them in turn, stopping on Young. "Look, agent, we're contract security. Pay-as-you-go. We're responsible for securing Section Five. But you gotta know, we haven't killed or hurt anyone. That's Smith and his oddball research team. Drainer and I post here every day. Never hurt—"

"Good. Now, you're going with Detective Spence back upstairs," Bear said. "The FBI will hold you until this is over."

Spence lifted the M4. "Anybody getting cute might get shot."

"How many others like you down here?" Young asked, looking toward two diverging corridors—one on either side of the security desk. "And where are they?"

Drainer thought a moment. "Three teams of two. There could be more coming from topside. There's a rear entry point. But that's a ways down the halls." Then he frowned. "There're rooms down both these halls. Way in, too. Maybe three on each side. But hurry, the other guys might not be as squeamish as us."

"They'll kill the families in here?" Young took one of the M4s from the floor. "How many families?"

"At least four that we've seen," Mitchell said. "But Smith and his people are pretty secretive. Even from us."

"Give me your access cards," Young said, holding up Munoz's he'd taken earlier. "I doubt this one works in here."

"It won't. Here." Drainer handed him a card. "They only work on certain doors, and the Command Post has to activate them each time we use it."

"Dual control," Mitchell said, handing his to Bear. "Keeps everyone honest."

"Yeah, honest." Young looked at Spence. "Spence, get these guys upstairs to me people. Then come back and protect our rear—bring more agents. Bear and I will each take a hallway and look for Professor Tucker and the others. "

"Copy." As Bear headed for the left hallway, he called back, "Don't take all day bringing backup, Spence. This could get ugly."

Chapter Fifty-Seven

After leaving Sally at ADRI to watch over Kerrie, I poofed onto the spook express to find Angel. This time, her fear was like a compass, and the moment I concentrated, I landed on a familiar rocky overlook deep in the Blue Ridge Mountains. It was the same place I'd joined Sally and her M35W crew earlier during my little jaunt back to 1864.

It was getting late, and the evening shadows cast the valley below in a blanket of blues and blacks, accented by the full moon and brilliant starlight. During my first visit, the valley was empty of any visible civilization. Now, there were thousands of lights dotting the valley where homes and businesses had grown the community in all directions.

The landscape had changed significantly, too. What had been a lush, wide valley had been transformed into a vast waterway. For the first time, it struck me how modern history might just have thwarted Smith's treasure hunt.

Back in the mid-sixties—the nineteen sixties—the Roanoke River had been dammed up to create Smith Mountain Lake. It was a twenty-one-thousand-acre man-made lake with more than five hundred miles of coastline. The coastline and surrounding area brimmed with life.

Tonight, the lake glimmered below me. It offered the overlook a spectacular, serene picture. If I hadn't been there to save Angel from a murdering traitor, I might have enjoyed the view.

Perhaps another time.

I landed just inside the trees, a dozen yards off the winding mountain road on the north end of the lake. On the other side, in the small clearing, were two of Smith's armed guards—probably hand-picked mercenaries named Jones and Jones. Altogether, there were six of them standing in a protective perimeter around me.

Smith stood at the rocky outcropping along the overlook. He held a heavy, multicell flashlight in one hand and a pistol in the other. He was focused on Charles Pellman, and Smith looked upset. Very upset.

Pellman was tinkering with the HEAP and refusing to look at anyone—Smith included. He kept his head down and focused on his work. When he finally looked around, he glanced at Angel, smiled a faint, embarrassed smile, and quickly looked away.

Did Charles Pellman have a crush?

Something tickled my thoughts—*Tuck, you're safe!*

Angel.

She sat on a large flat rock near the cliffside with one of Smith's men nearby. Piled around her were several hefty backpacks laden with outdoor gear. She looked terrified and dismayed all at the same time. But as I moved closer, her fear seemed to ebb away. She lifted her hands ever so slightly to show me her handcuffs.

"You all right, Angel?" I asked, stopping beside her. "How'd you get here?"

She nodded slightly and mouthed, "Helicopter. How are you? "

Smith stood over Charles and berated him. Twice, he nudged him with his foot and scolded him like a schoolboy. The security man by Angel was watching the discourse and moved closer to them. Maybe he felt sorry for Charles. Maybe he was ensuring there was no violent response from him.

He was out of earshot of Angel now.

Angel whispered, "I was with Mike Spence at White's compound. Smith was there and showed me a video of you in some kind of glass room. He said he captured you. I was terrified he'd killed you—for real. How'd you escape?"

"Later. I need to get you out of here. Spence?"

"He and I were separated at White's. It went badly. Bear and Nicholas were there and helping Smith. Smith took me hostage and told them to deal with White. First, he brought me somewhere near Dulles airport and then here by helicopter."

"Angel, I was there, too—at ADRI. They captured Sally and me."

"Oh, my God." Tears filled her eyes. "I've been terrified they'd kill you."

Yeah, me too. "Kerrie saved us."

"Little Kerrie?"

I shrugged. "More for later."

"Tuck, I think Bear…" she lowered her head. "I think he—"

"Later. Let's worry about you. What's going on here?"

She glanced around to make sure the guard still couldn't hear. "At White's compound, Smith took his family journal. It has clues to that silly Beale Treasure. They think it's real, Tuck. They're here to find it."

I remembered Sally jotting notes in a journal when I was here before.

"Angel, the treasure *is* real. Sally had a journal back in 1864. She made notes on the treasure's location. She knows where it is."

"I don't believe that." She gestured to Smith and Charles. Charles was cowering as Smith continued to badger him. "Tuck, the Pellmans are—"

"Triplets," I said. "Andrew is most likely dead—who killed him, I don't know. Aaron lost his mind, and Kerrie kicked his butt back at ADRI. This one, Charles, seems off, too."

"Poor Andrew." Angel lowered her eyes. "I think Bear killed him. Maybe Spence, too."

Jeez, Bear might have moved to the dark side a teensy-weensy bit—like treason and selling government secrets. That was bad enough. But murder?

"Aaron Pellman and Smith," she whispered, "have been stealing government secrets. White sells them to foreign buyers. They've both been trying to finance expeditions for that silly treasure. I don't know how Andrew or Charles fit into this. Andrew was a sweet, smart young man. Charles seems, well, a little shy and awkward. But he's here nonetheless."

Yeah, sweet and awkward. But the apples don't fall far from the grocery shelf.

I had a theory about sweet Andrew and awkward Charles. This ensemble of traitors and treasure hunters deserved each other. Aaron Pellman was batshit crazy and an evil genius. Bradley White was eccentric and power hungry. Someone needed to tell him the Civil War was over—that he lost a long time ago. As for Smith, well, he might be the sanest of the lot, and that was scary all by itself. Of course, he was the most evil. He was behind all this. He was a thief, traitor, murderer, thug, bastard, and a traitor. Oh, I said that one twice.

But Andrew and Charles?

The discourse between Smith and Charles grew. Smith belittled him for not having the HEAP ready—*after all, Aaron had prepared everything before they left ADRI*. Couldn't he follow simple instructions? When he compared him to Aaron, Charles glanced around, openly embarrassed. Smith didn't let up. He stood over him like an angry, disappointed parent. Charles worked on the HEAP, trying to block Smith out. Now and then, he'd look over at Angel and quickly return to his work.

I wandered over.

"Face it, it's gone, Colonel Smith," Charles stood and put his hands on his hips, looking at the ground. His face was awash in something odd—a mixture of embarrassment and disappointment? "What's the point? The treasure's gone. Smith Mountain Lake flooded it. It sunk the cabin, flooded the treasure's entrance, and obliterated any hope of finding it. The HEAP won't work underwater."

"Do what you're told." Smith stabbed at him with an angry finger. "The treasure vault could be underwater. We'll deal with that if it is. Do I need to get Aaron to do your work?"

"No." Charles walked away and dropped himself on a fallen tree. He dropped his head into his hands, pouting. "All my work—for nothing. You should have known. You should have—"

"How was I to know the markers would lead here?" Smith's voice became conciliatory. He tapped on his cell phone and a moment later, started to read. "But we have to try. Time is almost out. We have to find the markets and get the treasure. Now."

One of Smith's security men walked over. "Sir, I can take some men and scout out along the ridgeline and down the mountain. If there are markers, we'll find them. We're also SCUBA certified. If necessary, we can—"

"I can't swim. I can't." Charles jumped up in a panic, dropping the HEAP on the ground. "You can't leave me out of this. You promised. My brothers and I get our share. You promised. I want my share. But I can't swim."

Uh, oh, Charles Pellman was losing it.

Chapter Fifty-Eight

"Calm down, Charles. You'll get your shares. I'm sorry if I've been harsh," Smith gestured to Weaver. "Weaver, get your men and start the search. We'll worry about the lake later. Have one of your men secure the HEAP. Charles needs to rest."

Weaver, the chief guard, headed for Charles.

"No." Charles jumped back. His hands flew in front of his face in a defensive stance. "Don't touch me. Don't touch me. Stay away. Colonel Smith, tell him to stay away."

"Easy, Charles." Weaver patted the air and picked up the HEAP from where Charles had dropped it. "I'm just going to carry this for you. No one will hurt you. I'll give it back when it's time."

"Yeah?" Charles's face blanched, and his eyes dropped to the ground. He lowered his hands and backed away. "Promise?"

Weaver nodded. "Sure, kid. I promise."

I watched Charles quaking in his boots. "Angel, Charles is, er, not doing well."

"No, I see," she whispered. "He's nothing like Aaron or Andrew."

"I'm sorry, Colonel Smith. I'm sorry." Charles' voice was three octaves higher. "The HEAP is mine. You said so. No one can make it work but me. Don't let him take it away."

"Charles," Smith said with a calm voice. "Weaver's just going to carry it. You need to calm down."

"Promise?" Charles's face was scared and unsure. "Promise it's mine, and I can have some treasure?"

"Yes." Smith sounded like a consoling father. "My men will find the markers. If we need to dig it out with my—your—HEAP, you'll do that. After we find the treasure, we'll figure everything out."

Something told me that "everything out" included killing Charles and Angel. Once it was secured, I wondered how Weaver and the other Men-Wearing-Black would fare. You know, witnesses and all. My bet was they would get "figured out" too.

"Tuck?" Angel whispered. "They're all mad."

"Yep, but I have a plan." I didn't. But, at a time like this, she needed to think I did.

"No, you don't." So much for that.

Angel moved closer to Charles. When he turned and looked at her, she smiled a faint, friendly smile. "Charles, it'll be all right. I'm not sure the treasure's real. So go easy until we know. Okay?"

"No, Professor," Charles whispered, and glanced back at Smith. "The treasure *is* real. Sally said so. I heard her. Colonel Smith wants to hurt me and take the treasure for himself. I'm scared."

"Don't worry, Charles. I won't let them hurt you," Angel whispered back. "Stay close to me."

"Okay." He hesitated, then added, "I like you. You're nice to me."

"What are you two talking about?" Smith whirled around at her. "Sit down and shut up, Professor. I have enough to worry about."

"Do as he says, Angel." I felt a little breeze with the faint scent of jasmine blow through me. "Sally?"

She appeared beside me, seemingly indifferent to the others around us. "Oliver, there's another way to the treasure. Billy White and I found it days after discovering the main vault beneath the cabin. It's near the bottom of this ridge. It's very dangerous, but it can be used."

"Another way in?" I thought about that. "Why tell them? Why not just escape?"

"There are too many of them. They will harm Angela without reason to keep her safe. Use the information to protect her." She walked to the edge of the overlook and looked down over Smith Mountain Lake. She seemed distant just then. She sighed and closed her eyes. "I want to move on and let this all go. I died for the treasure's secret. Now, it's not a secret any longer. Let them have the treasure, Oliver. Help me go."

The glistening in Sally's eyes told me she was right.

I told Angel everything.

"Smith," Angel called. "There's a second tunnel to the treasure vault. I don't know if it's flooded like the main entrance, but you can try."

Smith eyed her with a suspicious glare. "How do you know?"

"Tuck told me. Yesterday." Angel was flying solo. "Sally confided in him. I know how to find it."

"Oh, you do?" Smith considered her warily. "A moment ago, you said the treasure was fake. Now you say there's another way to it."

"I still think it's fake." Angel shrugged. "But Tuck and Sally didn't. I'm not telling you everything all at once. I'm not stupid, Colonel."

Smith's forced laugh unnerved me. "I'm listening."

"I don't care about treasure," Angel said. "But if I help you find it, you let me go. As powerful as you are, I'll stay quiet. I know you could kill me anytime. No one would believe me anyway."

Smith seemed satisfied. "Professor, all I want is the treasure. My friends will deal with the aftermath. The treasure has much more than just monetary value. But first and foremost, it will allow me to escape and find sanctuary."

So, that was his hurry. He knew the feds were closing in. —Kerns murder proved that. And while he had some cash from the sales of secrets, he needed more. Wanted more. The Beale Treasure was that more. He must have known the feds were about to grab him.

"I can help you find it."

"It's mine, too." Charles stood alongside Angel. "Tell him, Professor. Tell him it's part mine."

"Of course, Charles." Smith patted the air again and tried to appease him. "But we have to find it first."

"Do we have a deal?" Angel looked hopefully at Smith.

Smith nodded.

Angel asked, "Charles? Okay with you?"

Charles looked between Smith and Angel several times. Then, Charles leaned close to her.

"Professor, don't trust him."

"I know, Charles." She put her arm around him. "Don't worry, I don't."

Smith pointed at him. "No whispering, Charles. No secrets. Remember?"

"Yes, sir." Charles looked at his feet.

"Good," Smith said. "Professor, you should take care of Charles. I need him to operate the HEAP if it comes to that. He's the only one who can. He's a child at heart. But he's a genius with electronics."

"All right, Colonel," she said. "I'll keep him close."

Smith stepped up to her. "I have Sally and your husband at ADRI. Don't forget that. Any trickery or attempts to escape, and I'll have Aaron kill them both—*permanently.*"

"Don't hurt him, please." Angel gave an Academy Award performance. "I promise—I'll show you the way to the treasure and won't go to the police. Just don't hurt him. Please. I beg you."

"If he only knew, Angel," I said. "Idiot."

Sally walked to Smith and looked him over head to toe. "This man bears a striking resemblance to Captain Little. He is as devious and traitorous, too. A fine family heritage."

"All right, Professor," Smith said. "We have an understanding."

Sally wandered to the overlook, trying to reorient herself. She seemed lost in nostalgia—staring out again and deep in thought. "Oliver, when I returned to Winchester back in sixty-four, I intended to keep all this to myself. I thought that would ensure my safety. No one knew but Billy and me about what we found—and where. Captain Little's men killed us before we could reveal anything."

I told Angel, and she repeated it for the others.

"You see, Colonel," Angel said confidently. "I'm the last link to the treasure. Any trickery or attempts to harm me or Charles would be the end of your Beale Treasure."

Chapter Fifty-Nine

Smith had planned well for this treasure hunt. He'd brought headlamps, flashlights, climbing gear, water, freeze-dried food, and other equipment. As his guards packed up, I couldn't help but think about Jules Verne's *Journey to the Center of the Earth*. Except we weren't going to the center of the earth. And we didn't have Hans the behemoth duck guy carrying all the heavy stuff. And I doubted there were dinosaurs waiting for us inside the mountain—geez, I hope there weren't any.

Oh, and we didn't have Gertrude the duck, either.

"Let's begin." Smith waved at his men. "Weaver, Cominsky, Allan, and Reynolds will accompany us. You other two will secure this site for our return."

Everyone gave the traditional, "Yessirs."

After gearing up, the descent down the mountain began. We picked our way down through the trees, descending at shallow angles, traversing lower and lower. In the dark, it was hard to tell just how far from the mountain's edge we were. We were in the trees, and at any moment, we could step over the edge into nothing and down.

Well, not me, of course.

I stayed close to Angel and helped her navigate without breaking an ankle or taking a fatal step. Luckily, I could see better than them even without a headlamp. And I had Sally guiding me.

Sally came and went. Mostly, she went. Oh, sure, whenever Angel needed to give a course correction to Smith, she popped up a few yards ahead of us. Then, after steering us, she poofed away again. When I asked her why she didn't just stay with us, she was vague and mysterious. What could she possibly have to do that was more important?

"I'll be close, Oliver. Do not fret."

This was a dangerous place. A precarious mountainside that offered loose rocks and narrow footing. The trees were thick and provided the perfect blind against the mountain's cliffs and ledges, where we might wander and plummet to our deaths. Well, they're deaths. There were rockfalls blocking the best path down. Double-backing offered no respite to the wary march, just added time.

But so far, no dinosaurs.

Our expedition weaved farther and farther down. One of Smith's guards led us, next was Angel giving directions, then Smith, Weaver, Charles, and three more guards.

After two hours, we found a small, level landing. It was just large enough for the entire group to drop their packs and relax.

"Oliver, come with me." Sally appeared and beckoned me through a thick stand of trees. On the other side, just a few steps through, was the mountainside's treachery. A ledge of fallen rocks with a dead drop over the edge. The fall below was a hundred feet.

"Tell Angela to be very careful coming through this area." Sally turned and looked back toward the others. "I would not warn Smith and his men. It would be a shame to lose them. No?"

"Gotcha." If push came to shove, I'd push and shove. "I understand."

We returned to the others in the clearing.

I went to Charles. He was clearly the odd child among Andrew and Aaron. I always thought Andrew was a bit odd, too—mostly because of his infatuation with Angel. But he was bright and outgoing and had no noticeable mad scientist traits. Aaron, well, he held all the Frankenstein genes. Charles was different. He was immature, often child-like in his adult body. I've heard that geniuses could be like that.

Smith had Charles along for one reason—the HEAP. After he operated that, Charles would most likely have an accident. Like a slip over the ledge accident.

Oddly, I felt bad for him.

Smith was focused on the treasure. Dangerously focused. That might give Angel a chance to escape. If not, I might have to arrange for Smith to enjoy the view of the lake during a hundred-foot rapid descent.

Would that be bad?

Weaver had reconnoitered through the trees where Sally and I had been. When he emerged again, he waved at Smith.

"Sir, there's a dangerous ledge through those trees. A fresh rockfall. We'll have to find another way down."

Smith glanced at Angel. "Professor? Did you steer us wrong? Remember my warning."

"Don't be stupid, Colonel," she said. "I didn't know there was a rockfall."

Sally appeared and said, "Return uphill for a hundred feet. I will scout ahead and find a path."

Instructions were delivered, and the expedition set off uphill.

Once we reached another easy stopping spot along our route, Sally appeared and began reorienting herself once more. I guess after one hundred sixty years, things were different.

"Oliver, turn north near the large rock overhang over there." She pointed through the darkness at a behemoth outcropping that jutted out from the mountainside like a monument. "It's very steep, but it's the only way to bypass that lower ledge."

I informed Angel, who explained to Smith.

He was not amused. "I thought you said you knew the way down?"

"I know what I was told." Angel crossed her arms. "It's dark, and finding the way is more difficult. I've never been here. I'm going by what Sally told Tuck."

Smith grabbed her by the arm. "Professor, you need to be very, very careful. If I doubt you—"

"No," Charles yelled and shoved Smith away from her. "Don't hurt Professor Tucker."

"Oh?" Smith's face twisted in amusement. "All right, Charles. All right."

I went to Smith, leaned close, focused with all my might, and whispered,

"Boo, asshole. Touch her again, and we'll meet on my side."

He startled backward and swiped his ear as though a bee had buzzed him. He turned back to Angel.

"Professor, is Detective Tucker about?" He glanced around nervously. "Is he?"

"Tuck? You have him." She looked at him with a wrinkled brow. "Why else would I be helping you?"

"Forget it." He swatted his ear again. "You will lead, Professor. If we walk into danger, you'll go over first."

"I'll go with you," Charles whispered. "I won't let him hurt you."

"Thank you, Charles." Angel patted his arm. "Stay close."

Angel moved carefully through the brush to the overhang. A narrow pathway, naturally cut through the rock and nearly impossible to see, lay ahead. At the rock base, crudely chiseled into the rockface was 'M35W.'

"Here, Colonel," Angel called back. "Proof."

Smith pushed past two of his men and shone his headlamp on the rock.

"Well, well, Professor. Very good. You might survive yet."

Sally appeared ahead of us again. "Tuck, follow that path. It is a steep slope down and turns several times. Once at the bottom, have Angela stop and stay away from the edge."

I told Angel. "Got it?"

She nodded and started off.

Angel picked her way down. She used the three-point climbing technique—with two hands and two feet, she always had three of those points secured. Only one moved at a time. It slowed descent considerably, but she was stable and unlikely to fall.

Smith was behind Cominsky, who followed Angel. He became impatient and shoved Cominsky ahead of her. "Move us faster, Cominsky. Tick tock."

Cominsky stumbled passed Angel. He tried to take short hops down the slope to increase the pace. On the third hop, he lost footing and began to slide. He fell sideways and grappled for a handhold. He looked back at Angel, and even in the dark, the terror in his face was palpable. For a second, he regained control. Then, as he tried to turn around and continue his descent, he slipped again.

"Don't move." Angel scurried down to reach for him. "Take my hand. Slowly."

He twisted sharply and thrust out his hand. His fingers reached for hers. They never touched.

Cominsky slid out of control another ten feet down on his back. He backpedaled, trying to brake himself. Then, with a gut-wrenching scream, he disappeared over the ledge. His voice reverberated for several seconds until his terror went silent.

"Oh, my God," Angel gasped. "No."

Charles grasped her arm and pulled her back, easing her against the trail wall.

"Angel, don't do that again." I caught up to them. "Don't try and save anyone. They'll pull you over, too."

Tears welled in her eyes and glistened in her headlamp light.

"All right, it's over. Move on," Smith barked, indifferent to Cominsky's loss. "We have to move on."

Angel cast a hateful glance at him and started down.

Thirty more minutes of agonizing, slow descent brought us to a small flat landing. It was riddled by a fresh rockslide. The landing was barely twenty feet long and five feet wide. An outcropping of trees blocked the ledge from the west side of the path adjacent to where we'd emerged. What was beyond was hidden in darkness.

"We're here, Oliver." Sally pointed to the tree outcropping. "There's a cave through there. Inside is the tunnel entrance. The treasure is deep inside and below us."

Chapter Sixty

"We're here." I gave Angel the news. She told Smith, and I waited for her to sit down and sip from a canteen of water. "Angel, you can't go into this mountain. It's too dangerous."

She turned her head so no one would hear. "What's your plan?"

"Ah, I'm working on it."

"Great." She turned to Smith. "We need to rest, Colonel. Then we'll find the opening."

"Good girl, buy me some time." I looked for Sally. "Sally, we need a plan." Nothing. Not even a whisp of a parasol.

We were much closer to Smith Mountain Lake now. It lay less than fifty feet below us. The blanket of stars and the bright moon made the water shimmer mysteriously. Though it was somewhere around midnight, there were still a few house lights breaking through the trees around the lake. Around us, the night cast long tree shadows like soldiers standing post—perhaps guarding the Beale Treasure. Perhaps planning to be our pallbearers if we continued searching for it.

As Smith and the others rested, a few bats swooped around us, eating bugs we disturbed. If I weren't dead, I would have freaked out and jumped.

Okay, I still jumped.

Charles sat alone several yards away, watching everyone. He was like a fly. His head twerked side-to-side. He looked at Smith, then each of his men, and back to Smith. He repeated it over and over. His eyes never stopped twitching.

"Charles," Angel said. "Are you all right?"

He turned to her. "Yes, Professor. I just know they're going to hurt me and steal the treasure."

His demeanor proved one thing—the promise of riches and treasure brings about one certainty—*paranoia*. Just as Humphrey Bogart. You know, *Treasure of the Sierra Madre.*

I sat with Angel and tried to formulate an amazing, brilliant plan. Considering the number of Smith's armed men, and Charles, too, I couldn't even come up with a mediocre plan.

Smith stood and surveyed the area. He wandered to an opening in the rock outcropping.

"Through here, Professor?" he said. "You're sure?"

"Yes, be careful. There's a cliff on the other side of the rocks. You have to get around it to reach a cave. It's very dangerous." Angel saw me frown, and then she whispered, "I won't be responsible for his death."

I, on the other hand, had no problem being responsible.

Smith pushed into the trees and scrub brush. When he re-emerged, he directed two guards back in his wake. "Mr. Allan, past the rocky outcropping is a narrow, steep ledge. Follow my path and find the cave entrance."

The men stood and followed orders.

Fifteen minutes ticked past.

Allan, a short, slender African American, emerged from the trees on the run. He was wildly out of breath like he'd run a marathon. His eyes were big and scared. When he reached us, he bent over to put his hands on his knees and gasped for breath.

"Sir, Reynolds is dead. We got around the cliff ledge. We found the cave opening like the professor said. Right inside the cave is a blind turn and a crevasse. Reynolds went into it. He's gone, sir."

"Unfortunate, Mr. Allan." Smith turned to Angel with a scowl. "Professor? Your doing?"

Angel sounded indignant. "No. Not any more than you killed Cominsky."

Smith shrugged.

"I didn't know about the crevasse." She went to Allan and handed him some water. When she turned back to Smith, her eyes were fiery. "I'd never intentionally harm anyone—not even you. It must be new since Sally was here. It's been a hundred and sixty years, after all. Perhaps—"

"Yes, perhaps." He studied her. He seemed to be deciding if she intentionally sent his men to be killed. Then, his face eased, and he cocked his head. "You did warn me, after all."

Angel folded her arms as fear simmered in her eyes. The thought of Reynolds' death weighed on her, despite our situation.

"It's not your fault, Angel," I said. "You warned them."

"Colonel Smith," Charles said, moving closer to the group. "I can use the HEAP to cut a new entrance to the tunnel. It won't take but a few minutes. The HEAP—"

"Slow down, Charles." Smith studied the mountainside where piles of fallen rock from previous slides had carried trees and debris around us. "No, Charles. The mountainside's unstable. You go blasting away, and it might collapse the tunnel inside. We'd never find our way through."

"Sure, sure, okay." Charles shifted his weight and looked at Weaver carrying the HEAP. "I'll save it for emergencies. I want to help. I can, you know."

"I know, Charles." Smith shook his finger at him. "I'm not going to hurt you."

Liar.

"Professor," Smith said. "Do you know the tunnel path to the vault?"

I flashed a warning look at Angel. "Say no. You can't go in there."

"Yes." She lifted her chin in a defiant gesture. "I do."

Oh crap. What was she thinking?

"You might have said so sooner."

She glared at Smith. "I'm not stupid, Colonel. I'm telling you a little at a time. Including the safest way *back* from the vault."

"I see." He laughed gruffly. "Then we'll take very good care of you *inside.*"

I asked, "Angel, what are you doing?"

She eyed me with a half-grin. She knew I had no plan. She was making her own.

I turned around, looking for Sally. She was nowhere still. "Sally? Come on, Grandma, I need your help. We have to—"

The breeze turned cold, and jasmine filled the air.

Sally poofed in near Angel and wagged a finger at me. "Call me grandma again, Oliver, and I'll give you a whippin', boy."

Gulp. "Yes, ma'am."

"Oliver, Angela will be fine." Sally walked to the trees where Allan had emerged. "Just follow my instructions—carefully. One wrong step in there can be deadly. Fear not. I have a plan."

"Tell me."

She faded as quickly as she'd arrived. "Stay to the right inside the cave entrance. Hug the wall as tightly as possible. There is a crevasse just inside, as Allan said. It is very dangerous. I will guide you further once there."

"Right. But what's your plan?"

She was gone.

I hoped she didn't lie about having plans like I do.

"Take it slow now, Angel. We have to wait for Sally's directions further in."

Smith suddenly waved at Weaver, Allan, and Charles. "Stay alert, men. We have to move quickly. Time is running out. Let's get moving."

"Those tunnels could be small, Colonel Smith." Charles gestured to Weaver, carrying the HEAP. "The HEAP might help open them a little. I'll carry it now."

"All right, Charles." Smith feigned a smile. "But do not use the HEAP unless I say so. We don't want to collapse a tunnel."

Charles was pleased. "Okay. Thank you."

Smith ordered some of the climbing gear donned. Everyone put on a helmet, knee pads, and heavy leather gloves. The remaining gear was stowed in their individual backpacks along with water and other equipment.

"After you, Professor." Smith pointed toward the trees. "Slowly."

Angel led us toward the cliff's edge—Charles behind her, Allan, Smith, and Weaver in line. I stayed alongside Angel, making sure she was steady and confident.

If only I were.

The mountain ledge was about two feet wide. The rock outcropping made it difficult to traverse, forcing them to go one handhold at a time. A large boulder jutted out from the mountain and partially blocked the ledge ahead of us. Easing inch by inch, Angel picked her way forward. Although Smith had already lost two men to falls, he pressed her to move faster.

She ignored him.

Reaching a large boulder, she found handholds shoulder high and began sliding her left foot ahead, hugging the rock. She found another and moved her left hand ahead. Her hand slipped, and she lost her footing. For a precarious few seconds, she hung by one hand and tried to regain her footing.

"Angel," I cried. "Hold on."

"I'm good," she called back, more for me than the others. "I'm okay."

Moving even slower now, she finally reached the narrow cave opening. There, Angel hesitated. The mouth of the cave was partially secreted between two halves of a large, jagged rockface. She inched ahead, keeping her body pressed into the mountain wall and prodding ahead with one hand—one handhold at a time. Finally, she reached the cave.

The cave entrance was barely wide enough for her to slip through. Smith was stocky and robust, and his men were nearly as bulky. They were going to struggle.

What a shame. Imagine if one got stuck and blocked the others?

"Colonel, I'm not sure all your men can make it through." Angel pressed herself against the wall. "You'll barely fit."

Smith moved up behind her and cautiously shone his headlamp inside. "We'll make it. It opens up just a couple feet inside. I'll go first, you second. Charles and my men last."

"We should tie ourselves in line."

"Not yet. Once I get inside, I'll secure a line for everyone."

"All right." Angel leaned backward to give him more room to pass without slipping off the ledge. "You're in charge."

"I am." Smith barked orders to his men. Then, he removed his small pack and stuffed it into the cave entrance. "Wish me luck."

"Not likely," I said.

I moved inside and called to Angel, "Angel, this place is creepy. When you come in, stay to the right. That crevasse is only a couple feet inside on the left."

The cave was a small chamber shaped like a hand with its five tunnel-fingers spreading out ahead. Some fingers were so narrow no one would make it through. One was a narrow crawlspace just above the floor. Two others were possibly the correct tunnel. The crevasse, about four feet wide, split the cave nearly in half. Anyone inside would have to jump over it to reach three of the tunnels.

Sally's voice popped into my head—*It's the tunnel on the far right just above the floor. You have to crawl. It opens about three feet inside. Be careful. Once you begin crawling, you cannot return.*

Of course, it was the crawly, scary tunnel. What did I expect?

A second later, grunting and breathing hard, Smith squeezed through the cave entrance and inside.

"There, it's not bad," Smith yelled back. "Come through, Professor. Pack first."

Angel's pack slid through the entrance and fell beside Smith's. A few seconds later, she inched in, easily slipping between the rocks. Inside, she stopped and turned slowly, letting her headlamp illuminate the cave. Her light stopped at the crevasse's edge. Without her headlamp, she would never have seen it.

"Colonel, we won't all fit in here at once," she said. "Not until we find the tunnel."

He agreed and called out. "Charles, you and Weaver wait until we find the treasure tunnel. Then you may join us."

A grunting, raspy voice—Charles—called, "Don't leave me, Colonel Smith. You promised. I'm coming."

A second later, Charles's pack crushed through the cave entrance and landed beside the other two. Then, muttering and gasping, Charles pressed himself through the opening. He got stuck momentarily as he reached the inner chamber. He grunted and forced himself through. He fell once inside, stumbled over his pack, and he crashed into Smith.

Smith yelled and tripped backward into Angel, sending her reeling.

"Tuck!" Angel crumbled to the ground and rolled into the crevasse.

Smith dove after her. He grabbed her arm the moment she slipped over the crevasse edge. But he was off balance and went down hard onto his knees. "I've got you, Professor."

"Hold on, Angel," I yelled and grasped Charles' headlamp. The surge of electricity was weak and didn't provide me with enough power to help. "Hold on."

Smith held her arm tight. He fought for balance to reset himself onto his feet and lift her up. He could find no leverage.

Angel slipped farther down. The darkness began to swallow her.

Chapter Sixty-One

Bear stalked down the corridor of ADRI's Section Five. CCTV cameras and odd, electronic light bars were positioned above every doorway. Each was red. It felt like he was moving through some spaceship in a science fiction movie. Each time he passed one of the doors, the light bars above the doorway flashed until he passed. Then, they returned to steady red.

The corridor was lined with high-security doors on both sides. Most of the doors were windowless, made of steel with heavy security locks and electronic keypads. Others were thick, heavy glass or transparent polymers. Each glass door had a keypad and a small speaker with push-to-talk controls on the side. The lights above those doors were also red/

He stopped and looked through one of the glass doors. There was only darkness and empty space inside.

He'd traveled deeper into Section Five. How deep, he didn't know. There had been at least two dozen steel doors and as many glass doors along the corridor. All the lightbars atop the glass doors were a steady red light and didn't change color as he passed, like the steel door's lights did.

"What the hell is all this?" He said to no one.

He continued to the far end of the corridor to a "T" intersection. Only darkness and rows of red lights waited on either turn to left or right. Neither was inviting.

He turned right.

There was a dim, white light ahead on the left side. He jogged to it and found one of the glass doors. The light above it was yellow and flashing slowly. Inside, instead of a dark, empty space, was a small apartment. It was furnished with a couch and two chairs. There was a television on one wall. Books were stacked on a coffee table in the center of the room. On the left side was an alcove with a small refrigerator and a round dinette table with two chairs. In the rear of the room, just beyond a short hallway, was a closed door. A bedroom?

This must be where Smith keeps his research subjects—prisoners by any other account.

He tried the glass door. It was locked. Then, he tried to call Young and Spence on his cell phone. No signal. He dared not use the commandos' radios for fear of bringing more of them to him.

Moving on, he came to another "T" intersection. This time, he turned left. There were three more white lights in the distance. Two on the left and one on the right. The door on the right had a steady green light above it. He jogged to that one.

Another little apartment identically furnished. This time, it was occupied.

A young woman, perhaps late twenties, sat on the couch watching the television mounted on the wall. On the floor at her feet was a young child of perhaps ten. The little boy was drawing pictures on a notepad.

Bear banged on the glass door and startled them. "Sheriff's Department. Open the door."

The woman's face froze in shock. She jumped up, came to the door, and shook the knob. She showed him it was locked. There was a speaker just inside the door similar to the one on Bear's side. He punched the talk button.

"I'm Captain Braddock," Bear said. "I'm here with the FBI to rescue you. Can you open the door?"

The woman pushed the speaker button on her side. "No. Only the guards can unlock the doors. You must leave. If they catch you down here, we'll be punished."

Punished?

He retrieved the access card Mitchell had given him. When he pressed it against the outside security lock, the light turned red. He dared not call the command center, or they'd know what he was up to.

Bear pointed to the back hall. "Go into the other room. I'm going to get you out."

The woman froze as he pulled out his handgun. Then, understanding what he was going to do, she turned, scooped up the little boy. She ran into the back room and slammed the door behind her.

Bear checked the hall in both directions. Then, he fired two shots from his nine-millimeter pistol into the electronic lock beside the door. The lock sparked and flamed. When the door didn't immediately open, he fired a third at the base of the door near its lowest hinge.

The door wobbled but didn't open.

"Not today." Bear fired another shot—another—into the glass.

Finally, the door succumbed and shattered onto the floor.

"Come out. It's safe."

Cautiously, the woman and little boy appeared from the rear room.

"Let's go." Bear holstered his pistol. "Are there others?"

"Yes, three others like us." The woman clutched the little boy close. "We only see them sometimes. Always the same three families. We know one of them—we've been tested with her. But please, we don't want any trouble."

Families? Tested? White hadn't lied. Smith was experimenting on these people.

"Mister," the little boy said. "I'm Simon. This is my mom, Celeste. We've been here for a long time. Are you really gonna save us?"

Bear knelt. "Yes, I am, Simon. I'm Bear."

"Hi, Bear. That's a funny name."

"It is." Bear gave his shoulder a comforting squeeze. "Why are they holding you here, Celeste?"

"Mom?" Simon looked to his mother. When she nodded, he looked up at Bear. "They make me do things. You know, with my mind. They make me try things all the time."

What? "Celeste, are you two all right?"

Slowly, she shook her head. "Not really. First, they promise us housing and money. All we had to do was let them test Simon. It's been six months.

It's so much more than just tests. We live like prisoners. We cannot speak to anyone but them."

No more. Smith and ADRI were going down in flames.

Bear said, "Let's go. Stay close behind me. Do you know where the other families are?"

"No," Celeste said, pulling Simon close again. "But the guards will. We have to be careful. They might have the others in one of the labs that way." She pointed farther down the hall to the right. "Some of the guards are friendly. Most are not."

"All right." Bear gestured down the hall. There's a lot of FBI and cops here. I'll get you to them. Then I'll search for the others."

"Thank you. Thank you." Celeste stepped into him and hugged him. Simon crushed into him from the other side. "We couldn't go on much longer."

"It's over." Bear let them hold on another moment. He was not accustomed to shows of affection. "It's okay. Let's go."

They walked silently down the hall and reached another turn. There, they started around to the right.

"Halt right there," a booming voice commanded. "Don't move."

Two heavily armed commandos stood just ahead of them. Two others stood behind them, standing on either side of a steel door. The light above that door was steady green.

"Hold on, I'm a cop." Bear eased Celeste and Simon behind him. He carefully lifted his badge out of his pocket and held it up high. "I'm Captain Braddock. I'm with the FBI Task Force. This facility is under a federal warrant. Drop your weapons and back away."

The two commandos facing him grinned and lifted their M4 rifles toward him.

"Yeah, we heard about your raid, pal," one of them sneered. "But we're at Security Condition 1. That means you don't mean shit. Now you drop your weapons and get down on the floor. All of you."

One of the commandos said, "And you brought them to us. Great. You saved us the trip of getting you two."

Celeste and Simon clutched each other. Simon began to cry.

"Easy, now." Bear considered his odds—impossible. With Celeste and Simon behind him, any resistance would get them all killed. He might get one or two of them, but not four with the firepower they had. "Okay, boys. Easy now. I don't want them hurt."

"Too late. That decision has already been made," the first commando said coldly.

"Broken Glass?" Bear asked.

"You know about that?" The commando prodded his M4 toward him. "You should have thought about that before you interfered then—"

The commando's eyes suddenly bulged. His M4 carbine flew from his hands and clattered onto the floor. His arms and legs splayed out from his body as he levitated onto his tiptoes and rose farther.

The second commando was beside him now—his weapon on the floor. His arms and legs expanded from his body, too.

The two men hovered there, a foot above the floor—eyes big and round and scared. They looked like marionettes waiting for their puppeteer to make them dance.

"What in holy hell?" Bear gasped. "Celeste, Simon, get back."

"It's all right, Bear." Simon released his mom and stood beside Bear. "It's just Kerrie."

Chapter Sixty-Two

"Please, don't let go." Angel's head was barely above the crevasses' darkness that threatened to consume her. She dangled there. Her feet scraped the crevasse wall, trying to find footholds. Her free hand gripped the rock edge but couldn't grasp it safely.

"Charles," Smith yelled over his shoulder. "For Christ's sake, help me."

"I… I…" Charles got to his feet and looked on. "I'm so sorry. It's my fault."

Angel's terror exploded in my head. It swirled around—frantic and helpless—begging me to save her. That's what I needed—her deep, consuming terror summoned lit the first surge of power inside me. Then, she called me again, aloud this time. "Tuck, please—where are you?"

Lightning.

With one leap, I was beside Smith. I grabbed her arm just below Smith's grasp and heaved upward.

"I'm here, Oliver." Sally appeared, grabbed Angel's free hand, and heaved. "You are all right."

Slowly, we—the three of us—lifted Angel up and over the crevasse's edge.

"Angel?" I stepped back into the darkness as Smith dropped on his haunches and breathed a heavy sigh. "Sally, thank you. How come you don't need juice or anything like me?"

"Really, Grandson?" Sally raised her eyebrows. "I do believe I've been around a tiny bit longer. I know a few tricks that perhaps you do not."

Yeah, she did.

"Professor, I'm so sorry," Charles cried out. Tears ran down his face. "It's my fault. I'm sorry."

"It's all right, Charles. I'm okay." Then Angel looked at Smith. "Colonel, you saved me. Thank you."

"Charles?" Smith stood and aimed an angry finger at him. "You little bastard. Were you trying to kill us both?"

"No, no." Charles crawled back against the cave wall. "I tripped. It was an accident. I'm sorry. I am. It was an accident. Don't hurt me."

Angel stood awkwardly, still shaken. "Colonel, it was innocent, I'm sure."

"I'm not." Smith descended on Charles and dragged him to his feet. He slammed him against the wall several times. "I ought to toss your sorry ass into that hole, boy."

Charles cowered and lifted his hands to his face. "Colonel Smith, it was an accident. I swear. Don't hurt me."

"Dammit, boy." Smith drove a deep punch into Charles' stomach and doubled him over. "Stay out of my way. One more 'accident' and you'll have one of your own."

"Stop this." Angel shone her light on Smith. "Leave him alone."

Smith growled something and turned his back. He shone his headlamp around the cave as he tried to calm himself and study the stone chamber.

When Angel went to Charles to comfort him, Smith considered her. "Professor, you called for Tuck just now. Why?"

"I did?" She shrugged. "I don't know. Silly, right?"

"Perhaps." He shone his light around. "I'd swear, though, that someone— something—helped me lift you out of there."

Angel shone her headlamp at the crevasse ledge. "No, Colonel. I got a foothold just as you started to pull that last time. I helped lift myself out. That's all."

"It's my fault," Charles whimpered. "I'm sorry. I am."

"Charles," Angel said, helping him stand. "It's all right. It's done."

Allan suddenly slithered into the cave behind us. He looked at Charles, whimpering, and then Smith. "What happened?"

Smith explained and concluded with, "Allan, you're the smallest except for Professor Tucker. You'll lead from here."

Sally stood near the far wall. "Oliver, the entrance is this small tunnel opening, just above the cave floor." She leaned down and pointed to a small opening just above the floor. "It is passable."

I translated to Angel and she to the others.

"More information you haven't shared before, Professor." Smith shone his light on the small opening. "Allan?"

Allan lay on his belly and examined the tunnel entrance low on the cave wall. It was only about four feet wide and no more than two feet tall. It sat a foot above the cave floor, nestled into a natural cavity in the rock. Without Sally's help, it might have been overlooked in the darkness.

Behind us, Weaver snaked into the cave by lying on the ground and crawling through. The opening was wider at the bottom and easier to traverse, given his muscled, powerful physique. When he stood, he held up a large, electric lantern that illuminated the cave into near daylight.

"You all look tense," Weaver said.

Allan updated him on Angel's near death and the plan to enter the small, narrow tunnel next.

"You all right, Professor Tucker?" Weaver asked, gesturing to her cuts and scrapes from the crevasse edge. "You look a little scraped up."

Angel began brushing herself off. "Thanks, I'm okay. Smith saved me."

"Oh, really? Great." Weaver eyed Smith with a strange, conspiratorial frown.

Allan was still examining the tunnel entrance. "It's small, Colonel, but I can get through. I'll pull a line with me we can use to pull the packs through, and anyone who gets stuck."

I said, "Angel, let two of them go ahead of you to make sure it's safe."

"Professor, I'll go after Allan. You follow." It was as if Smith heard me. "Weaver, Charles is your responsibility. He will follow Professor Tucker. You last."

The tunnel entry began.

Allan clipped a carabiner to his belt and tied a climbing rope to it. Then, he gave the other end to Weaver. It took him a few moments to negotiate through the narrow tunnel opening into the mountain beyond. When the scraping and grunting stopped, there was only silence from inside the opening.

Then, a light beam flashed out to us.

"It widens ahead, sir," Allan called. "Just a foot inside the opening, it gets wider at the top, and it's an easy way through. I'm in a larger chamber now."

Smith acknowledged him, knelt, and slipped headfirst after him.

"Clear," Smith yelled back. "Send the equipment next."

"Angel, are you sure about this?" I considered finding more power in Weaver's large, electric lantern and taking him out. "Smith and Allan are inside. You might escape."

She glanced back at Weaver and then Charles. She shook her head and knelt to look into the tunnel entrance.

Using a hammer and pitons from his pack, Weaver carefully hammered two eight-inch pitons into the cave floor. He positioned them on opposite sides of the cave. Then, taking the end of the rope Allan had given him, he affixed it through each piton and secured the rope.

He saw Angel watching. "Allan secured the other end inside. Now, it's a secure line just in case we have to pull ourselves, or something else, back through when we get out."

"Good thinking." She slowly slithered inside the opening. A moment later, she called back. "I'm in. It's easy, Charles. Just don't stop moving."

"Okay, Professor." Charles didn't look okay. He started through. "I'll be okay."

Weaver entered last.

The darkness was intimidating, even with all their headlamps and Weaver's larger lantern. Inside the mountain, the surroundings were daunting and dismal—the air dry and stale—eerily silent except for the sounds of the expedition's tense breaths and unsteady noises moving around.

At any moment, flesh-eating mutants could pounce on us from the shadows. No, really, it could happen.

Inside the tunnel, Angel sat in the larger chamber with the others. She looked around slowly, nervous and intimidated by the prospects lying ahead. I gave her a few one-liners to help ease her mind, and occasionally touched her arm for comfort. Oh, and I never once mentioned flesh-eating mutants. Though I'm sure they were on her mind, too.

When I was younger, I'd always wanted to go spelunking. Except I was afraid of tight spaces, falling, dying, getting lost, and cannibal cave-dwellers. I saw this movie once about an expedition that got lost in a cave. They were set upon by—yep—cannibal cave-dwellers.

Needless to say, I never went into my basement in the dark again.

Chapter Sixty-Three

"Who is Kerrie?"

Simon pointed toward the first two commandos levitating ahead of us.

Without a word, the two wobbled in the air, flew across the corridor, and smashed into the wall. They hit hard and slid down. Their eyes snapped closed.

"Her." Celeste gestured to a young, dark-haired girl holding a woman's hand several yards behind the commandos. "With her mom, Emily."

Kerrie had one hand outstretched at the other two commandos guarding the steel door. She aimed her fingers like a gun. The men were frozen, too. Their weapons lay on the floor. They were both splayed backward against the corridor wall. Their faces were pale and tight—eyes bulging in shock and terror. They hung there a foot above the floor as though they were pinned in place.

"Kerrie Garcia?" Bear recognized her from the Handley Library. "Celeste?"

"Kerrie's happening, Bear," Celeste said. "She's the most powerful of the children. No one can explain it. Not Emily or that bastard, Smith. Kerrie can do many strange things."

Simon tugged Bear's arm. "You need to help her, Bear. She'll get very tired. She can't do this a lot, or she gets sick."

"Sick?"

Celeste said, "No one knows what will happen if she overdoes it. The last time she got close, she was in a coma for weeks."

"Right." Bear snatched up one of the M4 carbines. "Kerrie, Emily. I'm Captain Braddock. Remember me from the library? I'm here with the FBI to rescue you. You can stop now."

Kerrie's eyes closed, and she lowered her hand. She sat down at Emily's feet and dropped her head to rest.

The two commandos pinned to the wall fell onto their knees. They quickly got to their feet and grabbed for their weapons.

"Don't touch them," Bear barked. He jumped forward and kicked the first guard in the back of the legs and tumbled him onto the floor. "Move, and I'll shoot."

The second guard raised his hands as Bear's M4 barrel poked him in the cheek. "Got it, mister. We give."

Kerrie opened her eyes, but they were tired and red. "I remember you, Captain Bear. Everyone thought you were bad. I knew you weren't. I'm so glad you came. We have to help your friend."

Bear made short work of disarming the commandos and zip-tying their hands behind their backs with their own restraints. He repeated the process with the first two men still unconscious behind them.

"My friend? Kerrie, do you mean Tuck?" Bear asked. "Where is he?"

"No." Kerrie lifted her hand in a slow, lethargic move and pointed at the steel door with the green light on. "Your other friend."

* * *

Cal's eyes could barely see. His limbs were numb. The sounds outside were louder now—the first time in a very, very long time. He couldn't recall when he'd heard anything other than the drone voice interrogating him and the rhythmic *tap—tap—tap.*

This was different.

There was no tap-tap-tap. No warning. The room unexpectedly flooded with brilliant light and pulled him from his stupor. He'd been lost in his darkness of solitude too long. For the first time in days—at least, he thought it was days—he heard a door open behind him and felt the sudden presence of someone in his lonely isolation chamber.

His eyes struggled to open against the brightness. Was this his imagination? Perhaps it was a delirious hallucination from the lack of food and water. The lack of human interaction. Silence. Emptiness.

When he finally focused, he knew his time in the chamber was over. No more tap-tap-tap. No more questions. No more haunting demands he could not—or would not—answer. There would be no more isolation.

Two figures stood in front of him, one held a rifle.

He'd done what he could. He'd protected Angel and Tuck as long as he could.

Now, it was over for him.

A peaceful satisfaction enveloped him as he resigned himself to fate.

"Cal, it's Bear." A voice broke through his malaise. "I've got you, partner. You're safe."

* * *

It took Bear and Celeste several minutes to bring Cal out of his fog. Emily took two large camel bags of water from the commandos. She used one to bathe Cal's face and allowed him to drink from the other in small sips.

"You'll be all right, Cal." Bear helped him to his feet, holding him as he wavered and nearly collapsed. He maneuvered him out of the room into the corridor. "Spence is here, and the FBI is all over this place."

"This place?" Cal wobbled but finally got his balance. He started to slip, so he leaned against the wall. "Where am I?"

"A government research center called ADRI. Though I doubt it's legit." Bear checked his eyes and his pulse. Then, he ran his hands over him, checking for breaks or injuries he might not see. "I gotta get you upstairs to a medic. Phones don't work down here."

"Down here?" Cal's words were weak and slurred. "How long—"

"Four days."

"Four... days?" Cal's face contorted, and he tried to smile. "Is that all?"

"Yeah." Bear laughed. "I'll pay you for it, but no overtime."

Cal's smile finally appeared.

Kerrie and Emily turned and looked down the corridor. Kerrie started walking, but slow and unsteady.

"Hey, hold on," Bear said. "Stay with us. We're going upstairs."

"Go, Captain Bear," Kerrie called back. "I'm not done. There are others."

"Okay, but wait for the FBI."

"No. The others can't wait."

Chapter Sixty-Four

"Professor?" Smith stood and donned his pack. "What is ahead? Be precise."

Angel stalled by drinking some water and adjusting her pack straps.

My brain tickled as Sally spoke to me.

Oliver, it's an easy downhill walk for several hundred feet. We are at the waterline of the new lake. The tunnel hasn't changed much. When I was here the first time, there was a beautiful, great cathedral. But, Oliver, it is very dangerous.

I repeated it all to Angel as Sally mind-melded it into me. She in turn gave a summary to Smith.

"It amazes me, Professor." Smith gazed at her through suspicious eyes. "That you have such details memorized. If I didn't know better—"

"But you do," Angel said. "There's not a lot to memorize, Colonel. This was a cavern system cut into the limestone. There are a lot of them in Virginia. Luray Caverns north of here, and of course, Dixie Caverns is not far either. The only thing to note are the turns and dangers that Tuck warned me about."

Charles moved close to her and whispered. "You're lying, Professor. But that's okay. Everyone is lying."

"I am not lying, Charles." Angel watched Smith's reaction. She needed him to believe her because she was lying like hell. "Let's focus on being safe."

Weaver and Allan carried heavy packs, easily seventy-five pounds of equipment and supplies. Angel's was near that, and Charles carried the

HEAP. Smith's pack was the smallest with virtually nothing in it. Everyone had a camel bag of water, too.

"We'll stop and break periodically," Smith said in his first display of concern. Then he ruined it. "I cannot afford to have you become worthless from exhaustion."

What a leader.

The tunnel ahead was a natural passageway carved through the limestone. There were twists and turns, low passages where we were nearly on hands and knees—they only lasted a few feet—and areas so wide we could walk side-by-side. Most rock walls and ancient formations were breathtaking. Some were utterly dark and terrifying.

Cave-dwelling cannibals lurked somewhere. And dinosaurs. Can't forget them.

"All this from water?" Weaver asked, flashing his light around. "Amazing."

"Yes," Angel said. "Millions of years carving the rock."

Weaver looked nervous. "What if the water comes back?"

"The water is long gone." She waved a hand toward the ceiling. "We might find some up closer to the large cavern ahead, but we're safe. Just ensure you can see where you're putting your feet. A crevasse or shallow hole could hide anywhere."

"I'll be careful." Charles gave her a pleasant, admiring look. "You too, Professor."

For a half hour, we wound our way deeper into the mountain. The passageway, although fascinating, was still dangerous. Sally hadn't appeared along the trip for a while—a sign no dangers lurked ahead. I told Angel that to comfort her. She was so captivated by the rock formations and passage around us, she seemed worry-free. Perhaps more to keep her mind off Smith than the science.

Despite the trek's fascination, she froze twice in tight bottlenecks when the walls temporarily closed on us. Each time she calmed herself—me talking her through it—eased forward and slipped through to the wider tunnel ahead.

Me, I was on guard for the mutants.

Thirty minutes later, we'd neared the end of the tunnel. We'd picked our way slowly and methodically, stopping every few yards to cast the powerful lantern ahead to check for hidden dangers. It was slow going, but no one got injured. When we stepped through a natural archway, a grand cathedral loomed ahead. All the headlamps and Weaver's lantern illuminated it at once.

It was breathtaking. Jules Verne had nothing on us.

The cathedral walls were a hundred or more feet apart in all directions. They were irregular with dark portals that appeared to lead into other chambers. There were rock outcroppings and narrow crevasses that gave the room a mysterious, mystical presence. Stalagmites and stalactites were everywhere, like little mutant cannibals waiting for us to come near. The cathedral ceiling, often obscured by irregular rock formations and stalactites—millions of them dangling like icicles—was easily fifty feet overhead. A dozen yards ahead of us was a flat, empty meadow of stone.

"Magnificent." Smith was the first to venture ahead. "You never said how wonderful this was, Professor."

"I didn't know." Angel followed him. "It's spectacular."

"It looks like a picture book." Charles was a child in a toy store, wondering and gawking at everything. "I have never seen anything like this. I'm going to take pictures."

"We're not here to sight see, Charles," Smith snarled. "Let's focus on the task. Time is short."

Nonetheless, Charles withdrew his cell phone from his pants pocket and began taking photos and videos. He turned around, recording everything and cooing like a child.

I didn't blame him. I felt like Axel, Professor Lidenbrock's nephew in *Journey to the Center of the Earth*, seeing the underworld for the first time. And no, I hadn't forgotten about the flesh-eating mutant cannibals. And now that I recall the story, Axel was nearly eaten by dinosaurs—twice.

Allan and Weaver caught up to us, and Allan jogged ahead, flashing his light at the cathedral in awe. He turned to Weaver, gave a child-like laugh, and jogged backward, looking at the ceiling overhead.

Five steps later, he disappeared.

"Allan?" Weaver flashed his lantern ahead. "Allan?"

Silence.

Smith and Angel ran ahead.

"Stop here, Oliver. Sally appeared where Allan had vanished. "It's water—a lake."

"Angel, stop," I yelled. "Stop."

She skidded to a halt just as Smith took his last step, disappearing as Allan had.

"Colonel?" Angel flashed her headlamp down and followed his tracks. "Weaver, it's an underground pool. They went into the water."

Two feet ahead of her was the edge of a large pool. It was black and still, camouflaged by the reflections from the cathedral roof overhead. Only a few ripples where Smith had disappeared made obvious its true nature.

"Where did they go, Professor?" Charles asked, stopping beside her. "They should have surfaced by now."

"Weaver, give me your rope," Angel called, dropping her pack. When Weaver tossed her an end to his climbing rope, she grabbed it and dove into the pool.

Before I could say, "Let them drown," she was gone.

I looked at Sally standing on the pond's edge. "Is she all right?"

"She should have let them go. It was not part of my plan, Oliver. She must not be so impulsive. What is she thinking?"

Yeah, what?

Several long moments ticked by. Finally, a few splashes and gasps filled the cathedral. Weaver flashed his lantern to the far end of the pool—some two hundred feet away. Angel had popped to the surface. She pulled Smith above the water and struggled to keep him floating.

On a dead run around the pool, Weaver pulled Angel and Smith toward the edge with the rope. Once there, he helped her and Smith onto the cathedral floor.

"Angel, are you all right?" I knelt beside her. "Here's your answer, Sally. Angel wants to escape, but not by letting them die."

Sally disappeared, but in her wake, she said, "Oliver, Angela is an amazing woman."

Yes, she is. *Dammit.*

"Are you all right?" I asked again. "How about Smith?"

She coughed and sputtered and nodded several times. She reached for Weaver's hand. "Thank you. I wasn't sure I could get us out. There's a strong undercurrent a few feet down. IT must be an underground stream or river feeding Smith Mountain Lake. We were caught in it."

"You okay, Professor?" Weaver asked, playing his lantern over the pool surface. "Allan?"

"Gone." Smith spit up a mouthful of water. He coughed and sat up. "I was too late. He was below me, and I saw him swept away. I nearly followed."

I said, "The weight of his pack was too much."

Angel repeated me and added with a loathsome tone, "You are lucky you had a light pack, Colonel."

"Yes, and lucky for you being here." Smith looked down and coughed again. "You saved me, Professor. Why?"

"Yeah, Angel, why?" If only she hadn't.

She first snapped a glance at me. She was about to answer when Charles ambled up and plopped down beside her. He looked at her with odd, sad eyes.

"What is it, Charles?" she asked.

"I'm sorry." He lowered his head. "I didn't help again. I'm so stupid. I'm sorry."

Smith coughed and stood. "You're useless, Charles. Just worry about keeping the HEAP safe. Let the rest of us do the real work."

Smith was an ass. Of course, that was established a long time ago. I doubt anyone would mind if I pushed him back into the pool. Holding a big rock. With a rope tied around his neck. Affixed to said rock. Nope. No one would care.

"Colonel," Weaver said, still looking at the pool. "Our ladder and some of the climbing equipment are gone. Allan was carrying it. Should we go back for—"

"No. We'll find the treasure vault. We'll map our way there and back. Then, I'll send you for the rest of our men and more equipment to carry it out."

Angel got to her feet, dripping wet. "After losing three men, you're still focused on the make-believe treasure, Colonel?"

"Yes. And you haven't answered my question, Professor. Why did you save me?"

"I don't know, Colonel." Angel didn't look at him with a smirk. "When I know why, you'll be the second to know."

Chapter Sixty-Five

It struck me that our odds were getting better. When we'd started, there had been six of Smith's armed men, him, and Charles. I wasn't all that worried about Charles. Smith left two men behind atop the mountain. He's lost three men. Now, there was only Smith and Weaver. She was still outnumbered, but things were looking up.

The treasure hunters took time for Smith and Angel to dry off. Smith broke out bags of dried fruit and granola and passed them around.

Such a great guy—always thinking of his troops.

His concern lasted five minutes. "All right, let's move."

Weaver barely finished a mouthful of granola. But when he started to object, Smith snatched the remaining bag and stuffed it into his own pack. Weaver got to his feet, dared glare at Smith a moment, and hefted his pack.

"I'm not dry yet, Colonel," Angel objected. "Surely a few more minutes—"

"We're moving, Professor." Smith threw a chin toward the rear cathedral wall. "How much farther? What is ahead?"

Angel stood and took her time organizing her pack and camel bag. "I don't know how much farther. Tuck didn't give me time or distance."

That was my cue. Before I could get the words out of my ethereal lips to call Sally, she materialized at the rear of the cathedral. There was a natural alcove where two passageways waited in the dark, partially concealed by an overhanging rock. One headed to the right. The other left.

"Oliver, take the left fork. It's not far now. Do not let anyone go down the right fork tunnel."

Okay, I had to ask. "What's down the right tunnel?"

She turned and walked into the right tunnel. "Me."

She had a plan.

Sally's directions were passed along.

"Angel, Sally's up to something. Be ready for anything."

Angel cocked her head and asked the unspoken question, "Ready for what?"

"I don't know. She has a plan." Sally was a Civil War spy. She had a devious, cunning plan, no doubt. Those traits run in the family. Well, most of the time, anyway.

Smith was in the alcove shining Weaver's big lantern into each tunnel entrance. Unlike the cathedral, the pathways were rugged and obstructed. Both were wide—perhaps six feet in places—but difficult to navigate through rock formations and stalagmites. The twists and turns formed by millions of years of rushing water had never been touched by human feet. Except, perhaps for Sally Mosby and Billy White.

"Professor, why not the right tunnel?" Smith took a few steps inside. "You aren't trying to trick me, are you?"

Angel walked into the alcove beside him. "Colonel, instead of tricking you, I would have just let you drown."

"She could have, Colonel Smith," Charles said, joining them. "You should trust her."

Smith ignored him. "I'd like to know for sure. Weaver, survey the right tunnel for, oh, a few hundred yards. Do it quick and return."

Crap. "Angel, try to talk him out of it. Sally doesn't want anyone down there."

She did, and it was pointless.

"Concerned, Professor?" Smith thrust a finger at Weaver and then pointed down the right tunnel. "Move out."

Weaver dropped his pack, took the lantern from Smith, and headed into the right tunnel. In moments, the light dimmed and went dark. He was out of sight. The tunnel had turned sharply one way or the other, no doubt. Not even the sound of Weaver's footfalls reached us.

After a few more minutes, Smith thrust his hands on his hips. When he turned toward Angel, he held a small semi-automatic pistol and aimed it at her.

"Professor, it isn't lost on me that without Weaver, you could attempt to escape. I cannot have that."

"You don't need a gun." Angel found a place to sit and wait. "But, have it your way."

"I will."

Smith walked into the right tunnel several yards and waited. All the while, he kept the pistol ready and continued to check on Angel over his shoulder.

Five more minutes. Ten. Twenty.

Weaver was gone.

Smith called out for him. He stopped and listened to the echoes. Then, called a second time and a third time. When the echoes stopped, only silence followed.

"Professor, what have you done?" He lifted his pistol again. "Explain."

"I warned you, Colonel." Angel's arms snapped closed. "I told you not to go in there. I don't know what happened. I just know I was told not to go."

Charles had been sitting on a rock outcropping. He stood and strapped the HEAP powerpack onto his back, then slung the HEAP over one shoulder and his camel bag on his opposite shoulder. He headed for the left tunnel, oblivious to Smith's pistol waving back and forth.

"Hold it, Charles." Smith jutted the pistol at him. "I want to know about Weaver before we go."

"He's dead." Charles' voice was cold. "Just like Allan and Cominski and Reynolds. You killed them. I guess you'll kill me next."

He was right. "Angel, Sally isn't around, and I don't know what happened to Weaver. I want to go see, but won't leave you."

Angel slowly nodded as she readied to go. "Colonel, Weaver could simply be too far in, or he's injured or dead. The only way to find out is to go in after him."

"Oh? Now we should go into the right tunnel?" Smith emerged from the tunnel and confronted her. "I don't know what you're doing, Professor. First, you don't want us to go in the right tunnel. Now you do. Perhaps you sent Weaver to his death just to lure the rest of us after him."

Huh? "Angel—"

"Enough." Angel flashed her hand at Smith. "I could have let you die. I didn't. Weaver saved me and you. I wouldn't repay him by killing him. Now stop it."

Smith was shocked by her onslaught. He lowered his pistol, turned, and looked down the right tunnel for a long moment, waiting. When he finally turned back to her, his face was grave.

"All right, Professor. We'll play along. I'll be watching you closely."

I know this guy has a reason to be paranoid, but really?

Charles whispered to her, "I'll protect you, Professor."

"Thanks." She forced a smile. "I know, Charles."

I considered going after Weaver. The treasure hunt club was down to Smith and Charles. As simple and juvenile as Charles was, I still didn't trust him. After all, he was Aaron's blood. Smith, well, he was just psycho. There was no way I was leaving Angel with the two of them.

As Angel started into the right tunnel, Smith shoved Charles in behind her and took up the rear. He stayed several yards back, pistol in hand.

"Remember, Professor, your dead husband isn't here to protect you. Any tricks and you'll never see him again."

"Silly man," I said, making Angel grin. "If he only knew."

Though the odds were in her favor, she was getting more nervous with each step. Her breath came faster, and her pace slowed. She knew we were getting close to the end—whatever that brought. That could mean a confrontation with Smith, or Charles, or both. I tried to reassure her with a few jokes. They fell flat. Weird, right?

As we climbed over rocks and around stalagmites, the air began to have a damp, sweet smell … water.

"Angel, do you smell that?"

She nodded. "Colonel, I smell water."

"Water? Good. We must be nearing the lake. Perhaps you're playing smart after all, Professor."

And perhaps I'll drown you in the lake, Smith.

Angel said, "Colonel, I think we've been under parts of the lake for some time. We've walked a long way and generally headed southwest. If not under the lake, we surely are quite near the edge."

"I can't swim, Professor," Charles said nervously. "Don't make me swim."

"Don't worry, Charles." Angel gave him a reassuring smile. "You won't have to swim."

We continued a steady descent through twists and turns, jumping over dark holes that might have been bottomless—well, for them, not me—and navigated outcroppings of rock and stalagmites. The tunnel suddenly straightened and had a sandy floor.

Angel's headlamp moved over the sand and tunnel walls until the tunnel opened into a large grotto.

Smith pushed past us and ran deeper inside.

"There's something ahead," he called back. "We have trouble—a huge rockslide. It looks new, too."

Charles followed Angel out of the tunnel. They played their headlamps around in all directions. It was much smaller than the cathedral and not as breathtaking. The ceiling was fifty or sixty feet overhead. The walls were the same on either side. On our left was a large rock outcropping, floor to ceiling. Ahead at the far end—another fifty feet or so—was a huge pile of fallen rock. It was piled floor to ceiling where the tunnel should have continued.

We were blocked.

Smith tucked the pistol into his belt. He climbed the rock pile with precarious speed and stopped a few feet below the ceiling. He shone his headlamp into a cavity in the rock pile. "I can smell water through here— much stronger. There's an opening at the top, and I can just see through it. We need to get beyond this rockslide. The tunnel continues on the other side."

I looked around. "Sally? Now would be a good time to give some sage advice."

Nothing.

"Sally?"

Nope. Maybe she was doing her hair and planning our escape. Surely, the mutant cannibals couldn't bother her.

"Angel, Smith put away his gun. He's fixed on the rock pile. Get ready to run."

She inched backward when Charles turned to her. "Don't go, Professor. Please. Don't leave me with him."

Angel saw his pleading eyes. "All right, Charles. But we might have to escape soon."

"Treasure first." Charles unslung the HEAP and called out, "Colonel, I can use the HEAP. Let me help."

Damn.

"I'm not sure it's safe to use in here, Charles," Smith called back, pulling rocks away from the opening and letting them roll down the pile. "Let me see what I can do first."

"Let me help. Please. I can control it. I can just cut slowly back and forth."

"Wait, Charles." Angel touched his arm as he began working the small keypad. "We have to be sure it's safe."

He ignored her and began mumbling as he tapped on the keypad.

Smith tried to move two large boulders but couldn't budge them. He cursed loudly and tried others. He met the same resistance.

"All right, Charles. Power it up. We'll cut through this pile of rocks a small layer at a time. Wait for me to come down."

Angel watched Charles, unease blanched her face. Charles had already powered the HEAP up and was arming the device.

"Charles, easy now," Angel said. "Wait for Colonel Smith to get clear."

Smith reached the bottom of the rock pile. "Charles, listen to me. Be careful. Go slow. Small cuts at a time. A foot deep."

It was time for my plan. Yes, this time I had one. I quickly explained it to Angel.

"Charles, wait," she said, watching him for a reaction. "Colonel Smith killed Andrew. Once you find the treasure, he'll kill you, too. He'll kill both of us. We should leave the treasure and escape. Now."

She's a brilliant lady, my wife. If she gets bored with history, she has a future on Broadway. What an actress—though, I'll have to keep that in mind the next time she says how wonderful I am.

"No, Professor. White killed his brother, Andrew." Smith jutted a finger at her and scowled. "I guess your dead husband failed to tell you. White used that buffoon, Braddock, to do his dirty work, too. A friend of yours?"

"No," Angel said. "I cannot believe that."

"It's true." Smith placed his hand slowly on his pistol. "Charles, don't listen to her. Andrew—"

"Andrew was weak." Charles spun the HEAP toward Smith and flipped a button on its side. It instantly hummed a deadly warning like a rattlesnake's tail. "Move near the Professor, Smith. Slowly."

Ah, what? "Angel, Charles—"

She opened her hands toward Charles. "Charles, what are you doing?"

"I'm sorry, Professor." His voice was stern and steady—confident. His eyes piercing and laser-focused on Smith. Whatever metamorphosis had just occurred was complete. The prey had become the hunter. "I truly am."

Earlier, I'd wondered what Charles' secret power was. It was clear now. He was a brilliant *trickster*.

Chapter Sixty-Six

"What's going on?" Angel stared at Charles with a strange, disbelieving look on her face.

"I'm sorry, Professor. I didn't want you to get hurt. You've been very kind to me."

"Listen to me, Charles," Smith growled, moving away from the rock pile. "I didn't kill Andrew. Point that damn thing away from me. We have to move fast."

"Angel, ease back to the tunnel," I said. "Be ready to run."

"Then you ordered his murder, Colonel." Angel tried to be calm. "It's the same thing as killing him yourself."

"Charles, we both know Kerns was onto us." Smith glanced sideways for a way out, but the HEAP settled on him, and he froze. "Andrew was going to work with Kerns."

Charles suddenly threw his head back and laughed raucously. "Going to the feds? I knew that. So did Aaron."

"You knew?" Smith seemed confused. "I thought—"

"That I was a dimwitted genius?" Charles cawed. "I am the intellect behind this HEAP. Aaron is good, but not like me. Andrew wanted nothing to do with us. All he wanted to do was get away from you—and us."

I wasn't totally clear on what was happening here. But it wasn't good. Suddenly, Charles Pellman seemed like a steady, brilliant guy. Still a bit nuts, but steady nonetheless.

"Listen to me, Charles." Smith stabbed the air with a finger and tried to regain control. "You work for me."

"Not anymore." Charles stepped forward and prodded Smith with the HEAP's barrel. "If not for Aaron and me, you'd never have the resources to be here now—your research, your little army, helicopters, everything. You set White up to keep your hands clean from the foreign sales. I guess you'd kill him once you got the treasure, right? Then Andrew, Aaron, and me."

"No, it isn't like that." Smith's arrogance was cracking. "You have to believe me, White killed Andrew."

Charles laughed again like a mad professor before throwing the switch on his evil ray gun and destroying the planet. Rather apropos, no?

"White didn't kill my brother." Charles waved the HEAP back and forth, keeping the barrel level and ready to fire. "You were setting Aaron and me up for those murders—the fed and his buddy the janitor. Who's next? White? Kill him and frame us for all of them?"

"No. No."

"Liar." Charles prodded him again with the HEAP. "I just got to them all first."

Wait a minute ... *no*. It was staring me right in the face. I missed it. Actually, it was staring at me from *three* identical faces. The Pellmans—Andrew, Aaron, and Charles—one patsy, one lunatic sadist, and one crazed murderer. Mother must be so proud—if she wasn't killed here, too.

"Angel, Charles killed them all." I explained my theory. "Use that. Stir him up."

"Charles?" Angel tried to project confidence and fearlessness. "You killed Agent Kerns and Mr. Downey? You killed—"

"Shut up, Professor." Charles turned sideways to look at her, too. "You should stay out of this. You might live longer."

She softened her tone. "You killed Agent Kerns because he came to the library to meet with Andrew. Mr. Downey caught you escaping, and you broke his neck. You're the Martial Arts expert, not Andrew."

"Andrew?" A strange, silly grin framed Charles's face as he laughed again. "Andrew, a Hapkido expert? Right. Andrew decided to tell the feds about me and Aaron—Smith, too. Andrew was stupid. The fed and janitor were listening in on White's meeting that day and were gonna take Andrew into protective custody. Andrew wanted Aaron and me to go with him—to get away from this asshole." He gestured to Smith.

"You didn't warn me?" Smith said. "I thought—"

Charles' face got angry. "You thought wrong. The HEAP is ours. We did it. I did it. Andrew was going to ruin it all. He was going to help them."

Angel said, "The police—"

"The police have nothing. I caught your detective pal at White's compound. I gave him to Smith. He likes to experiment on people. Sorry, Professor."

"You have Cal?" Angel turned to Smith. "Where? Is he all right?"

Smith shrugged. "Does it matter? It seems Charles has duped us all."

Something tickled my brain, and I had an idea. I told Angel.

"Charles, Smith is abandoning you. As soon as he gets the treasure, he'll kill you. Then he's leaving. He's taking all the money from selling secrets and the treasure and running."

Charles stopped and looked at her. "How do you know that?"

"Think about it." Angel opened her hands in front of her. "He left White behind at the compound and gave Captain Braddock orders to 'clean it up.' He left Aaron at the lab. He's going to leave you down here—dead. It's not about his family heritage or righting wrongs. It's just about money. Enough for him to leave the country before the authorities catch him."

Wow, that was a lot more than I'd told her. But she was on a roll, so I let her go."

"Don't play me, Professor," Charles sneered and turned to Smith. "Is that all true, Colonel? Are you running away and leaving Aaron and me to get caught?"

Smith's face contorted, and he looked like he was gonna be sick. "It's not really like that, Charles."

"Not *really* like that?" Charles growled. "How is it really?"

Sally's voice reached me—*Oliver, behind you, there is that large outcropping. It hides another tunnel—the right tunnel from the large cathedral opens behind it. Angela must get there.*

I explained to Angel. "Get ready, Angel."

"Okay, Tuck," she said out loud. "Got it."

Smith's eyes flared, and he opened his mouth, but nothing came out.

Saying my name got Charles' attention, too. He aimed the HEAP at her.

"Professor?" Charles demanded. "Don't try and trick me."

"I'm not," Angel said. "It's no trick, Charles."

"Detective Tucker is here?" Smith's eyes darted around the grotto. "He's out?"

Angel smiled a rueful smile. "You couldn't hold them."

"Them?" Smith spun, looking around in a frantic, jerky circle. "Them?"

"Us." Sally appeared at the base of the large rock pile. She stood in an aura of dim light that glistened off her blond locks and framed her as beautiful as in her living days.

All eyes fell on her.

Chapter Sixty-Seven

"Sally?" Smith's voice sounded fearful and uncertain. "How—"

"Why, Colonel Smith, you are speechless now that I am not your prisoner?" She twirled like a southern belle. "I knew your great-grandfather quite well. Captain Little was a sorrowful, traitorous scoundrel. As you are. I've waited for this moment a hundred and sixty-some years."

Smith's face froze. He tried to back away but stumbled over a rock and fell.

"No, no." Charles stared wide-eyed at her. "We captured you. Our containment was impenetrable."

"Yes, for a short while, Charles." Sally moved close to him. "A very, very short while. You young men are not quite as smart as you believe yourselves to be. Not unlike Captain Little. Your arrogance is your undoing."

Angel said, "Tuck? Is that—"

"Yes, it is. Great Grandma Sally Elizabeth Mosby."

I stood close to Charles and grabbed hold of the HEAP power tether leading to his backpack powerpack. The surge of energy was explosive—like nothing I'd ever experienced before. Lightning struck me and lifted me. It was brilliant. Blinding. So penetrating and vibrant it was nearly excruciating. But it was working. In a few seconds, every inch of me vibrated with strength and exuberance—invincibility.

As I released the tether, everyone in the grotto stared at me. *Me.*

"Detective?" Smith stuttered. "You?"

"Aaron's containment chamber failed?" Charles' face twisted. "Impossible. It was perfect."

"Don't take it too hard, Charles." I faced him. "You didn't consider an eleven-year-old little girl with a bad temper."

"Kerrie?" Smith got to his feet, flustered. "Kerrie Garcia freed you?"

"Why, yes. She is a sweet little thing." Sally walked to Charles and leaned close, holding his eyes. "She destroyed your little jail, too. Oh, and I don't know if poor Aaron made it out. Shame, really. But he was a repugnant little bastard. I am sure you will agree."

"Kerrie hurt my brother?" Charles's face went wild. His eyes were dark and hate-filled. The jaw muscles twitched. He thumbed on the HEAP's final switch, and the row of lights along its barrel turned green. "I don't believe you."

"No, Charles." Smith lunged at him. He grabbed the HEAP and grappled for control. "Think of the treasure. There's still time."

"The treasure, Smith? You were going to run away and leave me," Charles screamed and tugged on the HEAP. "You betrayed me like Andrew did."

"No, I was going to send for you. I was."

Charles, younger and more wiry than Smith, broke free from him, turned, and fired the HEAP. He didn't aim, and the energy beam struck a large stalactite overhead. It exploded and rained stone missiles down on us.

"Now, Oliver." Sally grabbed Smith by the arm and shoved him against the big rockpile. "Take Angela. Go."

I yelled, "Run to the tunnel on the left, Angel."

Angel spun on her heels and ran.

Charles laughed maniacally and lifted the HEAP, aiming at her. Seconds after she disappeared into the tunnel, he fired a short burst.

The grotto wall exploded in a burst of dust and smoke.

Angel?

"Charles, you forgot about me." I stepped in front of him. "I'm still here."

For an instant, he stared unblinking. His eyes flashed fear as his mouth opened with no words forming.

I was on him. With the HEAP's energy still raging inside me, I grabbed the weapon's barrel and spun him in a vicious arc. I whiplashed him into the rock pile beside Smith. I pounced and delivered two punches into his face that rocked his head from side to side. I wasn't sure what shocked him the most. The pain I delivered or that a ghost—a dead detective—had done so.

He screamed—a long, wavering, terrible wail.

"Detective, stop." Smith lay back on the rocks, watching in disbelief. He tugged his pistol from his waistband and aimed at Charles. "Detective, allow us to proceed. There's still time to reach the treasure. Charles, will you help me?"

Was he kidding?

I delivered a final punch into Charles' face, but he still wouldn't release the HEAP.

He screamed and ranted indistinguishably. He got onto one knee, lifted the HEAP, and jerked the trigger in rapid, uncontrolled bursts in all directions.

"Charles, no," Smith yelled. He tackled him and locked a death grip on the weapon. "Stop—there's still time. We can get the treasure and escape together!"

The walls shook violently. The room began to crumble. The roof rained stone and earth.

Charles and Smith battled for the HEAP's control. It fired bursts of energy here and there. As I backed away, the mountain began to cry.

"Oliver, go," Sally called. "Help Angela get out."

I didn't argue.

I caught up to Angel a few hundred yards up the tunnel. She was coughing and covered in dust and debris from the explosions. The grumble of a wounded mountain filled the air. That and a horrible, Godawful scream that reverberated for two minutes around us. It was an eerie, mournful sound—terror and sadness, anger and regret. Fear.

"Tuck? Is that—"

"Move, Angel. There's nothing back there."

Chapter Sixty-Eight

The right-side tunnel—the left tunnel as Angel escaped the grotto—had been Sally's secret weapon. Not because it was more dangerous or challenging. Because it wasn't. The passage was by far the widest—eight to ten feet in some places. Its ceiling was picturesque with brilliant rock formations with stalactites that looked like armies of dwarves marching along—others that resembled monsters poised for battle. Everything glistened in the Angel's headlamp light. The passage had virtually no precarious turns or hidden crevasses. No constricted, tight chokepoints to slow passage.

The climb was a steady and easy uphill trek.

Once a good half-hour up from the collapsing grotto that assuredly entombed Charles and Smith, Angel stopped to admire the natural beauty of the inner mountain. It was the first time I saw her relax and look safe.

"This is so magnificent." She rested on a small rock, admiring a formation of outcroppings ahead. "We could have saved so much time coming down this way."

A voice turned us around. Sally stood in the tunnel twenty feet behind us.

"Yes, Angela, it would have. I saved that knowledge for your escape. I needed time to stop Colonel Smith. I wished you to have a faster escape to the surface."

Before Angel could respond, Sally vanished.

"Tuck?" Angel asked.

"Yep, doesn't like long goodbyes. Or hellos."

Still, Sally's explanation made sense.

Another few minutes and we reached the grand cathedral. Angel dropped down on her belly at the water pool and splashed water over herself. Then, she drank the last of her camel bag and lay back to rest.

"It's not far now, Angel," I said. "Once out, we'll have to find a way home."

She didn't answer. She was asleep.

I let her rest for a half-hour before waking her to begin the last leg of our escape.

Her stamina was back, and her confidence restored. We moved at a faster pace, and even the tight openings that had intimidated her earlier caused no concern. She slipped through like an eel. It took only a short while, and she was pulling herself through the final opening into the cave just inside the mountain's edge.

She sat and caught her breath again. "Tuck, what will we find out there? What about Smith's other men?"

"I don't know. If they're loyal to him, we'll have a problem."

Outside the cave and into the coming dawn, Angel climbed carefully off the rockslide and into the trees. The darkness was quickly turning into dawn, and that sight was comforting.

A voice stopped us in our tracks. "Hold it right there, Professor Tucker."

Weaver walked out of the trees holding a pistol at his side. He was dirty and sweaty. A smear of blood matted his ear and cheek.

"Angel, don't move," I said. "Stay calm."

She said, "Weaver? You're alive? How'd you get out?"

"Are you all right, Professor?" He holstered his pistol. "Anyone else coming out?"

"No." Angel watched him cautiously. "How—"

Weaver dropped down onto a fallen tree on the edge of the clearing. He lowered his head for a short time. He coughed, wiped his brow, and looked up. His face showed exhaustion and something else… relief.

"Professor, I didn't sign up for this. Smith hired a few of us because of our Special Forces background. Things at ADRI got out of control. But this stupid treasure hunt was, well, it was all I could take."

Angel softened her tone. "I understand, Weaver. I do."

"Thanks." He leaned forward on his knees. "We lost good people on this trip—friends. When I went into that right tunnel alone, I knew Smith was sacrificing me. Halfway in, something hit me in the head, and I went down."

I said, "That would be Sally."

Angel nodded.

"Damnedest thing. When I came too, I'd swear I saw a woman. A beautiful blond woman. I figured it was a sign and retraced our path and got back out. Screw Smith and his psycho mad scientist."

Yep, Sally slowed him down. Part of her plan to thin Smith's herd.

"Are you all right?" Angel walked to him to check his wounds. "Let me see your head."

He waved her off. "I'm fine, Professor. I never wanted to see anyone hurt, let alone killed. Smith's nuts. Him and those two batshit-crazy Pellmans. I just wanted to earn enough on this gig to move on. I'm so sorry if I scared you or did anything—"

"You didn't. You saved me. Remember?" Angel carefully checked the contusion above his ear. "This isn't bad. But you should get checked for a concussion."

"Yes, ma'am." Weaver wiped his face with his sleeve again, and it came back bloody. "What about the others?"

She shook her head. "I cannot imagine they are alive."

"Good riddance to them. Crazy bastards." Weaver stood. "I'll make sure our guys up top don't bother you. I'll go back with you, Professor. I'll testify or whatever you need. I don't want this on me."

"I'll back you, too." Angel patted his shoulder. "Thank you. It's a shame. They all died trying to find that foolish treasure."

"Foolish treasure, Angela?" Sally appeared in front of us. She walked to Weaver and looked sadly at him. "I am truly sorry to have hurt him. I had no choice. I did not know he would help."

Angel fixed on Sally. "So, you're Sally."

"Yes, Angela. I am." Sally smiled and bowed slightly. Her long blond hair hung down over her shoulders and glistened in the fading starlight. "It is my sincerest pleasure to formally meet you."

"Who is Sally?" Weaver asked. "Who are you talking to?"

"I'll try to explain later, Mr. Weaver."

"No, never mind. The crazy shit I heard and saw down there. I'll chalk it all up to a concussion."

Angel laughed and turned back to Sally. "You helped me in the tunnels. Thank you. And you're so much more beautiful than Tuck said." Angel shot me a look that made me long for the tunnels. Then she looked at Sally again. "What now?"

Sally waved toward the overlook and Smith Mountain Lake glistening beyond. "The lake has saved many lives, you know—by concealing its secrets. It covered the entrance to the Beale Treasure."

I asked, "Isn't the treasure a myth?"

"Perhaps." She turned away as tears glistened down her cheeks. "It is a blessing that the lake was built. It stopped anyone who might have found our M35W markers and followed them. No one would have survived on the other side of that rock pile. That is why I put it there."

Sally caused that rockslide to stop us from reaching the treasure vault. That is, if there was one.

"Smith?" Angel asked, but her expression said she already knew the answer. "Charles?"

"No, Angela." Sally wiped her cheeks. "That odd young man with the strange weapon brought down the grotto. There was nothing I could do."

"It was Charles Pellman all the time." I thought about the possession at the Handley Library. "I suspected almost everyone at one time or another. But, Charles? He killed Kerns and Downey to keep out of prison. He killed Andrew to keep him silent—his own brother."

"Not unlike my war, Oliver. Brother killing brother. Still, we had history together—Smith, White, and me."

Angel said, "Yes, their ancestors caused a lot of pain and suffering. Both sides. White will go to jail for decades, and Smith's dead. All for the same greed that their ancestors had generations ago."

"Yes, greed and hubris," Sally said in a near whisper. "Those other men— those at the library. They died so tragically. I wish I could have stopped it."

I thought about that and went to her, putting an arm around her shoulders. "You did all right."

Angel said, "Sally? Will you be leaving for good?"

Overhead, a powerful spotlight flashed through the trees. The *thump-thump-thump* of helicopter rotor blades washed the air.

"No, Angela, it's not over yet," she said. "There is still a reckoning."

Chapter Sixty-Nine

Smoke plumed from ADRI's buildings as we arrived. Our FBI helicopter made a slow circle around the campus, awaiting approval to land. Finally, we began our descent onto a parking lot adjacent to the campus. The morning was alive with hundreds of emergency vehicles. The entire area was consumed with fire engines, ambulances, city and state police cruisers, and a dozen black, unmarked Suburbans. A hundred or more people scurried around.

It was nearing eight a.m. The sun was shining through a smoky haze, partially obscuring the chaos around us. Three hours earlier, when we'd emerged from the cave, we weren't sure what would happen next. How, we didn't know, but two FBI helicopters and tactical teams found us on that mountainside. They were secretive about their mission, and oddly enough, we didn't care.

Even Weaver was relieved. The agents took him into custody without any resistance. The second helicopter flew up the mountain to find the two remaining Men-Wearing-Black, but they had already vanished. I supposed they worried that Smith might give them an accident, too.

Once aboard the helicopter, Angel had asked, "How did you find us? Who sent you?"

"Ma'am," one of the agents had said, "this is all a need-to-know operation. You don't have that need."

The helicopter settled on the asphalt outside ADRI's complex, and the pilot powered it down. A female FBI agent wearing the traditional FBI raid jacket waited just outside the reach of the rotor blades. She watched as

Angel climbed out and was escorted to her.

"Professor Tucker, I'm Assistant Special Agent In Charge Paula Styres of the WFO. We're glad you're all right."

"Thank you." Angel looked at the mayhem surrounding us. "What's going on?"

"That, Professor Tucker, is a long story."

Angel pressed. "How did you find us—er, me? Why am I here? I want to go home."

"You will. I promise. Most of this is classified, ma'am," Styres said. "All I can say is we're dealing with national security. What's important is that you're okay. There's a lot of people worried about you."

"Like who?" I asked, smelling a tale of bull coming.

Styres led Angel to a large mobile trailer labeled "Tactical Command." Inside, it reminded me of the ADRI laboratory where Smith and Aaron Pellman had nearly killed Sally and me. There were rows of computers with video monitors on the walls. Facing them were communications workstations. In the center of the trailer was a small worktable and chairs.

Styres took a seat at the worktable and motioned Angel into a chair across from her. Someone brought coffee and a tray of breakfast sandwiches and fruit. Angel wasn't shy and dived into it.

Styres said, "Please tell me about Smith Mountain Lake."

"No." Angel stuffed an egg croissant sandwich into her mouth. "First, you tell me what's going on here. When I get answers, so might you."

I couldn't have played it better.

Styres barked orders, and the two FBI agents sitting at the workstations brought up video feed on the wall monitors. The first displayed ADRI from its perimeter—probably using its own fence surveillance cameras. Moments later, eruptions inside one of the rear campus buildings blew out windows and belched smoke and flames. Slowly, seemingly floor-by-floor, the building began to suffer an incursion. All around the compound, employees poured out of every building orifice into the parking lots and scurried away. A short time later, the first firefighters arrived, followed by a stream of other first responders.

It appeared a terror attack had been unleashed inside.

"They deserve this," I snorted. "But I hope no one was killed."

Angel had the same feelings. "What caused this, Agent Styres?"

"Terrorists." Styres was matter-of-fact. "An unknown number of perpetrators. They hit the building yesterday. It began in the sub-floors of Section Five—an underground facility performing highly classified research. It spread rapidly."

Yesterday? He couldn't mean … *no way... Kerrie?*

Angel watched the monitors as they transitioned through different CCTV coverage. The next stop on the tour was ADRI's main entrance. The camera ticker read late afternoon yesterday. A caravan of black SUVs swarmed the compound. FBI agents burst from the vehicles and deployed into the main building. Another vehicle arrived and skidded to a halt. Three men jumped out and charged inside.

Angel and I knew two of them. I recognized the third.

"Bear?" Angel stood and moved closer to the monitor. "Spence?"

I stood beside her. "And some guy Bear was in league with, Angel—Young. He was at the library and at White's compound. He's in on this."

"Young?" Angel said without thinking. "With Bear and Spence?"

"Special Agent Young is one of mine. He's a deep-cover operative," Styres said. "He and Captain Braddock were on a special assignment. Detective Spence joined in later."

"Bear's working for you?" Angel could barely say the words. "I thought—"

"Yes, you were supposed to think that." Styres joined her at the monitor. "I know they're friends of yours. I wanted you to see this first. They saved a lot of lives."

She stood silent.

I suddenly had a terrible feeling in my gut. I'd doubted Bear—though deep down I think I knew he was not guilty of the terrible things I feared. But I still doubted him—and broke trust.

"Angel, Bear didn't kill anyone. He wasn't on the take or gone rogue. It was all his cover."

Tears welled in Angel's eyes before making the embarrassing journey down her face.

"They saved friends of yours, Professor Tucker." Styres took control of the keyboard closest to her and tapped commands. The monitor showed a barren, dim hallway with two armed ADRI agents standing post outside a steel door. Another monitor displayed only a black screen. "This will explain a lot."

The dark screen turned on, and Bear, Spence, and Young stood outside a heavy security door. A few moments later, they entered. Inside, they confronted two armed commandos. There was an argument that ensued, and several minutes later, strangely, the commandos surrendered.

"Agent Styres, what's happening?" Angel asked.

"Based on evidence and testimony from Mr. Bradley White, in exchange for leniency on charges for treason and other federal crimes, a federal search warrant was executed yesterday late afternoon. We were looking for evidence against Aaron and Charles Pellman, Colonel Smith, and a ring of others stealing government research. Smith was selling it to foreign governments—several enemy states—through White."

"All to finance his crazy treasure hunt," Angel said. "And Smith's private army of enforcers. Then, Smith was going to escape. He knew you were all closing in on him."

"Yes, that's correct. Captain Braddock and Detective Spence assisted in the raid to find you, Detective Clemens, and others. After we lost Andrew Pellman—who was going to give us testimony and evidence against Smith and the others—we had nothing. After your abduction at Bradley White's mountain retreat, we interceded. White provided sufficient information enough to raid this facility. We got here just in time."

"Kidnapping and torture," I said.

Angel repeated me, adding, "And child abuse."

"I'm afraid it was headed worse." Styres looked somber. "Smith ordered the execution of all witnesses. The families he was researching included."

The CCTV images changed again, and the patchwork of images displayed Bear making his way down a dark hallway. He found a room where, after some effort, he rescued a little boy and his mother.

"That is Simon and Celeste," Styres said. "Then this happened."

The next few moments, while traversing dark hallways, the three encountered four more heavily armed ADRI commandos. What took place stunned us.

"What just happened?" Angel asked. "Play that again."

Styres did.

As Bear was confronted, the first two commandos were seized by some unseen force. They were raised above the floor—levitated there—disarmed and knocked out against the wall. The same fate befell the second set of commandos.

Kerrie Garcia and her mother stood a few yards behind the guards. Kerrie held her arms outstretched. When Kerrie twisted her hands, the men spun and slammed into the wall. Kerrie had defeated all four commandos—herself.

"Unbelievable." Angel stared, dumbfounded. "I met Kerrie at the Handley Library the other day. She did all this?"

Styres nodded. "Watch."

As Angel and I stood captivated by the recordings, the door the commandos were guarding flew open. Bear entered. A few moments later, he emerged, helping an African American man—soaked in perspiration and clinging to him for support—walk gingerly out of his cell.

"Oh, my God, Cal," Angel cried. "Is he all right? What did they do to him?"

"Detective Clemens is fine." Styres put a reassuring hand on her arm. "Badly dehydrated and hungry. That's all. He's in the hospital under FBI protection. It appears rogue elements inside ADRI were, well, using unique interrogation techniques on him. That's all I can say."

Unique interrogation techniques? "They were torturing him, Angel."

Then, on the monitor, Sally's reckoning began.

As Bear carried Cal down the hall, Kerrie and Emily Garcia went in the opposite direction. Three commandos appeared in the hall and charged them with weapons drawn. Kerrie stepped in front of her mom, lowered her head, and thrust her right hand toward them. In unison, the men split apart like bowling pins and crashed into the walls. Kerrie spun when two more commandos attacked them. She repeated her defense with identical results. Two lanes, two strikes.

"Kerrie?" Angel gasped. "Incredible."

Styres folded her arms. "She saved them all—Spence and Clemens, Agent Young and Captain Braddock. She also saved several other families imprisoned in Section Five."

"But the explosions? The fires?"

Styres turned off the monitors and faced her. "It was terrorists, Professor."

The hell it was. "Angel—"

"It was Kerrie," Angel snapped. "Don't give me any of that FBI cover-up. It was—"

"A *terror attack*, Professor." Styres took her shoulder. "Do you really expect us to report that an eleven-year-old girl with supernatural powers razed a billion-dollar government facility? All by herself?"

Angel dropped into one of the chairs at the table and buried her face in her hands.

"Angel, it'll be all right. It's just a cover story. It sucks, but it works."

"How does it work?" she asked without thinking.

I said, "Because he keeps Kerrie off the evening news."

Styres looked at her. "Because—"

"I get it." Angel let the tears rain. "Does anyone in the government ever tell the truth? Colonel Smith? You people? Anyone?"

As Angel and Styres sat at the table, I stood feeling stupid and traitorous. I was so convinced that Bear had turned against Angel and me, I'd missed the clues. He was undercover and trying to gain White's trust—trying to stop any more secrets getting into the wrong hands. No, wait … more … he was trying to protect me, too. Damn. Double damn, damn. He was protecting me. *Protecting Angel.*

My guts twisted with a mixture of embarrassment and regret. I was an idiot. Shame on me for doubting him. He deserved better.

"I feel like I betrayed Bear, Angel."

She looked at Styres. "Smith was a traitor. Little Kerrie is a hero who stopped ADRI. You call her a terrorist?"

"No, Professor." Styres' sly look widened. "Kerrie is a victim. Her and the other families held at ADRI were victims of a rogue research program. That was all, Colonel Smith. It is now classified above Top Secret, but you have my word, we'll take care of it all, and everyone left responsible. What you see here—outside—is that ADRI was destroyed by terrorists."

"Who were the terrorists?" I asked, and Angel repeated me.

Styres raised her chin. "The Pellman brothers, of course."

Chapter Seventy

"The Pellman brothers?" Angel wiped away tears. "Surely not, Andrew—"

"No, not Andrew," Styres assured her. "Aaron and Charles. Somehow, Charles learned Andrew was going to cooperate with us. Andrew was a terrible loss."

"Charles told us that Andrew tried to get Aaron and him to stop and turn themselves in." The words choked Angel, and she had to sit again. "Charles killed them all."

Styres looked painfully away. "Agent Kerns and Downey were DIA assigned to my task force. They were two good operatives."

"Jeez," I snorted. "How did this all start?"

Angel asked her that.

Styres sipped her coffee. "We learned about Smith a year ago. We saw him building his private army, we just didn't know it was for a treasure hunt—of all things. While Kerns and Downey were investigating the thefts, Agent Young and Captain Braddock were to identify all the buyers. It all led to Winchester."

Huh, imagine that. Murder and mystery in Winchester. Now treason and terrorism. Who would think?

Angel returned her attention to the CCTV monitors. She watched from monitor to monitor. Each showed a different area of ADRI and the carnage everywhere. The monitor closest to us was time-stamped shortly after midnight this morning. Kerrie and her mother stood in the atrium in the center of the ADRI complex. The buildings surrounded them like tall guards looking down. Kerrie began twirling in circles. As she did, the glass in the atrium walls shattered in all directions. Tables flipped or were mangled into twists of metal and wood. The surrounding buildings began to implode. Smoke and fire belched out and continued ADRI's obliteration.

Kerrie was unhappy being a lab rat. ADRI was paying the price.

Then, little Kerrie collapsed.

"Kerrie?" I yelled.

"Agent Styres." Angel jumped up. "Kerrie?"

"She's all right." Styres touched her arm. "We don't pretend to understand it, but Kerrie sort of, er, ran out of juice. She's resting at a nearby hospital—under protection. She'll be fine. It's the craziest thing I've ever seen. That little girl is amazing. Scary amazing."

"And later?" Angel searched the monitors. "Will she and her mother be safe?"

"Safe?" Styres actually laughed. "They were the safest ones in this place. Kerrie sent us to you, Professor. She told us exactly where to find you."

Angel turned to Styres. "Kerrie knew?"

"Yes, and more." Styres slid another coffee into Angel's hand. "She and Mom will be moved into protective custody as soon as Kerrie is released from the hospital. For a short time, I think we'll have you under protective custody, too."

"Angel, I have an idea." I explained it to her. "And no more experiments."

Angel repeated me word for word, adding, "They've been abused by ADRI, Agent Styres—our government abused them. I hope—"

"You have my word." Styres stood. "Under the circumstances, we can support your request. Presuming, of course, the Garcias agree."

"Were there many casualties?" Angel asked. "Here, I mean?"

Styres nodded. "Yes, but not many. Several injuries during the evacuation. Some smoke inhalation. A few broken ankles and cuts, and so forth."

"There're others." Angel lowered her head. "You'll need to add Colonel Smith, Charles Pellman, and several of his men to your list. It's a long story. Mr. Weaver can provide testimony, too."

"Yes, of course," Styres said. "I'd like to hear your story now."

After looking to me for an approving nod, she told her story covering the past several days. It took over an hour and two more coffees.

When she was done, Styres stared in disbelief. "Come on, Professor. That bullshit Beale Treasure is real?"

"Well, it's certainly not about space aliens," Angel quipped.

God, I loved this woman. "Ah, *humpf*, I was right about the ray gun."

Angel tried to conceal a grin and said, "People have been dying since the Civil War over that treasure."

"Did you find anything in the caves?"

"It's a hoax." Angel shook her head. "Everyone knows that."

Styres studied her for a long time. She looked like she was wondering just how true that was. "A hoax?"

Angel stood. "I'd like to speak with Bear and Spence now."

"They're being debriefed, Professor. They will not be discussing much with you afterward, either. This situation is highly classified."

"How convenient." Angel pointed a damning finger at her. "Our government is responsible for this."

"I know, Professor, we are," Styres said softly. "Now, though, I'm going to protect Kerrie. Better the public thinks this was terrorism than an eleven-year-old with paranormal abilities. She'd end up in a lab the rest of her life. Or worse."

Good point. A cover-up was just what the doctor ordered. After all, what's a few more secrets to bury?

The command trailer door opened, and I nearly fell over. I'm not sure what startled me more—that Poor Nic was voluntarily walking into an FBI lair or that he was holding Hercule's leash.

Woof. Wag. Woof... moan.

Poor Nic released him, and the big dog bound to Angel for a long embrace.

"My dear, I am so relieved that you are safe," the old gangster said. "I was so worried. Hercule has been, too."

"Nicholas? What ... how ..."

Poor Nic left his FBI escort at the door and walked to her. He took her in a solemn embrace. After a moment, he leaned back, held her shoulders, and scanned her slowly. Satisfied she was unharmed, he crushed her to him again.

"I'm all right, Nicholas. But, you…"

"It is simple, my dear." Poor Nic released her. "Captain Braddock had me retrieve Hercule while he cleaned up our operation. I simply had to bring this dear fellow to you."

"*Our* operation?" I asked. "Holy crap, Angel—Poor Nic's a federal snitch."

Styres waved Poor Nic's escort out of the trailer. When he was gone, she aimed a finger at Angel. "This is classified, remember that. Nicholas has been aiding us from the beginning. He knew—"

"He knew a guy who knew a guy." Angel hugged him again. "I understand."

Hercule woofed and demanded his time with Mom. That ended the "highly classified" discussions.

Outside, a helicopter powered up. Styres tapped her earpiece, listened, and affirmed the information over her radio.

"Professor," she said, extending her hand to Angel. "Your ride to Winchester is ready. Two of my men will escort you. I have enough for now, but tomorrow—the day after at the latest—you must be thoroughly debriefed. Can I count on your cooperation?"

Angel glanced over at me and waited for my nod. "Only if my request is granted."

"Of course." Styres thought for a long moment. "There will be rules, you understand. But I promise. No more research on Kerrie. Not unless her mother and she agree."

"None." Angel folded her arms. "I would hate to go on the news with this."

Styres grinned nervously. "None."

"Ah, Angel," I said. "I hate helicopters. I'll meet you in Winchester."

She nodded ever-so-slightly. "I'll hold you to your word, Agent Styres."

Chapter Seventy-One

Angel walked with Hercule and Poor Nic to the waiting FBI helicopter for her short flight home. A voice garbled in the propwash stopped her.

"Angela? Are you all right?"

She turned as Bear stepped around the command trailer. She ran from beneath the rotors and crushed into him. She stood there, enveloped in his arms, and cried heavily—embarrassment and relief.

"Hey, you okay?" Bear asked, moving her to arm's length. "What's wrong?"

She sniffled. "Me. You. Tuck. Dammit, Bear. We thought—"

"Yeah, I know. That was the hardest part of all this."

"The hardest part?"

"Lying to you. I had to for everyone's sake, including yours."

She wiped her face. "Yeah, we should have known. We didn't want to believe it all, but after Nicholas came to see me, and what Sheriff Millbert told Spence. It was just too hard to ignore."

"Poor Nic was helping me." He glanced over her shoulder and waved to him. "I didn't expect you and Spence to show at White's place. That nearly blew the entire operation. I gambled, and it paid off. But if anything had ever happened to you or Tuck—"

"We're okay."

"Where's Tuck? I need to make things right." Bear looked around. "Unless he doesn't want to."

"He will."

Chapter Seventy-Two

A week later, so much had changed. Angel finished her round of debriefings on Smith kidnapping her and the Beale Treasure hunt. It included, of course, all she knew about the Pellman brothers and Charles and Smith's demise. Then there was Bradley White. He made a sweetheart deal to stay out of prison for the rest of his life. All that in exchange for testimony against international arms dealers Ahmad El Fazi and Chen Liu. Oh, and for keeping the lid on the non-terrorist terrorist attack on ADRI. And no, he didn't get to keep the millions he'd made selling government secrets.

Angel was finally relaxing and getting back to normal. Normal included me clunking around the house with our new borders. I'm not talking about the two FBI agents assigned to protect her. I'm speaking of the little Asian-Latino girl with the supernatural power to destroy corrupt government buildings with a finger. Kerrie Garcia, not Kerrie Lee Garcia, and her mom, Emily Lee-Garcia, now occupied our guest bedrooms.

See, the FBI bought into Angel's recommendation. Although I'd call it a demand. Sort of like, "Let them stay, and you can guard all of us together. Or I go to the media—secrets or not." Funny how they thought it was a brilliant idea.

At the moment, about six in the evening, Angel and the master-barbecuer, Bear Braddock, were grilling steaks and veggies in our backyard. Hercule supervised, and Poor Nic sat nearby sipping my expensive bourbon.

Bear was nervous. I knew why.

I hadn't spoken to him since he fried my ethereal brain with his EMF meter. I wasn't mad for lying to me, or at least not telling me the full truth. It was that he had avoided me for a week while he helped the FBI mop up the ADRI case. I'm told he was offered a position in the Bureau if he wanted it. That killed me.

Time will tell if Bear becomes a G-man.

When he'd arrived earlier today, he made a beeline for my expensive bourbon in my den. Decanter in hand, he plopped himself out back in an Adirondack chair beside Poor Nic. They congratulated each other and did the toast thing. Everything was great... *for them.*

Except I wasn't invited. Truth was, I wasn't in on their operation. But Angel and I, as always, solved the real case.

"Oliver?" Doc Gilley summoned me into my den. "Please come here."

Please? Doc had never said 'please' to me in my life—or death. In fact, I don't think he's ever been polite to me.

I wandered in. "Yeah, Doc? What did I do wrong this time?"

The old surgeon stood across the room in his never-changed green surgical scrubs, stethoscope, and scowl. "Nothing, why would you think that?"

"Tradition?"

Doc folded his arms, grumbled something, and aimed a finger at me like a parent about to ground me for eternity. "You have done our family a great service, Oliver. You proved Sally Elizabeth was not a traitor, but a hero. Our family thanks you."

"Our family thanks me? How about *you* thank me?"

He cocked his head. "Oliver, to be honest, our family already knew the truth about Sally. We're all, how do I say it, connected in death. You were the only one who did not yet know."

"And the history books?" I sat behind my desk, put my feet up, and tried to milk this very rare moment of gratitude from my great-grandfather. "In truth, you want to thank me because I'll have Angel fix the history books."

Doc turned toward the door, refusing to look at me.

Got him.

"Oliver, how exactly do you plan on having Angela do that? She cannot tell the story of the Beale Treasure hunt. She cannot tell the story of your adventures to 1864. Hmmm?"

I started to object and stopped. Now, he had me.

"I'll find a way. Trust me."

Hercule bound into the room and saved him. Behind my butt-twisting dog came Bear Braddock.

"Oliver," Doc said, fading now. "Do repair your relationship with this big lug. He's been moping around since he arrived."

Crap. Yeah. It was time.

Bear stood in the doorway watching Hercule wag himself into a frenzy. Then, as Doc made his exit, Hercule jumped up into my best leather chair and stared at me across the room.

Woof. Woof. Grrrrr. Woof. Wag.

"Yeah, yeah, I know," I said. "Bear, let's talk."

Bear glanced around the room as though he didn't see me. Odd, too, since he could before this misadventure. "Tuck? Are you here?"

"At my desk. Can't you see me anymore?"

"Nope." He looked sad and withdrawn. "I guess you being so mad at me killed that connection. Huh?"

Did it? Now would be a great time for Doc's never-ending wisdom. Not that he ever gave it to me when I really needed it.

"Bear, it was, well, I thought you went bad, and I wanted to stop you and fix things."

Bear walked to the desk and looked at the chair I was sitting in. He looked awkward, like he felt silly doing that. "Yeah, I get that. I made it pretty hard not to believe it all."

No kidding. "Being a murder suspect and committing treason was the worst."

He lowered his eyes. "Look, Tuck. Maybe I played it too close with Spence and Angel at White's compound. I was really trying to save Angela."

"Save her?" I jumped up, more angry with him than I thought. "You gave her to Smith. How is that saving her?"

Bear lifted his head. His face was pale and his eyes sad. "Because I knew if she stayed, and things went bad with White and his men, she'd get hurt. The FBI team was late hitting the compound, or we would have had them all together. I took a chance she was safer with Smith—at least for a while."

Maybe he was right. He was in a lose-lose situation. "Okay, maybe. But—"

"But nothing, partner." Bear raised his voice.

Tears filled his eyes, and I can't recall ever seeing that. Not even when he arrived at my house the night I was murdered. I let him stew. Maybe that was mean, but there was something just below the surface he wanted to say.

And he did. "Tuck, I knew Smith had trapped you. I knew he would get your grandma, Sally, too. I let Angela go with him to save you, dammit. Smith would never hurt her in order to control you. Having her was his best play to force you to help him. You're already dead. It's not like he was going to make things worse."

If only Bear knew the truth—the torture Sally and I had endured. A sudden pang of guilt consumed me. It stabbed me a million times in my gut.

"Bear, I didn't see it that way. I'm sorry."

He turned away as the tears started a slow, embarrassing trek down his face. He wiped them away and stood with his back to me.

"Bear, I'm sorry."

"Damn you, Tuck. I kept you away from me to keep you safe from Smith."

"Okay, okay. I get it."

"No, you don't." He spun back around. "Kerns was a friend of mine. When I saw what that HEAP did to him, I knew how much danger you were in. I kept warning you off. You didn't listen, so I forced you away. They took Cal, and they had Kerrie Garcia and her mom. I had to find them without blowing the entire operation. Can you imagine the HEAP in the wrong hands?"

"Yes, I can. I saw it." I walked around the desk to face him. "I'm sorry, Bear. I didn't see it from your side. Just mine. You made the right calls—I think. Everyone's all right—everyone that matters. Smith and Charles Pellman, well, they're pancakes, now. You know how much I hate pancakes."

He laughed and wiped his face. "Damn, you partner."

"Yeah, probably." I stepped into him and did something I'd never done. I hugged him long and tight. "Thank you, brother. You saved me in so many ways."

Bear stood there a long moment. Finally, I felt his arms wrap around me. They tightened, and we connected between life and death. The connection lost when I'd lost my faith in him healed.

"Tuck, I can see you, and—"

"Whoa there." I pulled away. "Let's keep this man-hug to ourselves. Okay? Spence would have a field day."

"Agreed." He laughed, stepped back, and looked right at me. "I should have shot him when I had the chance."

"Yup."

A soft, feminine voice from the hallway turned us both around.

Sally stood in my den entrance. She was dressed in a beautiful yellow dress and a wide-brimmed bonnet—all very ladylike for the hardcore Union spy that she was.

"Oliver, I am going now. Thank you for helping me."

Helping her? "Sally, you saved us. Me. Angel. Thank you."

She walked in and kissed my cheek, winking over my shoulder at Bear, who stood there, gaping dumbfounded at her.

"Ah, Tuck? This is—"

I turned and gestured to Sally. "Captain Bear Braddock, please meet my great-many times grandmother, Sally Elizabeth Mosby."

"It is my honor to meet you, Captain Braddock." Sally did a little curtsy. "Why, you are just the man I thought you were. Big, strong, brave—"

"Okay, okay," I said. "He blushes easily."

Hercule bound in again with Angel in tow—woman's intuition, right?

The big dog walked around Sally, turned, and gave her a big woof and wag. When she bent to pat him, he dropped down and provided his belly for her to provide the required loving.

She giggled. "Why, Hercule, you are such a scamp."

"He is." Angel stood looking at her with an odd expression. Sort of the cat watching the canary cage. "Sally, are you leaving us?"

"Indeed, I am, Angela." She smiled warmly and turned to me. "Oliver, I tried for years and could never connect to anyone to help clear my name. Without you, I would forever be known only as a traitor. It's you, Oliver. You have some very unusual hold on this life."

Me, no. "Sally, I'm no different than you."

"You certainly are, Oliver." She wagged her finger at me. "That evening in the barn before we robbed that bank. Remember? You appeared to me. I saw you. I can't explain it, but you were there—even back then—you appeared. That's how I knew I had to reach you to stop all this."

Holy crap. Never in all my cases had anyone ever spoken to me in a vision. I had a lot of them, too. What did it mean? I asked her.

"I'm sure I don't know, Oliver. Perhaps one day you'll understand it all." She touched my cheek. "Doc Gilley tells me you and Angela will correct the history books. Thank you. Our family thanks you, too."

Angel said, "Sally, I'll set the record straight—somehow. I promise. You were hanged—murdered over treasure. It wasn't about the war. It was about greed and power. You died for a hoax."

She grinned. "Oh, you still believe the treasure is a hoax?"

"I do." Angel's eyebrows raised. "You told Tuck—"

"I'm a spy, Angela. I spread disinformation to get what I want." She twirled happily around. "Come now, if it were a hoax, where did young Kerrie Garcia get that gold piece that lured Oliver in?"

Crap. "Was the treasure down in that cave where Smith and Pellman died?"

"There are many hiding places under that lake, Oliver." She turned to Bear and handed him a large, heavy gold nugget. "Let them stay secret."

Bear's eyes flared, and he nearly choked. "Is this what I think?"

"It is, Captain Braddock." She leaned in and kissed his cheek. "A small gift for your superb assistance."

Bear looked from Angel to me. "Holy shit."

"Sally," I said, wondering if I should ask the big question. "You were murdered very young. How is it you're my great-grandmother a few times over?"

Her face washed with sadness. Tears flowed. She walked to me and hugged me warmly. When she stepped back, color had found her cheeks again. She had a faint smile.

"Oliver, before the war, I was married to a charming young man. We had two children—Benjamin and Elizabeth. My husband was killed in the war's early days, and my children went to live safely with family. After securing them, I went to war, too. I had to."

"Did you ever see them again?"

"Not in that life, Oliver. In time, I am most confident you will make my family's acquaintance."

"But—"

"No." Her voice was a mere whisper. "Some secrets are worth dying for, Oliver. Like you. You are a very valuable secret in this world. Stay safe."

Was she right? Did I really have a hold on this world? Maybe it was just dumb luck that has kept me among the living—able to continue some semblance of life with Angel.

Woof.

Yes, and Hercule, too.

Kerrie Garcia ran into the den, laughing and giggling as Poor Nic chased her—slowly. She stopped and looked at Sally with a big, beautiful smile.

"Hello, Sally. Is it time to go?" she asked. "I'll miss you."

Sally bent and kissed her cheek. "Oh, I may not be gone forever, little one. Mind those special things you do. And mind your mama."

"I will."

Sally was gone, leaving the faint scent of jasmine in her wake. Her secret kept her bound to that damned treasure far too long. She helped reveal its secrets. Those secrets set her free. Angel, Bear, and I, too, helped. White and Smith had terrible family secrets that killed Sally a long time ago. Not for their wartime causes—the North or the South—but for an unquenchable thirst for a treasure no man should ever possess. That cost them. Oh, not just Captain Little and William Stanford White, either. It also cost Bradley White and Colonel Smith, with a hundred and sixty years of interest due.

There were others, too, killed by those secrets.

In the end, I really did little to find the murderers. What I did was make it possible for the others—Angel, Bear, even Mike Spence—to solve those crimes. I protected Angel when she needed it and helped Kerrie Garcia—not Kerrie Lee Garcia, just Kerrie Garcia—find the will to fight back. And I discovered Sally's secret that she died for. Now, Angel will set that truth free, and along with it, Sally Elizabeth Mosby.

That's something, right?

All lives are filled with secrets—good and bad ones. People die because of them and often die to protect them. I'm no different. Sally thinks my life is full of secrets that bind me to this world.

Now, if I just knew what those secrets were.

Acknowledgments

Dying can bring out the best in people. It can also bring out the worst of secrets… So, if you want to know who your friends are, or what they're truly up to, kill one.

Naw, I think I'll just say thanks to my friends instead.

Tuck's newest adventure in this relaunched Dead Detective Casefiles comes on the heels of three of my favorite books that I've written. During the series, I racked up some pretty amazing support. This time around, I've added to it. Since this is the relaunch and the new adventure, I'll note them all:

Jean for being my biggest fan, eldest daughter, and best monster-wrangler (with my grandson). Wouldn't want to do this without you.

Nicci for being my second biggest fan and techno-edit guru, longest friend left around, and for buying lunches. Many a character and plot twist came from those salads.

Tikki "The Torch" M. A newcomer to my readers and fans. I turned to her to ensure Tuck's new adventure measured up to his others. Great advice and counsel. Thank you.

Gina B., Exec Director of The Friends of the Handley Library, for her support and interest in Tuck and the gang. Also, Barbara D. (retired) and Pat R. of the Handley Library. Also Ann W., Toby T. (Archives Assistant), and Carolyn B… Your openness and support doing research about Handley, the personal guided tour, and your willingness to support me helped immeasurably.

Gina H., one of the oldest supporters from book tours, and my newest friend and PR guru. Thank you so much for what you do—promos, reviews, edits, ideas, the heavy-lifts of social media…all of it.

Shawn R. Simmons and your Level Best Books team—you're an inspiration for many reasons. Most of all, a long-time friend and now publisher who really "gets" the spirit of authors who are fighting the good fight—uphill or not. It is so great to have your confidence and support. Lots to do and I'm already having more fun than ever.

Kimberley Cameron—as always, my hero, friend, spirit guide, and agent. Over the years you've continued to believe in me and my stories. You've always gotten me ahead and you made me feel like one of your biggest clients (and we both know that's not true). *Merci beaucoup*—you are the best.

About the Author

Tj O'Connor is an award-winning author of mysteries and thrillers. He's an international security consultant specializing in anti-terrorism, investigations, and threat analysis—life experiences that drive his novels. With his former life as a government agent and years as a consultant, he has lived and worked around the world in places like Greece, Turkey, Italy, Germany, the United Kingdom, and throughout the Americas—among others. In his spare time, he's a Harley Davidson pilot, a man-about-dogs (and now cats), and a lover of adventure, cooking, and good spirits (both kinds). He was raised in New York's Hudson Valley and lives with his wife, Labs, and Maine Coon companions in Virginia, where they raised five children who are supplying a growing tribe of grands.

AUTHOR WEBSITE:
   www.tjoconnor.com
   SOCIAL MEDIA HANDLES:

Web Site: www.tjoconnor.com
   Facebook: https://www.facebook.com/tjoconnor.author2
   Blog: http://tjoconnor.com/blog/
   Twitter:@tjoconnorauthor
   Instagram: https://www.instagram.com/tjoconnorauthor/
   Amazon: https://www.amazon.com/author/tjoconnor

Goodreads: https://www.goodreads.com/author/show/7148441.T_J_O_Connor

Youtube Channel: @tjoconnorauthor3905

Bookbub:https://www.bookbub.com/profile/tj-o-connor

Also by Tj O'Connor

Dying to Know

Dying For The Past

Dying to Tell

New Sins for Old Scores

The Consultant

The Hemingway Deception

The Whisper Legacy